WITNESS
TO
SURRENDER

WITNESS

SURRENDER

WITNESS
TO
SURRENDER

BY

SIDDIQ SALIK

1978

KARACHI
OXFORD UNIVERSITY PRESS
OXFORD   NEW YORK   DELHI

Oxford University Press

OXFORD LONDON GLASGOW
NEW YORK TORONTO MELBOURNE WELLINGTON
CAPE TOWN IBADAN NAIROBI DAR ES SALAAM
KUALA LUMPUR SINGAPORE JAKARTA HONG KONG TOKYO
DELHI BOMBAY CALCUTTA MADRAS KARACHI

First Published 1977

Second Impression 1978

ISBN 0 19 577257 1

78-8798

Printed by
Ferozsons Printers, Karachi
Published by
Oxford University Press, G.P.O. Box 442,
Haroon House, Dr. Ziauddin Ahmed Road,
Karachi-1.

To
The Memory of
United Pakistan

ACKNOWLEDGEMENTS

My sincerest thanks are due to Dr. P. D. Peters and Khwaja Shahid Hosain for their valuable help in finalizing the manuscript of this book. Dr. Peters, though thousands of miles away, remained as close to me as my heartbeat during various stages of writing. Khwaja Shahid Hosain, in spite of his heavy commitments, spared time for several sittings with me to dot the i's and cross the t's.

I am also indebted to innumerable fellow officers who answered my questions, both relevant and otherwise, with great patience and compassion.

Finally I would like to thank Mr. Rehman and Mr. Anwar for typing and retyping the manuscript.

CONTENTS

ILLUSTRATIONS

MAPS

PREFACE

20 December 1971. Dacca had fallen but four days before. A transport plane of the Indian Air Force waited at Dacca airport to fly our top brass, including Lieutenant-General Amir Abdullah Khan Niazi and Major-General Rao Farman Ali, to Calcutta, as prisoners of war. They were also allowed their staff officers, to share the air-lift and the subsequent ignominy. They all came and squeezed into the dark belly of the Caribou. The rickety machine jerked into life, groaned for some time, and finally took off. I was on board, too.

Two years earlier, a P.I.A. Boeing had landed me on the same tarmac. Life was very different then. The airport wore a gay look in the bright morning sun. The senior military officers were busy piloting the country to its democratic goal set by President Yahya Khan in his first address to the nation on 26 March 1969.

Those in the saddle then, were in shackles now. A great change had come about. Personally, I had survived it, but the country had not. It was painful to recall the process; impossible to forget it. In this hour of agony, I decided to record my experience of the change. Recapitulating the process, I have mainly concentrated on events rather than personalities. I leave it to history to distinguish devils from dervishes.

I am glad that neither General Headquarters nor the Government of Pakistan allowed me access to the official documents on the 1971 crisis. It has enabled me to retain my original impressions about the fall of Dacca. (The official documents quoted in the last part are only those which were available in Dacca even to the Indians after 16 December 1971). I shall welcome any official version which supplements, corrects, or contradicts my conclusions.

14 August 1976   SIDDIQ SALIK

PART I
POLITICAL

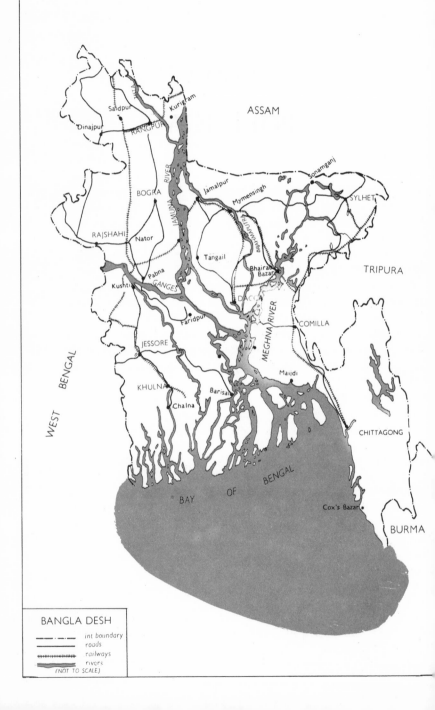

BANGLA DESH

— — —	int boundary
————	roads
▬▬▬▬	railways
	rivers

(NOT TO SCALE)

1

FACTS AND FEARS

It was the first anniversary of the second martial law in Pakistan.[1] Sheikh Mujibur Rehman was on his way to a rural town in East Pakistan to address an election rally. On the back seat of his rattling car sat with him a non-Bengali journalist who covered his election tours. He provoked Mujib on some current topic and quietly switched on his cassette tape recorder. Later, he entertained his friends with this exclusive possession. He also played it to me. Mujib's rhetorical voice was clearly intelligible. He was saying: 'Somehow, Ayub Khan has pitched me to a height of popularity where nobody can say "no" to what I want. Even Yahya Khan cannot refuse my demands.'

What were his demands? A clue was provided by another tape prepared by Yahya Khan's intelligence agencies. The subject was the Legal Framework Order (L.F.O.) issued by the government on 30 March 1970. Practically, it was an outline constitution which denied a free hand to Mujib to implement his famous Six Points. He confided his views on L.F.O. to his senior colleagues without realizing that these words were being taped for Yahya's consumption. On the recording, Mujib said: 'My aim is to establish Bangla Desh. I shall tear L.F.O. into pieces as soon as the elections are over Who could challenge me once the elections are over.' When it was played to Yahya Khan, he said, 'I will fix him if he betrays me.'[2]

I travelled light to Dacca in January 1970, but I carried heavy thoughts in my mind. My fears were not based on possible Indian aggression; rather, they lay in the realm of internal politics. Like many West Pakistanis, I had been told that Mujibur Rehman's Six Points were nothing but a veiled scheme for secession and the

[1] The second country-wide martial law was imposed by General A.M. Yahya Khan, Commander-in-Chief, Pakistan Army, on 26 March 1969. For details and political background, see Chronology of Events (Appendix I).

[2] G.W. Chaudhry, *Last Days of United Pakistan*, C. Hurst and Company, London, p. 98.

1968 Agartala Conspiracy was a practical step to implement it. I did not know the truth of either of these allegations. I thought that first-hand contact with my Bengali countrymen would clarify the issue.

On my way to Dacca, I also thought of the 25,000-strong military force I was going to join and 1,800 kilometres of Indian territory I was flying over. If ever India decided to invade East Pakistan, would our isolated garrison be able to repel the aggression? This was a very discomforting thought, which, as a loyal citizen of Pakistan, I did not want to entertain. Instead, I sought refuge in the sweet recollection of the reassuring cliches: that the All India Muslim League was founded in Dacca and that the historic Pakistan Resolution was moved by a Bengali. Hence there could be no danger to Pakistan!

Presently, I landed at Tejgaon airport. The airfield was hemmed by green fields and silvery clouds. The clouds were many, but they were scattered. They did not shut out the smiling sun. The atmosphere was mild and soothing. A few martial law officers had also arrived by the same flight. They lounged in the V.I.P. room while their baggage was stuffed into the silver-crested cars of Government House. The Bengali porters, hustling in the portico, did the job quickly and the officers drove off breezily. The dust settled down after a while.

I stood on the outer verandah waiting for some suitable transport to take me to the cantonment.[1] Eventually, a military vehicle offered me a lift. Its driver commanded a passing Bengali boy to load my suitcase into the jeep. The tattered lad did not like the command, but casting a resentful eye on his 'master', he obeyed. His white eye-balls, turned up to me, looked very poignant in the frame of his dark complexion. I tried to give him a few coins but the driver exclaimed: 'Don't spoil these bastards.' The boy gave yet another scornful look and went away. I boarded the jeep and left for the cantonment. The national flag, with its emblem of the crescent and star, fluttered high on the terminal building.

Those who failed to receive me at the airport turned up at the officers' mess in the evening. They greeted me warmly and expressed their regrets for the inconvenience at the airport. They also sympathized with me on my posting to East Pakistan at a time when

[1] The P.I.A. Trident flying me from Rawalpindi had been abandoned at Lahore owing to engine trouble. I had changed over to a Boeing but had not been able to inform my friends in Dacca.

things were 'hotting up'. Some of them even tried to 'put me wise' to the latest situation and offered pearls of advice: 'Martial Law practically doesn't exist here'; 'Don't go for heavy household goods, you never know how and when you may have to pack up'; 'Transfer your account to the National Bank, Cantonment Branch, instead of a commercial bank in the city'; 'Try to retain your predecessor's flat, it is as safe as a box, nobody can lob a bomb into it.'

Why should a Bengali throw a bomb into my house? I thought that my sympathizers' fears were mostly subjective. There seemed hardly any sign of abrupt violence. I cabled my reinforcements— my family—to join me, although my friends considered it a risky initiative. The family arrived within a few days and was deployed in the box-like flat. Soon a crowd of Bengalis raided our residence. But they were not bomb-throwing disruptionists. They were the job-seeking *ayahs* (maid servants) who preferred to work for West Pakistanis just as, before Independence, domestic Indian servants tried to find a place in a British house. I learnt next day that my wife had employed two *ayahs*. This appeared very extravagant but she explained that their total emoluments would come to less than we used to pay to a single servant in Rawalpindi.

After my wife's arrival in Dacca, I drove to the Pakistan Ceramic Industries at Tongi, about fourteen kilometres from Dacca, to order some crockery. On the way, a new dimension of reality dawned on me. I saw such scenes of poverty that the rush of job-seeking *ayahs* became understandable. The women had hardly a patch of dirty linen to preserve their modesty. The men were short and starved. Their ribs, under a thin layer of dark skin, could be counted even from a moving car. The children were worse. Their bones and bellies were protruding. Some of them toyed with a bell dangling from their waist. It was their only plaything. Whenever I stopped, beggars swarmed round me like flies. I concluded that the poor of Bengal are poorer than the poorest of West Pakistan. I started finding a meaning in the allegations of the economic exploitation of East Pakistan. I felt guilty.

I reflected on the advice of my friends who had recently put me wise to the situation. Yes, if these hungry mobs are roused to violence, they can loot the stores, storm the cantonment and even throw a bomb into my flat.

At the factory gate, I met a tall sturdy man in trousers and coat. He was Mr. Niazi, a West Pakistani, employed as a security assis-

tant in the factory. Our similar features were our only introduction.
He received me warmly and started talking in confidence. When
I told him my mission, he advised, 'Please, don't place the order
yourself. The Bengali labour here is very hostile to West Pakistani
officers. They deliberately spoil their orders . . . Leave it to me.'

On my return to Dacca, I described my day's experience to
Captain Chaudhry, an old friend from the Punjab. He was hardly
moved by the description of abject poverty that I had seen. Instead,
he started inveighing against the Bengalis for their lethargic habits.
'The only thing they are active in is violating the family planning
advice . . . I'll take you to the city (Dacca) to show you the other
side of the picture.'

At the first opportunity, he took me to the city and drove me
through a complex of magnificent buildings—the State Bank,
Government House, the High Court, the Engineers Institute,
the railway station, Radio Pakistan, the Provincial Secretariat,
the university campus, Baitul Mukarram, the stadium, New Market
and a number of private mansions. 'There was nothing here,' he
growled. 'All this has come up after 1947 in spite of annual floods,
cyclones and tornadoes. Somebody has to work out the figures of
foreign earnings and investment to blast Mujib's claim of economic
exploitation.'

When the facts are against Mujib, I thought, how can he sweep
the population to his side? Again, when there is Bhashani leading a
parallel force and the rightists emphasizing the Islamic bond between the two wings, how can Mujib have his way? Elections would
decide whether he really enjoyed majority support.

The preparations for the elections had started on 1 January 1970
when the ban on political activities was lifted. The leftist students
had hailed the new year with a torch-light procession at midnight,
shouting slogans in favour of a Red Revolution. Next day their
rival body, the East Pakistan Students League (which was affiliated
with the Awami League) held a public meeting where they declared: 'Six Points are the only road to emancipation'. The other
student bodies, which were known to enjoy patronage by rightist
parties such as the Jamaat-i-Islami, did nothing to show their
strength.

With the lifting of the ban, political parties like the Krishak
Sramik Party (K.S.P.), Pakistan National League (P.N.L.), Pakistan
Democratic Party (P.D.P.), the Jamiatul Ulema-i-Islam (J.U.I.)

and the factions of the Muslim League made a limping entry into the political arena, but their muscle-flexing only betrayed their inherent weakness. They were hardly impressive.

Soon, the three main political parties in the province formally launched their election campaign. The Awami League held its meeting at Paltan Maidan on 11 January, the Jamaat-i-Islami organized a big congregation a week later, and National Awami Party (Bhashani Group) staged a peasants' rally at Santosh near Tangail on 19 January.

The Awami League meeting was impressive by any standards. It was well-organized and well-attended. In journalistic parlance, it was a 'mammoth' meeting. In terms of thought content, it was no less memorable. Sheikh Mujibur Rehman, making his first election speech, said that the Bengalis had made a mistake in accepting parity in the 1956 Constitution.[1] He added that if anybody tried to force it on *Bangla Desh* now, he would launch a resistance movement.

Mr. Moinul Hussain, barrister-at-law, worthy son of the late Tofuzzal Hussain,[2] alias Manek Mia, later told me that during his father's life time it was possible to make the 1956 Constitution acceptable to Bengalis 'but now you are too late'. When I tested Mr. Hussain's claim with some of the old guards, they said, 'Yes, Manek Mia was the only sober influence on Mujib after Suhrawardy's death.'[3]

Next Sunday, the Jamaat-i-Islami held its first election meeting at the same maidan. The Jamaat, realizing its significance, tried to make it a complete success but it soon turned into a mêlée. Two persons were killed and fifty injured, twenty-five of them seriously. The party *amir*, Maulana Abul Ala Maudoodi, who had flown from Lahore specially to address the meeting, had to return abortively from the venue of the meeting. The Jamaat emerged from the skirmish as an aggrieved and disabled party.

The Jamaat blamed the Awami League for the bloody clash because the battle-field was filled with *Joi Bangla* (Long Live Bangla Desh) slogans. The Awami League, on the other hand, contended that violence, which could prejudice the prospects of polls, was

[1] The *Pakistan Observer*, Dacca, 12 January 1970.
[2] Proprietor and editor of a popular Bengali daily, *Ittefaq*, Dacca. He was an associate of Suhrawardy. He died on 30 May 1969.
[3] Mr. H.S. Suhrawardy, a former Prime Minister of Pakistan and a political mentor of Mujib, was found dead in a Beirut hotel in December 1963.

not in its interest. The arguments on both sides continued, but the role of the administration in this opening duel between two political parties remained very dubious. Where were the police? Why did not they intervene to restore order?

A senior martial law officer told me that before the meeting, he had offered government protection to the Jamaat but it was politely refused. 'We have made arrangements', he was told. The officer got the impression that the Jamaat wanted to prove that if the Awami League could hold a successful meeting unaided, so could they. Only the weaker party seeks government protection. When I mentioned it to a journalist close to the Jamaat, he said, 'No, Jamaat didn't refuse protection. The government sat on the fence to establish its non-partisan character.'

The third major event, the Peasants' Rally, commenced with a lot of fanfare. Although it was organized by the N.A.P. (Bhashani), invitations were issued to all other parties which professed socialism. The government ran special trains to Tangail and arranged a power supply at the site to make the rally a success. Some political owls in the Government House wanted the N.A.P. (B) to stay and develop as a political counter-weight to the Awami League.

The rally was not disturbed by any rival group. It collapsed because of its internal dissensions. Its only output was the currency of a few revolutionary slogans like 'Blood and Fire—Fire, Fire,' 'Ballot or Bullet—Bullet, Bullet'.

The ultra-revolutionary group led by the N.A.P.'s General Secretary Toaha vehemently opposed participation in the election on the plea that this might change the government but not the social system. A real socio-ecomic change, Toaha believed, could only be brought about through a Red Revolution.

A few days later, I happened to meet Mr. Toaha in a newspaper office. About his departure from the N.A.P. (B), he said: 'I left the Awami League because it had no spark. I, therefore, founded the N.A.P. with a revolutionary mission. It, too, has lost its creed. It is as sparkless today as the Awami League...... I will chart my new course after the elections.'

There were a few more political parties like Krishak Sramik Party, Pakistan National League, Nizam-i-Islam Party, Pakistan Democratic Party, Jamiatul Ulema-i-Islam and three factions of the Muslims League. But only one voice from this group was heard. That was the voice of Mr. Nurul Amin, the ailing chief of P.D.P.

He pleaded moderation, tolerance and fair play. But, in an atmosphere charged with the boisterous claims of the N.A.P. and the Awami League, this voice of sanity appeared to be weak and out of tune. In fact, political values were fast changing. Slogans prejudicial to national solidarity were becoming the norm of the day. But who could arrest this trend? Those who were supposed to, were either not aware of it or they deliberately turned a deaf ear to it.

After getting a feel of the political situation, I turned to the financiers and intellectuals who play a major role in framing a country's political destiny. A word about the economic aspect first.

During the course of my meetings with the Bengali businessmen— Rehman, Ahmed, Bhuiyya—they strongly argued that West Pakistan was developed with the money earned by East Pakistan. Pro-Awami League publications alleged that while East Pakistan provided 60 per cent of the total revenue, it received only about 25 per cent for its expenditure whereas West Pakistan, providing 40 per cent to the national exchequer, received 75 per cent. In addition, they dilated on the 'illogical and inconvenient' trade system which 'has its roots in West Pakistan'. They said, 'A ship carrying goods for East Pakistan (rubber, for instance) sails from the Far East—from under our armpit—to Karachi, from where the same goods are shipped back to Chittagong. It entails not only extra freight but also extra time.' On the flow of domestic goods, they said, 'Look at the camouflage jute nets used by the Army. Jute and jute factories are here. But the goods must travel to West Pakistan for dyeing before they are issued to army units in East Pakistan. Nothing seems to be fit for East Pakistan unless it enjoys the sacred touch of West Pakistan. It is true of politicians and administrators as well as commercial goods.'

On the intellectual front, the situation was equally grim. Among my first contacts in Dacca, was the Bengali Resident Director of the Pakistan Council for National Integration. He took me round the library. Stopping before the arts section, he pulled out a well produced book and said angrily, 'Look, this is what our Head Office (Rawalpindi) has sent us. What a waste of public money! Have you published any such art work on a Bengali poet?' His fury was caused by *Muraqqa-i-Chughtai*, a rare work of art illustrating selected verses of the world-famous Urdu poet, Ghalib. He next stopped before the political section and said, 'Here, we have a whole shelf of books on your *Quaid-i-Azam*.' I noted his accent on the word *your* and left.

A few days later, I attended a meeting of the film censorship board. The meeting was called to discuss ways to discourage plagiarism in our films. Representatives of the Dacca film industry, including film writers, directors and producers, were present. After a passionate plea against plagiarism had been made by the Chairman in the name of national prestige and identity, an eminent Bengali writer took the following line of argument:

'A high level seminar on the problems of the East Pakistan film industry was held in Dacca in 1965. It was decided then, in the interest of the industry, that the Government would not interfere with the traditional sources of its sustenance. I would suggest to the Martial Law Government that it stick to this earlier decision and keep the doors open to Calcutta. After all, how can we turn our back on our cultural *Ka'aba*!'

The Chairman of the meeting, with a reputation for dubious loyalties, gave me an ironic smile and, accepting the plea, called off the meeting.

My first impression after these preliminary contacts with the Bengalis was that a complete mental schism existed between East and West Pakistan. Would it be bridged or would it lead to a total break between the two wings? My mind immediately turned to the 25,000 troops who belonged to the national army—the ultimate guarantor of national solidarity!

2

STRAINS AT THE SEAMS

If politicians, businessmen, intellectuals and others had mentally fallen away from West Pakistan by early 1970, were the Bengali troops safe from this virus? Could they be relied upon to quell an internal disorder? How would they react in case of Indian aggression? Were they mentally and emotionally well integrated with the rest of the army?

I was not the first to face these questions. They had haunted people earlier, too. The General Officer Commanding (G.O.C.), Major-General Khadim Hussain Raja told me that he developed apprehensions in the 'local-non-local' riots of November 1969, when the Bengali troops, deployed on internal security duties, had acted with hesitation. He had, therefore, recommended to the General Headquarters (G.H.Q.) an increase in the strength of the West Pakistani troops and the distribution of the existing manpower of Bengali battalions to other infantry regiments. G.H.Q. seemed to ignore both the suggestions as they conflicted with the President's commitment in a broadcast to the nation on 28 July 1969, to 'double the quota of Bengalis in the defence services' The President had also declared that it was only a first step in redressing Bengali grievances.

The President who made the announcement was also the Commander-in-Chief of the Army. Either he did not know the psychological state of his troops or he deliberately worked on a different wave-length for some political reason.

Major-General Khadim Hussain, knowing that his suggestions were in the interest of national unity, pressed for their implementation. One fine morning, he received a secret letter from the General Headquarters. He opened it in the fond hope that perhaps it contained acceptance of his suggestions. Instead, it conveyed the Commander-in-Chief's order to raise two more battalions of

exclusively Bengali troops.[1] There were already seven in existence,
four of them posted in East Pakistan.

The General Officer Commanding was upset. He flew to Rawalpindi to explain the grave implications of the new order. He told
G.H.Q., 'If the intention is eventually to raise a Bengal army, go
ahead with the raising of exclusively East Bengal battalions; but if
you want to maintain the unity of the army—and the country—
please integrate the existing East Bengal battalions with the rest.'

It was a hard decision for the President to take. Political consider-
ations impelled him to augment the Bengali representation in the
defence services, while the man on the spot advised him to disinte-
grate gradually the exclusive Bengali battalions already in existence.
As many indecisive commanders do in such difficult situations,
General Yahya Khan tried to find a compromise solution. He
ordered the absorption of twenty-five per cent of the Bengali troops
in the existing battalions into the Frontier Force (F.F.) and Punjab
Regiments as an experiment. If it did not evoke any ugly repercussions either from the Bengali troops or from the Bengali politicians,
the policy could be pursued to its desired end. Meanwhile, the
raising of fresh East Bengal battalions was also to continue.

The 'induction parade' was held at the Fortress Stadium (Dacca
city) on 31 December 1969 to mark the integration of a company
of Bengali troops with 19 Frontier Force which already had
Pathans and Punjabis in equal numbers. The ceremonial parade,
which was held in full public view, passed off happily. But the
G.O.C. kept his fingers crossed because he feared that, if the Bengalis
mutinied in their new environment on any pretext, (a preference for
rice to wheat in the menu, for instance), the experiment was sure
to boomerang.

The Bengali troops, however, integrated well with 19 Frontier
Force and they jointly performed certain duties for internal security
until the battalion, on its normal turn of change-over, sailed to
West Pakistan. This reaffirmed the G.O.C.'s faith in his scheme for
national integration, but the President had ordered him to go slow
on it. The scheme stayed in the safe custody of steel cupboards.

On the other hand the President's directive to double the Bengali
quota was vigorously pursued. The publicity apparatus also jerked

---

[1] 8 East Bengal was to be raised in Chittagong and 10 East Bengal in Dacca.
GHQ was requested to change, at least, the venue of the raisings as Dacca
and Chittagong were the key cities—airport and seaport respectively. But
it had no effect.

into full activity. I, as one of its humble cogs, was asked to do an article on the subject, after consulting the commandant of the East Bengal Regimental Centre, Chittagong, which trained Bengali recruits for the army.

The commandant, Colonel (later Brigadier) Mozumdar was a stocky little fellow fired with Bengali nationalism. He had direct contacts with Mujibur Rehman, which gave him a rare combination of pride and prejudice: pride in Bengali nationalism, prejudice against West Pakistan. I met him on the flower-decked lawns of his office and apprised him of my mission. After an hour's conversation, I was convinced that his reputation was not groundless. He talked proudly about his importance, Bengali nationalism and injustices done to the Bengali people. He said, 'Why do you want to beat your drums about doubling the quota? Even if the President's order is fully implemented, it would mean only fifteen per cent representation for the Bengalis while they constitute fifty-six per cent of the national population.'

After this 'briefing' by Mozumdar, I had lunch with a West Pakistani officer. The conversation inevitably turned to the Centre commandant. My host related a small incident. He said that when the last batch of recruits was about to sail for Karachi, the colonel told them, 'You are proud Bengali soldiers now. You are not going there to polish the shoes of Punjabi officers. Soon they will be polishing yours.'

Mozumdar was not the only patron and guide of the Bengali troops. His burden was shared by a serving lieutenant-general and a retired colonel. I met both of them in early February when the second battalion of the East Bengal Regiment, the Junior Tigers, was to be presented with Regimental Colours at Joydebpur, north of Dacca. Officially, Lieutenant-General Wasiuddin, the colonel commandant of the East Bengal Regiment, was to give the colours and take the salute but the real spirit behind the occasion was Colonel M.A.G. Osmani who led a 'retired' life in Dacca by taking an active part in Awami League politics.'[1]

Two days before the function, I was summoned by these two officers to the V.I.P. suite of the 14 Division officers' mess where they finalized General Wasiuddin's speech for the occasion. I was given a copy of this address which profusely eulogized the services

[1] He later won a seat in the National Assembly on the Awami League ticket and became a minister in Mujibur Rehman's Bangla Desh cabinet.

of Colonel Osmani and advised the Bengali troops to count always
on his advice in adversity. Later, the printed copies of this speech
were distributed to all Bengali troops in both wings.

Colonel Osmani was a small, worn-out man. The only white
feature on his sun-burnt face was the brush of white moustache
on his upper lip. A fellow officer often described him as 'a man
attached to a pair of moustaches'. (His role in the crisis figures later
in this book.)

Major-General Khadim, as commander of the troops, was aware
of the possible impact that General Wasiuddin, Colonel Mozumdar
and Colonel (ret.) Osmani might have on the troops. Even without
this, he knew that the total immunity of troops to current political
movements was never possible. He remembered that Muslim soldiers
in undivided India had developed an emotional commitment to
Quaid-i-Azam Mohammad Ali Jinnah's movement for Pakistan.
If Pakistan's independence had come before the discipline of the
British Indian Army could collapse due to the political motivation
of troops, this did not mean that Bengali troops would passively
and indefinitely wait for autonomy through peaceful means. He
feared that some day they could be agitated to rebellion. His fears
were strengthened by the Agartala Conspiracy which envisaged the
capture of unit armouries (*kotes*), disarming of West Pakistani
troops and taking over the cantonments. He therefore privately
summoned all his brigade commanders (non-Bengali) and asked
them to keep part of their arms in the unit lines, instead of the *kotes*.
'They would certainly be handy in an emergency,' he said. He did not
follow it up with any written orders, 'because the matter was too
sensitive,' he told me later.

Was the G.O.C. obsessed with imaginary fears? Would it not
create mutual distrust if it did not exist already? Maybe these were
no more than mere fantasies but we were so badly caught in them
that we interpreted every incident in their light. For instance, I
once walked into the office of my Bengali colleague, and found
him engrossed in a discussion with another Bengali officer.
When I entered the room they broke off immediately. Some
awkward moments ticked by. I said, 'What is happening?' By then,
my host had recovered from my surprise visit. He said, 'We were
planning a fishing trip for next Sunday.' I said, 'May I join you on
the trip?' He paused and said,'No, the programme is not final yet.' I
thought they were discussing the prospects of Mujib's Bangla Desh.

In my next meeting with the corps commander, Lieutenant-General Sahabzada Yakub Khan, I told him about the loss of faith between Bengali and West Pakistani officers. He, wiser than I, did not necessarily interpret my experience the way I had done. He 'enlightened' me with a sophisticated intellectual disquisition. I returned to my office.

The general and I, perhaps, represented two categories of officers. The juniors, with their limited comprehension, made mountains out of molehills while the seniors, gifted with depth and vision, turned mountains into molehills. Whether, in fact, it was a mountain or a molehill was not clearly known. Everything was masked by the heavy crust of army discipline. The Awami League and its sympathizers had the whole election year to erode this crust.

3

MUJIB RIDES THE CREST

Bengali nationalism, spread by the Awami League, continued to infect the Bengali troops as well as the civilian population, although its impact was more vivid and immediate on the latter. To promote this virus, the Awami League made every effort to suppress national occasions like Pakistan Day (23 March), Independence Day (14 August), *Quaid-i-Azam's* birth and death anniversaries (25 December, 11 September) and played up provincial events like Sergeant Zahoorul Haq's death anniversary, Language Day and Tagore's birthday.

Sergeant Zahoorul Haq, co-accused with Mujibur Rehman in the 1968 Agartala Conspiracy case, died in military custody in 1969. The first anniversary of his death was celebrated on 15 February 1970, mostly at the behest of the Awami League, in seventeen out of the nineteen districts of East Pakistan. Dacca vibrated with new life on this occasion. His portrait and biographical details occupied the front-page columns of important Dacca dailies. His services were eulogized at several public meetings where it was pledged that 'his blood would not go to waste'.[1] Sheikh Mujibur Rehman, addressing one of these meetings said, 'Zahoorul Haq was a great patriot who would be remembered by the people along with the great patriots like Titumir and Surja Sen.'[2]

A week later was Language Day—an event of great emotional importance for the Bengalis. The occasion was celebrated 'as a day of inspiration'. The newspapers brought out special supplements to pay homage to those who laid down their lives in the 1952 language movement. A large number of people visited the 'martyrs' graves in Azimpura. The boys and girls of the College of Arts and Crafts tastefully painted the entire road from the Central Shaheed Minar to the Azimpura graveyard.

[1] The *Pakistan Observer*, Dacca, 16 February 1970.
[2] The *Morning News*, Dacca, 22 February 1970.

Sheikh Mujibur Rehman paid tribute to the martyrs by making a midnight pilgrimage to the Shaheed Minar. Earlier, at a meeting, he demanded that the Bengali language be introduced in all government departments at all levels.[1]

Then came 8 May, the 109th anniversary of the birth of Rabindranath Tagore, a Bengali poet, whose works had been banned from the government-controlled radio and television because they 'promoted secular Bengali nationalism'. The Dacca press front-paged large portraits of him, lauded his literary achievements and published translations from his works. The Bengali youth chanted Tagore's songs with ecstatic relish. They held musical soirées to pay homage to his memory. Mujib himself hummed his verses in public and private.

The Awami League espoused every cause that weakened inter-wing links and stressed the character of Bengali nationalism. For instance, the students campaigned against a government prescribed book, *Desh-o-Krishti* (The Land and the People), because it emphasized ideological links with West Pakistan. They defended Kamaruddin's *'Social History'* against the government ban because it promoted cultural links with Calcutta. The student movement was supported by all prominent poets, writers and intellectuals. Mujib lent his full weight to their cause saying, 'Previous movements for the Bengali language (1952) had defied all force and this attack on the cultural property of Bengalis will also be resisted.'[2]

The Awami League also struck at every other initiative by its rivals to strengthen feelings of inter-wing unity. It demolished the Jamaat-i-Islami meeting in January mainly because it stressed the bonds of Islamic unity between the two wings. The League repeated the same high-handed tactics during the rest of the campaign period. It destroyed P.D.P. meetings in Dacca on 1 February, in Chittagong on 28 February, in Saidpur on 7 March; Convention Muslim League meetings in Comilla on 10 March, in Barisal on 15 March and in Dacca on 12 April. It also disrupted several other meetings organized by different political groups.

Mujib's rivals, like Fazlul Qader Chaudhry, Khan A. Sobur Khan, Mr. Nurul Amin, Professor Ghulam Azam and Maulvi Farid Ahmed lacked the political sinews to challenge him on a

---

[1] The *Morning News*, Dacca, 23 February 1970.
[2] The *Pakistan Observer*, Dacca, 23 February 1970.

public platform. The only man who could roar at Paltan Maidan with equal verbosity was the same old Bhashani who did not believe in building up a sustained campaign to achieve a particular end. He could roar in public, retire in private and shift his stand at will. He first threatened to launch a mass movement on 1 August. When 1 August came, he postponed it to 8 September, then to 2 October and finally nothing happened. Thus, he let his awesome presence lose its impact on East Pakistan politics.

The rise of Mujib's campaign for Bengali nationalism and the gradual fall of his political opponents left little doubt in our minds about the future course of events. It was apparent that Mujib would muster enough support, by the polling date, for his Six Points. Would Pakistan stay in its present shape if the Six Points were implemented? If they were really secessionist in intent, how could the trend be arrested?

Vice-Admiral S. M. Ahsan, Governor of East Pakistan, raised this issue of the Six Points versus national integrity at one of the Cabinet meetings presided over by General Yahya Khan. He said, 'Before we proceed, let me get one thing clarified. Is propagation of his Six Points a violation of Martial Law Regulation 16 (which prohibited any talk against national integrity)?' He was told, 'Don't worry.' But many in the country did. It was perhaps to allay public fears that the President, in spite of his *ex-officio* engagements, found time to come on the air on 30 March and declare, 'I would not accept anything that cuts across the basic principles of our nationhood.'[1] He followed his announcement, next day, by issuing the Legal Framework Order (L.F.O.) which laid down the fundamental principles of the future constitution to guarantee the 'inviolability of national integrity' and the 'Islamic character of the Republic'. I was relieved to read the L.F.O. because it cut across the Awami League politics which preached the secular character of the Republic and its division into virtually self-governing provinces.

The Legal Framework Order irked Mujib sorely. He was particularly irritated at Sections 25 and 27 which vested powers of authentication of the future constitution in the President. It implied that Mujib would not be free to implement his Six Points, even if he obtained majority seats in the National Assembly (Parliament) unless his Constitution Bill received the President's

[1] The *Pakistan Times*, Rawalpindi, 31 March 1970.

approval. It is on this issue that Mujib had said, 'I shall tear L.F.O. into pieces as soon as the elections are over.'

The President flew to Dacca to handle the situation himself. He invited Mujib, on 4 April, for a friendly chat. I was there when Mujib arrived. He was received with a lot of warmth and courtesy. As they settled down for a tête-à-tête, I withdrew. An hour later, I was sought out from a friend's house to draft a press note on behalf of the Cabinet Division amending L.F.O. in those parts (Sections 25 and 27) to which Mujib had taken exception. I drafted the note and handed it back. Luckily, it was not issued because somebody had, meanwhile, advised Yahya Khan not to disarm himself completely against the politicians.

When Yahya Khan was about to fly back to West Pakistan on 10 April, he faced the Dacca press on the disputed clauses of the L.F.O. at the airport. I was present, too. When pressed hard on the issue of the President's powers 'to veto the Constitution Bill passed by the people's representatives', Yahya Khan said, 'That's a procedural formality only. I have no intention of using them.' A pro-Awami League journalist whispered over my shoulder, 'He has assured Sheikh Sahib (Mujib) that he would not exercise them. They are like certain constitutional formalities vested in the Queen of England.'

I do not know what 'assurances' General Yahya Khan received in return for this commitment to Mujib. I do know that it further confirmed the Awami League chief in his belief that he had attained a height of popularity where 'even Yahya Khan cannot say 'no" to what I want.'

Within two months of this Yahya–Mujib understanding, Mujib felt confident enough to show his hand a little more openly. On 4 June, he declared, 'My party is going to participate in the ensuing elections taking it as a referendum on the Six Points programme.'[1] Mr. Nurul Amin, P.D.P. Chief, challenged this next day saying that if the elections were a referendum on the programme and if the programme received no support from West Pakistan, 'in that case East and West Pakistan would fall apart'.[2] This provoked Mujib to be more explicit the following day when he said, 'We won the 1946 referendum in spite of opposition from Gandhi, Nehru and their British overlords.

The *Pakistan Observer*, Dacca, 5 June 1970.
Ibid., 6 June 1970.

And we are going to win this time, too, in spite of Mr. Nurul Amin and his overlords (West Pakistan).'[1]

The historical parallel drawn by Mujib was very ominous. It implied that he was following in the footsteps of the creator of Pakistan who won the 1946 referendum as a prelude to the establishment of an independent state. Was Mujib working for a similar end? He was questioned on this issue privately by one of Yahya's representatives in Dacca, but he denied the implications. It was not his first political somersault, nor was it his last. I recall several such occasions when he appeared a terror in public but turned tame in private. This duality helped him in coercing the masses into his fold, while convincing the authorities of his pious intentions. Skilfully riding his political surfboard, he climbed the crest of popularity.

[1] Ibid., 7 June 1970.

4

THE MOCKERY OF MARTIAL LAW

The civil and martial law administration in Dacca passively watched the political ebb and flow—the flow of the Awami League, the ebb of its rivals. It did little to influence the course of events except by certain acts of omission which allowed a free hand to Mujib in coercing the silent majority into submission. This was, perhaps, in keeping with Yahya Khan's soft attitude towards the Bengali leader.

There was wide-spread speculation on Yahya's motives. Many people wondered why a dictator should show so much accommodation ('one man, one vote', for instance) to a politician who was tried by his predecessor on charges of treason. The popular guess was that Yahya Khan wanted to win over Mujib so that he could continue as the President even after the lifting of martial law. Yahya Khan himself, however, gave a different reason for it. He said several times in my presence, 'I have to carry the majority province of East Pakistan with me. If not Mujib, who else represents East Pakistan?'

Whatever Yahya Khan's compulsions, the fact remains that the Awami League employed, without interruption, all fair and foul means to establish its supremacy in East Pakistan. The Martial Law Headquarters and Government House, headed by Lieutenant-General Sahabzada Yakub Khan and Vice-Admiral S. M. Ahsan respectively, did nothing to bridle the Awami League horse or urge on rival political steeds to win the race. It was, perhaps, due to a deliberate policy: stay neutral in the election campaign.

Since 1 September 1969, Governor S. M. Ahsan (rather than Martial Law Administrator Yakub Khan) had been made responsible for all provincial matters including the maintenance of law and order. The martial law apparatus was to move only when the normal civil machinery had collapsed or was rendered ineffective. They were both answerable direct to Yahya Khan who was the President, Chief Martial Law Administrator, Supreme Commander of the Armed Forces and Commander-in-Chief of the Army.

General Yakub, with his intellectual outlook and soft manners, was an apt choice to implement Yahya Khan's 'slow pedal' policy towards East Pakistan during its political resuscitation. His personal charm was an added asset. Vice-Admiral Ahsan who was installed, much against his will, as the Provincial Governor after his removal from the prestigious command of the Pakistan Navy, was not temperamentally suited to the new job. The Governor's task, in those critical days, called for extraordinary political sagacity, firm administrative skill and an extrovert temperament. Ahsan, on the other hand, had the aloofness of a hermit, delicacy of a scholar and formality of a diplomat. These qualities, which would have been his strong points elsewhere, were weaknesses in his present position.

To make it worse, he enjoyed neither the confidence of the President nor the command of troops—the two poles of martial law authority. His relations with the President remained strictly official. He dutifully received the Chief Executive at the airport, escorted him to the President's House and himself retired to the safe sanctuary of Government House. He would only return to the President's House when summoned for some official purpose. And that happened very infrequently.

As a result, Ahsan had to lean heavily on his Bengali Chief Secretary, Mr. Shafiul Azam, who had the rare talent of pleasing simultaneously the Awami League, Martial Law Headquarters and Government House. He looked like a tortoise—a long neck (quick to stick out, quick to scuttle back in), thick skin and a steady pace. He knew how to win the Awami League race against the speeding generals. The Awami League was happy to see him in this key position. Some people even speculated that President Yahya Khan had accepted him as the Awami League nominee in the provincial administration. The net result of this weak administration was the absence of effective control in East Pakistan. Martial law proved weaker than the ordinary law it had replaced. Explaining his ineffectiveness as Governor, Admiral Ahsan told me later, 'It was a martial law regime. All major offences were cognizable under martial law orders and regulations which I had no powers to enforce. The Martial Law Administrator

alone could do that. And, mind you, he was answerable to
Yahya Khan, not me.'

The growing weakness of the administration and the rising
strength of Mujibur Rehman had some inevitable effects. The
law and order situation, as well as industrial, commercial and
educational life, became uncertain, erratic and chaotic. The worst
hit were the factories and mills which suffered from frequent
strikes, lock-outs or lay-offs. Sometimes they closed in such a
surprising sequence that one felt as if some magic hand controlled
their shutters. The result was that industrial concerns like the
Adamjee Jute Mills, Nishtar Jute Mills, Khulna Jute Mills,
Chittagong Steel Mills, Vikrampur Jehangir Steel Mills and
Khulna Newsprint Mills only opened occasionally to become a
battle-field between rival labour groups or labour and management. The Martial Law Administration, at times, put some hot
heads behind bars but it hardly eased the situation. It further
infuriated the striking labour. Some 10,000 labourers even tried,
on 29 and 30 May, to break open the Khulna jail gate to release
their comrades. A week earlier, another group of labourers killed
the Assistant Superintendent of Police, Mr. Fazlur Rehman
Chaudhry, who tried to break their picket outside a steel mill. His
body was dragged and mutilated because he had chosen to be a
'stooge of West Pakistan'. Mujib did not utter a word of sympathy
for the deceased. His support lay with the anti-government forces.

In this atmosphere of industrial confusion, I went to a famous
fabrics shop on Eskaton Road. I was impressed by advertisements
boasting of their modern machinery and high quality products.
The manager took this opportunity to air his grievances to me.
He said, 'We have installed the most modern equipment with
an investment of Rs. 12.5 million. It has the capacity to produce
goods worth Rs. 125 million annually. After laying aside goods
worth Rs. 150,000 for home consumption, we entered into export
deals with foreign firms. But owing to the unending labour
problem, we are not in a position to honour our commitments.
The representative of a client firm from Singapore is in town
for one week to ensure the shipment of goods which his firm,
in turn, has promised to the buyers. I can't help him. He is
sympathetic to our problems but insists that a fresh but firm
date should be given. How can I give him a firm date when I
don't know when the factories will open and for how many

days?' 'Have you apprised the authorities of your problems?'
I asked. 'Several times. When I go to the martial law authorities
they say it is a civil matter. When I approach the civil government
they put me off with sweet promises but take no action. It seems
there is no government. At least, there is none that can help me.'

Besides the labour, the students also contributed to the disturbed
conditions in East Pakistan. Early summer was the season for
examinations. They boycotted the examinations on one pretext
or another. They did not even hesitate to *gherao*,[1] manhandle
or stab dutiful invigilators and examiners. When they were on
the rampage, they smashed window panes, light shades, flower
pots and burnt the college furniture.

When there were no examinations, they had their standing
eleven points to lash the government with. These points, shorn
of any educational content, were essentially political demands
for provincial autonomy and Bengali nationalism. It was interesting
to note that teachers, who at times opposed the students for
using unfair means in examination halls, thought it quite fair
to support their eleven points.

The spirit that animated industrial labour and university
students soon permeated Class IV government servants. Over
16,000 of them went on strike in early July to press for the
acceptance of their nine-point demands. The government declared
their strike illegal but Mujib lent his support openly to the
striking government employees and sent a telegram to the
Governor urging him to 'accept their demands immediately'.[2]
It confirmed the growing impression among the employees that
Mujib, and not the government, was sympathetic to their demands.

Soon other groups, including jewellers, tannery workers,
journalists, family planning workers and tea-garden employees,
were jumping onto the band wagon of agitators. Their demands
were formulated into points which numbered from three to
fifteen. The crowning moment came on 4 September 1970, when
beggars formed their East Pakistan Beggars' Association and
held a public meeting at the famous Paltan Maidan to press for
the acceptance of their five-point charter of demands.[3]

As if this dual onslaught of strikes and demands were not
enough, Bengali nationalists also launched a terrorist movement

---

[1] Literally to surround in order to obtain terms under duress.
[2] The *Morning News*, Dacca, 6 July 1970.
[3] The *Pakistan Observer*, Dacca, 5 September 1970.

with a series of bomb blasts. They chose, quite symbolically, the premises of the Pakistan Council for National Integration on Topkhana Road for the inaugural blast on 5 May. It occurred at 7.30 p.m. in the presence of several persons who obeyed the command of three bomb throwers and vacated the library room for the act. While the readers idly watched the furniture blow up, the terrorists leisurely mounted the jeep and drove off. Nobody tried to capture them nor later volunteered information to the investigating authorities.

Bomb explosions occurred with measured frequency. As soon as calm began to return to the city, another burst tore it to shreds. Khulna, Chittagong, Rangpur and other towns also experienced the blasts. But their real impact was felt in the provincial capital, Dacca — the nerve centre of East Pakistan.

These wanton acts, coupled with industrial chaos, created a reign of fear and insecurity. Peaceful citizens liked to stay in their homes rather than venture out in the alleys of death. I remember my visit to Mr. Zahurul Haque, an Urdu poet, who lived in old Dacca city. I was accompanied by a poet from West Pakistan. We knocked at his iron gate several times before we were heard. From behind the iron protection, a servant made sure of our good intentions before he opened the gate. Once inside, we were entertained with *pan* and *ghazal*. His poetic compositions sounded like the plaintive notes of a caged nightingale. When we were about to leave, he said to me, 'You army people don't come this side. You are the custodians of our life and honour but have declared the city out of bounds for all ranks. You don't know how heavily time is weighing on us.'

On my way back, I dropped into a newspaper office where I met a Bengali barrister who wrote legal notes for the paper. Naturally, the prevailing conditions came under discussion. He said, 'Don't make a mockery of law—even martial law. Either enforce it properly or lift it.'

During one of my informal meetings with General Yakub I apprised him of the general talk about the 'toothlessness' of martial law. He registered the point and took it up at his next monthly meeting with the editors of the Dacca papers. He explained this 'toothlessness' of martial law as follows (I paraphrase):

For people in Pakistan, martial law is an image of terror. But they forget that the martial law regime is also leading the country to democracy. In fact, democracy and martial law are incompatible. Martial Law, in its traditional sense, would not let democracy take root. So to let democracy grow in this land, martial law has to lose some of its classical bite. We have to keep a balance between over-action and inaction. Some times you may think that we are under-acting but we have to judge whether that, too, is not over-action? The inverse is also true. To borrow a metaphor from aviation, a pilot might imagine that his aircraft is banking and, while trying to right it, crash into the neighbouring cliffs, although the machine would otherwise have passed the valley safely.

The editors were impressed by the argument as well as by the metaphor. They praised the general's eloquence and wisdom but still felt that the craft of state was tilting dangerously and, if it were not righted in time, it would crash and perish.

The civil or the martial law government, however, did not take any corrective steps. The law and order situation continued to deteriorate. Industrial life showed no improvement. Educational institutions remained closed for educational purposes. Awami League chauvinism continued to grow. One after the other, most of its rivals withdrew from the political contest.

It was in this atmosphere that East Pakistan approached the general elections of December 1970.

5

THE FREE-FOR-ALL ELECTIONS

The Awami League had practically won the elections before the polling day. 7 December was only to formalize the *de facto* victory of Mujibur Rehman. By the end of November, many people had started showing their reaction in anticipation of the Awami League success.

The General Manager of the Dacca television station told me on 1 December, 'I must go and explain my position to *Sheikh Sahib*. I have not been able to cover all his public meetings in the mofussil[1] areas because Rawalpindi had restricted coverage to the main cities. *Sheikh Sahib* must surely be displeased. When he comes to power, he may not touch you (in uniform) but he won't spare me.' A Deputy Superintendent of Police, Dacca, had similar apprehensions. He said, 'I ordered the police lathi-charge[2] on pro-Mujib labourers in the Postogola incident on 22 May. They must have told him my name; and *Sheikh Sahib* has an excellent memory.' A Bengali civilian, Mr. Rehman, summed up the common sentiment when he said, 'The country is heading for trouble. If the Awami League is voted to power, it will make life unbearable for all the dissidents. If it is not, it will resort to violence as it is fully keyed up to rule the country.'

These fears were not confined to the civilian population alone. They also found expression in military circles. I remember a senior officer of military intelligence saying, 'After assuming power, if *Sheikh Sahib* sends for all the papers on the Agartala Conspiracy case, he will surely find my name at several places ... And Mujib is not liberal enough to forgive and forget.' Those army officers who had never offended Mujib at any stage of their career, also started loud canvassing in favour of the Six Points. They tried to outdo each other in counting the merits of the Awami League programme. But they were generally those

---

[1] Mofussil: outside the capital or main towns.
[2] Lathi-charge: use of heavy sticks by the police to control or disperse crowds.

who thought that this strategem would endear them to the future rulers or wanted to cover their deep-rooted aversion to the dubious content of the Six Points.

When everybody was trying to readjust his relationship with the Awami League, taking its victory for granted, the party itself developed some apprehensions. Will the elections be allowed to be held? Will the Awami League get a chance to reap the harvest of its campaign? These were imaginary fears—the product of a highly tense and uncertain situation. The fears led to a rumour that General Hamid, Chief of Staff of the Pakistan Army, had deposed Yahya Khan and assumed full power. He would announce the cancellation of the polls and begin anew. Both of them were in Dacca then.

I received several queries—oblique as well as direct. They were addressed to other quarters also. But the Awami League could not obtain a satisfactory answer. Finally, a foreign journalist helped it by putting the question direct to President Yahya Khan when he was about to board the plane for Rawalpindi on 3 December 1970.

The journalist said, 'Mr. President, are you in full control of your country?' 'Yes...yes...absolutely...,' said the President batting his heavy eye-lashes. 'But there are strong rumours that...' The President lost his patience and said, 'It is fantastic...it is rubbish.' Then he abruptly turned to his left, where I was standing with other officials and said, 'Who shares power with me...? Nobody moves me unless I move...' Waving his baton and squeezing his lips in displeasure, he boarded the P.I.A. Boeing. It set the rumours at rest.

As the election day drew nearer more than one hundred foreign correspondents and media men assembled in Dacca. I had not seen such a large crowd even during the worst national calamities like floods and cyclones. The Ministry of Information and Broadcasting arranged a dinner in their honour on 6 December at Hotel Purbani, to which I was also invited.

I sat at the dinner table with three Western correspondents. The subject of conversation naturally turned to the polling that was to take place next day. One of them asked me, 'Major, which party are you going to vote for?' I said, 'There is only one party and that is the Awami League.' He seemed to take the joke seriously.

After the dinner, I dropped into the Martial Law Headquarters at the Assembly Chambers when the suitability of imposing Section

144 (which prohibits the assembly of four or more men and the carrying of arms) on the election day was being debated. Some officers favoured it in order to maintain peace on the historic day while others opposed it on the grounds of impracticability. As soon as I entered the spacious office, somebody shouted ironically, 'Here comes our public opinion expert. Let's ask him.' I assumed the mantle of an expert and said solemnly, 'My assessment of the prevailing opinion warns me against any restrictive measures. It would only pack more tension into an already over-charged atmosphere. The Awami League is sure to win. It will, therefore, also keep the peace.' They accepted my advice. I was amused to discover that a novice can command opinion if he behaves like an expert!

It had been announced from Rawalpindi earlier that the armed forces (mainly the Army) would supervise the polls. But the instructions that reached Dacca were: (a) don't involve yourself with polling; (b) keep a watch on key points; (c) stay in the background so that your public appearance does not provoke an angry reaction; and (d) act only to quell a riot.

An 'operations room' was set up in the Martial Law Headquarters to co-ordinate the Army supervision of the polls. General Yakub flew over important polling stations in an army helicopter. I rode with him. He was pleased to see the orderly crowds and peaceful atmosphere.

I spent the rest of the day in the 'operations room'. The atmosphere there was tense initially but when no reports of violence arrived from any quarter by midday, everybody relaxed and gossiped. Only one staff officer seemed to be busy receiving telephone and wireless calls—all confirming the peaceful progress of the polls. Queries from the headquarters of the Chief Martial Law Administrator (Rawalpindi) were accordingly answered in a reassuring manner.

The army had contributed to the peaceful conduct of the polls by the expedient of leaving the polling stations in the total control of the Awami League and its sympathizers. The polling and presiding officers also did not want to annoy their future rulers.

In fact, the candidates contesting against the Awami League had a tough time. They had neither the party strength to counter the Awami League volunteers nor the protective umbrella of the Government. Some aggrieved candidates approached the Army but got no redress because the Army had instructions not to involve itself in the polls unless large-scale violence erupted. I cite two typical cases.

A twelve-year old boy, raising *Joi Bangla* slogans, advanced to the polling booth at Chaumuhani (in Noakhali district). He was grabbed by a non-Awami League candidate and produced before Captain Chaudhry who waited with his platoon in the rear of the building. The candidate complained that (a) the boy was too young to vote and (b) he was raising slogans within the polling station, violating the rules. The captain said, 'Go and report to the presiding officer. I am not supposed to intervene in such matters.'

The second incident pertains to Tangail where one Rehman was brought before Major Khan with the complaint that he was going to cast his vote for the fifth time with the connivance of the polling officer. The major said, 'You may be right but that is not my headache. Tell me, is there any riot?'—there was no riot, thanks to the Awami League *goondas* (strong-arm boys).

By the end of the day when polling was over, General Yakub walked into the office of Major-General Rao Farman Ali who was in charge of civil affairs at the Martial Law Headquarters. General Yakub said with a visible air of pride, 'I am glad everything was peaceful... The polls were fair and free.' Farman quietly said, 'Yes... they were *free*, free-for-all.'

Four days later (11 December), President Yahya Khan sent the following message to the Service Chiefs: 'I acknowledge and appreciate the impartiality, devotion to duty and firmness with which all ranks of the armed forces ensured peaceful atmosphere during the general elections.'[1]

The Awami League had benefitted most from this 'peaceful' atmosphere. It had bagged all except two seats in East Pakistan. As soon as the unofficial counting was over, the European correspondent with whom I had shared the dinner table on 6 December rang up from his hotel room to say, 'Congratulations, Major! Your party has swept the polls.' I pocketed the compliment. Who disowns a winning horse!

What would be the Awami League's attitude now? Would it be flexible after it had capitalized on popular sentiment? I recalled my meeting, a month earlier, with Dr. Kamal Hossain, Mujib's chief *aide* on constitutional affairs.[2] I had suggested to him in the

---

[1] The *Pakistan Observer*, Dacca, 12 December 1970.
[2] He later won a seat in the National Assembly and became a cabinet minister in independent Bangla Desh.

air-conditioned bar of the Hotel Intercontinental, 'Now that the Awami League victory is a foregone conclusion, it would be better if you improve upon Sheikh Mujibur Rehman's image by projecting him as a national (rather than provincial) leader. It would do both him and the country good if he were to visit West Pakistan and address public meetings in important cities there in order to win the acceptance of the people as the future prime minister of Pakistan.' He said, 'That is a good suggestion but we will implement it after the elections. So far we have conducted our campaign on the Six Points and Bengali nationalism. If we change our stance now, we might lose the elections. Once we have converted the public sentiment into solid votes, we will amend the Six Points to make them acceptable to West Pakistan.'

After the election, I met him again and reminded him of his promise. He had changed like the whimsical weather of East Pakistan. He said, 'No, the Six Points cannot be changed. They are now public property. Any amendment would amount to a betrayal of the people's confidence.'

His party chief, Sheikh Mujibur Rehman, was equally adamant. He declared only two days after the polls: 'The election, for the people of Bangla Desh, was above all a referendum on the vital issue of full regional autonomy on the basis of the Six Points and the eleven-point programme...Therefore, a constitution securing full regional autonomy on the basis of the Six Points formula has to be framed and implemented in all respects.'[1]

That was the verdict of the majority-party leader in the National Assembly. If he chose to go it alone, could anybody stop him from becoming the undisputed ruler of Pakistan? Would the Army gracefully withdraw from the helm of affairs and leave it to the elected leaders to do their job? These were some of the questions that agitated our minds in Dacca immediately after the polls.

The answer to these questions was provided by a General in Yahya's confidence who came to Dacca in late December. After a sumptuous dinner at Government House, he declared during an informal chat, 'Don't worry... we will not allow these black bastards to rule over us.'

The remark seemed to have trickled down to Mujibur Rehman. While publicly thanking Yahya Khan for honouring his commitment to hold elections, he said that there was a section among

[1] The *Pakistan Observer*, Dacca, 10 December 1970.

Yahya's subordinates which was still conspiring to undo the election results. He added that some of these conspirators came to Dacca recently and held a secret meeting. He warned the President to restrain these conspirators, 'otherwise the people of Bangla Desh will confront those elements with bamboo sticks.'[1]

The real elements of confrontation, however, lay elsewhere.

---

[1] The *Pakistan Observer*, Dacca, 4 January 1971.

General A.M. Yahya Khan
President of Pakistan

Sheikh Mujibur Rehman
President of Awami League

6

THE MAKING OF A CRISIS

The Awami League duly triumphed in the elections by capturing 160 of the 162 seats in East Pakistan but it failed to secure even a single seat in the west wing where Z. A. Bhutto's Pakistan People's Party (with no candidates in East Pakistan) won 81 of the 138 seats. It created a very interesting but delicate situation.

I have referred earlier to the stiffening attitude of Mujibur Rehman after his victory. Mr. Bhutto who commanded the majority in West Pakistan, mainly in the important provinces of Punjab and Sind, also showed few signs of flexibility in his post-election utterances. He said in Lahore on 20 December: 'No constitution could be framed nor could any government at the centre be run without my party's co-operation.' He also said that the Punjab and Sind were bastions of power in Pakistan and since P.P.P. had emerged with a sweeping majority in these provinces, his party's co-operation would be essential for any central government. On the same occasion, he assured the people that 'the P.P.P. would not deviate an inch from its declared aims and objectives and would implement its programme in letter and spirit if and when it came to power.'[1]

The statement evoked a sharp rejoinder from Mr. Tajuddin, General Secretary of the Awami League. He said:

'The Awami League is quite competent to frame a constitution and form the Central Government. That would be done with or without the support of any party... The Punjab and Sind can no longer aspire to be the "bastions of power". If we are to move towards a better future, such claims should be avoided as they generate unnecessary and harmful controversy.'[2]

This post-election confrontation between East and West Pakistan was most worrying to us in Dacca. I felt its impact even on the junior army officers who rarely burden their minds with complex political issues. Some of them who saw in Mr. Bhutto a champion of their aspirations said, 'How can one province rule over the entire

[1] The *Pakistan Observer*, Dacca, 21 December 1970.
[2] Ibid., 22 December 1970.

country.' Others who had a genuine feel of the local situation commented, 'We have dominated them (the Bengalis) for a good twenty-three years. It is now their turn. We should not be always jockeying them.'

Whatever our feelings, the summit where the destiny of the nation would be decided was far removed—and snow-capped. There appeared some signs of a thaw by the turn of the year. The initiative came from the People's Party leader, Zulfikar Ali Bhutto. He intended to open a dialogue with the Awami League. We in Dacca saluted him *in absentia* for this important move. He sent his emissary to Dacca on 2 January 1971 to convey his personal felicitations to Mujib on his electoral victory and to prepare the ground for future talks with him. Bhutto also struck a conciliatory note in his statement of 27 December: 'We welcome the East Pakistan majority in the government and express our confidence in it.'[1]

Mujib apparently responded to these moves by declaring at a Dacca rally, 'Being the absolute majority party in the Assembly, I would not like to say that we do not want co-operation from representatives of West Pakistan in framing the Constitution. Surely, we want it.'[2] Now there seemed to be some movement in the right direction. A protégé of Yahya Khan attributed it to the benign influence of the President who was both umpire of the political game and a participant of influence. I did not bother who took the credit as long as dangerous confrontation was avoided.

I was pulled out of my rosy dreams on 3 January by an Awami League rally at Dacca where all the Awami League M.N.A.s and M.P.A.s (417 in number) took an oath of allegiance to the Six Points. They affirmed:

—'In the name of Allah, the Merciful, the Almighty;
—'In the name of the brave martyrs and fighters who heralded our initial victory by laying down their lives and undergoing the utmost hardship and repression;
—'In the name of the peasants, workers, students, toiling masses and the people of all classes of this country;
We, the newly-elected members of the National and Provincial Assemblies, do hereby take oath that we shall remain wholeheartedly faithful to the people's mandate on the Six Points and the eleven-point programme.'

[1] The *Dawn*, Karachi, 28 December 1970.
[2] The *Pakistan Observer*, Dacca, 31 December 1970.

It appeared we were back to square one. The Awami League had publicly tied down, on oath, its elected members to the Six Points, cutting off all hopes of give and take. I mentioned this to a Bengali journalist close to Mujibur Rehman and said, 'I feel that this period (between the elections and the Assembly session) should be used to mollify public sentiments roused during the year-long election campaign so that a negotiated agreement on the Constitutional Bill can be reached.' He replied, '*Sheikh Sahib* cannot let public sentiments cool off. That is his only weapon to counter your guns and tanks.'

The day following the Dacca Rally was the twenty-third anniversary of the founding of the East Pakistan Students League. The students seemed to be more impatient than Mujib for the realization of their goal. They pressed him hard to yield to their wishes but he, counselling patience, said, 'If necessary, I will give you a call for revolution. Till then you should wait.'[1]

The earlier hopes of a thaw were thus belied by Mujib's hardening attitude. He seemed to have spurned Bhutto's initiative.

If anybody could intervene to break the deadlock, it was President Yahya Khan. He flew to Dacca on 12 January 1971. He used this occasion to come to a 'thorough understanding' of the Six Points. Mujib and half a dozen of his senior colleagues were invited to the President's House to 'present' their Six Points. Lieutenant-General S.G.M. Peerzada, Principal Staff Officer to the President, summoned Governor Ahsan to attend the meeting. Ahsan, who had always been ignored in important political decisions about East Pakistan, reluctantly came over. He thought it was too late to attempt a 'thorough understanding' of the Awami League programme. It should have been done much earlier so that necessary steps could have been taken in time. Now when the entire province had voted for it, this move would be of little help.

Yahya, Peerzada and Ahsan sat on one side of the discussion table while Mujib, Khondkar Mushtaq, Tajuddin and their colleagues sat on the other. On the Awami League side, Mujib did most of the talking. He presented his Six Points one by one. After explaining each point, he said, 'You see, there is nothing objectionable in it. What's wrong with it? It is so simple.' Yahya and his *aides* listened. General Peerzada made an observation here and there but Mujib very sweetly overruled him. Yahya Khan, in the end, said,

[1] The *Pakistan Observer*, Dacca, 5 January 1971.

'I accept your Six Points. But there are strong feelings against them in West Pakistan. You should carry West Pakistan with you.' Mujib readily said, 'Of course, of course, we will carry West Pakistan with us. We will consult them. We will frame the constitution. We will frame it on the Six Points. We will show a copy of our constitution to you. There will be nothing wrong in it.' Yahya Khan batted his heavy eye-lashes, puffed at his foreign cigarette and remained silent.

I owe this version to Vice-Admiral Ahsan. Another account of the same meeting is given by the Central Communications Minister, Professor G. W. Chaudhry, who accompanied President Yahya Khan to Dacca on this historic mission. He tells us that the President was badly hurt by Mujib's betrayal. He says:

'As soon as the (Mujib–Yahya) meeting was over, I received and answered a summons from the President's House to see Yahya. I found him bitter and frustrated. He told me, "Mujib has let me down. Those who warned me against him were right; I was wrong in trusting this person." ...When I specifically asked him, "Have you reminded Mujib about his pledges made on the eve of the elections?" Yahya's reply was made with deep anguish. "You and I are not politicians—it is difficult for me to understand their mind and way of thinking. Let us pray and hope for the best." '[1]

General Yahya Khan left for Karachi on 14 January in the same disturbed mood. I was present at Dacca airport when he answered journalists' questions. He seemed to have lost all hope for the future. No reply, comment or 'aside' gave the slightest hint about his plans. He seemed impatient to throw the burden of further decisions onto Mujibur Rehman. In reply to a question, he said, 'Ask him (Mujib), he is the future Prime Minister of Pakistan. When he comes and takes over, I won't be there. It is going to be his government soon.'[2]

After his departure, a Bengali journalist said to me, 'The key sentence in the President's statement is "I won't be there" because the Awami League has refused to assure him of his continued presence in the President's chair under the democratic arrangement, unless he promises to authenticate the Awami League's draft Constitution.'

[1] Op. cit., pp. 149 and 151.
[2] The *Dawn*, Karachi, 15 January 1971.

The selfish broker, after a day's relaxation in Karachi, flew to Larkana as Mr. Bhutto's guest. The P.P.P. Chairman, who had naturally kept a watchful eye on the Mujib–Yahya meeting in Dacca, extended his traditional hospitality to the President and his *aides*. Among those who joined the President on this 'duck shooting' trip was the Army Chief, General Hamid. His presence at once inspired fearsome speculation in Dacca. The Awami League felt that a conspiracy was being hatched, with the active support of General Hamid, to punish Mujib for his unbending attitude in the recent talks.

Then appeared an important picture on the front page of Dacca papers showing Yahya and Bhutto enjoying a stroll on the spacious lawns of *Al-Murtaza*. It was in sharp contrast with the tense atmosphere in which the Dacca meeting was held. A Bengali journalist close to the Awami League, said to me, 'Look at this. When Yahya comes here, one of his staff officers rings up Mujib, the majority-party leader, to come and report to the President at the President's House but when he goes there, he stays with Bhutto, the minority-party leader. Is this the respect that the Army has for democracy?'

Let us hear the gist of the Larkana parleys from Bhutto himself:

'On his return from Dacca, President Yahya Khan and some of his advisers came to Larkana, my home town, on 17 January. The President informed us of his discussions at Dacca, in which he told Mujibur Rehman that three alternatives were open to the Awami League, namely to try and go it alone, to co-operate with the People's Party or to co-operate with the small and defeated parties of the West Wing; and that in his opinion, the best course would be for the two majority parties to arrive at an arrangement. For our part, we discussed with the President the implications of the Six Points and expressed our serious misgivings about them. We, nevertheless, assured him that we were determined to make every effort for a viable compromise, and said we were to visit Dacca in the near future to hold discussions with Awami League leaders.'[1]

After 'duck shooting' in Larkana, the President and his advisers left for Rawalpindi. Equipped with the President's briefing and guided by his own light, Bhutto left for Dacca on 27 January. He was accompanied by his *aides*.

Mr. Bhutto found the clouds of the 'Larkana Conspiracy' sur-

[1] Z.A. Bhutto, *The Great Tragedy*, p. 20.

rounding him in Dacca. It would have been better, it seemed, if he with his team had met Mujib and his advisers without having entertained Yahya and his party in his home town. Now the Dacca atmosphere had changed for the worse. Yet the Awami League tried to create favourable conditions for the visit because it felt that, after Yahya, it was the People's Party whose co-operation they should seek to make the President's veto ineffective. How could Yahya Khan refuse authentication to a Constitution Bill supported by the majority parties of both East and West Pakistan? But would Bhutto ignore the interests of his base of power in West Pakistan? If so, what advantage could accrue to him from this?

Mr. Rehman Sobhan gives us the Awami League version of the talks. He says, 'Mr. Bhutto came to Dacca in the last week of January. He had a direct session with Mujib, and then his 'constitutional team' met their Awami League counterparts. As the talks proceeded it became clear that the P.P.P. had, as yet, not prepared their draft, and were merely probing the Six Points as Yahya had done before them. This made formal negotiations impossible, since negotiations imply alternate sets of positions and an attempt to bridge the gap between them.'[1]

This version appeared six months after the talks. But I heard one comment from an Awami League source (the barrister Moinul Hussain) immediately after the talks. He said, 'You see, we had to strive very hard to make Bhutto acceptable to Dacca. But he showed no interest in the basic constitutional issues. He spent all his time discussing his share in power and the allocation of portfolios.'

Professor G.W. Chaudhry adds, 'He (Bhutto) and his party arrived there (Dacca) on 27 January. I was there to watch the outcome, if any, of the political dialogue between the two leaders who had emerged as the leaders of East and West Pakistan. There were three days of talks but, due to their lack of mutual understanding, there could hardly be any progress towards political settlement... Mujib made it clear to Bhutto, as I gathered from various sources, that he was not prepared to modify the six-points plan, while Bhutto made it clear that his party could not agree to a veiled scheme of secession under the plan.'[2]

[1] Rehman Sobhan, *Negotiating for Bangla Desh:* A Participant's View, The South Asian Review, London, July 1971.
[2] Op. cit., p. 19.

We have a fuller version from Bhutto, who wrote:

'On 27 January 1971, the leaders of the People's Party left for Dacca. In our discussions with Sheikh Mujibur Rehman we found him intractable on the Six Points. He told us plainly that he had received a mandate from the people on the Six Points and that he was not in a position to deviate one inch from the Six Points. We explained to the Awami League President that the People's Party had not received a mandate on the Six Points... We tried to put forward certain constitutional proposals, but the Awami League leaders refused any discussions till the Six Points were accepted *in toto*. We pointed out to Mujibur Rehman that public opinion in the West Wing was against the Six Points. We told him that the general impression of the people of the West Wing was that the Six Points spelt the end of Pakistan and that in our opinion the people's assessment was not far off the mark... The Awami League leader fully understood our difficulties but he was not prepared to accept them. He had chalked his strategy and our request did not suit his plans. The strategy was to bring the National Assembly to session without loss of time in order to give legal sanction to his Six Points to thrust a Six Points constitution on the country before full awareness of its implications could grow in the West Wing or, for that matter, in the East Wing itself.'[1]

Bhutto and his *aides* returned to West Pakistan on 30 January. A solution seemed to be nowhere in sight. The distance between the two wings looked wider than ever before.

India also contributed its share in widening this gulf. She banned overflights, using the pretext of a hijacked Indian Fokker.[2] P.I.A. flights which previously took two hours were now routed via Ceylon (Sri Lanka) taking about six hours. I have no evidence to support my impression that India had hatched this conspiracy well before 30 January but had timed it to coincide with the outcome of the abortive Bhutto Mujib talks. Subsequent developments, however, have strengthened my conviction in this regard.

By the end of January, the Awami League knew where it stood. So did Yahya and Bhutto. We had come to a complete impasse. Mujib pressed hard for convening the Assembly without delay,

---

[1] Z.A. Bhutto, *The Great Tragedy*, p. 22.
[2] Two Kashmiris had brought the Fokker to Lahore on 30 January. Judicial inquiry later confirmed that it was an Indian conspiracy to create a pretext for the ban.

at the latest by 15 February, while Bhutto argued for more time to influence public opinion in West Pakistan so as to reach some sort of a general agreement with the Awami League. Yahya, with his advisers, formulated his own schemes. No light was visible on the horizon.

In this hour of black depression, I turned to General Yakub whose vision had always been a source of strength to me. I asked him for his analysis of the situation. He said, 'I am trained in the profession of arms. My mental antennae are quite sensitive to all military moves. For instance, when they despatch an Indian Mountain Division from Kashmir to West Bengal apparently to supervise the elections, I can at once read all its implications, namely: has it really come for the declared purpose or has it some other role? Has it brought its mountain equipment or not? Is it deployed defensively or is it poised aggressively? But my political antennae are very dull. When Mujib makes a political move, I fail to understand its full implications... I really don't know. He (Mujib) tells one thing to me and quite another to his people. I don't know what he means.'

After about ten days of apprehensive silence, we heard some movement in the western wing. The new development began to unfold at measured intervals of two days: Mr. Bhutto had a long session with the President in Rawalpindi on 11 February; two days later it was announced that the Assembly would meet at Dacca on 3 March; after another two days Mr. Bhutto addressed a press conference in Peshawar (15 February) where he expressed his party's inability to attend the National Assembly session in the absence of an understanding, compromise or adjustment on the Six Points. 'I cannot put my party men in a position of double jeopardy (by sending them to Dacca),' he said and threatened 'a revolution from the Khyber to Karachi,'[1] if the People's Party were left out.

Two days after Bhutto announced his decision, Yahya Khan dismissed his civilian cabinet. It marked the end of civilian involvement in his regime and a reversion to pure Martial Law rule. Two days later, he called his military governors and martial law administrators for a conference in Rawalpindi. Lieutenant-General Yakub and Vice-Admiral Ahsan were to attend from East Pakistan. They were to meet on 22 February.

General Yakub called me on 19 February for an informal exchange

[1] The *Dawn*, Karachi, 16 February 1971.

of views. He made two points. Firstly, he said that Mr. Bhutto had kept his stand flexible. He would attend the Assembly session if he were assured by Mujib or the President that his views would be accommodated. 'I think General Yahya is fully armed with the Legal Framework Order to make his word effective.' Secondly, he said that if the deadlock continued and eventually culminated in a military situation, it would be catastrophic. It may appear that Yahya Khan is delaying the process of secession but in fact he will be hastening it. Then, emphasizing that we were discussing only a hypothetical situation, he asked my views on the military action if it became inevitable. I said, 'It has to be quick like a surgeon's knife. And it should be followed by massive action for political and economic healing.'

Before their departure for Rawalpindi, General Yakub and Admiral Ahsan met Mujib who assured them that 'the Six Points are negotiable.' A tricky fellow! He had the extraordinary guile to shift his position to suit new developments. But perhaps that is what is known as politics.

I do not know what they discussed and decided in Rawalpindi but I know the impact of their deliberations in Dacca. The news that reached us there was that Mujib would be given one more opportunity to prove his good intentions otherwise 'Martial Law would be reimposed (that is, enforced) in its classical role.' This implied two things. One, that renewed efforts for a political dialogue with Mujib would be made. Two, that military plans for regaining control would be finalized. Work on both commenced simultaneously in Dacca immediately after the return of General Yakub and Admiral Ahsan. Ahsan held rounds of talks with Mujib trying to convince him that he should climb down from his position on the Six Points to make them acceptable to West Pakistan. Ahsan told him, 'You preach the Six Points for East as well as West Pakistan whereas the people in the West Wing have strong feelings against them. You, therefore, should make a big gesture to wipe out the popular sentiments against them.' Mujib, according to Admiral Ahsan, promised to make the gesture. He announced a few days later that he would not insist on the application of the Six Points to the West Wing. As to the contents of the Six Points vis-a-vis East Pakistan, he did not budge an inch.

General Yakub also ordered his staff to finalize the operational plan 'BLITZ' which was originally prepared by Headquarters 14

Division for internal security. I, too, was asked to put the final touches to my mini-plan for a total press censorship in East Pakistan. It was to be incorporated in the main 'BLITZ' plan. 'Prepare it in such a way that on the green signal, you enforce complete censorship without raising any queries,' said the brigadier. 'But may I ask one question now?' 'Yes,' he replied. I said, 'What is the basis of this plan? Should I assume that the civil servants are on our side—because censorship is normally carried out with the help of civilian press officers?' He said rather angrily, 'I don't know. It is your job to assess their reaction and find an answer to your problem... But don't get it (the plan) typed. Make only one copy in your own hand and deposit it with me today.'

Two infantry battalions—22 Baluch and 13 Frontier Force—started flying in by P.I.A. on 27 February. The process continued till 1 March. The local Brigade Headquarters (57 Brigade) was asked to receive the additional troops and integrate them into the new operational plan. The Bengali brigade major was kept out of this arrangement for reasons of security. But hundreds of troops landing at Dacca, an airport manned mostly by Bengalis, could not be kept a secret.

As the situation on the military side drifted towards the 're-imposition' of martial law, the Awami League began to waver—a grave reckoning was approaching. Mujibur Rehman, as one of his *aides* put it, faltered in his resolve, becoming reluctant to accept responsibility for the death and destruction that would follow his intransigent attitude. Perhaps the foreign patrons who were covertly backing his moves were not yet ready for a show-down. The Awami League, therefore, tried desperately to get to General Yahya Khan to avoid armed confrontation or at least to buy time to oil its own confrontation machinery.

I received a call on 25 February from the Bengali editor of an influential daily. He pressed for an urgent meeting with me. I knew that he was very intimate with the Awami League high command and the matter could not be anything other than the latest situation.

I drove to his office at 11 a.m. and was introduced to two Bengali gentlemen who, I discovered later, were members of the Awami League Executive Committee. They said that President Yahya Khan should be asked to visit Dacca immediately. I said, 'Sorry, I don't control the President's movements.' 'But you can be heard

at the highest level. The matter is very urgent.' Then they disclosed that if the President came, the Awami League would honour
his visit by making substantial concessions. 'Publicly, we will
stick to the Six Points but, in fact, we will include certain riders
which will make the Six Points acceptable to you,' they said. To
add weight to their suggestion, they said that they talked on Mujib's
authority. The amendments they suggested were as follows:

1. Foreign trade will remain a provincial subject. Trade delega-
   tions will be sent by the provinces. They will explore and
   negotiate trade deals. *But no trade agreement will be effective
   unless it is ratified by the Centre.*
2. A province's income, from domestic and foreign sources,
   will remain in the Provincial Reserve Banks *but the money
   would not be spent on any project unless it was approved by a
   Central Co-ordination Committee which will have equal representation from all federating units.*
3. Levy of tax and its collection will be a provincial subject *but
   if the Central Government wants to retain its own machinery
   for collection of taxes, it will be allowed to do so.*
4. *We do not insist on a separate currency.*

They concluded by stating that they were prepared to give a
written commitment on these points. I promised to convey their
views to the appropriate authorities and suggested that even
now there was time for Mujib to pay a visit to West Pakistan.
'I am sure it will help,' I said, 'though I hold no brief on the subject.' They promised to discuss this proposal with Mujib at lunch
and let me know the results in the afternoon.

We met again at 4 p.m. in the same office. They conveyed Mujib's
reaction to my proposal as follows: 'I (Mujib) have held very
satisfying talks with Governor Ahsan recently. He dropped no
hint to the effect that the President needs me in Rawalpindi. My
hands are full with arrangements for the party convention on
27 February and I cannot leave unless I am assured that there
has been some fresh development on which urgent talks are
required.'

In the evening, I briefed General Yakub on my day's experience.
He took out the office copy of a long telegram he had already
sent to the President urging him to visit Dacca without further
loss of time. It appeared that what had been fed to me by the

Awami League representatives had already been conveyed to General Yakub.

We all hoped and prayed for the President's visit with desperate sincerity. We thought there was still time to avert the crisis. I even saw some junior officers tying up normal security details for the President's visit so that if he suddenly turned up he would not miss the usual ceremonial treat.

The President did not come. Something more ominous came instead.

7

MUJIB TAKES OVER

Lieutenant-General S. G. M. Peerzada, Principal Staff Officer to President Yahya Khan, made an ominous phone call to Governor Ahsan on 28 February to break the news that the President had decided to postpone the Assembly session to allow more time to the political parties to hammer out an agreement on the draft constitution outside the Assembly Chambers.

As desired by Peerzada, Mujib was summoned to Government House at 7 p.m. the same evening and, after a long preparatory talk, Ahsan apprised him of the President's decision. Surprisingly, Mujib did not let fly. He retained his sweet reasonableness and said, 'I will not make an issue out of it provided I am given a fresh date. It is very hard for me to handle the extremists within the party. If the new date is some time next month (March), I will be able to control the situation. If it is in April, it will be rather difficult. But if it is an indefinite postponment, it will be impossible.' Before leaving Government House, he said to Major-General Farman, 'I am between two fires. I will be killed either by the Army or extremist elements in my party. Why don't you arrest me. Just give me a ring and I will come over.'

The same evening Rawalpindi was informed of Mujib's reaction. It was followed up by earnest entreaties to Rawalpindi to include the new date in the postponement announcement. Rawalpindi cabled back a cold reply, 'Your message fully understood.'

Dacca interpreted this message as a tacit acceptance of its proposal and hopefully waited for the fresh date. The announcement was broadcast on 1 March at 13.05 hours (East Pakistan Standard Time). Anticipation and emotion kept us glued to our radio sets. I sat in the monitoring section so that I didn't miss a word. To our surprise, and horror, the announcement said nothing of the new date. Many ugly scenes began to hover before my eyes.

What surprised me, besides the omission of the date, was the absence of the President's voice which had jarred our ears several times before to announce relatively unimportant developments. Did this mean that he was not a party to the announcement? This, at least, is what Professor G. W. Chaudhry wants us to believe. He says, 'Yahya was only a signatory to it.'[1] Who then, was the author? When I checked up details of this important development with Major-General 'I' who was on Yahya's personal staff, he said, 'The President was in Karachi then. We were all downstairs. Major-General 'H' and Major-General 'O' were going up and down. They painted such a picture to the President that he had to agree to the draft already prepared.' Is this a sufficient defence for General Yahya Khan? Yahya was under pressure from the hawkish generals, Mujib from his extremists and Bhutto from the electorate! Who was then a free agent? How much one yields to such pressures and how much freedom of action one retains, gives the measure for a man who seeks the responsibilities of a national leader.

The reaction to the postponement in Dacca was instant. Advance knowledge of the decision allowed time to Mujib to organize his reaction. Within half an hour after the announcement, angry crowds brandishing bamboo sticks and iron rods thumped the city streets spitting anger wrapped in abusive slogans. The city seethed with fury. Shops, mainly those of non-Bengalis, were looted and vehicles destroyed. The cricket match between the BCCP (Board for Control of Cricket in Pakistan) XI and an International XI was wrecked at the City Stadium and the players, narrowly saved, were whisked away to the M.N.A.'s Hostel.

The Awami League Parliamentary Party met the same afternoon at a local hotel to consider the latest situation. Later in the evening, Mujib addressed a crowded press conference to declare, 'We cannot let it go unchallenged.'[2] He called for a complete hartal in Dacca on 2 March and throughout the province on 3 March. Allowing the next three days for the government 'to think and decide', he promised to spell out his future course of action at a public meeting on 7 March.

After showing his strong face to the public, he drove to Government House to plead once again for a fresh date. He said, 'I assure you there is still time. If you get me a new date even

[1] Op. cit., p. 159.
[2] The *Pakistan Observer*, Dacca, 2 March 1971.

now, I will be able to control the public fury tomorrow. Thereafter, it will be too late.'

The top brass in Dacca put their heads together the same night and tried to speak to President Yahya Khan on the telephone. But they could only get to Peerzada who refused to lend an ear to the Dacca tune. Then they tried to locate General Hamid (who had gone out of Rawalpindi) so that he could be persuaded to prevail upon his old pal, Yahya Khan. General Hamid listened to the crisis talk and promised to speak to General Yahya Khan. But nothing came of it. Later that night, General Peerzada rang up General Yakub and asked him to take over from Admiral Ahsan. The Admiral was eased out of Government House most unceremoniously.

The country was plunged into deep chaos. In my view, this development finally confirmed Mujib's fears of the existence of a conspiracy. He slammed all doors on negotiations, launched a 'non-violent non-cooperation movement' and set out upon the war path.

The Bengali staff of P.I.A., Dacca, were the first to boycott their work. They refused to handle the flights which brought troops (22 Baluch and 13 Frontier Force) from Karachi. Two Bengali youths even tried to blow up a Boeing but they were forestalled by the Pakistan Air Force, which took over the flight handling and airport management duties on 1 March and carried them out most successfully throughout the subsequent turbulence.

The incoming troops confirmed Mujib's misgivings and he protested that the Boeings which should have brought M.N.A.s were flying in troops to 'suppress the aspirations of the Bengali people'. General Yakub requested Rawalpindi to stop forthwith the further dispatch of troops, as they would do more harm than good.

Mujib was now spitting fire. How soon it would envelop the whole province, or the country, was anybody's guess. The local martial law administration tried to contain the flames by issuing a Martial Law Order (number 110) which prohibited the press from publishing news, views or pictures against the integrity and sovereignty of Pakistan. The flames burnt this scrap of paper because the journalists could comply with its content only at the peril of their life and that of their dependents. The Awami League *goondas* (strong-arm boys) cracked down heavily on those who failed to conform to their tactics. The administration, on the other hand, was unable to provide the requisite protection to all the threatened journalists and their families. The result was obvious.

In this critical situation, Chief Secretary, Shafiul Azam, proved very helpful to the Awami League, whose game now was to compound the chaos and to render Yahya's Government ineffective in East Pakistan. It made a calculated move spear-headed by Shafiul Azam. He rang up Major-General Farman, in charge of civil affairs, to 'request' that the army should be called out to control the situation. Farman replied, 'It's not as simple as that. It has serious implications. You had better employ your normal law-enforcing agencies.' 'No, *General Sahib*,' insisted Mr. Shafiul Azam, 'They can't control the situation. The army has to step in.' Similar telephone calls were made by the Home Secretary and the Inspector-General of Police to senior martial law officers. A few minutes later Shafiul Azam again phoned General Farman and pressed for acceptance of his 'request'. General Farman said, 'Have you consulted *Sheikh Sahib*?' 'Yes, I have. I am speaking with his approval,' said Shafiul Azam.

The army agreed — and fell into the trap. As soon as the curfew was announced and the troops moved in (2 March, evening) to enforce it, the Awami League sent out its workers to violate it. A platoon of 32 Punjab was lifted by helicopter from the cantonment and lodged inside Government House to protect it from the violent mob. The troops were under strict orders not to open fire. The Awami League volunteers seemed to be under equally strict orders to provoke firing. These were very trying moments. Brigadier 'A' left his troops under the command of his officers and rushed to the Martial Law Headquarters to protest his predicament. He said, 'You have tied my hands and thrown me into the fire. Troops are jeered at and abused. They are still obeying orders not to shoot. But their patience will soon reach its limits.' I also heard his protest. He seemed far more perturbed than I had seen him during the 1965 war.

Later that night, pressure mounted and the troops' patience wore out. The troops and the mob clashed. While the soldiers sustained only minor injuries (from brick-bats and similar missiles), the mob lost six persons. Of them, three had been killed outside Government House which they tried to swarm and ransack.

Zulfikar Ali Bhutto
Chairman of Pakistan People's Party

Lt.-Gen. S.G.M. Peerzada
Principal Staff Officer to the President

Gen. Abdul Hamid Khan
Chief of Staff, Pakistan Army

Six deaths in one night! Shafiul Azam and his patrons had carried the day! This would not only complicate the army's position but also give a new fillip to the Awami League movement.

Next day, they carried these dead bodies in a procession on the main city roads. Then Mujib, placing the corpses in front of him, displayed his best talents as an orator. His fiery speech worked up the processionists to such a pitch that they would willingly have undertaken the deadliest tasks for his sake. Later he issued a four-page press statement calling upon all sections of society, including government servants, to rise against 'the unlawful government' and recognize 'people's representatives' as the 'only legitimate source of authority'.[1]

This provocative statement reached the newspapers and the Martial Law Headquarters at about the same time, shortly before midnight on 2 March. A 'wise' martial law officer suggested that the press should be asked to black it out. I said, 'That is possible. But beware of its repercussions. It will further infuriate Mujib and he will lash out more savagely at the government tomorrow.' Then General Yakub called me to his office and enquired, 'What do you suggest?' Knowing that he enjoyed some sort of equation with Mujib, I said, 'If you persuade Mujib to withdraw the statement or at least tone it down, it will solve the problem.' He spoke to Mujib for forty minutes in my presence from eleven-thirty to ten minutes past midnight. He used all his tact, persuasive eloquence and diplomacy to convince Mujib, but without avail. The General would say, '*Sheikh Sahib, aap khud siyaney hain.*[2] You know the situation is very tense. A statement like this will only worsen it.' Mujib argued back, 'No, there is nothing inflammatory in it. It is just another political statement.' So the debate continued. Mujib refused to oblige. After he had put down the telephone receiver, General Yakub looked across his shining table towards me and said, 'He was saying: "I cannot tone it down. I am under pressure. You'd better come and arrest me. It will solve my problem!" I was about to say that it won't solve mine. But, perhaps, that was not the occasion ... O.K., where do we go from here?'

Then he called a 'mini war council' of Major-General Khadim, Major-General Farman and Brigadier Jilani, which I also attended.

---

[1] The *Pakistan Observer*, Dacca, 3 March 1971.
[2] 'You are yourself a sensible person.'

It was decided to forewarn the troops, all over the province, to be ready to meet anv upheaval that the statement might evoke in their areas.

Next morning, General Yakub again pleaded with Rawalpindi to take some decision or authorize him to do so because the situation was fast deteriorating. The President's reply was, 'I trust your judgement and you may exercise it *if telecommunications between Dacca and Rawalpindi fail.*' But real communication between Dacca and Rawalpindi had already failed. Only the wire service remained physically operative.

Meanwhile, the law and order situation continued to deteriorate. Spirited mobs clashed in Dacca with law-enforcement agencies, including the Army, resulting in a number of casualties. Similar reports poured in from Chittagong, Jessore, Khulna, Comilla, Sylhet and Rangpur. Where there were no troops, the mob played with the life, property and honour of non-Bengalis.

President Yahya Khan was kept posted on the developing situation. Initially, he did not budge. But when he was sure that the situation had reached a point of no return, he declared his intentions. He wanted to meet all the politicians in Dacca on 10 March. Word was sent in advance to Mujib to assess his reaction. Mujib agreed. His assent was flashed to Rawalpindi. But when the President's proposal was announced, Mujib flung back a sharp reaction. He said, 'NO MORE R.T.C., NO MORE FARCE.'[1] After he had spent his fury, he was asked about this volte-face. He said, 'What I had agreed to was Yahya's meeting with individual politicians or their small groups. I did not, and do not, favour any form of Round Table Conference where I have to sit at the same table with people like Bhutto who is responsible for the shedding of Bengalis' blood.' Mujib made no secret of his allegation that Bhutto was behind all the trouble in East Pakistan.

Casualties were mounting every day. On 3 March 155 wounded persons were admitted to Dacca Medical College Hospital and the Mitford Hospital. Next day, eight persons were killed—four on the spot, four dying in hospital. Mujib visited the hospital and gave a call for blood donations.

The troops had hardly stayed for two days in the city—at

---

[1] Reference to President Ayub Khan's Round Table Conference held in Rawalpindi from 11–13 March 1969.

Shafiul Azam's request, made with Mujib's consent—when their presence was termed 'provocative to the people'. Mujib now wanted them to go back to their barracks, as if he had merely wanted to 'test their effectiveness'. But who would maintain law and order? Mujib replied, 'Leave it to me. I will use my volunteers. If necessary, I will call Ansar (provincial paramilitary force) and Police help. But I don't need your army. Send it back to the barracks.'

Mujib's offer was seriously considered at the Martial Law Headquarters. The general impression at the meeting was that it was impossible to maintain peace without the active co-operation of the Awami League. Therefore, reference was made to Rawalpindi and a decision was obtained to the effect that the troops would be withdrawn to the cantonment. It amounted to assigning the peace-keeping role to blood-thirsty Awami League volunteers. But the troops were withdrawn to their barracks!

So the government voluntarily abdicated in favour of Mujib, who now became the absolute ruler of East Pakistan. Life for non-Bengalis, under Mujib, became miserable. Many of them sought refuge in the cantonment—the only island of safety in a sea of torture. There was hardly a house in the Dacca Cantonment which did not have five to fifty refugees from the city. They lay on verandahs, in backyards, servants quarters, galleries and even kitchens. Those who could afford to buy a ticket to safety, flew to West Pakistan. But the majority of them had to endure the ordeal.

General Yakub, sensitive to human misery, rang up General Peerzada on 4 March to say that the President must visit Dacca without any further delay because every hour that ticked by, took us away from a possible solution. Peerzada, after having a word with the President, rang back that the President would be visiting Dacca soon but it was difficult to give a firm date immediately. General Peerzada also disclosed that the President would talk to Mujib 'right now' and tell him 'not to make things difficult'. Yahya contacted Mujib on a private telephone which was not listed in the telephone directory.

This development greatly relieved General Yakub and all those whom he took into confidence. The same night (4/5 March), Governor Ahsan who had handed over to General Yakub on 1 March was due to fly to West Pakistan. He was invited to a

farewell dinner at General Yakub's house. Major-Generals Khadim
Raja and Farman Ali were also present. After they had seen off
Vice-Admiral Ahsan, the three generals sat down and discussed
the President's impending visit and its anticipated favourable
impact on the situation. At 9.10 p.m. a telephone call interrupted
their conversation. The President was on the line. He wanted to
speak to General Yakub. While he walked to the telephone appre-
hensively, General Raja, General Farman, their wives and Begum
Yakub waited in suspense. Yahya said, 'I have changed my mind.
I am not coming to Dacca.' General Yakub tried to put in a word
or two but the President remained adamant. He said, 'No, I cannot
come because I am convinced that it won't bring me anywhere
near the solution.' With that, he hung up.

The immediate reaction of the three generals was that of despair
and desolation. What could be done? The President had extinguished the only flicker of hope. Immediately, General Yakub
put in a call to General Peerzada. He was through in a minute.
He said, 'Peer, if the President cannot be persuaded to come
(to Dacca), I may be relieved of my responsibilities. I will send
you my formal resignation tomorrow morning.' As soon as the
telephone call was over, Khadim and Farman also offered to
resign but, according to these two gentlemen, General Yakub said,
'Thank you for this gesture of support. But this is no trade union.
It is the Army. You carry on.'

Before they dispersed, it was decided to send General Farman,
by the midnight flight, to the headquarters of the Chief Martial
Law Administrator (Rawalpindi) to apprise Peerzada and the
President of the gravity of the situation. Once on board, he had
about eight flying hours to contemplate his delicate mission.
The following morning (5 March), General Yakub sent his resignation by signal (telegram) to Rawalpindi. The resignation text also
contained, typically, an admirable pen-portrait of the prevailing
situation.

Before the resignation reached the President, the latter had
taken the next decision. He had summoned Lieutenant-General
Tikka Khan, a corps commander and martial law administrator
(Punjab) to Rawalpindi to assign him to his new task in General
Yakub's place. General Farman and General Tikka, travelling
from different places and charged with different missions, landed
at Rawalpindi together. Each was given a separate audience by

the President. General Tikka Khan was briefly told of his new job and he readily accepted it as a true professional soldier. When General Farman discussed the East Pakistan situation with the President and pleaded for prompt decisions to arrest the drift General Yahya said, '*Bachu*, I have to think of my base. I have to think of West Pakistan. I cannot destroy my base.'

Meanwhile, more blood had been shed in East Pakistan. The victims were mostly the unarmed non-Bengalis who could not defend themselves against Awami League terrorists. The bloodiest spot was Pahartali, a part of Chittagong, where 102 non-Bengalis were killed in one day (3 March). Brigadier Mozumdar, the Centre Commandant who had been made martial law administrator there, apparently did nothing to prevent this butchery.

The situation in Dacca itself had grown far worse. Nobody felt secure. The agony of impending death weighed heavy on most of the non-Bengali civilians. Many of them sold their household effects to buy a passage to Karachi. Some rich residents of the Gulshan and Banani colonies willingly parted with their brand new cars in exchange for a P.I.A. seat—the normal fare was only Rs. 250. The airport had long queues of waiting men and women. Many of them spent days and nights there to maintain their 'seniority' in the row. They presented a pathetic scene— like tragic sea-farers thrown on a cold alien shore by a tidal wave.

The Awami League volunteers established check-points on all major routes leading to the airport to 'stop the outflow of Bangla Desh wealth'. The strongest picket was at the Farm Gate on the city airport road. A Pathan, travelling by rickshaw, was stopped there for a search. He resisted. The result: instant and cruel death. His body was dragged and thrown into a nearby ditch. This happened in broad daylight, just a few hundred metres from the Dacca City Martial Law Headquarters. The Army sent a detachment of troops to recover the body and bury it in the cantonment—the only safe place for the living as well as the dead.

As the crucial 7 March—the day Mujib was to address a public rally at Ramna Race Course—approached, Dacca became restive with rumours, fears and apprehensions. It was widely anticipated that Sheikh Mujibur Rehman would make a unilateral declaration of independence (U.D.I.) for Bangla Desh. Many people thought that it would only formalize a *de facto* situation, but others felt that it would mean the outright break-up of Pakistan which the armed forces would not allow.

The Awami League was also aware of the grave consequences of such a declaration. Its extremist elements still pressed for it but the moderates pleaded against it. Mujib is said to have oscillated between the two, weighing the pros and cons of this extreme step.

The Awami League went into session on 6 March, after dinner, to take the final decision. All eyes of the government were focussed on the meeting. The headquarters of the Chief Martial Law Administrator was also informed of the anticipated 'bombshell'. The meeting was adjourned at midnight without a decision. It was to meet again early next morning.

Meanwhile, two important developments took place. President Yahya had had a long telephone conversation with Mujib on 6 March persuading him 'not to take a step from which there would be no return'.[1] Later, he sent a teleprinter message for Mujib. It arrived in the Martial Law Headquarters Dacca at about midnight in my presence. I read it briefly before it was passed on. Later I recorded its contents from memory, in my diary:

Please do not take any hasty decision. I will soon come to Dacca and discuss the details with you. I assure you that your aspirations and commitments to the people can be fully honoured. I have a scheme in mind which will more than satisfy your Six Points. I urge you not to take a hasty decision.

The message was carried personally to Mujib's Dhanmandi residence by a brigadier who, on his return, was voluble about Mujib's hospitable and courteous mood and the festive look of his house where dozens of cars and scores of visitors basked in the sparkling festive atmosphere.

To say that the President sent the message on the advice of the Dacca authorities to 'build up sufficient strength to act decisively against the Awami League'[2] is sheer fabrication. Dacca had, in fact, advised against any build up of forces during this period. Even the normal change-over of troops was stopped. What lay in Yahya's mind is another matter.

[1] G.W. Chaudhry, *The Last Days of United Pakistan*, p. 153.
[2] Robert Jackson, *South Asian Crisis: India–Pakistan–Bangla Desh*, Chatto and Windus, London, p. 29.

The same day (6 March), President Yahya had announced that the National Assembly would meet in Dacca on 25 March. If this had been done a week earlier, the situation would have been different.

The second important development of the night took place at the G.O.C.'s house in Dacca cantonment. He was woken at 2 a.m. by his intelligence officer who was accompanied by two representatives of the Awami League. Mujib's emissaries said, 'Sheikh Sahib is under immense pressure from extremists. They are forcing him to make the U.D.I. He doesn't find enough strength to refuse them. He suggests that he be taken into military custody.' The G.O.C. replied, 'I am sure a popular leader like Mujib knows how to resist such pressure. He cannot be made to act against his will. Tell him I will be there (at the Ramna Race Course) to save him from the wrath of the extremists. But tell him, too, that if he talks against the integrity of Pakistan, I will muster all I can—tanks, artillery and machine-guns—to kill all the traitors and, if necessary, raze Dacca to the ground. There will be no one to rule, there will be nothing to rule.'

Next morning (7 March), the U.S. Ambassador to Pakistan, Mr. Farland called on Mujib. A Bengali journalist, Mr. Rahman, phoned me a little later to say that the U.D.I. had been averted. G.W. Chaudhry tells us more about Farland's call on Mujib. He says, 'The U.S. policy was made clear to Mujib by Ambassador Farland who advised him not to look towards Washington for any help for his secessionist game.'[1]

Then the crucial hour struck. Mujib's speech was to commence at 2.30 p.m. (local time) and the Dacca station of Radio Pakistan, on its own initiative, had made arrangements to broadcast it live. The radio announcers were already speaking from the Race Course telling the listeners about the unprecedented enthusiasm of the million-strong audience.

The headquarters of the Chief Martial Law Administrator intervened and directed Dacca to stop this 'nonsense'. I conveyed the orders to the radio station. The Bengali friend at the receiving end reacted sharply to the order. He said, 'If we can't broadcast the voice of seventy-five million people, we refuse to work.' With that, the station went off the air.[2]

[1] Op. cit., p. 120.
[2] It resumed its transmission next morning when it was allowed to play the tape of Mujib's speech.

Mujib who, in the morning, had allowed student leaders to hoist the national flag of an independent Bangla Desh at his residence, refused to unfurl it at the public meeting. Tense and coiled, he mounted the dais and surveyed the sea of humanity waiting for his long awaited declaration. Mujib started in his usual thunderous tone but gradually scaled down the pitch to conform to the contents of his speech. He did not make the U.D.I. but laid down four preconditions for attending the assembly session on 25 March. These were:

1. The lifting of Martial Law;
2. The transfer of power to the people's representatives;
3. The return of the Army to barracks; and
4. The establishment of a judicial enquiry into the killing of Bengali people.

At the end of his speech, he counselled the people to remain peaceful and non-violent. The crowds that had surged to the Race Course dispersed like a receding tide. They looked like a religious congregation returning from mosque or church after listening to a satisfying sermon. They lacked the fury which might have motivated them to charge on the cantonment—as many of us had apprehended. The reaction to the speech in the Martial Law Headquarters was that of relief. A senior officer, replying to a telephone call from Headquarters, Chief Martial Law Administrator said, 'This is the best speech under the circumstances.'

Now that the immediate crisis had been averted, analysts started probing for the factors that influenced Mujib's decision. They listed three reasons. Maybe, he had grasped the olive branch held out by the President; maybe Farland's visit had tilted the balance; maybe it was the G.O.C.'s threat that had done the trick. Maybe all three influences had worked together. But nobody was prepared to attribute it to Mujib's genuine love for Pakistan.

After the storm had receded, Lieutenant-General Tikka Khan arrived at 1540 hours. Lieutenant-General Yakub, Major-General Khadim Raja and other senior military officers went to receive him. I was there, too. General Tikka Khan, wearing a blue suit and a white collar, descended from the plane beaming vitality and confidence. He was in sharp contrast to the fragile and fatigued figure of Lieutenant-General Yakub who, dressed in khaki uniform, flogged the flaps of his trousers to hide his emotional convulsions. The two looked so different; so were their roles. As the motorcade left the tarmac, the spring sun cast its last rays on the glittering top of the black Mercedes. Night was falling fast.

Major-General Khadim Hussain Raja accompanied General Tikka Khan in the same car. On the way General Tikka said to Khadim, 'What mess have you created here?' The G.O.C., who had weathered several storms, both political and meteorological and hoped for a word of cheer, was stung by this unexpected remark. He jumped to the edge of his seat and said, 'Mind your words, Sir. We have been through hell here. Is this our reward? Please hold your remarks till you have seen the situation yourself.' General Tikka kept quiet. The schism created between the two, on the first day, took several weeks to mend.

The same evening, General Tikka Khan was officially briefed on the situation. I was told to be available in the adjoining room during the briefing, but nobody sent for me. At about 7.30 p.m. General Yakub emerged from the briefing and, placing his affectionate hand on my right shoulder, said,

نہیں کھیل اے داغ یاروں سے کہہ دو   کہ آتی ہے اردو زباں آتے آتے

'One doesn't realize the full significance of a problem at first sight.'

At 8 p.m., a signal was sent to Rawalpindi saying that General Tikka Khan had taken over. Now he wore three hats: those of Governor, Martial Law Administrator, and Commander of Eastern Command. He inspired confidence among us for his soldierly qualities. We also respected General Yakub, a linguist and intellectual, who, we knew, had bowed out because he could not bow down to a policy of deliberate crisis and consequent repression.

But Mujibur Rehman still reigned in the province and General Tikka Khan could not find a judge to swear him in as the Governor of East Pakistan. Mr. Justice Siddiki, Chief Justice of the East Pakistan High Court, refused to administer the oath for 'reasons of ill health'. In fact, he could not afford to annoy the Awami League, the *de facto* ruler of the province. A few days later, the Dacca Bar Association passed a resolution complimenting Mr. Siddiki on his bold stand.

The martial law officers in Dacca tried to make alternative arrangements. But according to the legal parchment issued by the President, the swearing in ceremony was to be performed by the Chief Justice of the concerned province. His nominee or a local judge of the Supreme Court could not administer the oath unless the parchment was amended. General Tikka himself rang up his Chief Secretary, Shafiul Azam, to arrange this ceremony but he, on one pretext or the other, refused. Thus he maintained his allegiance to the Awami League without losing his job as Chief Secretary.

Meanwhile, the Awami League consolidated its rule by issuing a series of directives (31 in all) which were obeyed by all sections of society including government departments, industrial units, state and commercial banks, educational institutions and the rest. Even government-controlled radio and TV obeyed Mujib's commands. Mujib's rule engulfed the entire province except seven pockets within the military cantonments where officers and men spent their oppressed days and nights. Though pent up emotionally, they adhered to the demands of discipline. But Mujib left no provocation untried. He even asked the people to deny the use of roads and railways to the armed forces. The local contractors stopped their supplies. The officers and men lived on their reserve of dry rations. And yet they obeyed all orders.

Some of them still stood guard with police and the East Pakistan Rifles (E.P.R.) on important buildings like banks, the radio and television stations, the power-house and telephone exchange. The mobs often rebuked, jeered and abused the troops on duty and obstructed their local movements. At times, it led to a clash between the mob and law enforcement agencies. The result was casualties on both sides; a few to the government troops, several to the mob.

An official hand-out issued on 7 March admitted the week's casualties as 172 dead and 358 wounded. It said, '...out of them, 78 were killed and 205 injured in clashes between the rioters themselves at Pahartali, Feroze Bagh Colony and Wireless Colony in Chittagong. The army killed only five and injured one while two fell to E.P.R. bullets... 41 persons were killed due to police firing in the local–non-local clashes in Khulna on 3 and 4 March... They killed three persons and wounded 11 at Rangpur in their effort to quell the local disturbance... Four persons lost their lives and one sustained injuries due to police firing when a train was derailed near Khulna on March 4... 341 convicts and under-trial accused tried to escape by breaking open Dacca Central Jail on March 6. The police had to resort to firing, killing 7 and injuring 30... The violent mob attacked telephone exchanges at Jessore, Khulna and Rajshahi on March 3 and 4. The army troops guarding these vital installations had perforce to resort to firing which resulted in 8 deaths and injuries to 19 persons. Three persons were killed and some were injured when troops had to fire while they were attacked by a mob on their way from Jessore to Khulna on March 5... In discharge of their duties, the law enforcing agencies also suffered casualties which included one officer killed and one wounded... In the Nawab-pur Thatari Bazar incident on the night 2–3 March, E.P.R. killed 6 persons and injured 53. An E.P.R. personnel fired in self-defence killing 4 persons and injuring three... The province-wide casualties by the army are 23 killed and 26 wounded. Of these, six persons were killed when a mob attacked the army at Sadarghat (Dacca) on night 2–3 March. One person was killed while the army tried to protect the local television station from a violent mob on 3 March.'[1]

The Bengalis did not believe these figures. They thought that the hand-out understated the facts. Rather they believed in the blaring newspaper headlines which said, 'Several Hundred Rushed to Hospital with Bullet Injuries', 'Thousands Being Mowed Down by Army Bullets', 'Innocent Women and Children Among the Sufferers.'

What the hand-out, as well as the newspapers, failed to report was the agony of non-Bengalis (including West Pakistani civilians) who continued to suffer at the hands of Awami League terrorists. It was suggested to the authorities that they give out details of these Awami League atrocities during its *de facto* rule, but they refused to do so. They gave two reasons for this. Firstly they said that it would 'disprove' the two-nation theory (Muslims killing Muslims). Secondly, it could provoke reprisals in West Pakistan where a large number of Bengalis lived a peaceful life.

The matter was referred to Headquarters, Chief Martial Law Administrator with the advice that if the atrocity stories were issued later they would be taken as an after-thought. Rawalpindi, too, kept the lid tight on this boiling barrel of blood. The President still marked time at Rawalpindi. Was he perhaps waiting for the situation to deteriorate sufficiently to ensure that his visit would not improve the prospects for the assumption of power by the Awami League?

Mujib, meanwhile, organized his armed strength for a show-down with the President if the latter refused to recognize the realities of the situation. Colonel (ret.) M.A.G. Osmani became Mujib's

[1] The *Pakistan Observer*, Dacca, 8 March 1971.

de facto commander-in-chief. His private army consisted of Awami League volunteers, university students and ex-servicemen. They were provided with weapons by looting arms shops and laying open government armouries. All the Ansar rifles, held by the Provincial Government, were issued to them. Caches of arms funnelled from abroad (mostly India) with relief goods during the post-cyclone operations augmented the indigenous resources. University boys and girls made crude 'bombs' in their laboratories. They also rehearsed the making of road blocks and the erecting of barricades. When an old Awami Leaguer, not in active politics, warned Mujib that 'You cannot fight a professional army like this,' he said, 'Oh, I know the Army's worth. It could not even enforce a curfew in Dacca. What can it achieve if seventy-five million people, though crudely armed, rise against it.'

On Mujib's instructions, Colonel Osmani also established contact with the Bengali police, the East Pakistan Rifles and East Bengal battalions to co-ordinate their action on a given date and time. The military team of the Awami League high command met regularly. Some serving Bengali officers also attended these meetings.[1] This development was reported to the authorities but they refused to take action. When I mentioned to a senior officer that Bengali troops may betray us, he said severely: 'Keep your mouth shut. You are casting aspersions on the discipline of the Pakistan Army— the best in the world.'

These were the broad features of the first fortnight of Mujib's rule. We waited to see what difference the President's visit would make.

Several Bengali officers, during their interrogation later, admitted their involvement in the military preparations of the Awami League. They included Brigadier Mozumdar, Commandant, East Bengal Centre: Lieutenant-Colonel Masudul Hasan, Commanding Officer, 2 East Bengal; and Lieutenant-Colonel Yasin of the Governor's Inspection Team. Several others, who escaped arrest, loudly boasted of their prior knowledge of the pre-arranged reaction. They included Major (later Brigadier) Musharraf, Major Jalil and Major Moin.

8

TRIANGLE

I have seen many arrivals of Presidents and Heads of State but I will never forget the atmosphere in which President Yahya Khan landed in Dacca on 15 March. All entries to the airport were sealed. Steel-helmeted guards were posted on the roof-top of the terminal building. Every inmate of the airport building was scrupulously screened. A heavy contingent was posted at the P.A.F. Gate—the only entrance to the tarmac. A company (nearly one hundred men) of an infantry battalion (18 Punjab) mounted on trucks fitted with machine guns waited outside the gate to escort the President to the city. Only a handful of officers, carefully picked, were allowed inside the airport. Special security passes were issued to them, including me.

There were no bouquets of flowers, no civil officials, no rows of 'city elite', no hustling of journalists, and no clicking of cameras. Even the official photographer was not admitted. It was a strange, eerie atmosphere charged with a deadly stillness. We all waited, in a bunch, outside a small control office near the P.I.A. hangar. There were still five minutes to go before the President's arrival. An Allouette III of Army Aviation fluttered up and down, about a hundred metres away, practising landing and take-off. It had been positioned there to fly the President to the President's House—three kilometres away in the city—in case he decided to avoid the dangerous road route. Those who waited for the President included Lieutenant-General Tikka Khan, Major-General Khadim Raja, Major-General Farman and Major-General A. O. Mitha, the Quartermaster-General of the Pakistan Army.

We looked at our watches, then to the western horizon. But the President's Boeing was still out of sight. Meanwhile, a vulture emerged from the left and flew past over our heads; and the Bengali Superintendent of Police, Dacca, came panting up with the 'happy news' that *Sheikh Sahib* had very graciously agreed to remove the Farm Gate check-point 'to avoid embarrassment to his guest'

Earlier, Mujib had declared publicly that President Yahya 'is we come as a guest of Bangla Desh'.

The President arrived at 3 p.m. Squadron Leader Qazi of P.A.F drove the gangway to the aircraft and the President descended, hi plump face radiating health and vitality. He talked casually bu confidently. Referring to the male crew that had flown him via Sr Lanka, he said, 'They are brave boys. Well done.' Then he shool hands with everybody, even me. There seemed to be no burden on his mind or conscience. He looked as vacant as he would when visiting a routine army unit. There was no sign of his awarenes of the tragic situation in which we had lived from day to day, hour to hour and, at times, minute to minute.

Meanwhile, the car with a four-star plate had pulled up in from of the V.I.P.s. General Tikka Khan, looking at the helicopter, said to the President, 'Would you like to go by car?' 'Do you doubt it?' 'No, I mean the helicopter is ready, too.' 'No, I will go by road.' General Tikka Khan accompanied him in the same car, others followed. The company of 18 Punjab assumed the escort duties. Wireless messages reported the progress of the President's journey to the city: He has safely crossed Farm Gate... Now he is approaching the V.I.P. building... The motorcade has now negotiated the last bend before the President's House... The President has safely reached his destination. Many heaved a sigh of relief. A major hurdle had been crossed peacefully.

The same evening, General Yahya Khan summoned his local senior military officers for an on-the-spot situation report. Generals Tikka, Khadim, Farman and Air Commodore Masud, among others, attended it. The briefing started in typical army fashion and sailed through the prescribed procedure: describing the mission, the magnitude of the problem (in terms of law and order only), the quantum of available forces and their distribution to various areas. Like all briefings, it ended on a confident note.

The President was not presented with any study in depth of the complex political situation. Nor were any recommendations made. When I later asked one of the senior officers to account for this omission, he said, 'The President never asked for it. He had his own advisers. He relied on their analysis. He didn't care a fig for the opinion of the men on the spot.'

At the end of the briefing, the President said, 'Don't worry. I will line up Mujib tomorrow... will give him a bit of my mind...

shall cold shoulder him and won't even invite him for lunch. Then I will meet him the day after and see how he reacts. If he doesn't behave, I'll know the answer.' There was a silence. After a few awkward moments, a tall wiry fellow stood up like a wing strut and asked for permission to make a submission. The request was granted with a nod. 'Sir,' he opened, 'The situation is very delicate. It is essentially a political issue and it needs to be resolved politically, otherwise thousands of innocent men, women and children will perish...' Yahya listened with rapt attention, the others with apprehension. The President, batting his lashes and nodding his head said, 'Mitty, I know it... I know it...' Mitty sat down. (A few days later, he was quietly relieved of his duties. He only retained the burden of moral courage.) The meeting dispersed. That was the last military conference Yahya Khan held in Dacca. He then turned to his political task.

He met Mujib at the President's House next day. There were no *aides* on either side. It was understood to be an informal attempt to re-establish the broken contact. It didn't take Yahya long to discover that Mujib had something up his sleeve and he didn't respond to the President's overtures as openly as he had done in pre-election days. The President was dismayed. Amazingly, he had (apparently) failed to see the snake in the grass for one full year, although it is said that leaders should be sensitive enough to hear the grass grow.

The preceding half month had, in fact, eroded all common ground for a negotiated settlement. Mujib, during this period, had ruled the province with a firm hand. His hold over the civil administration and people was absolute. This *de facto* control was backed by the people's massive mandate given in the last election. Why should Mujib part with power voluntarily? He could, however, show some accommodation to a guest from West Pakistan provided the guest reciprocated by endorsing his draft constitution.

On the other hand, General Yahya still believed that he held absolute power, since he was President, Chief Martial Law Administrator, Supreme Commander of the Armed Forces and Commander-in-Chief of the Army. Why should he accommodate a regional political leader without getting adequate concessions from him? That was the basic conflict. Both of them talked from different premises. Each thought he was asked to make concessions.

Yahya and Mujib held full-dress talks on 17 March. It was a

tough session. Both sides presented their views with no discernible areas of compromise. The Awami League had briefed its team well but it could not convince the President's advisers of its standpoint.

After the meeting, when Mujib emerged from the President's House flying a black flag on his white car, he was stopped by the waiting journalists at the gate. I was present but Mujib took no notice of my uniform. He seemed obsessed, and highly agitated. I stood close to his left shoulder looking at his face. It was ashen. His entire frame quivered and his lips trembled with excitement. He dismissed all questions with a snappy 'yes' or 'no' and drove off rapidly to his Dhanmandi residence. The journalists followed him. I stood bemused under the sprawling banyan tree. The iron gate of the President's House had clanked shut. Only the bayonet of the guard could be seen from outside.

Back in the cantonment, I learnt that the G.O.C. had gone to General Tikka Khan to learn the outcome of the day's talks. General Tikka Khan said, 'Khadim, I know as little as you do.' 'But, Sir, it is your right, as the man on the spot, to keep in touch with developments so that you are not caught unawares.' The same evening, General Tikka Khan's staff car entered the President's House. Yahya Khan reportedly told him, 'The bastard is not behaving. You get ready.' Tikka Khan rang up the G.O.C. at 10 p.m. to say, 'Khadim, you can go ahead.' It was taken to mean that planning and paper preparations for army action could start— as the army always readies itself for all contingencies—but that the action would depend on the progress of political talks. The Army in Dacca was not forcing the President's hand for a crack-down. It still longed for the political settlement which was being attempted at the President's House. Preparations, it should be emphasized, do not necessarily indicate intentions. If one digs out the military files of any country, one will find offensive as well as defensive plans against the country's potential enemies. It was just a contingency plan.

It is therefore, at best, ill-informed and, at worst, most malicious to allege, as some foreign writers have done, that the Dacca talks were continued only to allow time to build up forces and to finalize plans. I personally know that no additional troops were flown into Dacca from West Pakistan or from within East Pakistan during the twenty-five days of Mujib's *de facto* rule. Moreover, planning for a military action didn't take as many as ten days (Yahya's arrival on

15 March and the subsequent crack-down on 25 March). In fact it did not take even ten hours. And I will tell you how and when, it was prepared, presented and approved.

On 18 March (morning), Major-General Khadim Raja and Major-General Rao Farman Ali met in the G.O.C.'s office to draft the basic operational plan. Both of them agreed that the basis of operation 'BLITZ' (that is, the people's co-operation) was no longer relevant, as had been amply demonstrated since 1 March. They also agreed that the aim of operation 'BLITZ' (to enforce martial law in its classical role), had likewise been superseded by events. Now, if and when any action was taken, it would have to aim at overthrowing Mujib's *de facto* rule and re-establishing government authority.

In the same sitting, General Farman wrote down the new plan on a light blue office pad, using an ordinary school pencil. I saw the original plan in General Farman's immaculate hand. General Khadim wrote its second part, which dealt with distribution of resources and the allocation of tasks to brigades and units.

The plan, christened 'Operation SEARCHLIGHT', consisted of sixteen paragraphs spread over five pages (See Appendix III). It presumed that all Bengali troops, including regular East Bengal battalions, would revolt in reaction to its execution. They should therefore, be disarmed. Secondly, the 'non-cooperation' movement launched by Mujib should be deprived of its leadership by arresting all the prominent Awami League leaders while they were in conference with the President. The plan also listed, as an annexure, sixteen prominent persons whose houses were to be visited for their arrest.

The hand-written plan was read out to General Hamid and Lieutenant-General Tikka Khan at Flag Staff House on the afternoon of 20 March. Both of them approved the main contents of the plan but General Hamid struck out the clause pertaining to disarming the Bengali troops as 'it would destroy one of the finest armies in the world'. He, however, approved the disarming of paramilitary forces like the East Pakistan Rifles and the Police. He asked only one question, 'After distribution of these troops for various tasks, are you left with any reserves?' 'No, Sir,' was the prompt reply from the G.O.C.

Later, the President also deprived the plan of one of its fundamental features. He refused to agree that the Awami League leaders should be arrested, on the appointed day, while they were in conference with the President. 'I don't want to kill the people's confidence in political negotiations. I don't want to go down in history as a traitor to democracy.' These were his very words reported to me by an eye-witness. What was eventually left in the plan was only the allocation of tasks and areas of responsibility to various brigades and battalions.

On the other hand, Mujib's *de facto* commander-in-chief, Colonel (ret.) M.A.G. Osmani, also brushed up his plans for military action against Yahya's government. He secretly contacted the Bengali troops, including those in the regular Pakistan army, to get ready for action on a call from Mujib. According to Major-General (ret.) D.K. Palit,[1] Colonel Osmani's plan included the following courses of action:

(a) Capture of Dacca airport and Chittagong seaport to seal East Pakistan.
(b) East Pakistan Rifles and the Police, aided by armed students, to control Dacca city with a base at Dacca University.
(c) Defecting East Pakistan Rifles/East Bengal Regiment personnel to storm the cantonments and occupy them.

Thus, both sides prepared for the worst. Who would strike first or would deliver the pre-emptive strike was not yet known. Both sides, it appears, wanted to try the political course first.

The Awami League's talks with the President and his advisers brought the parties no closer to a solution till 18 March when some progress was reported. Mujib also confirmed this indirectly when he said that he would not have continued the talks if there had been no progress.[2] This positive development was conveyed to General Tikka Khan and, through him, to Major-General Khadim Raja. It also trickled down to some of us who lived in a dark tunnel called the cantonment. Perhaps any light reaching them is magnified for the men in a tunnel. We felt happy and sanguine about the future. Some of us gave up the idea of sending our families to West Pakistan. The more realistic among us, however, did send their dependents to West Pakistan.

The Yahya–Mujib parleys focussed on the Awami League proposal that martial law be lifted immediately and power transferred to

---

[1] *The Lightning Campaign*, published within a few weeks of the 1971 war as publicity unofficially sponsored by the Government of India.
[2] The *Pakistan Observer*, Dacca, 19 March 1971.

the five provinces without effecting a change, for the time being, in the central government headed by General Yahya Khan. As to constitution-making, the Awami League suggested that the National Assembly be divided *ab initio* into two committees, each comprising M.N.A.s from the East and West Wings. The committees, meeting in Islamabad and Dacca, would prepare separate reports within a given period. Then the National Assembly would meet to discuss these reports and find a compromise between the two. Meanwhile, the 1962 Constitution could be amended and promulgated, assuring full autonomy to East Pakistan on the basis of the Six Points. The West Pakistan provinces were free to work out their own quantum of autonomy. This scheme for the transfer of power was to be promulgated by a Presidential Proclamation. The President saw one good point in it: it did not affect his position. He would still be President, assisted by advisors of his own choice. This was the basis of hope and progress reported in the press.

But the scheme had grave implications. If martial law were lifted, the Yahya regime would lose its legal sanction and the provinces would be free to claim independent status. Yet the President gave an undertaking to Mujib that the scheme would be accepted if Bhutto did not raise any objections to it. So Bhutto was asked once again to come to Dacca. He was still in Karachi, watching the situation. From there, he had already sent a telegram to the President saying that if any decision was reached bypassing the Pakistan People's Party, it would not work.[1] Bhutto refused to visit Dacca because, he said, he had already made his point of view clear to the President. On the other hand, Mujib was averse to Bhutto's presence at a conference table because of his alleged role in causing bloodshed in East Pakistan. Bhutto insisted on an assurance that Mujib would be prepared to discuss the political situation with him.

While telephonic and teleprinter efforts continued to try to persuade Bhutto to fly to Dacca, I visited the Dacca Press Club where I met Mr. Hussain, a senior journalist close to Mujib. He said, 'Bhutto is irrelevant as far as we are concerned. Once we have convinced Yahya, it is for him to persuade Bhutto. And if Bhutto does not obey him, he should crack down on him.' He was obviously unaware of the political realities in West Pakistan. Yahya would have destroyed his own 'base' through such action.

---

[1] The *Pakistan Times*, Rawalpindi, 11 March 1971.

On my way back, I dropped into the office of the *People*, a virulent daily, notorious for publishing fantastic stories maligning the Army. In the news room, I found three Awami League barristers who began to cross-examine me on the role of the army and its intentions in the present crisis. One of them, Shahabuddin by name, if I remember correctly, said, 'Don't you think the Army has the right to rule the country because it has to defend it with its blood?' 'No, I don't think so. Most of the officers and men claim for themselves no better role than the defence of the borders.' 'Then, why don't you leave it to the people's representatives to rule. Why don't you accept the Awami League's draft constitution?' 'It is for the President and the politicians to accept it. The rank and file of the Army have no say in the matter.'

The second barrister, who wore a white shirt and powerful black-rimmed glasses, picked up the argument: 'I suggest you give the Awami League constitution a trial. If you find it prejudicial to the national interest, as you fear, abrogate it. You will still have the guns as well as the argument of acting in the interest of national solidarity.' 'I don't think a Constitution should be accepted only to abrogate it later. It is a sacred document which, once adopted, must be protected,' I argued. He said ironically, 'Since when has the Army become the protector of the Constitution. You now lecture us on the sanctity of a constitution, after abrogating two in a decade.'

The third barrister was yet to join the argument when I asked the editor's permission to leave, despite 'the very enlightening discussion', as it was getting late. I drove back to the cantonment with a burdened mind. I peeped into the officers' mess where some officers were still watching television. The programme, as usual, reflected the true spirit of the Awami League movement and the spirited young men and women sang full-throated liberation songs. The young officers at once turned to me to hear 'the latest from the town'. I told them of my experience with the barristers. Captain Chaudhry commented, 'The President is dragging it out too much. He has simply to give the order. One company (of troops) is enough.'

Bhutto and his principal *aides* arrived on 21 March. The Awami League considered it its duty and privilege to receive all visitors to Bangla Desh. It therefore insisted that reception and security arrangements for the P.P.P. leaders should be made by the Awami League volunteers. The Army, however, had its doubts about the effectiveness of the Awami League measures. It therefore made alternative arrangements of its own, but let the Awami League handle the guests in the first instance. Chaos soon surfaced, however, and the Army took over the duties from the Awami League the same afternoon.

The President faithfully conveyed the salient features of the Awami League's scheme for the transfer of power to Bhutto, saying that it awaited his approval for implementation. Bhutto's reaction, in his own words, was:

'I acquainted my colleagues with the two-committee proposal. They expressed their misgivings and suggested that I should not accept the proposal as it contained seeds of two Pakistans... We also agreed that [the scheme] had to be put to and approved by the full knowledge of the people. Two or more political leaders could not ignore the existence of the entire Assembly vested with constitutional and legislative power.'[1]

So the awaited approval by Bhutto was not forthcoming. The fateful triangle persisted.

Thus dawned 23 March—the anniversary of the historic Pakistan Day which commemorates the passage of the Pakistan Resolution in 1940. The Awami League used it as a 'Resistance Day'. They burnt the Pakistan flag, tore down the *Quaid-e-Azam* Mohammad Ali Jinnah's portrait and burnt his effigy. Instead, they flew the new flag of independent Bangla Desh and displayed portraits of Sheikh Mujibur Rehman. The Radio and Television played Tagore's *Sonar Bangla* as the new national anthem. It was not just a student prank. Mujib was a party to it. He received a delegation of student leaders at his residence in the morning, allowed them to hoist the Bangla Desh flag on his roof-top (the *de facto* President's House) and took a salute from the student rally in front of his house.

The whole city was covered with the new maroon and golden flag. The Pakistan flag could be seen only at two places—Government House and the Martial Law Headquarters. In fact, some clever Bengali boy had managed to stick a small Bangla Desh flag on the western gate of Government House; but the symbol of united Pakistan still fluttered high on the main building. It looked lonely, though.

Z.A. Bhutto, *The Great Tragedy*, p. 41.

Bengali youth thumped the city streets raising *Joi Bangla* slogans. It was a virtual Independence Day for them. Only a few irritants had to be removed; and Mujib was doing his best to do it without bloodshed.

On 24 March, the Awami League came out with new proposals. It abandoned its previous proposal of Constitution Committees and insisted, instead, on Constitution Conventions. These Conventions were to draw up two Constitutions for East and West Pakistan, and the National Assembly was to meet to integrate these constitutions into a 'Confederation of Pakistan'. Bhutto met the President the same day. Both of them agreed, perhaps not for the first time, that the Awami League had progressively raised its stakes from provincial autonomy to the constitutional break up of Pakistan. Whatever course of action they might have contemplated or decided upon to protect national solidarity, it was announced that the talks were still continuing. Tajuddin Ahmed, General Secretary of the Awami League, declared in the evening, however, that his party 'had submitted its *final* proposals and had nothing to add or negotiate.'[1]

The West Pakistani politicians, experts and advisers, including Bhutto's *aides*, started flying back to Karachi, as wise birds flee to their nests before the coming storm.

The Awami League had its own means of determining the latest trends but later on one of its sympathizers complained to me, 'We still hoped that the negotiations were continuing. Nobody ever said that the talks had failed. Nor had anybody dropped a word of caution that we were crossing the limits beyond which lay death and destruction.' I asked, 'Do you think there was still some hope left after the confederation proposal had been made?' He replied, 'That is where we miscalculated. We thought, and our sources inside the government confirmed, that the Army was giving in. So we pressed on, forgetting completely that Bhutto had arrived on the scene.'

When the West Pakistani leaders were catching a P.I.A. flight, General Farman and General Khadim boarded two helicopters to pass the instructions to the Brigade Commanders (outside Dacca) to get ready for army action. (Until then, the plan for operation SEARCHLIGHT, though approved, had not been issued). They briefed Brigadier Durrani (Jessore) and Brigadier Iqbal Shafi (Comilla) respectively. Farman returned to Dacca, while Khadim

[1] The *Pakistan Observer*, Dacca, 25 March 1971.

went to Chittagong from Comilla. Chittagong was a very tricky place, because the only senior officer there was Brigadier Mozumdar who was known for his collusion with the Awami League. The G.O.C. handled the situation tactfully. He quietly passed the orders to Lieutenant-Colonel Fatimi, the most senior non-Bengali officer there, and asked him to hold his ground to allow time for Brigadier Iqbal Shafi to arrive from Comilla. In addition, he convinced Brigadier Mozumdar that 2 East Bengal, which had shown some signs of restiveness at Joydebpur (north of Dacca) needed a pep talk from 'Papa Tiger' to pacify them. He brought Mozumdar to Dacca. That was the end of Mozumdar's command in the Pakistan Army.

Other emissaries, usually the senior staff officers, flew to other cantonments like Sylhet, Rangpur and Rajshahi on the same mission. H-hour was to be communicated later on by telephone because the President had not yet given the order. Officially, the talks were still open. Meanwhile, 57 Brigade in Dacca carried out a reconnaissance of its target areas as unobtrusively as possible. They used civilian clothes and vehicles.

The President decided to leave on the evening of 25 March. He was to address the nation from Islamabad. He was handed a draft speech written by Major-General Farman Ali. Its main points were:

Mujib should not be branded a traitor, but a patriot in the hands of extremists.
Mujib has not been arrested for any crime but only taken into protective custody.
The speech should clearly spell out a quantum of provincial autonomy for East Pakistan.

The President's speech broadcast on 26 March 1971, however, ignored this brief completely and declared that Mujib's act of treason (in running a parallel government) 'would not go unpunished'. It echoed Mujib's thunderous call on 1 March when he had said 'This (postponement of the National Assembly session) would not go unchallenged'.

The President's departure from Dacca was kept a secret—a greater secret than his arrival ten days earlier. A small drama was staged to deceive the public. The President drove in state to Flag Staff House (in the cantonment) for afternoon tea. Before the light started fading, the President's cavalcade drove back to the President's House with the usual fanfare—the pilot jeep, outriders, the President's car with four-star plate and flag. But the President was not in the car. Brigadier Rafiq deputised for him. This blind was considered a great success, although Mujib's spies saw through the game. Lieutenant-Colonel A. R. Chaudhry, who was on Yahya's staff, saw the Dodge carrying the President's baggage to the airport and informed Mujibur Rehman. When General Yahya Khan entered the P.A.F. Gate to board the plane at 1900 hours, Wing Commander Khondkar, who watched the show from his office, passed the word to Mujib. Fifteen minutes later, a foreign correspondent rang me from Hotel Intercontinental saying, 'Major, could you confirm that the President has left?'

By then, the night had already set in. Nobody knew then that it would be a night without a healing dawn at its end.

PART II

POLITICO-MILITARY

9

OPERATION SEARCHLIGHT—I

Major-General Khadim Hussain was brooding over the possible outcome of political talks on 25 March when his green telephone rang at about 11 a.m. Lieutenant-General Tikka Khan was on the line. He said, 'Khadim, it is tonight.'

It created no excitement for Khadim. He was already waiting for the fall of the hammer. The President's decision coincided with the second anniversary of his assumption of power. General Khadim passed the word to his staff for implementation. The lower the news travelled, the greater the sensation it created. I saw some junior officers hustling about mustering some extra recoilless rifles, getting additional ammunition issued, a defective mortar sight replaced. The tank crew, brought from Rangpur (29 Cavalry) a few days earlier, hurried with their task to oil six rusty M-24s for use at night. They were enough to make a noise on the Dacca streets.

The general staff of Headquarters 14 Division rang up all the outstation garrisons to inform them of H-hour. They devised a private code for passing the message. All garrisons were to act simultaneously. The fateful hour was set at 260100 hours—1 a.m. 26 March. It was calculated that by then the President would have landed safely in Karachi.

The plan for operation SEARCHLIGHT[1] visualized the setting up of two headquarters. Major-General Farman, with 57 Brigade under Brigadier Arbab, was responsible for operations in Dacca city and its suburbs while Major-General Khadim was to look after the rest of the province. In addition, Lieutenant-General Tikka Khan and his staff were to spend the night at the Martial Law Headquarters in the Second Capital[2] to watch the progress of action in and outside Dacca.

---

[1] Full text is printed as Appendix III to this book.
[2] A complex of surrealistically modern red-brick buildings, designed by the famous American architect Louis Kahn. Still incomplete, it had been started during the Ayub Khan regime (October 1958–March 1969) as a sop to mounting Bengali resentment sharpened by the construction of a new federal capital at Islamabad in West Pakistan. The Second Capital stands on the south-western fringe of Dacca airport.

A few days earlier, General Yahya had sent Major-General Iftikhar Janjua and Major-General A.O. Mitha to Dacca as possible replacements for Khadim and Farman in case they refused to crack down'. After all, they had formed General Yakub's team until very recently and might still share his ideas. General Hamid had even gone to the extent of questioning Khadim's and Farman's wives to assess their husbands' views on the subject. Both the generals, however, assured Hamid that they would faithfully carry out the orders.

Junior officers like me started collecting at Headquarters, Martial Law Administrator, Zone 'B' (Second Capital) at about 10 p.m. They laid out sofas and easy chairs on the lawn and made arrangements for tea and coffee to last the night. I had no specific job to perform except 'to be available'. A jeep fitted with a wireless set was parked next to this 'outdoor operations room'. The city wrapped in starlight, was in deep slumber. The night was as pleasant as a spring night in Dacca could be. The setting was perfect for anything but a bloody holocaust.

Besides the armed forces, another class of people was active that night. They were the Awami League leaders and their private army of Bengali soldiers, policemen, ex-servicemen, students and party volunteers. They were in communication with Mujib, Colonel Osmani and other important Bengali officers. They were preparing for the toughest resistance. In Dacca, they erected innumerble road blocks to obstruct the march of troops to the city.

The wireless set fitted in the jeep groaned for the first time at about 11.30 p.m. The local commander (Dacca) asked permission to advance the H-hour because 'the other side' was hectically preparing for resistance. Eveybody looked at his watch. The President was still half way between Colombo (Sri Lanka) and Karachi. General Tikka gave the decision. 'Tell Bobby (Arbab) to hold on as long as he can.'

At the given hour, Brigadier Arbab's brigade was to act as follows:

13 Frontier Force was to stay in Dacca cantonment as reserve and defend the cantonment, if necessary.

43 Light Anti-Aircraft (LAA) Regiment, deployed at the airport in an anti-aircraft role since the banning of overflights by India, was to look after the airport area.

22 Baluch, already in East Pakistan Rifles Lines at Pilkhana, was

to disarm approximately 5,000 E.P.R. personnel and seize their wireless exchange.

32 Punjab was to disarm 1,000 'highly motivated' policemen, a prime possible source of armed manpower for the Awami League, at Rajarbagh Police Lines.

18 Punjab was to fan out in the Nawabpur area and the old city where many Hindu houses were said to have been converted into armouries.

Field Regiment was to control the Second Capital and the adjoining Bihari localities (Mohammadpur, Mirpur).

A composite force consisting of one company each of 18 Punjab, 22 Baluch and 32 Punjab, was to 'flush' the University Campus particularly Iqbal Hall and Jagan Nath Hall which were reported to be the strong points of the Awami League rebels.

A platoon of Special Service Group (Commandos) was to raid Mujib's house and capture him alive.

A skeleton squadron of M-24 tanks was to make an appearance before first light, mainly as a show of force. They could fire for effect if required.

These troops, in their respective areas, were to guard the key points, break resistance (if offered) and arrest the listed political leaders from their residences.

The troops were to be in their target areas before 1 a.m. but some of them, anticipating delay on the way, had started moving from the cantonment at about 11.30 p.m. Those who were already in the city to guard the radio and television stations, telephone exchange, power house and State Bank etc., had also taken their posts much before the H-hour.

The first column from the cantonment met resistance at Farm Gate, about one kilometre from the cantonment. The column was halted by a huge tree trunk freshly felled across the road. The side gaps were covered with the hulks of old cars and a disabled steam-roller. On the city side of the barricade stood several hundred Awami Leaguers shouting *Joi Bangla* slogans. I heard their spirited shouts while standing on the verandah of General Tikka's headquarters. Soon some rifle shots mingled with the *Joi Bangla* slogans. A little later, a burst of fire from an automatic weapon shrilled through the air. Thereafter, it was a mixed affair of firing and fiery slogans, punctuated with the occasional chatter of a light machine gun. Fifteen minutes later the noise began to subside and the slogans

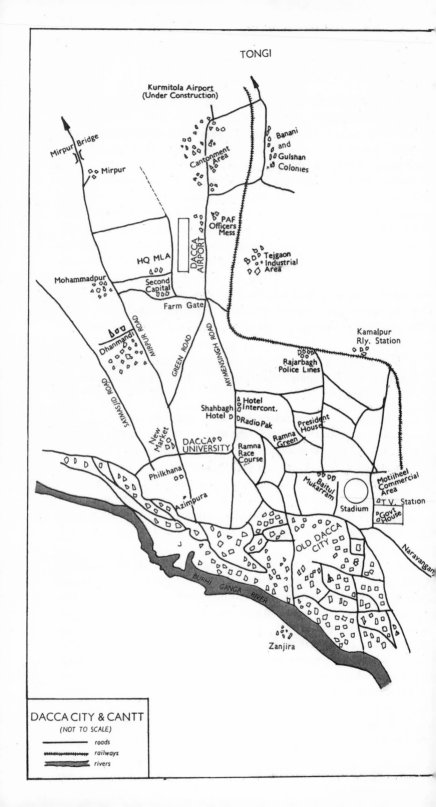

started dying down. Apparently, the weapons had triumphed. The army column moved on to the city.

Thus the action had started before schedule. There was no point now in sticking to the prescribed H-hour. The gates of hell had been cast open. When the first shot had been fired, 'the voice of Sheikh Mujibur Rehman came faintly through on a wavelength close to that of the official Pakistan Radio. In what must have been, and sounded like, a pre-recorded message, the Sheikh procliamed East Pakistan to be the People's Republic of Bangla Desh.'¹ The full text of the proclamation is published in *Bangla Desh Documents* released by the Indian Foreign Ministry. It said, 'This may be my last message. From today Bangla Desh is independent. I call upon the people of Bangla Desh, wherever you are and with whatever you have, to resist the army of occupation to the last. Your fight must go on until the last soldier of the Pakistan occupation army is expelled from the soil of Bangla Desh and final victory is achieved.'²

I didn't hear this broadcast. I only heard the big bang of the rocket launcher fired by the commandos to remove a barrier blocking their way to Mujib's house. Lieutenant-Colonel Z.A. Khan, the commanding officer, and Major Bilal, the company commander, themselves had accompanied the raiding platoon.

As the commandos approached Mujib's house, they drew fire from the armed guard posted at his gate. The guards were quickly neutralized. Then up raced the fifty tough soldiers to climb the four-foot high compound wall. They announced their arrival in the courtyard by firing a sten-gun burst and shouted for Mujib to come out. But there was no response. Scrambling across the verandah and up the stairs, they finally discovered the door of Mujib's bedroom. It was locked from outside. A bullet pierced the hanging metal, and it dangled down. Whereupon Mujib readily emerged offering himself for arrest. He seemed to be waiting for it. The raiding party rounded up everybody in the house and brought them to the Second Capital in army jeeps. Minutes later, Major Jaffar, Brigade Major of 57 Brigade, was on the wireless. I could hear his crisp voice saying 'BIG BIRD IN THE CAGE... OTHERS NOT IN THEIR NESTS... OVER.'

As soon as the message ended, I saw the 'big bird' in a white

¹ David Loshak, *Pakistan Crisis*, London, pp. 98-9.
² Op. cit., Vol. 1, p. 286.

shirt being driven in an army jeep to the cantonment for safe custody. Somebody asked General Tikka if he would like him to be produced before him. He said firmly, 'I don't want to see his face.'

Mujib's domestic servants were released immediately after identification while he himself was lodged in the Adamjee School for the night. Next day, he was shifted to Flag Staff House from where he was flown to Karachi three days later. Subsequently, when complications arose about the 'final disposal' of Mujib (such as international pressure for his release), I asked my friend Major Bilal why he had not finished him off in the heat of action. He said 'General Mitha had personally ordered me to capture him alive.'

While Mujib rested in the Adamjee School, the city of Dacca was in the throes of a civil war. I watched the harrowing sight from the verandah for four hours. The prominent feature of this gory night was the flames shooting to the sky. At times, mournful clouds of smoke accompanied the blaze but soon they were overwhelmed by the flaming fire trying to lick at the stars. The light of the moon and the glow of the stars paled before this man-made furnace. The tallest columns of smoke and fire emerged from the university campus, although some other parts of the city, such as the premises of the daily *People*, had no small share in these macabre fireworks.

At about 2 a.m. the wireless set in the jeep again drew our attention. I was ordered to receive the call. The Captain on the other end of the line said that he was facing a lot of resistance from Iqbal Hall and Jagan Nath Hall. Meanwhile, a senior staff officer snatched the hand-set from me and shouted into the mouth-piece: 'How long will you take to neutralize the target?...Four hours!...Nonsense... What weapons have you got?... Rocket launcher, recoilless rifles, mortars and... O.K., use all of them and ensure complete capture of the area in two hours.'

The university building was conquered by 4 a.m. but the ideology of Bengali nationalism preached there over the years would take much longer to subdue. Perhaps ideas are unconquerable.

In the rest of the city, the troops had accomplished their tasks including disarming the police at Rajar Bagh and the East Pakistan Rifles at Pilkhana. In other parts of the city, they had only fired a sniping shot here and a burst there to create terror. They did not enter houses, except those mentioned in the operational plan (to arrest the political leaders), or those used by rebels as sanctuaries.

Before first light on 26 March, the troops reported completion of their mission. General Tikka Khan left his sofa at about 5 a.m. and went into his office for a while. When he reappeared cleaning his glasses with a handkerchief and surveying the area, he said, Oh, not a soul there!' Standing on the verandah, I heard his soliloquy and looked around for confirmation. I saw only a stray dog, with its tail tucked between its hind legs, stealing its way towards the city.

After day-break, Bhutto was collected from his hotel room and escorted to Dacca airport by the Army. Before boarding the plane, he made a general remark of appreciation for the Army action on the previous night and said to his chief escort, Brigadier Arbab, 'Thank God, Pakistan has been saved.' He repeated this statement on his arrival at Karachi.

When Bhutto was making this optimistic remark, I was surveying mass graves in the university area where I found three pits—of five to fifteen metres diameter each. They were filled with fresh earth. But no officer was prepared to disclose the exact number of casualties. I started going round the buildings, particularly Iqbal Hall and Jagan Nath Hall which, I had thought from a distance, had been razed to the ground during the action. Iqbal Hall had apparently been hit by only two, and Jagan Nath Hall by four, rockets. The rooms were mostly charred, but intact. A few dozen half-burnt rifles and stray papers were still smouldering. The damage was very grave—but not enough to match the horrible picture I had conjured up on the verandah of General Tikka's headquarters.

The foreign press fancied several thousand deaths (in the university area) while army officers placed the figure at around a hundred. Officially, only forty deaths were admitted.

From the university area, I drove on the principal roads of Dacca city and saw odd corpses lying on the footpaths or near the corner of a winding street. There were no mountains of bodies, as was alleged later. However, I experienced a strange and ominous sensation. I do not know what it signified but I could not bear it for long. I drove on to a different area.

In the old city, I saw some streets still barricaded but there was no one to man the road blocks. Everybody had shrunk to the sanctuary of his house. On one street corner, however, I saw a shadow, like a displaced soul, quickly lapsing into a side lane. After a round of the city, I went to Dhanmandi where I visited Mujib's house. It was totally deserted. From the scattered things, it appeared that it had been thoroughly searched. I did not find anything memorable except an overturned life-size portrait of Rabindranath Tagore. The frame was cracked in several places, but the image was intact.

The outer gate of the house, too, had lost its valuable decoration. During Mujib's rule, they had fixed a brass replica of a Bangla Desh map and had added six stars to represent the Awami League's Six Points. But now only the black iron bars of the gate, with holes for the metal fixtures, were there. The glory that had quickly dawned, had quickly disappeared.

I hurried back to the cantonment for lunch. I found the atmosphere very different there. The tragedy in the city had eased the nerves of defence personnel and their dependents. They felt that the storm after a long lull, had finally blown past leaving the horizon clear. The officers chatted in the officers' mess with a visible air of relaxation. Peeling an orange, Captain Chaudhry said, 'The Bengalis have been sorted out well and proper—at least for a generation'. Major Malik added, 'Yes, they only know the language of force. Their history says so.'

10

OPERATION SEARCHLIGHT—II

Although Dacca had been benumbed overnight, the situation in the rest of the province continued to be fluid for some time. Chittagong, Rajshahi and Pabna, in particular, gave us anxious moments for several days.

The total number of Bengali and West Pakistani troops in Chittagong was estimated at 5,000 and 600 respectively. The former consisted of trained recruits at the East Bengal Centre (2,500), the newly raised 8 East Bengal, East Pakistan Rifles Wing and Sector Headquarters, and the police. Our troops were mainly the elements of 20 Baluch whose advance party had sailed back to West Pakistan. A senior non-Bengali army officer in Chittagong, Lieutenant-Colonel Fatimi, was ordered to hold ground to allow time for reinforcements from Comilla to arrive.

The rebels initially had all the success. They effectively blocked the route of the Comilla column by blowing up the Subapur bridge near Feni. They also controlled major parts of Chittagong cantonment and the city. The only islands of government authority there were the 20 Baluch area and the naval base. Major Ziaur Rehman,[1] the second-in-command of 8 East Bengal, assumed command of the rebels in Chittagong in the absence of Brigadier Mozumdar (who had been tactfully taken to Dacca a few days earlier). While the government troops clung to the radio station, in order to guard the building, Major Zia took control of the transmitters separately located on Kaptai Road and used the available equipment to broadcast the 'declaration of independence' of Bangla Desh. Nothing could be done to turn the tables unless reinforcements arrived in Chittagong.

The G.O.C., Major-General Khadim Hussain, learnt about the stoppage of the Comilla column about fifty minutes past midnight on D-day. He ordered Brigadier Iqbal Shafi to cross the

---

[1] Later in August 1975, he staged the *coup* which deposed Mujibur Rehman and resulted in the killing of the Sheikh and his family. He subsequently became President and Chief Martial Law Administrator of Bangla Desh.

nullah (ravine), leaving the bridge in hostile hands, and make his way to Chittagong at the earliest opportunity. Brigadier Iqbal Shafi, however, could not make any headway without taking the bridge. This he did next day by 10 a.m. The column moved, but again it was pinned down by hostile fire at Comeera, about twenty kilometres short of Chittagong. The advance company suffered eleven casualties including the commanding officer, who was killed. The column lost contact with Brigade Headquarters (Comilla) as well as with Divisional Headquarters (Dacca).

The lack of information about the column raised much apprehension in Dacca. It might have been butchered! If so, what would be the fate of Chittagong? Would it remain with the rebels? With Chittagong in hostile control what would be the outcome of operation SEARCHLIGHT?

The G.O.C. decided to locate the missing column himself in an army helicopter next day. He would fly to Chittagong first and then follow the Chittagong–Comilla Road so that, if the column had meanwhile made any progress, he might find it on the outskirts of Chittagong. As his helicopter fluttered close to the Chittagong hills to land in the 20 Baluch area, it attracted small arms fire from the rebels who had taken up positions on the high ground. The chopper was hit but sustained no serious damage. It managed to land safely. The G.O.C. got down for a quick briefing by Lieutenant-Colonel Fatimi on the Chittagong situation. The Colonel triumphantly reported his success in controlling the East Bengal Centre by killing 50 and capturing 500 rebels. The rest of Chittagong, however, was still with the rebels.

As the G.O.C. walked to the helicopter to continue the search, he saw a terror-striken woman with a baby in her arms. She was the wife of a West Pakistani officer desperately seeking to be evacuated to Dacca. She was accommodated.

The helicopter was in the competent hands of an ace pilot, Major Liaquat Bokhari who was ably assisted by Major Peter. They flew the G.O.C. along the Comilla Road, but could not see anything because of the low cloud formation. When they were approximately over Comeera, the G.O.C. studied the quarter-inch map spread on his knees, looked out and ordered the pilot to go down through the clouds. As the helicopter descended and the G.O.C. craned his anxious neck to locate the column, a quick splash of bullets sprang up from the ground. The pilot pulled up instinctively. Nevertheless, his machine was hit. One bullet grazed the tail while another pierced through its belly, only inches away from the fuel tank. Major Bokhari, apparently unperturbed by the incident, said to the G.O.C. 'Sir, do you want me to make another attempt.' 'No, make, for Dacca direct.' The mission had failed. The column was not located.

Meanwhile, General Mitha had sent a commando detachment (ex 3 Commando Battalion) from Dacca to Chittagong by air with the same mission—to link up with the column. The detachment did not know the location of the missing column or the rebels' position. They had to rely on their own intelligence. A Bengali officer, Captain Hamid, appeared from nowhere and said to the commanding officer of the commandos, 'I have come from Murree to look up my parents in Chittagong. I know the area. May I go with you as a guide?' His offer was accepted.

The day (27 March) the commandos were to undertake the search/link up operation, the G.O.C. moved his tactical headquarters to Chittagong and sent a column of 20 Baluch on the same mission but on a different route. The success of the operation hinged on a link up of these three columns. The 20 Baluch column got involved with the rebels soon after leaving its unit area but the commandos dashed to the target, the Bengali officer with them. They had not got very far when they came under cross-fire from the hills flanking the Chittagong—Comilla Road. Thirteen of them were killed including the commanding officer, two young officers, one junior commissioned officer and nine other ranks. The effort had proved both abortive and expensive.

At the other end, Brigadier Iqbal Shafi had himself assumed the command of the column after the Comeera incident. He sent for a battery of mortars which joined him from Comilla on 27 March. He planned a dawn attack for 28 March. The attack was successful. He broke the resistance and cleared his way to Chittagong. He finally reported his presence at Haji Camp, the pre-embarkation resting place for pilgrims, on the edge of Chittagong City.

Next to Haji Camp were the Isphahani Jute Mills where, before the arrival of our troops, an orgy of blood was staged by the rebels. They collected their helpless non-Bengali victims—men, women and children—in the club building and hacked them to death. I visited the scene of this gruesome tragedy a few days later and saw blood-spotted floors and walls. Women's clothes and the children's toys lay soaked in a congealing pool of blood. In the adjoining building, I saw bed sheets and mattresses stiffened with dried blood.

While this happened the Pakistan Army was still attempting a link-up of the three columns. The link-up was effected on 29 March and the happy news was radioed to Dacca, where tense officers in the operations room heaved a sigh of relief. But it was too late for the victims at the Isphahani Mills slaughter-house.

The only success in Chittagong so far had been the unloading of 9,000 tons of ammunition from the ship which had been *gheraoed*,[1] by the Awami League volunteers since mid-March. Brigadier M.H. Ansari, who had flown from Dacca, had mustered all available resources—an infantry platoon, a few mortars and two tanks—and formed a task force. The Navy had lent the support of a destroyer and a few gunboats. He had achieved this success with marvellous skill. Later an additional battalion was also flown from Dacca to Chittagong.

Although the situation with regard to the availability of resources had improved, the main battle for Chittagong had yet to be fought. The radio transmitters, East Pakistan Rifles Sector Headquarters and the Reserve Police Lines in the District Courts area (the concentration point for the policemen, ex-servicemen and armed volunteers) remained to be cleared before the general flushing out of the area could be undertaken.

General Mitha was the first to have a go at the transmitter building. He sent a commando detachment to blow it up. His troops approached the target from the flank, following the river-route. They soon came under fire while still in country boats. Sixteen of them were killed. Mitha's second attempt too proved abortive and highly expensive.

Major-General Khadim then sent a column of 20 Baluch under Lieutenant-Colonel Fatimi. Once again, Fatimi managed to involve himself in some sort of engagement with the rebels on the way and never reached the transmitters. Finally, two F-86s (Sabres) from Dacca had to knock them out. I visited the sight a few days later and found the building well fortified with pillboxes and foxholes—all interconnected with a fine network of trenches. The building was intact.

The other principal target was the East Pakistan Rifles Headquarters where 1,000 armed rebels were well entrenched. Located

1 Literally, to isolate and cordon a target.

n high ground, they had artfully laid their defences along the
mbankment with holes and slits to facilitate small arms fire. Our
roops knew the odds and prepared a massive attack to neutralize
hem. The attacking troops, approximately in battalion strength,
ad the support of a naval destroyer, two gunboats, two tanks and
. heavy mortar battery. The battle raged for three hours before the
lefiant rebels could be subdued. This happened on 31 March—the
ixth day of operation SEARCHLIGHT.

The next target was the Reserve Police Lines where 20,000 rifles
were reportedly stocked, to be used by an assortment of rebels.
A battalion-strength attack was launched there, too, but the defenders proved less dogged than the East Pakistan Rifles personnel and
.oon withdrew towards the Kaptai Road.

The key role in neutralizing these points of resistance was played
oy Brigadier Ansari. His gallant services were later recognized by
he award of the *Hilal-i-Jurat*[1] and promotion to the rank of
Major-General (although earlier he had been superseded).

The main operations in Chittagong were over by the end of
March, but the mopping up action continued until 6 April. The
other two towns where the rebels had an upper hand were Kushtia
and Pabna. Let us see how our troop fared there.

Kushtia, about 90 kilometres from Jessore, is an important road
and rail junction. Our troops were not permanently located there
but, on the D-day, 27 Baluch (Jessore) had sent one of its companies
·just to establish our presence there'. For want of proper briefing
the company carried only small arms, a few recoilless rifles and a
limited quantity of ammunition. They thought that they were going
on normal internal security duty, which usually did not involve
heavy fighting.

The company commander distributed his manpower in small
groups and assigned them the task of guarding the telephone
exchange and V.H.F. station. He also sent small parties to arrest
the local Awami League leaders—but they had all left. He established his presence, after killing five rebels on the first day (26
March). Thereafter it was only enforcement of curfew and collection of arms from the civilians. Two days passed peacefully.

On 28 March, at about 9.30 p.m., the local Superintendent of
Police, pale with fear, came to the company commander, Major
Shoaib, and reported that the rebels had gathered in the border

1 Pakistan's second highest gallantry award.

town of Chuadanga, about 16 kilometres from Kushtia and were about to attack the town at night. They were also threatening to kill all 'collaborators'. The company commander passed a word of caution to his platoons, but the troops did not take it very seriously. They did not even bother to dig their trenches.

The attack commenced at 3.45 a.m. (29 March) with heavy mortar shelling. It jolted our troops out of all illusions of safety. They soon realized that the attackers were none other than the troops of 1 East Bengal which had been sent out from Jessore cantonment 'for training'. They had been joined at Chuadanga by the Indian Border Security Force (B.S.F.). (Four Indian B.S.F. soldiers were captured near Jessore and two near Sylhet.)

The scene of the battle was the police armoury occupied earlier by our troops. The rebels managed to climb into the adjoining three-storey red brick house of a local Judge and used it as a vantage point. From there they sprayed bullets into the police building. At dawn, five of our men lay dead in the compound. By 9 a.m., the toll had risen to eleven. In the next half hour, nine more had fallen. Only a few survivors managed to escape to the company head-quarters about a kilometre away. Shortage of ammunition and lack of cover were the immediate causes of the disaster.

The other posts in Kushtia town—the telephone exchange and V.H.F. station—had simultaneously come under equally severe attack. So neither of the posts could reinforce the other. In the company headquarters, eleven lay dead at one place and fourteen at another. In all, twenty-five out of sixty men had been massacred in the early part of the engagement. Frantic messages for help were sent to Jessore and even an air strike was requested, but nothing reached Kushtia. The last message received from Jessore by the end of the day said, 'Troops here already committed. No reinforcement possible. Air strike called off due to poor visibility... *Khuda Hafiiz!*'

Major Shoaib collected the remnants of his command to re-organize them. He found that only 65 had survived out of 150. He decided to abandon Kushtia and take the survivors to Jessore. He lined up one three-ton truck, one Dodge and six jeeps. The convoy left at night with the company commander in one of the leading jeeps. They had travelled barely 25 kilometres when the leading vehicles, including the one that carried Major Shoaib, caved into a culvert which had been cut by the rebels in the centre

ceptively covered from the surface. As soon as the convoy stopp-
d, it came under intense fire from both sides of the road. Our troops
umped down and hit the ground but bullets continued to rain on
hem. Only nine out of the sixty-five managed to crawl out and
isappear into the country-side. Most of them were later captured
y the rebels, and subjected to a barbaric end.

The story of the Pabna action has many features in common
vith the Kushtia catastrophe. Here, a company of 25 Punjab had
een sent from Rajshahi 'just to establish our presence'. The 130
nen had arrived in Pabna with only first line ammunition and
hree days rations. On arrival, the company was split into small
letachments, which were posted at vulnerable points like the power
nouse and the telephone exchange. They also visited the residences
of local political leaders but found no one. The company established
ts presence without any resistance and lived in peace for the first
hirty-six hours. Then at about 6 p.m., on 27 March, all the posts
ame under intense fire from across the *nullah* (ravine). The rebel
orce consisted of an East Pakistan Rifles Wing (900 men), 30
Policemen and 40 Awami League volunteers. They didn't know our
strength. They therefore kept on firing from a distance without
assaulting our positions. Our troops also opened up but shortage
of ammunition imposed heavy restrictions on the volume of fire.
One N.C.O. and two other ranks were wounded in this initial
encounter.

Captain Asghar, who was being constantly harassed by a rebel
light machine-gun, decided to silence it. He took a few volunteers
with him and charged its position. He knocked it out with a hand
grenade which exploded right inside the post. But at the same time,
another light machine-gun sent a burst into Captain Asghar.
Badly hit, he swerved around to take cover behind the pillar of the
gate, but collapsed. The raid was called off. Another attempt
was made by Lieutenant Rashid, who also died in action.

Meanwhile, all the posts were wound up except that at the
telephone exchange. The rebels also regrouped, then launched
an all-out attack. The lightly equipped defenders realized their
folly, but too late. They had to pay very dearly for it. They lost
two officers, 3 J.C.O.s and 80 other ranks. One more officer and
32 other ranks had been wounded. Repeated calls for help were
sent, in consequence of which a helicopter came to evacuate the
wounded, but could not land. Major Aslam from Rajshahi, how-

ever, managed to reach Pabna with eighteen soldiers, one recoilless rifle, one machine gun and some ammunition, and managed to extricate the survivors. He loaded the wounded into the Dodge and sent them to Rajshahi across country, to avoid possible resistance on the way. He took the able-bodied with him to fight his way back to Rajshahi by road. Meeting heavy resistance on the way he took to the countryside, where they had to wander for three days without food or water. When this column finally reached Rajshahi on 1 April at 10 a.m. it consisted of only eighteen soldiers. The rest, including Major Aslam, had been killed en route.

Thus Chittagong, Kushtia and Pabna turned out to be the towns where we suffered the severest casualties. These places were cleared on 6 April, 16 April and 10 April respectively. In other areas where we were in strength, we regained control wihout much resistance.

The rebels did not settle the score with West Pakistani soldiers only. They also killed civilian dependents with equal barbarity. It is not possible here to document all such cases but I quote an episode to illustrate this point.

2 East Bengal, which had a sprinkling of officers, J.C.O.s and N.C.O.s (technical trades only) from West Pakistan, was located at Joydebpur in an old palace about 30 kilometres north of Dacca. As a part of the general scheme, the East Bengal battalions had been kept away from the cantonments, to avoid trouble with West Pakistani units. Three companies of 2 East Bengal had moved to Ghazipur, Tangail and Mymensingh 'for training'. The fourth company was in the battalion headquarters located in the old palace building at Joydebpur. This is same place where I had witnessed the colour-presenting ceremony in February 1970.

The battalion revolted on 28 March after exchanging information with other Bengali units. Their first action after this change of loyalties was the massacre of their West Pakistani colleagues and their families. One Subedar Ayub, who had served the battalion for over twenty years, managed to escape from this systematic butchery and reached Dacca contonment about midday on 28 March to break the news. I saw him when he arrived in the headquarters—pale with fear, with spots of white forth settled at the corners of his dry lips. Everybody tried to console him but he was too shaken to accept a cup of tea or piece of advice. He asked for help—immediate help.

A company of Punjab Regiment was despatched. A few young
icers accompanied the reinforcements voluntarily. As the rein-
'cements reached the battalion headquarters, they saw the most
.esome sight of their lives. On a heap of filth lay five children,
butchered and mutilated, their abdomens ripped with bayonets.
.e mothers of these children lay slaughtered and disfigured on a
.arate heap. Subedar Ayub identified, among them, members of
. family. He went mad with shock—literally mad.

Inside the palace compound was parked a jeep fitted with a
reless set. The tyres were flat and the seats were soaked in blood.
few splashes of blood had settled on the wireless itself. 'Search-
hting' the interior of the building, they found blood-stained
.othes in the bathroom. They were later identified as the garments
' Captain Riaz from Gujranwala. In the family quarters of the
her ranks, they saw a young mother lying dead, an infant trying
. suckle the withered breasts. In another quarter was huddled a
rror-stricken girl, about four, who cried out at the sight of the
.ldiers, 'Don't kill me, don't kill me please till my father comes
.me.' Her father never came home.

Similar stories were reported from other stations. Some of them
.unded too melodramatic to believe but they were all essentially
ue.

General Hamid, Chief of Staff, Pakistan Army, told me a few
.onths later that the blame for this suffering must lie on Lieuten-
.nt-General Yakub 'who had opposed the arrival of West Pakistani
'oops in early March. Had he allowed us to build up the forces
. time, there would have been West Pakistani troops in all major
.wns to prevent these wild killings.'

General Yakub, it may be recalled, had opposed the move at a
.ery delicate stage of political negotiations. If General Hamid had
.ade his mind clear to Yakub on the eventual crack-down, I
.elieve General Yakub's reaction would have been different.

Now that General Yakub was no longer on the scene and the
.rmy crack-down, with all its ugly repercussions, had commenced
.here was no bar to the despatch of troops. Operation GREAT FLY-
.N was thus started as early as (but not before) 26 March.
.he arriving troops were quickly despatched to areas under
.ressure.

Once the situation had stabilized in the key cities, strong columns
.f troops were sent to provincial towns. Let me describe here the

march of one column from Dacca to Tangail on 1 April, which
accompanied. The main column, loaded in trucks fitted wi
machine-guns, moved on the main road while two compani
spread out over about five hundred metres on either side of t
road. These foot columns were equipped for all contingencies
both animate and inanimate. Nothing was to escape their wrat
Behind the infantry column was a battery of field guns which fir
a few shells at suitable intervals in the general direction of the mov
The artillery bang was enough to scare away any rebels in the area

The infanty column opened up on the slightest pretext or susp
cion. A stir in a bunch of trees or a little rustle in the *bari* wa
enough to evoke a burst of automatic fire or at least a rifle shot.
remember that a little short of Karatea, on the Tangail road, the
was a small locality which hardly rated a name. The searching troop
passed through it, putting a match to the thatched huts and th
adjoining bamboo plants. As soon as they advanced ahead,
bamboo stick burst with a crack because of the heat of the fir
everybody took it as a rifle shot by some hidden 'miscreant'. Thi
caused the weight of the entire column to be rivetted on the localit
and all sorts of weapons fired into the trees. When the source o
danger had been 'eliminated', a careful search was ordered. Durin
the search, the column stood at the ready to shoot the 'miscreant
on sight. The search party found no sign of a human being—aliv
or dead. The bamboo crack had delayed the march by abou
fifteen minutes.

Karatea was a modest town surrounded by a thick growth o
wild trees. It boasted a local bazaar consisting of a single row o
shops. The people had already fled their homes. Where had they
gone? It was difficult to investigate. The column halted there,
surveyed the town, burnt the bazaar and set fire to some kerosene
drums. Soon, it developed into a conflagration. The smoky columns
of fire smouldered through the green branches of the trees. The
troops did not wait to see the fruits of their efforts, they soon moved
on. When we reached the other end of the town, I saw a black lamb,
tied to a spike, trying to wriggle out of its gutted abode but with no
success because the rope was tightening round its neck with every
additional attempt at liberation. It must have strangled itself to
death.

A few kilometres further on, we saw on the road-side two V-
shaped trenches, newly dug but hurriedly abandoned. Probably

e rebels had prepared these positions to meet us but after hearing
e bang of guns, had decided to leave. Whatever the case, the
olumn could not advance without flushing the area. As the troops
anned around, I walked into a mud hut to see how the people
ere lived. The interior was neatly plastered with clay—a mild
ey shade. A framed portrait of two children, probably brothers,
ung on the front wall. The only furniture in the hut was a *charpoy*
ad a mat of date leaves. On the mat was a handful of boiled
ce which bore the finger prints of infant eaters. Where were they
ow? Why had they gone?

I was awakened from these disturbing thoughts by a loud argu-
ent between the soldiers and an old Bengali civilian whom they
ad discovered under the banana trees. The old man had refused
o divulge any information about the 'miscreants' and the soldiers
reatened to kill him if he did not co-operate. I went to see what
as going on.

The Bengali, a walking skeleton, had wrapped a patch of dirty
nen round his waist. His bearded face wore a frightened look.
My eyes, following his half-naked body down to his ankles, settled
n the inflated veins of his dusty feet. Finding me so inquisitive, he
urned to me and said, 'I am a poor fellow. I don't know what to do.
A little earlier, they (the miscreants) were here. They threatened to
ut me to death if I told anybody about them. Now, you confront
ae with an equally dreadful end if I don't tell you about them.'
'hat summed up the dilemma of the common Bengali.

The column, maintaining its diligent pursuit on the way, finally
eached Tangail in the evening. It replaced the Bangla Desh flag
rith the national flag on the Circuit House, fired eight shells in the
nvirons to announce its arrival and settled down for the night. I
eturned to Dacca.

The widespread killings zestfully reported by a hostile world
ress, did not take place in the initial phase of operation
SEARCHLIGHT. They occurred in the subsequent period of
rolonged civil war. Infantry columns on clearing missions were
ent from Comilla, Jessore, Rangpur, Sylhet and other places.
Usually, they moved along the metalled roads, leaving the option
o the rebels to slip into the countryside or recede to the borders
nd eventually into the lap of their Indian patrons. The speed of
hese operations depended on the availability of troops and their
esources.

Additional manpower and resources became available betwee
26 March and 6 April. During this period there arrived two division
headquarters (9 Division, 16 Division), five brigade headquarter
one commando and twelve infantry battalions. They had all le
their heavy equipment in West Pakistan as they were to quell
rebellion rather than fight a proper war. Three more infantry ba
talions and two mortar batteries arrived on 24 April and 2 Ma
respectively. The paramilitary forces funnelled into East Pakista
between 10 April and 21 April included two wings each of Ea
Pakistan Civil Armed Forces (E.P.C.A.F.) and West Pakista
Rangers (W.P.R.), besides a sizeable number of Scouts from th
North West Frontier. They were mainly taken in place of defectir
East Pakistan Rifles and police.

Whatever reinforcements arrived from West Pakistan, were use
to complete operation SEARCHLIGHT which was never formall
closed but was deemed to have achieved its end by the middle c
April when all major towns in the province had been secured.[1]

I have not been able to collect the figures of casualties suffere
or inflicted during operation SEARCHLIGHT except those I hav
mentioned in the course of this narration. But I can vouch for th
strength of my assessment that the number of lives lost in the clashe
barely touched the four figure mark. If the foreign press made th
world believe that several million people perished, the blame lie
with those who expelled the foreign press from Dacca on 26 Marc
(evening) and forced them to base their stories on the fantasy c
Indian propagandists or the whims of opinionated tourists. If th
foreign journalists had been allowed to stay in East Pakistan afte
25 March, even the most biased among them would have witnesse
a reality which, though tragic, was far less gruesome than wha
appeared in their stories.

---

[1] The major towns were secured on the following dates:
Paksy (10 April), Pabna (10 April), Sylhet (10 April), Ishurdi (11 April),
Narsindgi (12 April), Chandarghona (13 April), Rajshahi (15 April), Thakur-
gaon (15 April), Kushtia (16 April), Laksham (16 April), Chuadanga (1'
April), Brahamanbaria (17 April), Darsana (19 April), Hilli (21 April),
Satkhira (21 April), Golundu (21 April), Dohazari (22 April), Bogra (2:
April), Rangpur (26 April), Noakhali (26 April), Santahar (27 April), Siraj-
ganj (27 April), Maulvi Bazar (28 April), Cox's Bazar (10 May), Maulvi
Hatia (11 May).

11

AN OPPORTUNITY LOST

Pakistan started receiving an adverse press abroad soon after the expulsion of foreign correspondents from Dacca on 26 March. The military bureaucracy was so involved in internal affairs that it did not pay much attention to this vital problem. I suggested on the last day of March 1971 that the only way to counter the blame of killing 'unarmed innocent civilians' was to disclose the defection of the East Bengal Regiment, East Pakistan Rifles and the East Pakistan Police. I received a sharp rebuke in return. I was asked, 'Do you want to destroy the image of the finest army by telling the world that its discipline has collapsed?'

I could not muster enough support for my proposal. So it remained unimplemented until circumstances forced the authorities, on 1 May, to find a correspondent to circulate our version, highlighting the heavy odds due to large scale defections by the Bengali troops.[1]

I was not the only one who lost this battle of reason. Major-General Farman Ali also suggested in early April that a general amnesty should be declared to encourage the defecting personnel to return to our fold rather than give them no option but to unite in the Indian sanctuaries. A general senior to him said tauntingly, 'Oh, we know your political approach. But the time for politics is over.' They declared a general amnesty five months later (September) when India had organized the rebels into the *Mukti Bahini*— 'the liberation army'—which facilitated the task of the Indian Army later in open war.

The high command in Rawalpindi, however, accepted one piece of advice: to send another general to Dacca to share General Tikka's burden as the commander of troops, zonal martial law administrator and provincial governor. They picked Lieutenant-General A.A.K. Niazi who had been decorated with the Military Cross in World War II, and the *Hilal-i-Jurat* in the 1965 War. He

---

[1] Anthony Mascarenhas's story published in the *Sunday Times*, London, 1 May 1971.

enjoyed the reputation of a 'tiger' and seemed to be an apt choice to tame the Bengal Tigers. His failings, which were to be highlighted by the December debacle, were then generally hidden from the people. Had he succeeded, I am sure, his foibles would have been ignored by the nation. But foibles and failings he did have.

I met him in the gardens of Flagstaff House on 11 April. He had taken over Eastern Command the same morning. The new appointment had brought him the new rank of lieutenant-general, which he enjoyed wearing with full ribbons and war distinctions. He seemed quite confident about his new job. General Khadim Raja, the G.O.C., told me later that when he had handed over the command of troops, General Niazi had asked him, 'When are you going to hand over your concubines to me?'

After assuming command, General Niazi addressed his staff in Eastern Command Headquarters where he criticized the 'doves' in the Army for their past laxity, and poured his wrath on the Bengalis, particularly Hindus and the intellectuals—the two classes which, in his opinion, nurtured Bengali nationalism.

On the operational side, he obtained a brief from the out-going G.O.C. and followed it till 10 May, when the last border town (Cox's Bazar) was reached by the troops. Major-General Rahim Khan, reputedly one of the Yahya regime's finest generals, replaced General Khadim Raja. General Niazi now had three fresh divisional commanders: Major-General Rahim (14 Division), Major-General Shaukat Riza (9 Division) and Major-General Nazar Hussain Shah (16 Division). He divided East Pakistan into three zones and made each general responsible for one of them. Broadly, 9 Division got the entire eastern border; 16 Division, northern Bengal; and 14 Division the rest of the province.

With these troops, it did not take General Niazi very long to break the backbone of the Bengali resistance. He secured all major towns by the end of April. The following month was devoted to minor operations aimed at clearing the suspected pockets. But this period of relative peace and absolute control was not used for launching any constructive campaign to win over the Bengalis. Instead their wounds were continuously abraded by the invasion of private houses in what were known as 'sweep operations'.

These operations were only a partial success because the West Pakistani troops neither knew the faces of the suspects nor could they read the lane numbers (in Bengali). They had to depend on the co-operation of the local people. The Bengalis, by and large, still cherished the hope of Mujib's return and assumed an attitude of passive indifference. The only people who came forward were 'the rightists like Khwaja Khairuddin of the Council Muslim League, Fazlul Qader Chaudhry of the Convention Muslim League, Khan Sobur A. Khan of the Qayyum Muslim League, Professor Ghulam Azam of the Jamaat-i-Islami and Maulvi Farid Ahmed of the Nizam-i-Islam Party.

They had all been defeated by the Awami League in the 1970 elections and carried little appeal for the Bengalis. The people generally felt that they were outdated coins being given currency by the Army once again. But the Army, out of sheer necessity, valued their presence and followed their advice. I suggested in one of the meetings that instead of propagating the statements of these 'outdated coins', it would be better to seek the co-operation of teachers, lawyers, artists and intellectuals who command respect in their respective fields. The suggestion was approved and I was ordered to obtain supporting statements from prominent people in various walks of life. I had some success with lesser known people but the intellectuals, the fountain-head of Bengali nationalism, received me with reservation. An instance of this is my experience with Justice Murshed, a former Chief Justice of the East Pakistan High Court. He admitted me to his marvellous study (Gulshan Colony) and entertained me with the choicest books and the rarest manuscripts. He freely quoted from Rumi, Sa'adi and Iqbal— the great oriental poets and writers. In this scholarly setting, I requested his co-operation. After a long, winding talk, he said: 'Allow me three months to think.' 'Three months to think!' I exclaimed in surprise. 'Yes,' he said, 'a minimum of three months to see whether you have really re-established your authority. Where is Farland these days, by the way?' When I narrated my experience at the next meeting, a 'patriotic' intelligence officer said, 'We can pick up Murshed at night and get you any statement you like.' He was, I am pleased to say, spared this distinction.

Justice Murshed was not the only intellectual who doubted the effectiveness of Army action. Many others cherished hopes of Mujib's return and the 'liberation' of their homeland, as my experience with radio and television was to show. Soon after the crack-down, I was assigned the task of 'reactivating' the radio station to broadcast fresh martial law orders to give an impression of 'normalcy'. To begin with, I thought it safe to allow them to play instrumental music in the intervals between martial law announcements. They began to play dirges, lamenting the death and destruction caused by army action. I ordered them to play *Hamd* and *Na'at* (hymns in praise of God and his Prophet) instead, to revive the Islamic bonds between the two wings. They cleverly put this famous devotional song on the air:

اے مولاعلی اے شیر خدا میری کشتی پار لگا دینا

(Row my boat to the safety of the shores, O Ali, my Lord!)

Incidentally, the boat was the election symbol of the Awami League.

Similarly, I asked the television station to produce short plays on the heroes of the Pakistan Movement to highlight the need for independence from Hindu and British domination. They selected a prominent name—Maulana Mohammad Ali Johar—and used the occasion to televise a forceful play on the virtues of independence. It called upon all the freedom fighters (*Mukti Bahini*) to spare no sacrifice for the great cause!

Instead of eradicating these germs of independence, the authorities thought it wise to perpetuate the reign of terror 'to keep the Bingos under control'. They frequently resorted to 'search and sweep operations' on information provided by 'patriotic' Pakistanis. Some of them were genuinely interested in the integrity of Pakistan and they risked their own lives to co-operate with the Army, but a few of them also used their links with the Army to settle old scores with pro-Awami League people. For instance, a rightist politician arrived one day in Martial Law Headquarters with a teen-aged boy. He met me by chance on the verandah and whispered in confidence that he had some vital information to impart about the rebels. I took him to the appropriate authority where he said that the boy, a nephew of his, had managed to escape from a rebels concentration in Karaniganj across the Burhi Ganga river. The boy added that the rebels not only harassed the locals but also planned to attack Dacca city at night.

A 'clearing operation' was immediately ordered. The commander of troops was briefed. The field guns, mortars and recoilless rifles were readied to 'soften' the target in a pre-dawn bombardment. The troops were to make a pincer move to capture it at day-break.

I watched the progress of the action in the operations room where the gun-fire was clearly audible. Soon some automatic weapons also joined the battle. Many people feared that the attacking battalion might not be able to bag all the 5,000 rebels reported in the locality. The operation was over after sunrise. It was confirmed that the target had been neutralized without any casualties to our troops.

In the evening, I met the officer who carried out the attack. What he said was enough to chill my blood. He confided. 'There were no rebels, and no weapons. Only poor country-folk, mostly women and old men, got roasted in the barrage of fire. It is a pity that the operation was launched without proper intelligence. I will carry this burden on my conscience for the rest of my life.'

While these search and sweep operations were in progress, Radio Pakistan, the press and television harped on the 'normalcy' that was fast returning to the province. It happened at times that members of a household, while listening to a 'normalcy' broadcast from Radio Pakistan, were raided by a search party sweeping everything that came in its way. Thus Radio Pakistan, like the other government-controlled media, lost credibility with the Bengali listeners who preferred to tune in to All India Radio (A.I.R.) or any other foreign station. The A.I.R. and its Western sympathizers had their own fantastic stuff to inject into Bengali ears. The Indian station missed no opportunity to foment Bengali hatred and persuade the people to leave their homes 'if they wanted to save their life and honour'. The large-scale exodus of the population took place later in July and August, when the insurgency was in full swing.

Those who decided to stay put in their homes, in spite of the uncertain conditions, thought it wise to cultivate the friendship of an army officer, or any person in uniform. A khaki uniform and a Punjabi or Pushto dialect were considered a shield against harassment and victimization. Many of us were pleased to 'patronize' one Bengali family or another. A family gifted with beautiful girls earned the patronage of several officers at a time.

I was invited by a prosperous Bengali editor to his house although during the previous year of our contact, he had never relaxed his formal exterior to allow me even a peep into his personality. He took me with him on the plea that my visit would sustain the morale of his family who were completely shaken after a recent night attack in their neighbourhood. After a formal introduction to his mother, married sister and other relatives he left me with his beautiful bride in the air-conditioned drawing room, to pick up a guest from the Hotel Intercontinental. The silence soon began to weigh heavily. I attempted to open a conversation with my elegant hostess, by saying, 'I am sorry for all that has happened but...' She cut me short: 'You are sorry *now* after destroying so much property, killing so many people and raping so many women...' I tried to intervene but she stormed on, 'You should be ashamed of yourselves... I hate khaki to its every thread. Barbarity is written large on the face of every West Pakistani soldier... I do not know why my husband brought you here. You certainly belong to the brutes who visited my sister's house last night.' I quietly rose and walked out.

Nothing was done to root out this hatred. No need was genuinely felt to give attention to the psychological healing of the patient. Whatever efforts were made, were confined to the restoration of law and order, repairing of railways, working of ferries, transportation of goods and operation of domestic flights.

Leaving aside the major task of bridging the mental and emotional gulf, the material problem itself was too gigantic for the pygmies who attempted to solve it. They lacked comprehension of the magnitude of the problem. They were like a mouse who, while riding an elephant's back, may consider itself master of the area it occupies but can hardly claim to have grasped the elephant as a whole.

They sent a reinforcement of about two dozen bureaucrats and 5,000 policemen from West Pakistan to control the elephant. Both the police and their bosses were familiar with the imperatives of running a normal administrative unit but lacked the ability of putting together the limbs of a chopped body and infusing new life into it. Bureaucrats were not the Messiahs who could perform this miracle. It was essentially a job for statesmen—but rarely do they grow in the arid land of martial law.

12

INSURGENCY

The Indian involvement, which climaxed in the open aggression of December, was not a secret in March 1971 (at least to us). Prominent Indian leaders and writers had declared their support for the rebels soon after the Army action. Mrs. Indira Gandhi told the *Lok Sabha* as early as 27 March, 'I would like to assure the honourable members who asked whether timely decisions (about the East Pakistan crisis) would be taken, that it is the most important thing to do. There is no point in taking a decision when the time for it is over.'[1] Four days later, the Indian Parliament passed a Resolution saying, 'This house wishes to assure them [the rebels] that their struggle and sacrifices will receive the whole-hearted sympathy and support of the people of India.'[2] The same day, Mr. K. Subramanyum, Director of the Indian Institute of Strategic Studies, elucidated the Resolution at a symposium organized by the Indian Council of World Affairs in New Delhi. He said: 'What India must realize is the fact that the break-up of Pakistan is in our interest, an opportunity the like of which will never come (again).'[3] In the same speech, he called it the 'chance of the century' and expressed the Indian resolve to destroy Pakistan, its enemy number one.

India backed this verbal support with practical steps. Her Border Security Force took part in fighting the Pakistani troops. Six of them had been captured near Jessore and Sylhet in early April, several kilometres inside Pakistan territory. The Inspector-General of the Border Security Force called his troops 'the first official hosts of the rebels'. Many officers of the Indian regular army operated in East Pakistan in civilian clothes to organize resistance against the Pakistan Army. Two of them, on separate occasions, boasted to me later (while I was a prisoner of war in India) that they were in East Pakistan throughout March and afterwards.

[1] *Bangla Desh Documents*, Vol. I, p. 669.
[2] Ibid., Vol. I, p. 672.
[3] *The Hindustan Times*, New Delhi, 1 April 1971.

If this was the extent of their involvement, why did the Indians miss the opportunity to intervene militarily and clinch the issue in late March or early April, when we were very vulnerable? Major-General D.K. Palit, India's official historian of the 1971 war[1] says that the Indian Army Chief had refused to accept the responsibility, because the armed forces were still in the process of re-equipping and re-organizing. General Palit says that the Rs. 50,000 million Five-Year Defence Plan was being implemented and many measures had yet to be taken to tone up India's war machine. He says:

'In the Army, manpower provisioning had not been fully achieved and many units were still under strength. Some armoured regiments had not completed raising and re-equipping. There were shortfalls in administrative and logistic units required for the conduct of mobile operations. In the Air Force, the production programme of MIG-21 fighters had still not gone into full swing and lack of spares had reduced some squadrons to a state of low serviceability. In the Navy also, re-equipment projects had not yet been completed. A few more months of crash programming were required before the armed forces could be brought up to full war readiness... More serious than that was the upset in the Army's balance of forces caused by demands for internal security. Two Divisions (minus their heavy equipment) had been deployed in West Bengal and one Division each in Nagaland and Mizo Hills. The air arm would also find itself handicapped at this stage because our bases had not been developed for operations in Bangla Desh. Kurigram airfield at Silchar, which would have to be used for operations over the Comilla sector, was not operationally adequate.'[2]

Later Mr. K. Subramanyum, as a co-author of *The Liberation War*, fixed nine months as the minimum period for full-scale war with Pakistan. He says, '...nine months was the time we required to carry out all preparations, prepare international public opinion, get the Soviet Union's commitment etc. before such a successful action could be launched.'[3]

Besides the military preparations, India also needed time to neutralize diplomatically the chances of Chinese intervention, and to create a favourable world opinion. She started work on all

[1] D.K. Palit, *The Lightning Campaign*, p. 42.
[2] Ibid., pp. 40-2.
[3] Mohammad Ayoob and K. Subramanyum, *The Liberation War*, New Delhi, p. 177.

these fronts simultaneously. While her Service Chiefs hurried with reorganizing and re-equipping their armed forces, her Foreign Ministry dug out an earlier proposal for an Indo-Soviet 'Treaty of Peace, Friendship and Co-operation' and signed it on 9 August 1971. To influence world opinion in her favour, she exploited and magnified the presence of refugees who had fled to India because of the uncertain conditions in East Pakistan.

Meanwhile, India did not allow the Pakistan Army a free hand in quelling the rebellion. She organized a rebel force, commonly known as the *Mukti Bahini*. The East Bengal Regiment and East Pakistan Rifles personnel who had defected from East Pakistan provided the backbone of this force. These were supplemented by students, Awami League volunteers and able-bodied refugees. Colonel (ret.) M.A.G. Osmani became their Commander-in-Chief.

To provide a political umbrella for this rebel force, India used the presence of the Awami League leaders who had fled to Calcutta in the wake of army action on 25 March. Prominent among them were Tajuddin, Qamaruzzaman, Mansur Ali and Mushtaq Ahmed Khondkar. They were grouped to form a government-in-exile with the mission to 'liberate Bangla Desh' with Mukti Bahini help and Indian patronage.

The Indian warlords laid down the following course of action for the Mukti Bahini;

'Deployment in their own native land with a view to *initially* immobilizing and tying down the Pakistan military forces for protective tasks in Bengal, *subsequently* by gradual escalation of guerilla operations, to sap and corrode the morale of the Pakistan Forces in the eastern sector and *finally* to avail the cadres (*sic*) as ancillaries to the Eastern Field Force in the event of Pakistan initiating hostilities against us.'[1]

The Mukti Bahini was accordingly prepared to carry out this mandate in phases. In the first phase, they were trained for four weeks in sabotage work, sniping, grenade throwing and rifle shooting. Later, the training was extended to eight weeks and covered wider tasks including the handling of all small arms. Finally, 30,000 of them were armed and organized to fight a conventional war side by side with the Indian regular army, while the remaining 70,000 were to carry on guerilla warfare.

[1] Pran Chopra, *India's Second Liberation*, Delhi, p. 155.

The insurgency operations in East Pakistan can be summarized in three phases:

Phase I (June–July): They operated in border areas where Indian troops were close by to support them morally and materially. The rebels, during this phase, behaved very timidly and retreated quickly to their sanctuaries at the slightest sign of detection or counter-action. Their main achievements included the blowing up of minor culverts, mining abandoned railway tracks, lobbing a grenade or harassing an insignificant political adversary.

Phase II (August–September): They showed improvement in their training and a method in their operations. They seemed to be more confident, better motivated and better led. Now their exploits included ambushing army convoys, raiding police stations, blowing up vital installations, sinking river-craft and assassinating prominent political leaders. Their operations extended right up to Dacca.

Phase III (October–November): They were fairly active both on the borders and in the interior. Backed by Indian troops and artillery, they mounted pressure on the border outposts and fomented trouble in important towns and cities. This dual attack overtaxed our resources and strained our mental energies. It is during this phase that the Indian Army established some important bridge-heads which they profitably used in the war.

With the increase in their role, the number of training camps for the Mukti Bahini also grew from 30 in May, to 40 in August and 84 in September. Each camp had the capacity to train between 500 and 2,000 rebels in one training cycle. Their total strength had risen to 100,000 before the war.

Initially, India had some problem in finding weapons and equipment for the rebels but, after signing the treaty with the U.S.S.R., she had the resources of a super power available to her. 'Indian arms deliveries to the guerillas were stepped up after the Soviet Union assured India that it would replace Soviet weapons sent on to the rebel forces.'[1] A British journalist told me in Dacca that she had seen the rebels with obsolete Soviet equipment of World War II vintage which previously had lain dumped in Eastern Europe. In addition, the Bangla Desh Government-in-exile purchased, with

[1] *News Review on Pakistan,* The Institute of Strategic Studies and Analysis, New Delhi, November 1971.

Indian help, some sophisticated weapons, with contributions collected by Bangla Desh envoys abroad.

How did Pakistan meet the challenge? She had 1,260 officers and 41,060 other ranks to counter the mounting menace of insurgency. This manpower had to cover an area of 55,126 square miles. T.E. Lawrence, the legendary guerilla leader, lays down the ratio of twenty persons per four square miles.[1] He fixed this figure in the, context of desert warfare where observation is not obstructed by abundant vegetation as in East Pakistan. Even by the desert formula Pakistan needed 375,640 men to control the situation, about seven times more than the available troops. David Loshak, a foreign correspondent, estimated the number of required troops at 250,000.[2] Yet Pakistan effectively kept the widespread insurgency in check for nine full months until the war broke out.

Pakistan maintained her presence by holding the sensitive border outposts and important district and sub-divisional headquarters. She occupied 90 out of 370 border posts and almost all the major towns. With their bases in towns, the troops operated in adjoining areas mostly on reports of rebel activity. As usually happens in such cases, the rebels disappeared before the punitive troops could crack down on them. In a later phase of insurgency, however, the rebels at times resisted the clearing troops and left their hideouts only when they feared their total extinction by reinforcing columns.

Our troops were very active from April to June, when the insurgency was in its infancy. As the menace grew, the commanders became indifferent and acted only when it was unavoidable. In the last phase (October–November), they generally preferred to stick to their bases and did not risk their command. There may be several reasons for this, but the principal among them was the prolonged irregular war without any relief.

The Bengalis' behaviour followed the fluctuations in the fate of insurgency operations. They usually sided with the winning party. If our troops were around, the people were apparently with us, but when they were withdrawn, they welcomed their new masters (the Mukti Bahini) with full warmth. Some prudent fellows kept two sets of flags—Pakistan and Bangla Desh—to hoist on their rooftops to suit the occasion. But it was not a simple matter of hoisting one flag or the other. They suffered heavily if they were found on the wrong side of the fence. Here is a typical instance.

[1] T.E. Lawrence, *Seven Pillars of Wisdom*, London, p. 192.
[2] David Loshak, *Pakistan Crisis*, London, p. 130.

It happened in the Noakhali district in August. A subaltern was deputed with seven men to clear a rebel-infested area. The young officer, using 'tact and flexibility' as ordered, got five of his men butchered by the rebels. A strong reinforcement was sent under a captain. The rebels, well stocked and well entrenched, decided to offer resistance. The captain saw a few dead bodies of the earlier detachment and visualized a similar fate for his troops if he tried to deal with the situation leniently. He loud-hailed a couple of warnings to the rebels, but to no effect. He then cordoned off the whole locality and pounded it heavily with all the weapons he had. Loud cries and dense columns of smoke began to rise. After some time an old man appeared, carrying a white flag, to request a truce. The offer was accepted, but many lives had been lost in the process.

The rebels inflicted similar punishment, sometimes more severely on 'collaborators' with the Pakistan Army.

The main problem was to isolate the rebels from the innocent people. They usually mixed like fish in water. It was suggested to General Tikka Khan that the 3-kilometre border belt be depopulated so that the troops could shoot all suspects in the area. General Tikka Khan, however, turned down the suggestion. He felt that it would aggravate the rehabilitation problem and he was already occupied with the resettlement of refugees returning from India in response to the general amnesty announced on 4 September.

So the rebels and their hosts continued to mix. It was difficult to distinguish one from the other as all of them looked alike. A rebel carrying a sten gun under his arm could, in emergency, throw his weapon in the field and start working like an innocent farmer. On the other hand, a harmless-looking fisherman could suspend his work to plant a mine in the way of an approaching convoy and disappear. Here is an actual incident to illustrate the point.

A report was received in Rajshahi that rebels had entered the Rohanpur area and were forcing the people to give them food, money and shelter. A group of soldiers searched the area but found no one except three farmers working in the fields. They were about to return when they found a bearded man and forced him, at bayonet point, to reveal the rebels' whereabouts. On his indication, the troops rounded up the three farmers and recovered several grenades, a sizeable quantity of explosives and some propaganda leaflets from the field. All the three turned out to be staunch members of the Mukti Bahini.

They employed several other techniques to hoodwink the Army. For instance, two soldiers on routine patrol duty between Benapol and Ragunath (Jessore sector) in July saw a miserable looking fellow carrying a bagful of vegetables. As they did not find any rebels to occupy their time, they casually shouted at the man, 'What are you carrying, *Baba*?' The old man started trembling with fear. When they unpacked his load, they found it full of time fuses (for sabotage) covered with a sprinkling of vegetables. Similarly, Lieutenant Farrakh, while searching the 'char' area in Brahmaputra, apprehended a boat laden with seasonal fruits. Underneath, it was full of mines and grenades.

The insurgents also employed different routes to avoid detection. Generally, they operated through the countryside while we used the main roads. The rebels knew this and made full use of it. A letter written by a rebel in Rangpur to his comrade-in-arms across the border, said, 'The Pakistan Army can never detect us. They guard only the main approaches, popular ferries and principal *ghats* whereas we use only bye-lanes, side paths and unfrequented routes. Again, they search the body of the boats without caring to know what is trailing underneath. Our sanctuaries are the private houses of Imam Masjids (local religious leaders) or prominent members of Peace Committees, as the army does not suspect them of disloyalty. Our ways are subtle, our aims high. We will triumph.'

As time passed, their sabotage work attained some degree of sophistication. For instance, in the beginning, they used booby traps and safety valves but when we learnt to neutralize the danger by moving an empty cart or a railway bogey ahead of the main convoy, they changed to electric detonators with remote control, which enabled them to blast a moving target at will. When their dynamos were detected, they started using dry battery cells which were easy to smuggle in ordinary torches or bamboo barrels.

The same was the case with operations in the estuary. They started with crude explosives tied to a ship, barge or coaster; but, by August, they turned to a liberal use of limpet mines which could be easily planted with their magnetic face on any part of the target. When this, too, became hazardous for them, they employed divers who could swim undetected to the ship, plant the mine on it and come back. The Indian Navy had trained 300 frogmen for this purpose.[1]

[1] D. R. Mankekar, *Pakistan cut to size*, Delhi, 1972, p. 133.

At times, they used a reed to provide an air pipe to the divers under water. Later, they supplemented this by sending limpet mines with a floating object—a bamboo stick or a banana trunk—towards the target, to which it would be automatically attracted by its steel-plating.

Their sabotage inventory included damage to, or destruction of, 231 bridges, 122 railway lines and 90 electric installations. They could not reach this figure without a high degree of motivation. Here is an example of their spirit. A Bengali lad was arrested in Rohanpura area (Rajshahi District) in June 1971, for an attempted act of sabotage. He was brought to the company headquarter for interrogation but refused to divulge any information. When all other methods had failed, Major 'R' put his sten-gun on his chest and said, 'This is the last chance for you. If you don't co-operate, the bullets will pierce through your body.' He bowed down, kissed the ground, stood up and said, 'I am ready to die, now. My blood will certainly hasten the liberation of my sacred land.'

It was not an easy job for the Army to stamp out insurgents so sophisticated in technique and so highly motivated. Yet it tried its best. In the beginning, it sent out columns by road but after a few explosions, the troops operated through the countryside. This exposed them to sniping and ambushes. In the monsoon season, they used country boats to track down the rebels but could not master the required skill in spite of 'watermanship courses' run by the formations. At times, the boats sank on their own or capsized as a result of rebel action. Then we resorted to foot-slogging through mud and slush, only to be teased by weeds and leeches. Leeches were a sufficient harassment to men from the plains. I saw one lieutenant, Shahid by name, with several leech bites on his legs. He carried the sores long after the war.

During these operations, some troops, to the shame of all, indulged in looting, killing and rape. Nine cases of rape were officially reported and the culprits were severely punished—but the damage had been done. How many such cases there were in all, I do not know—but I firmly believe that even if just one soldier committed rape it was enough to destroy the good work of the entire Army.

The stories of these atrocities naturally alienated the Bengali population. They were not very fond of us before, but now they hated us bitterly. No serious effort was made to arrest this trend or diminish the hatred. Hence, there was no question of mass co-operation by the Bengalis. Only those people joined hands with us who, in the name of Islam and Pakistan, were prepared to risk everything.

These patriotic elements were organized into two groups. The elderly and prominent among them formed Peace Committees, while the young and able-bodied were recruited as *Razakars* (volunteers). The Committees were formed in Dacca as well as in the rural areas and they served as a useful link between the Army and the local people. At the same time, they earned the wrath of the rebels and 250 of them were killed, wounded or kidnapped.

Razakars were raised to augment the strength of the West Pakistani troops and to give a sense of participation to the local population. Their manpower rose to nearly 50,000 as against a target of 100,000. In September a political delegation from West Pakistan complained to General Niazi that he had raised an army of Jamaat-i-Islami nominees. The general called me to his office and said, 'From now on, you will call the Razakars *Al-Badr* and *Ash-Shams* to give the impression that they do not belong to one single party.' I complied.

The *Al-Badr* and *Ash-Shams* groups were a dedicated lot, keen to help the Army. They worked hard and suffered hard. About 5,000 of them or their dependents suffered at the hands of the Mukti Bahini for the crime of co-operation. Some of them displayed a sense of sacrifice comparable to the best troops in the world. For instance, a Razakar from Galimpur in Nawabganj Police Station had gone as a guide with an army column to sweep a rebel hideout. When he returned, he found his three sons killed and a daughter kidnapped. The loss only confirmed his loyalties to the Army and to Pakistan. Another Razakar, while guarding a road bridge in Gomastapur (Rajshahi), was overpowered by the rebels who tried to force him to say *Joi Bangla* but he continued shouting *Pakistan Zindabad* till he was bayoneted to death.

In terms of training and weapons, however, the Razakars were no match for the Mukti Bahini. They had two to four weeks training while the Mukti Bahini went through an intense eight-week training cycle. The former were armed with obsolete .303 rifles while the latter carried sophisticated weapons, including automatics. Thus the Razakars were an asset as long as they were deployed with the Army, but could not be relied upon for independent assignments.

The main brunt of insurgency, therefore, had to be borne by the regular troops, who suffered the odds with fortitude. Their plight cannot be measured in terms of casualties alone. The deeper damage was in the psychological field. What affected the morale of the troops most was the fact that neither could the wounded always be evacuated to military hospitals for treatment nor the dead be flown to West Pakistan. The wounded at times lay for days in the border outposts awaiting evacuation by helicopter, as the road link to the border outposts was usually mined and covered by fire. And the helicopters could not be detailed unless the Regimental Medical Officer (R.M.O.) had certified that the casualty was serious enough to warrant an airlift. The R.M.O., on the other hand, could not reach the casualty because he was located in the battalion head-quarters several kilometres to the rear. If the casualty could not be evacuated by road because of ambushes or mines how could the doctor travel to the post?

A few lucky fellows, however, managed to reach the Combined Military Hospital, Dacca. One could hardly bear their sight. Some had their limbs chopped off, others were completely defaced with burns. Some were permanently blinded or deafened. Most of them, even if cured, would lead a crippled life. Many others carried the burden of their duty in the field in spite of minor wounds, foot rot, fungus and leech sores. They had known no rest, relief, or recreation for several months.

As to the dead, we flew them to West Pakistan initially, but when by July and August their numbers began to soar, we stopped sending them to their relatives for fear of 'creating an unnecessary scare'. When the attention of the visiting Chief of General Staff was drawn to this unpopular decision, he is reported to have callously remarked, 'The dead are as useless in the West as in the East.'

The relatives in West Pakistan, however, always wanted their dead to be flown home. I remember a letter written by an officer's sister to the commanding officer of 31 Frontier Force. She said, in part, 'I gave my handsome brother to your care when you left Karachi. If you cannot bring him back in the same good shape, do not forget to bring him back dead.' She never saw her brother again alive or dead.

13

POLITICS, AT HOME AND ABROAD

President Yahya Khan went on a long mental holiday after ordering the army crack-down on 25 March. Apparently he lost interest in the fate of East Pakistan and took no advantage of the time bought by his troops with their sweat, blood and lives.

Several explanations, some of them conjectural in nature, have been advanced for Yahya's inaction. Professor G.W. Chaudhry says that during these months, Yahya 'looked vacant and seemed unable to talk to me.'[1] He gives the impression that Yahya Khan, a delicate soul, was shocked by the barbarity of his troops and did not know how to condone it. On the other hand, a general on Yahya's staff told me that the President planned to visit East Pakistan in June and flew to Karachi but 'got involved there with that bitch...' (Apparently one of the females in whose company he frequently relaxed). A hawk in Yahya's coterie, however, gave yet another reason. He said loudly during one of his visits to Dacca, 'There can be no political settlement with the "Bingos" till they are sorted out well and proper.' Yahya himself said to a journalist, 'Everytime I make up my mind to go to Dacca, my staff tells me that the visit would serve no useful purpose.'

Yahya could have taken prompt political decisions even without visiting East Pakistan, but he didn't. In eight months of protracted guerilla warfare, he took only two decisions: the replacement of Governor Tikka Khan and the grant of a general amnesty to the rebels. He exercised his political discretion only after repeated suggestions from friendly quarters.

President Yahya Khan is understood, in the first instance, to have offered the governorship of the province to Mr. Nurul Amin, an aged Bengali M.N.A. and former Chief Minister of the Province but he refused to accept the responsibility for reasons of health. Then the choice fell on Dr. A.M. Malik, an equally ancient figure from East Pakistan. Dr. Malik, 74, was a dentist by education, a

[1] Op. cit., p. 191.

trade unionist by practice and superannuated politician by career. He shouldered the task.

It was suggested that General Tikka Khan be retained in Dacca, either as commander of troops or as zonal martial law administrator. General Farman advised the President to combine both offices in General Tikka Khan and pull back General Niazi. But the President had his own preferences.

General Tikka Khan himself was not pleased with his removal. At the farewell dinner given in his honour on 1 September 1971 at the officers' mess, he said in the presence of all of us (I paraphrase):

'I was hurriedly summoned to Rawalpindi on 4 March to take over East Pakistan. I am suddenly asked now to make over my charge to Dr. Malik. I don't want to comment on this decision as the President alone knows the whole situation. As far as I am concerned, I am sorry to leave you in mid-stream. I would have preferred to complete the task assigned to me. Anyhow, don't lose heart. You have an experienced commander [Niazi] who will provide you with the necessary guidance. But keep one thing in mind: don't relax your hold. Keep the lid tight. Otherwise your lives will become miserable...'

Next morning, we all gathered at the airport to see him off. A handful of civil servants were also there. He was not the same buoyant general who had landed at the same airfield six months earlier, beaming with hope and confidence. Now he was in a far more sombre mood.

The new governor was sworn in at 4 p.m. on 3 September. Among those who attended the ceremony were the élite of the town, prominent civil servants, members of the diplomatic corps and some old politicians like Sobur Khan, Fazlul Qader Chaudhry and Monem Khan. During the ceremony, I watched the stooping figure, misty eyes and drooping jaw of the new Governor who was stepping into the shoes of an ironman like Tikka Khan.

Dr. Malik's assumption of office visibly lessened the tension in the city. The Bengalis were not exceptionally fond of him, but they preferred him to any West Pakistani general. The new governor also struck a placatory note by visiting the *mazars* (tombs) of H.S. Suhrawardy, Fazlul Haque and Khwaja Nazimuddin. He also offered his Friday prayers at Baitul Mukarrum, the biggest mosque in the city.

Lt.-Gen. Sahabzada Yakub Khan
Commander, Eastern Command and
Martial Law Administrator, East Pakistan

Vice-Admiral S.M. Ahsan
Governor, East Pakistan

Lt.-Gen. Tikka Khan
Governor and Martial Law Administrator
East Pakistan

Maj.-Gen. Khadim Hussain Raja
General Officer Commanding East Pakistan

The non-Bengalis, particularly the Biharis, however, felt insecure after General Tikka Khan's departure. They thought that, with a weak governor in Dacca, the rebels could disrupt life more often and cause incalculable damage to property. On 4 September, a Bihari journalist phoned me for help in some private matter and I advised him to contact the civil government. He said sorrowfully, 'For us, there is no civil government. *Our* governor has flown to West Pakistan.'

The second important decision—amnesty—was announced on 4 September. The amnesty order pardoned all 'miscreants' and provided for the release of all those under detention. However, this did not apply to those who had been charge-sheeted. The decision, though well intended, proved ineffective because it came too late. By now, the rebels had been grouped, trained and indoctrinated by India. The Awami League leaders, ninety of them, who were in East Pakistan in early April and were willing to co-operate with us on a simple guarantee of personal security, had finally gone to India to help fight the 'liberation war'. The successes of guerilla war and rumours of Mujib's release also made the amnesty offer unacceptable to the rebels.

What the amnesty order did achieve was the release of about two hundred *detenus*. One hundred and sixteen of them were set free in my presence from the Joydebpur cells while eight more were released in Dacca. Others were freed in the mofussil districts. All of them had been screened and declared 'white' (harmless) by the Inter Services Screening Committee (I.S.S.C.). Eighty-seven more prisoners, categorized as 'grey' (doubtful cases) were also released.

To the best of my knowledge, no hard core member of the Mukti Bahini returned to us under the lure of amnesty. In fact, they used the opportunity to increase their traffic of explosives, mines and grenades. The reception camps set up along the border received only a sprinkling of returning refugees while trained saboteurs, taking advantage of the amnesty, flooded along unauthorized routes. They travelled empty-handed and collected their arms and explosives from fixed points in East Pakistan.

Some Bengalis were hopeful that the amnesty decision also applied to Mujibur Rehman. Their hopes were further kindled by widespread rumours that some influential world capitals were pressing Yahya Khan to drop the trial of Mujib and release him. A general in Yahya's confidence arrived from Rawalpindi and gave some credence to these speculations. He said, 'It would perhaps be better to finish Mujib politically than to kill him physically because a dead Mujib would be more dangerous than a living Mujib.' He added that Mujib was prepared to sign a commitment of loyalty and declare his allegiance to united Pakistan. 'Don't you think it would take the wind out of the sails of the so-called liberation movement?' I said, 'First, the President is already committed on the matter of Mujib's fate. Secondly, what is the guarantee that once Mujib is released he will not do a volte-face, on one pretext or another.' The general avoided further discussion saying, 'Oh, I was just discussing a hypothetical situation.'

But it was not a purely hypothetical situation. Some informal meetings were arranged, by a friendly country, between representatives of Bangla Desh and Pakistan. Yahya was understood to have assured a wealthy neighbour that Mujib's life would be spared, but that the timing of his release must be left to him (Yahya).

A German journalist flew into Dacca in October 1971, after seeing Bhutto in Larkana. He told me that a new political arrangement was in the offing in West Pakistan and Bhutto gave him the impression 'that if he came to power, he would release Mujib' because he was not publicly committed on this issue.

As a corollary to the new political arrangement, by-elections were ordered to fill 78 Awami League National Assembly seats from East Pakistan. Major-General Farman Ali was put in charge of this. He wanted to reward the rightist politicians who had co-operated with the Army during the crucial period following the Army action. The seats were few, the aspirants many. He, therefore, asked the rightists to put up a consolidated list of their candidates. They gave their bids as follows: Pakistan Democratic Party, 46; Jamaat-i-Islami, 44; Council Muslim League, 26; Convention Muslim League, 21; and Nizam-i-Islam Party, 17. Farman then tried to work out a formula to satisfy all of them, keeping in mind the President's desire to give sufficient seats to Mr. Nurul Amin so as to enable him to form a coalition government at the centre.

While Farman worked at the figures, he received a fresh order from General Peerzada who said, 'Give 21 to Qayyum League and 18 to Pakistan People's Party also.' 'Then how can I accommodate all the rightists?' 'O.K. Make it 13 for P.P.P.' Later on, I learnt that the President was playing with three politicians—Nurul Amin,

Qayyum and Bhutto—giving the lure of Premiership to each. I don't know how his game progressed in Rawalpindi but as far as Dacca was concerned, the by-elections were a sheer hoax. In practice, the seats were distributed by General Farman.

A retired air marshal also arrived in Dacca to assess the prospects of his party in the by-elections. I met him with another journalist at the Hotel Intercontinental on 1 October at 5.30 p.m. When he asked my opinion on the by-elections, I said, 'I suggest you take a trip to the countryside to see the plight of the common man. The people by and large are not interested in by-elections. They are worried about their survival.' This developed into a long argument. 'If the problem is as complex as you say, then who, in your opinion, can retrieve the situation?' 'It is certainly beyond generals, air marshals and field marshals. The country badly needs a politician of national stature.' 'I think Mujib is the answer,' he said, 'he should be released forthwith. It is already very late.' 'But he is a traitor. He is responsible for all this,' I objected. 'If your Army can pardon all the murderers (by the amnesty), it can also stomach the release of Mujib who hasn't killed a single soul with his own hands. I tell you West Pakistan is ready to accept his release.' He returned to Rawalpindi without any prospect of getting representation for his party in East Pakistan.

While other politicians struggled for a share in the East Pakistan by-elections, Bhutto insisted outright on the transfer of power to the 'people's representatives' on the basis of the 1970 elections. The demand sounded out of place to local observers in the context of the serious crisis at hand, but those who knew the state of the junta's mental bankruptcy prayed for an early change of government so that the best could be made out of a bad situation. As far as the level of understanding of Yahya and his colleagues was concerned, it had been sufficiently exposed.

We saw some prospects of hope when we learnt that the President had decided to send a high-powered delegation, under the leadership of Mr. Z.A. Bhutto, to the People's Republic of China. We knew that Bhutto, as Foreign Minister, had been the main architect of Sino-Pakistani friendship and hoped that somehow he would pull the chestnuts out of the fire. The inclusion of Air Marshal Rahim Khan, P.A.F. Chief and Lieutenant-General Gul Hasan, Chief of the General Staff, in the eight-member delegation made it amply clear that China's military help was also being sought.

The delegation visited Peking in early November and held wide-ranging talks with the Chinese leaders. During the visit, Bhutto was able to declare that 'the result of this meeting should be a deterrent to aggression'.[1] This confirmed the earlier declaration by President Yahya Khan about Chinese help in the event of aggression against Pakistan. In addition the press statements made then by Pakistani and Chinese leaders, encouraged one to believe that Chinese help would be forthcoming in the event of war. When I tried to confirm my optimism with a source close to Bhutto's delegation, he said, 'Yes, the Chinese are great friends. They have advised us to win over the people of East Pakistan.'

Washington was also asked whether the United States would honour her obligations under the bilateral treaty signed with Pakistan in the 1950s. But there too, we got the same advice instead of a firm commitment of help. 'Yahya showed me his correspondence with Nixon and the Chinese leaders, who were keenly hoping that a political settlement with the Bengalis might be possible.'[2]

India achieved better diplomatic results than Pakistan. She followed up the Indo-Soviet Treaty with intense efforts to neutralize the threat of intervention by China or the U.S.A. She invoked Articles 5 and 9 of the Treaty which make it obligatory for the signatories to consult each other 'in the event of either party being subjected to an attack or threat thereof'. Indian writers later confirmed that 'there is a military underpinning to the Agreement.'[3]

Consequently traffic between Moscow and New Delhi increased greatly. A five-member diplomatic mission headed by Soviet Deputy Foreign Minister Nikolai Firubin and a six-member military delegation led by the Chief of Air Staff, visited India in quick succession. The climax was a visit by Marshal Grechko, the Soviet Defence Minister, himself. There were also reports that an Indo-Soviet liaison office had been established in New Delhi and Soviet experts and pilots were permanently associated with it.

Indira Gandhi herself undertook a tour of important countries like the U.S.A., West Germany and England from 24 October to secure their support or at least to neutralize any possible help for Pakistan from these quarters.

The world watched with concern this drift towards armed confrontation between India and Pakistan but seemed unable or

[1] The *Pakistan Times*, Rawalpindi, 7 November 1971.
[2] G.W. Chaudhry, *The Last Days of United Pakistan*, p. 192.
[3] D.K. Palit in the *Hindustan Times*, New Delhi, 20 October 1971.

unwilling to act effectively to avoid the catastrophe. The General Assembly of the United Nations, during its twenty-sixth session, considered Pakistan's complaint of Indian interference in her internal affairs and proposed posting U.N. observers on both sides of the East Pakistan border to defuse the situation. Pakistan readily agreed but India refused. India, in fact, did not approve of any initiative which was likely to ease the situation in East Pakistan. She did not want to miss her 'chance of the century'.

14

CLOSER TO CATASTROPHE

The East Pakistan situation was not affected by either domestic or international politics. It continued to deteriorate without any interruption as if it followed a pre-ordained course. Neither the installation of Dr. Malik's civilian cabinet nor Pakistan's supplications abroad made any difference.

Life in Dacca itself became very difficult. Hardly a day passed without an incident of looting, arson, political murder or bombing. The following are but a few typical examples. The former governor, Abdul Monem Khan, was shot dead at his residence in broad daylight on 23 October. A few days later, a provincial minister's car was blown up in the university area. Then a stolen car, loaded with explosives, went up in flames in the Motijheel commercial area, killing five and injuring thirteen persons. The following day, a bomb exploded in the massive State Bank building. Then the Dacca Improvement Trust building, housing the television station next to the Governor's House, caught fire.

People became inured to such incidents when they became a daily event. The rebels had, therefore, to achieve something extraordinary to draw the attention of people at home and abroad. They did it by blowing up the toilet section of the Hotel Intercontinental, bringing down a major portion of the building. It took several weeks to repair the damage.

On 11 October the rebels introduced a new element into their operations. They used mortars for the first time in Dacca. I heard the bang myself at 1.40 a.m. near the P.I.A. kitchen adjacent to the airport. Two shells were fired inaccurately, without the sight, towards the airport but they fell short of their target. Nevertheless, the incident upset the local administration because it was feared that next time the shots might not be so inaccurate.

The suburbs of Dacca, too, seemed to be infested with rebels. In fact, the outlying areas were relatively safe for them because we usually concentrated our search operations on the city proper.

The Sidhirganj incident is a case in point. Rebels damaged the main power house there and cut the outgoing cables. No Bengali worker was willing to repair the damage. So a team from the Water and Power Development Authority—two assistant engineers, one line superintendent, one assistant foreman and one lineman—was sent from West Pakistan. While working on the site, they were attacked by the rebels, in broad daylight, on October 30. All five were killed. The rebels took away the body of the assistant foreman, Badr-i-Islam, as a trophy. The other four corpses were recovered and despatched to West Pakistan on 31 October at 5 p.m.

Travelling from Dacca and its suburbs towards the interior, one could not help feeling that one was passing through an enemy area. It was impossible to move without a personal escort which, in turn, served as a provocation for the rebels. They ambushed the party or mined its path. If one reached one's destination safely, one could look back on the journey as a positive achievement.

The local commanders in the mofussil areas had no relief or respite from the turbulent situation. They had to solve numerous problems with only a handful of troops. Their responsibilities included maintaining public order, protecting government property, working industrial units and clearing suspected areas. The troops posted there were usually in platoon or company strength but generally their area of responsibility was so wide that they had to be further divided into small detachments. The smaller the detachment, the greater the danger of its elimination by rebels. To augment their strength some Razakars, East Pakistan Civil Armed Forces (E.P.C.A.F.) personnel, West Pakistan Rangers or police were posted with them. This heterogeneous crowd did not make a very cohesive fighting force. But there is always some moral strength in numbers. Therefore, when a post had thirty men, instead of ten, it was considered more secure and tenable.

In practical terms, the posts were not fully secure or fortified. Some of them, particularly those held by paramilitary forces, were a temptation to the rebels who frequently attacked and usually eliminated them. This created a general scare and the timid or disloyal among them abandoned their posts without facing any attack by the rebels. For instance, 32 of the 39 Razakars at Nawabganj police station abandoned their post on 29 October. The remaining seven were overpowered by the rebels next day and the police station went into hostile hands. Again, in Lohaganj police station, we had fifty-seven Bengalis cleared by the Inter Services Screening Committee (I.S.S.C.) and freed under amnesty. Posted with them were thirty riflemen from the West Pakistan Police and Rangers. On 28 October, all fifty-seven Bengalis ran away. Next night, they returned with reinforcements and killed the thirty West Pakistanis. Thus this police station, too, went under rebel control. Several other police stations suffered a similar fate, mostly those located in Noakhali, Faridpur and Tangail districts.

Advancing to the borders, one frequently heard the bangs from the Indian artillery which constantly shelled the border outposts and the adjoining areas. This practice, originally started in late June, intensified in September and October with the rise in rebel activity. The number of rounds fired into our territory ranged from 500 to 2,000 per day. The shelling had three objectives. First, it formed a part of the India's policy of 'controlled escalation' of hostilities. She wanted to keep the borders hot. Secondly, it served as a tonic to the rebels operating in the border areas. Thirdly, it achieved a tactical goal. It helped the rebels and their patrons to occupy some indefensible bulges, salients and enclaves. Trying to eject them, we invariably came under artillery fire or ran into an ambush and suffered heavy casualties. They gradually nibbled away several curves and bulges in our border.

Yet the President of Pakistan, in his radio broadcast on 12 October, gave this commitment to the nation, 'Your valiant armed forces are fully prepared to defend and protect every inch of the sacred soil of Pakistan.'[1] By then, about 3,000 square miles of border bulges had already gone under Indian control.

General Niazi considered it his duty to back the President's announcement with exaggerated claims of victory. He declared several times that if war broke out, he would take the battle to Indian territory. In his loud fantasies, his attack sallied, at one time, towards Calcutta and, at another, towards Assam. When I requested him, as his P.R. man, not to raise unattainable hopes, he said, 'Don't you know that bluff and trickery are the evil geniuses of war?'

It was not a matter of bluffing the enemy. He was only bluffing himself. I remember my exclusive interview with him on 24 October, 1971, in his office. He said, 'What do your friends [the foreign correspondents] say?' 'They say that war is round the corner.'

[1] The *Pakistan Times*, Rawalpindi, 13 October 1971.

'Oh, I am ready for it. My defence works are complete. I have 70,000 armed men. I am very strong on the ground.' 'But you have very little Air and Sea support.' 'I have planned to fight the war without the Air Force and the Navy.' 'Still, I don't think you have enough to fight insurgency as well as external aggression. I fear...' 'What do you fear?' 'We are deployed all along the border. The enemy is both inside and outside. We are like the filling in a sandwich. All they have to do is pierce our defences at a point of their choosing and link up. That will spell our doom.' 'Your fears are absolutely unfounded. You seem to go by numbers. In war, it is not the numbers but generalship that counts. And do you know what generalship is? It is the art of positioning the right number of troops at the right place and at the right time.'

Bluff was not the exclusive prerogative of President Yahya Khan or his commander Niazi. Those down the line also indulged in similar exercises. I always accompanied General Niazi on his tours to divisional and brigade headquarters and attended almost all the military briefings. All the divisional commanders and the brigade commanders, except one major-general and one brigadier, invariably assured General Niazi that, despite their meagre resources and heavy odds, they would be able to fulfil the task assigned to them 'Sir, don't worry about my sector, we will knock hell out of the enemy when the time comes,' was the refrain at all of these briefings. Any comment different from this was taken to imply lack of confidence and professional competence. Nobody wanted to jeopardize his prospects for future promotion.

Quite contrary to the wishful optimism of their commanders, the troops were in a low state of training, equipment, and morale. They had been through eight long months without seeing any improvement in the situation. They had had no time for training to fight a conventional war. They had known no rest or relief for several months. Many of them did not have boots, socks or *charpoys*. Worst of all, several of them had no heart in the operations. There was no point, they thought, in laying down one's life for the Bengalis who had chosen to side with the Hindus to kill their fellow Muslims.

It is said that three quarters of command lies in knowing what is going on in the minds of your troops. But our commanders generally ignored this important psychological factor and counted only the heads and rifle butts under their command. When they were told that we had lost 237 officers, 136 junior commissioned officers and 3,559 other ranks in counter-insurgency operations, they preferred to count those who had survived. Little did they realize that the psychological casualties in their command were several times higher than the physical losses.

As a result of this low state of morale, the troops had lost aggressiveness in patrolling and tenacity in fighting. The patrolling of border areas had relaxed correspondingly. A detachment of troops occasionally went out, once a week or so, to scan its area of responsibility and returned to its base for a night's sleep. On 12 November one such detachment, on routine patrol duty in the Dharmadaha area (about one and a half kilometres from the border in Jessore Sector), discovered that the place was occupied by a platoon of the 1 Naga Battalion of the Indian Army. The intruders had quietly crossed the border on 5 November and lay there undisturbed for one week. They were ejected on 13 November. Four of them were captured and remained with us till after the end of the war.

We got a similar surprise in Belonia Bulge, south of Comilla, where we discovered that by 10 November half of the bulge had been nibbled away by the rebels and their patrons. A few days later, a night operation was launched to unhinge their defences. It was a success. The same week another enemy force crossed the border near Boyra (Jessore Sector) on 13 November. It stayed there undetected for seven days, during which the Indians built up the force to two complete battalions—Jammu & Kashmir and 2 Sikh Light. We learnt about their presence as late as 19 November. The local brigade (in Jessore) was assigned the task of dislodging the intruders. Two companies, from 22 and 38 Frontier Force, were ordered to attack. The attack failed, with heavy losses to us. Later the enemy attacked and our 38 Frontier Force troops were forced back from their defences, leaving behind all their equipment.

The incident proved, on the one hand, that our troops had lost their staying power and, on the other, that the enemy was fully determined. It needed a really serious effort to eject him. The Division made available the Divisional troops—21 Punjab (R&S) and 6 Punjab—for the attack. Task force 'Alpha' and task force 'Bravo' were organized and placed under Lieutenant-Colonel Imtiaz Waraich and Lieutenant-Colonel Sharif respectively. They were also given a squadron of tanks and the fire support of a field regiment of artillery.

The attack was launched at 6 a.m. on 21 November. It progressed well initially but when the attacking force advanced towards the enemy position in a grove of trees, enemy tanks opened up from hidden positions. This was a major surprise for us because we had always regarded it as an 'untankable' area. The enemy artillery also joined the battle from across the border. We sought P.A.F. help. Three Sabres soon appeared overhead. They were met by Indian MIGs. We lost two aircraft and all the tanks. The attack was called off. The enemy did not leave the ground but we cordoned him from three sides to restrain him from further expansion. The cordon continued till all-out war started on 3 December. It was trumpeted as a major achievement, although tactically we had played into enemy hands. Since the major force of the Division was concentrated at one 'sore' point, it opened immense opportunities for the enemy to achieve a breakthrough at any ill-defended point in the divisional area. Luckily though, till then the enemy had a limited aim.

In public, we termed the 21 November battle as an enemy attack supported with MIGs, armour and artillery. In fact, it was an attempt on our part to throw back the enemy who had occupied the area since 13 November.

During the same week (20 25 November,) India attacked Zakiganj and Atgram in Sylhet area, Hilli in Dinajpur and Pachagarh in Rangpur district. The enemy wanted to occupy some vantage points in the border areas to use them as a spring-board for future operations. But we cried ourselves hoarse that an all-out invasion of East Pakistan had commenced. Some of the defending troops in Sylhet and Rangpur sectors were also driven back, as 38 Frontier Force had been in Jessore Sector, and forced to abandon their positions without being able to salvage their equipment and cooking utensils.

These three incidents greatly displeased General Niazi who, in my presence, censured the defaulters and gave the following order, 'No withdrawals without suffering seventy-five per cent casualties. Then, too, the withdrawals will only be permitted by the G.O.C. himself.' This verbal order was later confirmed in writing.

General Niazi visited the border areas almost daily from 22 November to 2 December. I accompanied him throughout these trips. While on a visit to Hilli area on 27 November, General Niazi met a batch of journalists who were being taken to the site of the

Indian attack on Hilli where a disabled Indian tank lay on our side of the border. The press interview continued informally for about half an hour. At the end, a journalist asked, 'When do you think all-out war is coming?' Raising his head from a plate of chicken *tikkas* (pieces), he said, 'All-out war for me has already started.' Nobody was convinced by this answer because we all knew that if India had unleashed its full military might—planes, armour and artillery—General Niazi would not have been cracking jokes with journalists over a plate of chicken.

When the press party left for Hilli, General Niazi took off for Dacca without the slightest fear of interception by enemy jets. He carried with him a young lady journalist for an exclusive interview at Flagstaff House.

PART III

MILITARY

15

DEPLOYMENT FOR DEFEAT

General Niazi's claim, in late November, of fighting an all-out war was contradicted by the deployment pattern of his troops. Strung along the border as they were, in penny packets, it seemed that their main aim was merely to check rebel infiltration or Indian incursions. The imperatives of war, however, demanded a different deployment. Before we examine the options of deployment open to General Niazi, it may be useful to consider the territory he was about to defend.

East Pakistan, separated by more than 1,600 kilometres from West Pakistan, was surrounded on three sides by hostile Indian territory. On the fourth side lay the Bay of Bengal, which could easily be dominated or blocked by the Indian Navy. Only a small tip on the south eastern border had an opening towards Burma. The Chittagong Hill Tracts region, situated along this opening, was a hilly area dominated by the jungle, Mizos and wild animals. It was not fit for any military operations except infiltration and insurgency.

The rest of the province was of alluvial soil, divided into four natural zones by the mighty Jamuna, the Padma, the Brahmaputra and the Meghna. Each zone was further criss-crossed by a number of waterways resembling the work of a linear artist. The patches of land between the waterways were covered by a thick foliage of trees, shrubs and crops. In addition, there were two formidable forests, the Sunderbans in the south-west and Madhupur in the north, near Tangail.

Climatically, East Pakistan was very moderate, except in the rainy season, which officially started in mid-May and ended in mid-September. In reality, the rains started a month earlier and ended a month later. Floods seldom missed their annual visit to the province. They inundated vast areas, disrupting all means of communication except water transport. Even when the flood water receded and normal road and rail communications were restored

the terrain remained wet, rendering it unsuitable for military man-
oeuvres till the middle of November.

The riverine terrain, with its prolonged season of floods, put
certain restraints on India. She could not launch a 'lightning
campaign' during the summer. However, she used this period to
wear down our troops, physically and morally, by prolonged
insurgency. Meanwhile, she also oiled her military machine
and deployed eight divisions of fresh troops around East
Pakistan.

Two Indian divisions, under II Corps, were deployed in West
Bengal against our Jessore Sector while three more divisions, under
XXXIII Corps, were earmarked for operations against North
Bengal.[1] In the middle of our northern border stood her 101
Communication Zone, which had been converted into a fighting
formation and placed under a major-general. On our east were
deployed three divisions under IV Corps. These three corps, consisting of eight divisions and one communication zone, had their
full complement of armour and artillery with them. They had 10
medium and 48 field regiments. Later, they were increased to 12
and 60 regiments respectively.

The Indian artillery included 130mm Russian guns which could
effectively engage a target as far away as 30 kilometres. Her armour
complement consisted of a regiment of T-55 tanks and two regiments each of PT-76 and Sherman tanks. In addition, she had two
independent squadrons of PT-76 tanks and enough armoured personnel carriers to carry two battalions. Most of her tanks had night
capability. They could also ford river obstacles.

Her air power consisted of ten squadrons of MIG-21s (intercep-
tors), Canberras (bombers), Gnats (ground support aircraft) and
SU-7s (fighter-bombers). She had specially laid a network of airfields round East Pakistan from which to conduct offensive operations in the area. She had also massed a large number of transport
planes and helicopters to air-bridge the sprawling East Pakistan
rivers.

India had created, for her eastern theatre, a powerful aircraft
carrier task force. The carrier *Vikrant* had 6 Alize (reconnaissance
aircraft), 14 Sea Hawks (fighters) and 2 Sea Kings (anti-submarine
helicopters) besides an escort of three destroyers and frigates.

---

[1] This was taken to include the north-western part of the province, demarca-
ted by the Ganges to the south and the Jamuna in the east.

Dr. A.M. Malik
Last Governor of East Pakistan

Maj.-Gen. Rao Farman Ali
Adviser to Governor
East Pakistan

Lt.-Gen. Amir Abdullah Khan Niazi
Commander, Eastern Command

The task force also included   four warships,[1] two subm
one minesweeper, five gun-boats and three landing craft   . ...
force had the ability to effect a total naval blockade of East Pakistan.

In addition, India had one brigade of paratroops and three brigade groups. Among her assets should also be counted 29 battalions of Border Security Force and the 100,000-strong Mukti Bahini. As far as the seventy-five million people of East Pakistan were concerned, they had generally turned hostile to us and could render valuable help to the enemy.

For our part, we had three lightly equipped infantry divisions, one squadron of F-86 Sabres and four gun-boats to meet this huge Indian force. (More planes without additional airfields would have been meaningless). Besides this military strength, we had about 73,000 paramilitary personnel including East Pakistan Civil Armed Forces, Scouts, Mujahids and Razakars. How we could use these resources to our greatest advantage, depended largely on the correct appreciation of enemy intentions.

What was the Indian objective in East Pakistan? Today, the question seems stupid and the answer quite obvious; but in 1971 many Pakistani strategists assessed that India aimed at nothing higher than capturing a 'sizeable chunk of territory to establish Bangla Desh' so that she could shift the headquarters of the Bangla Desh Government from Calcutta to East Pakistan and transfer the bulk of her refugee burden to the 'liberated area'. It would be a constant irritant for Pakistan—much to the relief of India. That is all we had by way of strategic anticipation.

The troops were, therefore, deployed to deny this 'sizeable chunk of territory' to the rebels or their Indian patrons. They fulfilled this role for about eight months, and deserve all credit for it. But during this period, India did not unleash her mighty war machine to slice off any sizeable territory. She knew this would mean total war. And this she did not want unless she had tied up all loose ends. She, therefore, worked on the limited objective of aiding the rebels, wearing down our troops and establishing bridgeheads.

The mission given earlier to Eastern Command, however, was 'to defend East Pakistan'. On paper, this mission remained unchanged and H.Q. Eastern Command worked hard—again, on

[1] I.N.S. *Beas*, I.N.S. *Brahmaputra* (Leopard Class), I.N.S. *Kamorta* and I.N.S. *Karartti*, (Petya Class).
[2] I.N.S. *Khandari* and I.N.S. *Kalvari*.

paper—to fulfil it. How best could East Pakistan be defended, was a question that had agitated the minds of General Niazi and his predecessors. Four strategic plans had been advocated from time to time. It is worth examining each of them briefly to determine whether Niazi chose the best.

One way to defend East Pakistan was to concentrate on the defence of Dacca, which would determine the fate of the entire province. The Dacca defences could be best arranged along the home banks of three mighty rivers—the Ganges, the Meghna and the Brahmaputra—which circumscribed the strategic triangle commonly called the 'Dacca Bowl'. This strategy had two obvious disadvantages. First, it meant that all territories lying outside the bowl—Jessore, Kushtia, Rajshahi, Bogra, Rangpur, Sylhet, Bhairab Bazar, Comilla and Chittagong—would have to be surrendered to the enemy without making him fight for every inch. Secondly, by narrowing our defence perimeter, we would permit India to divert at least four of her eight divisions to the West Pakistan border where, for the first (and possibly the last) time in history, we had a near parity of forces. It goes without saying that the situation on the Western border had to be kept as favourable as possible because 'the defence of East Pakistan lay in the west'—according to the traditional concept of national strategy.

The second course open to the defenders of East Pakistan was to deploy troops on the border and gradually withdraw them to the 'Dacca Bowl'. It was a reasonable strategy but one major consideration proved it impracticable: enemy air domination during the day and intense rebel activity at night would make withdrawal from the border to the bowl impossible.

The third alternative advocated 'mobile warfare' which, according to its proponents, was ideally suited to conditions in East Pakistan. Its opponents, however, argued that if this strategy were adopted, we would be hunted down by the rebels as well as the invaders.

The fourth, and final, course open to General Niazi was to adopt the 'fortress' concept of defence which meant converting important border towns, particularly those falling on the main axis of enemy advance, into fortresses (like Tobruk) and defending them to the last. This concept, though outdated in modern strategy, had two major advantages. First, it precluded voluntary surrender of our vast territory. Secondly, it concentrated our resources which were not sufficient to permit the fighting of an open conventional war. It was felt that these 'fortresses' would prove a great hindrance to the enemy advance. He would either have to neutralize them or bypass them. In order to neutralize them he would have to employ a force several times greater than that of the defenders. It would be like a hammer falling on an anvil, the arms wielding the hammer would be exhausted before any appreciable damage could be done to the anvil. In order to bypass the fortress, he would have to detail at least an equal force to besiege it. This, it was calculated, would not allow him sufficient spare troops to continue his advance.

General Niazi chose this fourth course and ordered that the following towns be developed into fortresses: Jessore, Jhenida, Bogra, Rangpur, Jamalpur, Mymensingh, Sylhet, Bhairab Bazar, Comilla and Chittagong.[1] Before occupying these fortresses, which were to be stocked with ammunition for 60 days and rations for 45 days, the troops were to fight on the borders to prolong the war.

So the operational plan evolved by Eastern Command envisaged the following course of action:

The troops deployed on the border would fight on till they are ordered by the G.O.C. to withdraw.

While withdrawing to the fortresses they would fight delaying actions so as to 'trade space for time'.

Finally, they would occupy and defend the fortresses to the end.

The plan sounded very reasonable, under the circumstances. Nobody raised any serious objections to it. It was presented to General Hamid during one of his visits to Dacca. He accepted it in principle. Later, it was submitted to G.H.Q. where it was approved with the following recommendations:

Offensive action against English Bazar (opposite Rajshahi) should be reinforced in the plan.

The plan should incorporate a commando action to destroy or damage Farakka Barrage.

One infantry battalion should form the nucleus in Chittagong (to be reinforced later by sea).

Dacca should be treated as the lynch-pin for the defence of East Pakistan.

---

[1] Other important towns in the border area were to be developed as 'strong points'. These points were to be selected by the local commanders.

General Niazi confirmed to G.H.Q. that all the recommendations had been incorporated in the plan. That seemed to settle the matter.

Eastern Command also evaluated the gravity of the threat and worked out certain hypotheses as to the direction of enemy attack. It concluded that the main attack would come from the west (opposite Jessore Sector) with a subsidiary effort from the east (opposite Comilla Sector). The available resources were distributed accordingly.

Jessore Sector: 9 Division under Major-General M.H. Ansari with headquarters at Jessore.

107 Brigade with headquarters at Jessore; 57 Brigade with headquarters at Jhenida; two field regiments of artillery; one reconnaissance and support (R&S) battalion.

North Bengal: 16 Division under Major-General Nazar Hussain Shah with headquarters at Nator.

23 Brigade with headquarters at Rangpur; 205 Brigade with headquarters at Bogra; one field regiment of artillery; two mortar batteries; one R&S battalion; one armoured regiment—the only one in East Pakistan.

Eastern Border: 14 Division under Major-General Abdul Majid Qazi, with headquarters at Dacca.

117 Brigade with headquarters at Comilla; 27 Brigade with headquarters at Mymensingh; 212 Brigade with headquarters at Sylhet; one field regiment of artillery; two mortar batteries; four tanks.

Chittagong Sector: 93 Independent Brigade under Brigadier Ataullah with headquarters at Chittagong.

In addition to these regular troops, each Division was given E.P.C.A.F. personnel, Mujahids and Razakars to augment their strength. They were employed with army personnel to 'thicken the defences'. They proved the weakest link during the war.

As the clouds of war began to gather, General Niazi attempted another big bluff. He suddenly created two *ad hoc* divisional headquarters and four *ad hoc* brigade headquarters. The divisional headquarters were located in Dacca and Chandpur under Major-General Jamshed, Director General, E.P.C.A.F., and Major-General Rahim Khan, Deputy Martial Law Administrator, respectively. Jamshed got two infantry battalions, shed from 27 Brigade which had moved from Mymensingh to Bhairab Bazar while Rahim was given 53 Brigade which had been earmarked for

Dacca. 117 Brigade (Comilla) was taken out of 14 Division and placed under Rahim. The *ad hoc* brigades, their location and role will be discussed in subsequent chapters.

General Niazi was very proud of this 'creation'. 'You see, the enemy will be flabbergasted to see these additional headquarters. He will mentally multiply our strength accordingly. It will certainly be a deterrent to him.' He often boasted in this vein in my presence but the creation of these *ad hoc* formation headquarters could not compensate for the inadequacy of troops and, by the middle of November, General Niazi had to send Major-General Jamshed and Brigadier Baqar Siddiqui, his Chief of Staff, to Rawalpindi to plead for additional troops. By that time pressure on the borders had increased, most of the salients had been lost and many areas in the interior had fallen into enemy hands. The team presented its case to G.H.Q. and asked for two more divisions. It got a promise of eight infantry battalions. Five of them arrived by the last week of November; the remaining three battalions never came. The fresh battalions, on arrival, were divided into companies and despatched to the areas under extreme pressure. They thus lost their identity as cohesive fighting units.

19 November, the eve of the great Muslim festival of *Eid*, was an important day. On this day, G.H.Q. passed an important message to Eastern Command. It said that, according to the latest information, the main enemy offensive would come from the east (Comilla) with a subsidiary attack from the west (Jessore). It also said that the probable day of attack was *Eid* Day, when the troops and their commanders would be busy with festivities. G.H.Q. is understood to have advised Eastern Command to readjust its positions accordingly.

The message was taken seriously and the border positions, particularly in the eastern sector, were quickly examined. It was found that the belt between Comilla and Feni was very vulnerable, so 53 Brigade was quickly moved from Dacca to Feni. General Rahim moved, with his martial law staff, to Chandpur to defend this sensitive sector. With a brigade each at Feni and Comilla, he seemed quite confident. A word of caution was passed to Major-General M.H. Ansari in Jessore Sector, where the subsidiary attack was expected. All other commanders were also informed.

Eastern Command, however, failed to readjust its defences for the prosecution of the war. At this point it was deployed all along the 2,700-kilometre border, mainly to check infiltration and incursions. This arrangement was not changed, despite the advice from Rawalpindi.

Luckily, the enemy did not open the all-out war on *Eid* Day, he only intensified the pressure on certain sectors. By containing this pressure, Niazi thought he had stemmed the tide which, in fact, had not yet started to flow. Dacca remained absolutely undisturbed by Indian jets. Buses, railways and ferries continued to operate as normally—or abnormally—as before. General Niazi followed his schedule of daily visits to the border areas in his helicopter, and continued to thrive on bawdy jokes and plentiful chicken *tikkas*.

Nevertheless, General Niazi insisted that all-out war had started for him on 21 November (the Boyra incident) and that he was successfully fighting it out. During the same press interview mentioned earlier, he had defended his border deployment as 'a forward posture in defence'. Explaining it to foreign correspondents, he said, 'My troops in the border outposts are like the extended fingers of an open hand. They will fight there as long as possible before they fold back to the fortresses to form a fist to bash the enemy's head.'

I was fascinated by the simile. But I recalled his latest decision prohibiting any withdrawals unless seventy-five per cent casualties had been sustained. When three out of four fingers are broken or wounded, is it possible to form a fist? I can't form one if I have so much as a damaged nail!

That was a novice's way of analysing General Niazi's operational strategy, the professionals considered it as 'undue confidence in his capabilities'. The fact remains that he refused to admit that he was deployed for defeat.

16

THE RECKONING BEGINS

General Niazi's last trip outside Dacca was to Mymensingh on 3 December. After the tour, I was writing the day's story in my office when Brigadier Baqar, his Chief of Staff, rang me up at about 5.10 p.m. He was very upset. He nearly shouted at me, 'What sort of a press officer are you? Radio Pakistan has announced the outbreak of war and you haven't informed me?' I said, 'I thought I would hear the news from you.' 'Don't find excuses...Come over to the TAC H.Q.[1] immediately.'

TAC H.Q. was situated about half a kilometre away in an unpopulated part of the cantonment. Headquarters, Eastern Command, had moved there on 19 November when the scare of war was first created by G.H.Q. The underground TAC H.Q., about three metres below ground, was built under a sprawling *sheesham* tree. I stepped down about six stairs, turned to the left and, passing three cubicles on each side, entered the big room at the end of the corridor. This was the 'operations room' of the TAC H.Q.— the nerve centre of military operations in East Pakistan.

When I entered, General Niazi was addressing his officers. He wore summer trousers, a grey bush-shirt and a silken scarf. All the walls of the four by seven metres operations room were covered with huge operational maps. On one side of the room was a row of tables for telephones and wireless sets. General Niazi was standing in the centre of the room with his back to the wall. In front of him sat about thirty officers, including Major-General Jamshed, Major-General Farman and Rear-Admiral Shariff.

It was not a formal address. He talked to them casually, strolling on a narrow beat between the wall and his audience. There was no sign of worry or commotion on his face. But the atmosphere was so solemn that every word he uttered sank deep into the hearts of his audience. The main theme of his talk was that the long-awaited hour of open war had struck. Now, there would be no holds barred,

[1] Tactical headquarters.

no restrictions on crossing international borders and no limits on chasing the intruders back into their territory. All the clouds had lifted.

After the talk, I noticed conspicuous signs of relief among the officers. They had fought too long the slushy war of insurgency without sighting its end. Now it would end, they thought. It would allow our forces in West Pakistan to demonstrate the strategic concept that 'the defence of East Pakistan lies in the West'.

When everybody had left the operations room, General Niazi summoned me to his office and asked me to draft an 'Order of the Day' for him. The Order, he said, must emphasize two points. First, it should tell the troops that now they were free to strike the enemy wherever they found him, without any regard for the international border. Secondly, it should remind them that they must fight unto their last as there was no land, air or sea route by which we could withdraw from East Pakistan. The Order of the Day was drafted, approved and duplicated next day, but it could not be distributed to the troops for lack of transport. All the copies had later to be burnt.

Although on the West Pakistan front, P.A.F. jets had attacked seven I.A.F. bases and land forces had crossed the border·at several points before dusk on 3 December, we in Dacca did not receive any Indian retaliation till the small hours of the following day. I was disturbed from my sleep at about 2.40 a.m. by the noise of anti-aircraft guns and Indian Canberras. I watched the tracer bullets for an hour from the window of my bedroom. The enemy aircraft tried to bomb the airport with full fury but they were constantly beaten back by the determined gunners of Light Ack-Ack Regiment. Several other weapons like machine-guns and light machine-guns also opened up to add to the volume of fire from the ground. The concerted effort managed to scare away the night intruders without any damage to the airport. The P.A.F. Sabres did not participate in this duel because they had no night capability.

By daybreak, there was a lull in the aerial attacks. I shaved, changed and went to the TAC H.Q. but found little activity there, except a morning conference to which we will turn later. Let us first discuss the Navy and the P.A.F. and the brief.role they had in East Pakistan.

The first to be tested was the Pakistan Air Force. I.A.F. jets came again at breakfast time and continued their attacks throughout the day. To beat back these waves of enemy attacks, we had a total of 14 F-86E Sabres, 14 fighter pilots and 14 days ammunition. On the first day, P.A.F. flew 32 operational sorties and expended 30,000 rounds of ammunition. It was the heaviest per day per aircraft expenditure in the history of the Pakistan Air Force. Likewise, the ground weapons employed in an anti-aircraft role used up some 70,000 bullets. It was feared that, at this rate, the ammunition stocks would hardly last for seven to ten days. Strict measures were therefore adopted to conserve the ammunition, in the expectation that we would have to fight a prolonged war. But when the end came unexpectedly soon, the reserve stocks had to be burnt.

India lost ten to twelve aircraft on the first day, without causing any damage to the runway. Only four bombs fell in the vicinity of the airport and these did not affect our operational capability. It forced India however, to change her air strategy from direct bombing of the runway to dislocation of our lines of communication. SU-7s and Hunters, instead of MIG-21s, were therefore employed to strafe ferries and ghats, besides giving close fire support to Indian land forces in the border areas. This shift in Indian strategy decreased the pressure on Dacca airport on 5 December, enabling P.A.F. to fly a few sorties to Comilla and other areas to support our ground troops. There was no close quarter combat because our Sabres had less endurance (35 minutes for aerial combat) than the Indian SU-7s and Hunters. Twenty sorties on the second day, therefore, involved an expenditure of hardly 12,000 rounds.

Throughout the day (5 December) and the following night, the ack-ack guns kept the intruders away from Dacca airport. On 6 December, when our Sabres had just returned from a ground support mission and the airport was without C.A.P. (combat air patrolling) ten Indian MIG-21s, escorted by fighters, came over. The anti-aircraft guns tried to meet the challenge but in vain. The enemy bombers released six modern Russian bombs, weighing 500 kilograms each, two of which fell on the runway.

Each sleek bomb had a composite frame and carried a delayed fuse system which enabled it to explode a quarter of a second after penetration into the ground. They fell on the vital intersection of the runway, 1,200 metres apart, rendering it unusable. Each crater was about ten metres deep and twenty metres wide. It would be impossible to use the runway unless one of its damaged ends could be repaired. The Indian Air Force had thus succeeded in its aim of denying the use of the airport to our Sabres, after suffering a loss of twenty-two to twenty-four aircraft in two days—about seven to P.A.F. and the rest to 6 Light Ack-Ack Regiment.

Repair work on the damaged parts of the runway was undertaken in all earnestness. The military engineering services of the Air Force and the Army made relentless efforts to fill the craters. They were joined by the troops of the local engineering battalion and a handful of Urdu-speaking civilian labourers. Their efforts were interrupted by intermittent air strikes, but they boldly carried on their work. In the process, eleven of them died and twenty were wounded.

The following night (6/7 December) hectic efforts were made to repair the craters quickly so that our jets could take off next morning. By 4.50 a.m., 7 December, the major part of the work was over and it required only six to eight hours more to cement the surface. But as the day dawned, a fresh wave of enemy aircraft came and caused craters at three more intersections of the runway. It now required at least 36 hours of uninterrupted hard work to finish the job. So much respite was never given by the invading aircraft and the runway remained unusable for the rest of the war.

Another airport was under construction at Kurmitola, about five kilometres from Tejgaon (Dacca). Its main runway had been completed but some work was yet to be done at the ends. The enemy paid equal attention to this incomplete airport and successfully bombed it on the first day.

When the old as well as the new airport had been put out of action, somebody suggested that the broad roads of the Second Capital should be used as runways, but the P.A.F. Base Commander ruled this out because of technical problems and inaccessibility. That sealed the fate of the P.A.F. in East Pakistan. It remained grounded from 10 a.m. on 6 December till the end of the war.

P.A.F. fighter pilots, whose services could no longer be utilized in Dacca, were sent to West Pakistan through a friendly country. Ten of them were flown out on 8 December and four on the following day. The pilots of helicopters and trainers, like those of Army Aviation, stayed behind.

The P.A.F. had no regrets. It had survived for sixty hours, against its anticipated lease of life of twenty-four hours. It had survived so long by its sheer grit, determination and professional competence.

In the absence of the P.A.F., the air defence of Dacca became he exclusive responsibility of anti-aircraft guns which were the irst to open and the last to fall silent in East Pakistan. I personally watched their performance from a gun-pit. The gunners stood undaunted, in their grey berets, behind their guns. Their eyes constantly scanned the skies. As they saw an enemy aircraft speed-ng towards Dacca, they quickly 'zeroed' their guns towards it and ired blast after blast in its direction. They reinforced their gunfire with spirited shouts of *Naara-i-Takbir, Allah-o-Akbar*. It was an inspiring experience to spend some time with them.

The Navy in East Pakistan was in no better shape than the Air Force. Its total strength consisted of four patrol boats[1] and one rear-admiral. The latter, though a gifted commander, had no re-sources to meet the challenge of India's Naval Task Force which consisted of one carrier and several destroyers, frigates and many other war vessels. The patrol boats, originally purchased for anti-smuggling operations, were fitted with 40/60mm guns and had a crew of twenty-nine men each. The gun range was limited to only 5,000 metres. The fastest cruising speed was about twenty knots. They could be easily outgunned, outdistanced and overtaken by all the craft in the Indian Task Force.

Admiral Shariff had acquired seventeen boats from civilian sources, fitted them with 12.7mm or 20mm guns and added them to his fleet. Some of these 'improvised' boats had .50 or .30 Brown-ing machine guns which were a help during counter-insurgency operations. But they were of little use in full-scale warfare.

The Navy had an impossible task in East Pakistan. The coast-line extended for nearly 600 kilometres from Teknaf on the Burmese border to Passar near the Indian coast. The sea lanes to Karachi, measuring several thousand kilometres were dominated by the Indian Navy. The inland waterways were so many that they alone required several hundred boats to patrol them. Admiral Shariff had, on several occasions before the war, made it clear to every-body that the Navy with its existing resources would not be able to play a significant role in the defence of East Pakistan. It was pro-bably because of this frank appraisal that General Niazi had 'plan-ned to fight the war without the Navy'.

The Navy organized coastal defences at the ports of Chittagong

[1] *Comilla, Rajshahi, Jessore* and *Sylhet*.

and Mongla, leaving the rest of the coastline to God's care. It deployed two guns of the Coastal Defence Battery (4-inch guns with 12,000 metres maximum range) at Chittagong port, while an *ad hoc* battery looked after Chittagong airport. In addition, 400 men of a marine battalion and a naval platoon kept watch on the area west and east of the port respectively. The Mongla port was in the hands of one garrison company (equipped with small arms), an E.P.C.A.F. Company, three improvised gun-boats and two 25-pounder guns.

The sudden outbreak of war, on the afternoon of 3 December, found the patrol boats scattered all around. The improvised gun-boats based at Khulna had sailed out on routine patrol duty while the *Rajshahi* from Chittagong base was cruising in the Sandwip Channel, the only link between Chittagong and the rest of the province. The *Sylhet* was already confined to the dockyard with a technical defect. The *Comilla* was the only boat secured alongside the jetty.

The Navy had issued orders well in advance that in the event of an all-out war, the gun-boats would shrink back to the safe sanctuary of the harbour. It was a very simple order for the boats to obey; but what about the twenty-three foreign ships and seven coasters waiting at outer anchorage? They could neither be hidden nor protected in the open. No orders could be passed to them immediately because they opened their communication sets only during fixed hours. The only way to establish contact with them was to visit them physically. A bold officer took a boat with a hand-picked crew and finally managed to disperse them. They flew their foreign flags to avoid air strikes.

Chittagong received the first impact of war at 2 a.m. on 4 December when an enemy aircraft hit an oil reservoir. The next day, a harmless-looking light aircraft approached from the direction of the sea and lazily droned over the city. The Razakars manning the coastal guns did not realize the danger until it blew up the Chittagong refinery. Next came a wave of five Canberras. The *ad hoc* anti-aircraft battery was able to shoot down two of them. The other three dropped their load near the naval base, the airport and the refinery and made their way back.

Meanwhile, unconfirmed reports reached Chittagong of a night landing by the enemy near Kutubdia Island. The commodore in charge of Chittagong base thought it wise to send out

Comilla, Rajshahi and (the improvised gun-boat) Balaghat to check the landing because he found no point in hiding the boats while the enemy knocked at the door.

When Rajshahi reached the reported landing area, she found no sign of enemy troops. She was, however, overtaken by four enemy Hunters. She tried unsuccessfully to ward them off with her 40/60mm guns and received six direct hits. Her engine caught fire and water started gushing into the main compartment. Fire and water, traditional enemies of each other, joined forces in an attempt to sink this hapless vessel. Seven members of the crew, including the commanding officer, had been wounded (one of them later died). But they did not let the vessel go down so easily. Some tried to control the fire while others checked the incoming water. Luckily, the enemy aircraft, seeing her ablaze, had gone back. The hectic efforts of the crew finally succeeded in saving the boat and they brought her back to the harbour.

The Comilla, about half a kilometre away, could not come to the help of Rajshahi as she, too, had been attacked—this time by nine aircraft. The pilots practised their target shooting on this poor thing. Like a light-weight boxer turned giddy by the repeated blows of an unequal opponent, the Comilla finally began to list. The crew, though wounded, continued to struggle for her life till another hit on the fuel tank made short work of it. The commanding officer realized that in the next few moments, six hundred rounds of ammunition would catch fire and everything would be blown to pieces. So he ordered the two officers and twenty-one crew members to put on life-jackets and abandon ship. As he and his crew jumped into the sea, a big explosion tore the vessel apart. It soon heeled over and sank.

The Balaghat, which had escaped enemy attention, finally rescued the Comilla crew and brought them to Chittagong base. Once the Rajshahi and the surviving crew of the Comilla were at the base, no vessel was sent outside the harbour either to check landings or to attempt anything nobler. In fact, there was no vessel worth sending out.

The Khulna base, smaller in size and importance, received less punishment. It had one proper gun-boat, the Jessore, and four improvised boats. On the first day of the war, two boats were destroyed in an air attack and the remaining three were forced to take shelter in the nearest jungle.

That was practically the end of war for the Navy in East Pakistan. For the remainder of the war the Navy used its manpower, in collaboration with army troops, to guard the coast and later defend the 'fortress'. Some boats helped in transporting the troops through inland water channels and, in this role, they continued to ply till the end of the war.

With the Navy and the Air Force thus eliminated in the initial days of the war, the fate of East Pakistan hinged on General Niazi and his 45,000 military and 73,000 paramilitary troops. The general's moral courage and the physical courage of his troops were to decide the issue.

I saw General Niazi in a very buoyant mood in the early days of the war. He regularly held a morning conference at 8.30 and cheerfully met any officer who came in contact with him. I was surprised to find that he, during this period, showed more interest in the progress of war in the West Wing than in his own area of responsibility. He had a one-inch map of the West Pakistan front fixed on a wall of the operations room. Every morning, before Niazi's arrival, a staff officer diligently marked the map to show the battle picture as depicted in the latest G.H.Q. signals. (G.H.Q. had arranged to circulate daily a heavily-censored version of the war situation).

The Indian and Pakistani forces were represented on the map by red and green pencils respectively. The West Pakistan map had three or four green dots a few centimetres across the international border indicating our penetration into the enemy territory. Although they did not look very impressive to me, the experts insisted that the gains were substantial.

When I entered the operations room about midday on 4 December I found it bubbling with the happy news that Amritsar had fallen and that our troops were somewhere near Ferozepur. Rear-Admiral Shariff, who was close by, realistically asked, 'If the news is correct, why don't they (G.H.Q.) say so in the signal?' 'Oh, they don't want to commit themselves in writing or in radio broadcasts till they have stabilized their gains,' he was told.

When the news reached General Niazi in his cubicle, I was with him. Although seated in his chair, he leapt up and down like a wrestler. He turned to me and said, 'You always advised me not to raise high hopes by saying that I will take the war to

Indian territory. Now, you see, if not I, my big brother (West Pakistan) has taken the war to Indian territory.' He quickly dialled the Governor and informed him about this great development. He also ordered that the information should be flashed to the troops as 'it would be good for their morale' but Admiral Shariff advised that its full authenticity should be first checked.

I was asked to check it back with the officer who had first heard it. When I contacted the officer, he said that Air Marshal Rahim Khan, the P.A.F. Chief, had presumably passed the news to the P.A.F. base, Dacca. When I rang up the base, they denied having received any such news from the Air Chief. 'But you heard this news?' I asked. 'Yes.' 'Where from?' 'From the operations room of Headquarters, Eastern Command.' A telephone call was made to Rawalpindi but it too failed to confirm the story. Eventually, it turned out that the rumour was false. The hopes it had generated suddenly slumped into despondency.

Next morning brought no happy news. The green pins showing our gains on the West Pakistan border remained where they were twenty-four hours earlier. We tuned in to Radio Pakistan and listened to all the news bulletins but they said nothing more than 'fortifying our defences'.

By 6 December, General Niazi had lost all hope of a break-through on the West Pakistan borders. He therefore stopped the reading of extracts from G.H.Q. signals at the morning briefings and ordered the removal of West Pakistan maps from the wall. He shrank back into his own shell of East Pakistan and studied the operational map with greater intent. Here the arrows showing troop movements were far larger than the puny pins on the western border. These arrows generally depicted the routes of enemy advance and our withdrawal.

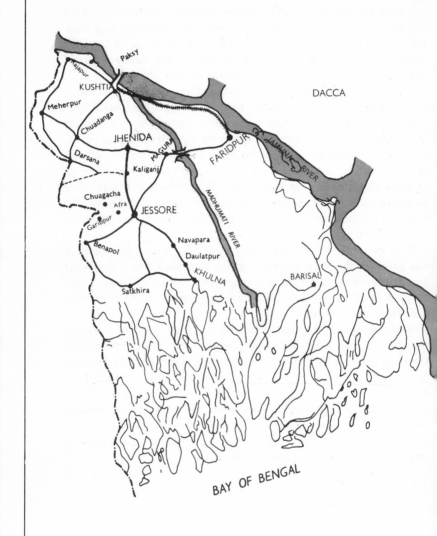

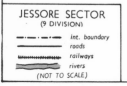

JESSORE SECTOR
(9 DIVISION)

—·—·—·—	int. boundary
————	roads
▬▬▬▬▬	railways
▬▬▬▬▬	rivers

(NOT TO SCALE)

17

THE FIRST FORTRESS FALLS
(9 Division)

The 9 Division area was like a neatly cut slice of cake. It was cut from the north by the Ganges (Padma) and from the east by the Jamuna. Contiguous with the Indian province of West Bengal, it contained important towns like Khulna, Jessore, Jhenida, Kushtia, Barisal and Faridpur.

The divisional border with India, about 600 kilometres long, extended from the southern bank of the Ganges to the Bay of Bengal. Almost parallel, between fifty to eighty kilometres from the border, ran the road connecting Khulna, Jessore, Jhenida and Kushtia. Further in from the border flowed the Madhumati river, about half a kilometre wide, which, in emergency, could serve as a good defensive line. The rest of the area was relatively dry, allowing free movement of troops, trucks and tanks.

About half of the northern border, from Rajapur to Darsana, was entrusted to 57 Brigade under Brigadier Manzoor with headquarters at Jhenida, while the lower length from Jibbanagar to the Bay was placed under 107 Brigade commanded by Brigadier Makhmad Hayat. The brigade headquarters was located in Jessore. The Division too had its peace-time headquarters in Jessore but, on the first day of war, it moved to Magura, almost half way between Jhenida and the Madhumati. An *ad hoc* brigade, which consisted of some E.P.C.A.F. personnel and Razakars, was centred on Khulna.

According to the operational plan, the troops were to delay the enemy at the Benapol–Darsana–Rajapur border line, then 'trading space for time', were to fall back on Jessore and Jhenida —the two fortresses in the area. It was calculated that the enemy would not venture to stick his neck out very far without neutralizing one or both of the fortresses. If he decided to invest them, he would have to employ one division at each fortress which would not leave enough troops to him to achieve a breakthrough.

It was also calculated that the enemy could use any one of the three main axes: Calcutta–Benapol–Jessore, Krishnagarh–Darsana–Chuadanga or Murshidabad–Rajapur–Kushtia. Each of them could take a divisional force, but the best and the shortest of them was the Benapol axis. Thus it was also the most likely approach; and a wise·enemy, they say, does not follow the most likely course. He hits where he is least expected.

India used none of these three axes. She decided, instead, to take advantage of the lodgements already established on our side of the border. One of these lodgements, as mentioned above, was located in the Garibpur area where we had cordoned the enemy forces since 21 November. The other lodgement, created by the end of November, was near Darsana close to the boundary between the two brigade districts. The first lay in the territory of 107 Brigade and the second in that of 57 Brigade.

The Garibpur lodgement, about 150 square kilometres, was barely eleven kilometres away, as the shell flies, from Jessore cantonment. Since November, enemy guns had been firing sporadic shots into the cantonment and airfield areas, but their intensity was tolerable. After the outbreak of war, they stepped up the shelling and tried to breach the cordon at Burinda, 8R (as it is commonly known) and Mohammadpur. But our troops held their ground: our force consisting of 6 Punjab, 12 Punjab, 21 Punjab (less one company) and a company of 22 Frontier Force, successfully contained the enemy for a good sixty hours. It was, however, feared that if the enemy did achieve a breakthrough, he would directly hit Jessore without allowing time for the brigade commander to withdraw his troops from the border and organize a fortress defence. His nearest troops were at Benapol and the farthest at Satkhira, about forty-three and ninety kilometres from Jessore, respectively.

Brigadier Makhmad Hayat, a thorough-going professional, saw this danger and asked his G.O.C.'s permission to fold back his extended fingers in time to form a fist at Jessore (which had no regular troops). General Ansari, sitting forty-five kilometres to the rear, refused permission, citing General Niazi's orders that no withdrawals were to take place unless seventy-five per cent casualties had been sustained on the border.

Brigadier Hayat reckoned that, should the Garibpur defences on the Afra axis be withdrawn, it would be better to lure the enemy

owards Khulna rather than meet him at Jessore. He therefore
ordered that part of the ammunition stock be transferred from
Jessore to Khulna. He also had the option of withdrawing to
Magura where the divisional headquarters lay. After fighting a
delaying battle there, he could fall back on the Madhumati river
and offer prolonged resistance to the enemy. He had sufficient
dumps of ammunition and rations available at Faridpur, only a few
kilometres to the rear.

Brigadier Hayat's officers argue that the Madhumati line of
defence was never mentioned in any operational plan. The 'Line
of No Penetration' indicated to them, they say, had been fixed at
the Jessore-Jhenida road. Brigadier Baqar, General Niazi's Chief
of Staff, however, insists that the Madhumati line of defence was
discussed and finalized with General Ansari but it was not incorporated in the operational plan, lest faith in the 'Line of No Penetration' be weakened and the defenders start looking back. Whether it was in the plan or not, Brigadier Hayat ruled it out and stuck
to his original idea of withdrawal towards Khulna, but kept it a
secret till the last moment. He shared it with only one commanding
officer in his confidence. He told him in Pushto on 5 December
at about midday, 'Don't be caught napping. If we leave Jessore,
we go to Khulna.'

The enemy, meanwhile, had enlarged his Garibpur lodgement
by pushing back 12 Punjab, 21 Punjab and a company of 22 Frontier
Force by about three kilometres. Our new defence line was now
Kaeemkola-Santoshnagar-Amrit Bazar but the collar of contain-
ment was still round the enemy neck.

The new defence cordon necessitated a change in the position
of the neighbouring 22 Frontier Force which guarded the Benapol
axis. The company at Benapol was withdrawn to Sarcha, four
kilometres to the rear, and the second company at Ragonathpur
was moved to Jhingergacha, with the battalion headquarters, on the
Jessore road.

The enemy put the entire weight of his 9 Division on the Afra
axis on 6 December. The morning attempt was abortive and a
second attempt at about 11 a.m. was equally unproductive. The
third attempt, made soon after lunch, met with partial success.
They overran a platoon on the right of the Afra axis. It was a small
breach, but it could not be plugged because there were no reserves.
Major Yahya, second-in-command of 8 Punjab, thought it wise

to inform the brigade headquarters about this development. He sent a message that enemy tanks and armoured personnel carriers were rushing through the gap towards the Jhenida–Jessore road. The message reached Brigadier Hayat at about 1500 hours when Lieutenant-Colonel Shams, the commanding officer of 22 Frontier Force was with him. He ordered Shams to withdraw his battalion from the Benapol–Jessore Road and make for Navapara, nineteen kilometres towards Khulna, leaving a company at the T-junction in Jessore city to ensure the safe passage of other battalions. All commanding officers were informed accordingly.

The brigade headquarters left Jessore at about 5.30 p.m. on 6 December, abandoning the fortress without firing a shot. They did not even destroy the rich ammunition dump. The enemy, who anticipated a bloody battle for Jessore, however, did not occupy it till 11 a.m. next day. Even two days after the fall of Jessore, Eastern Command continued to claim that a battle was still raging there. Meanwhile, many foreign correspondents, who had entered Jessore with the Indian troops, reached Dacca and ridiculed our unrealistic claim. They said that they had seen our brigade commander's vacant tent, with his half-burnt cigarette in the ash-tray, as well as our abandoned brigade headquarters, where the clerks had not had time to pull out the paper from their typewriters.

Many officers used the Jessore–Jhenida road as well as the Jessore–Magura road till late in the evening on 6 December and found no signs of enemy presence on these possible routes of the brigade's withdrawal. In fact, Lieutenant-Colonel Ehsan saw a detachment of our Military Police posted at the ferry on the Magura road to direct the retreating traffic towards Magura. Similarly, our Supplies and Transport (S&T) vehicles freely plied on the Jhenida road, without any interference from the enemy. This only proves that Brigadier Hayat could have used either of these routes for his brigade's withdrawal to Magura.

The night between 6 and 7 December was very hectic for the troops under 107 Brigade. Mentally tuned to withdraw to the sanctuary of the Jessore fortress, they were now ordered to hitch-hike to Navapara, a destination never seen or talked about before. They withdrew in great confusion, and the company commander at the T-junction later told me that it was quite a job to clear traffic jams and direct the vehicles towards Khulna.

At about midnight, an ambulance was seen speeding towards

Garibpur instead of Navapara. An officer stopped the vehicle and shouted to the driver, 'Hey, Goof! Don't you know which way is Khulna? You are going in the opposite direction.' 'Yes, Sir,' he said politely, 'I know the Khulna route but I have promised a wounded soldier in Garibpur to pick him up on the second trip. He will be waiting for me.'

107 Brigade did not reach Navapara, near milestone 20[1] in one hike. It first stopped at milestone 30, then at milestone 25, but the dazed troops in the new environment did not stick to their temporary defences. They fought their first battle on this axis at milestone 20 (Navapara) on 10 December and withdrew to milestone 9 (Daulatpur) on 11 December. They were about to withdraw to Khulna on 16 December when the war ended in Dacca. Cease-fire orders were passed to Brigadier Hayat, who deserves all credit for successfully fighting his private war.

The *ad hoc* brigade at Khulna was never put to the test. In fact, it did not feel confident of holding Khulna after the fall of the Jessore fortress. So it set off for Dacca during the night of 6/7 December, using all available means of transport. Commander Gul Zarin, in charge of the Khulna naval base, also took a gun-boat and escaped seaward, leaving much to chance. The evacuation of Khulna was premature, notwithstanding the sudden abandonment of the Jessore fortress.

Headquarters, Eastern Command, did not know that day about the departure of the Khulna troops or Commander Gul Zarin. It still fancied prolonging the life of the Khulna garrison which, it knew, did not have the ammunition required by the retreating 107 Brigade. It provided helicopter-loads of valuable ammunition, which the gallant pilots of Army Aviation flew by night to Khulna, at great risk—and all to no avail.

Let us now turn to Brigadier Manzoor's 57 Brigade, which faced 4 Indian Mountain Division. The brigade had 29 Baluch, 18 Punjab, one company of 12 Punjab (Reconnaissance and Support) and two companies of 50 Punjab, besides a regiment of artillery and a squadron of M-24 tanks (corps reserve). Brigadier Manzoor, a commander of mild disposition, was lounging in his headquarters (Jhenida) when he learnt that the enemy was pressing hard to enlarge his bridgehead in the Jibbanagar area threatening Darsana, an impor-

---

[1] At this time, Pakistan had not yet converted to the metric system except in currency notes.

tant border town. If Darsana were to fall he appreciated that
Chuadanga, Governor A.M. Malik's native town, would be deprived of defensive cover. The enemy would be free to race for
Jhenida or Kushtia. He therefore went personally to the area to
ensure that the enemy would be delayed as long as possible on the
border. But, in spite of his presence, Darsana fell on the opening
day of the war. Brigadier Manzoor collected his troops from the
border posts and grouped them in Chuadanga to receive the enemy.

But the real direction of the enemy advance could not be ascertained. He did not show up on the Chuadanga road. Possibly
he had chosen to proceed to Kaligani to cut the Jhenida–Jessore
road and join forces with the other column which had broken
through our defences on the Afra axis. A task force of 38 FF and
50 Punjab (minus)[1] was therefore formed under Colonel Afridi,
Colonel Staff of 9 Division, and placed near Kaligani to check
the enemy advance. Surprisingly, the enemy did not go for Kaligani either. Instead, guided by the Mukti Bahini, who knew every
inch of the terrain, he moved across country and cut the Chuadanga–Jhenida road at Sadhuhati, about half-way between Chuadanga
and Jhenida. An infantry company and a troop of tanks reached
this point by midnight on 4/5 December but Brigadier Manzoor
did not discover this till about 10 a.m. the following day, when
some administrative vehicles plying from Chuadanga to Jhenida
bumped into the road block.

Brigadier Manzoor, with his entire brigade at Chuadanga, now
had two options. First, he could quickly neutralize the road block
and occupy his Jhenida fortress. Secondly, he could stay in Chuadanga, a divisional 'strong point', and remain a source of worry to
the enemy pushing eastward. He did neither. Instead he made a
half-hearted attempt at Sadhuhati. He first despatched an officer
to confirm the existence of the road block, then sent a weak
detachment to clear it. Finally, on 6 December, he ordered a platoon under Major Zahid to clear out the enemy but called it back
prematurely when he learnt that the enemy had, meanwhile, built
up a battalion and a squadron of tanks there. He thought it would
be too big a task for an infantry platoon.

The Indian Major who manned the Sadhuhati road block admitted later to Major Zahid that, for the first twenty-four hours,
he trembled in his shoes and cursed his superiors who had placed

[1] Less than a battalion.

him, with only one company, between two jaws—Jhenida and
Chuadanga—of the Pakistan Army. But, luckily, Indian troops
had reinforced him before he was contacted by the Pakistanis.

6 December was a crucial day for both the brigades of 9 Division.
In one sub-sector, Brigadier Manzoor lost hope of clearing his
way to Jhenida, while in the other, Brigadier Hayat abandoned
Jessore. The G.O.C., who spent most of his time on his prayer
mat in Magura, rang up Manzoor's brigade major in the evening
and said, 'Jaffar, what is happening?' 'Nothing in particular,' he
replied. 'O.K. I think you should come back to Magura. Jessore
has already fallen. Tell Afridi also to fall back. There is nothing
to defend divisional headquarters here.' Colonel Afridi's force
withdrew from Kaligani to Jhenida the same night and Jhenida was
abandoned the following morning, without a fight. Our last vehicle
left this 'fortress' at 11 a.m. The enemy occupied it late in the
evening.

Meanwhile, Brigadier Manzoor took his brigade to Kushtia,
close to the Hardinge Bridge on the Ganges (Padma). He reached
there by last light on 8 December and hurriedly deployed his troops
in the perimeter defence of the town. Headquarters, Eastern Command, asked him to force his way to Jhenida, or move to Magura
along the railway line but he expressed his inability to achieve
either. He preferred to stay in Kushtia. He spent the night of 8/9
December there. Next morning, he was contacted by the enemy
from the direction of Jhenida. Manzoor sent a company of 18 Punjab under Major Zahid, with half a squadron of tanks under Major
Sher-ur-Rehman, to check the enemy. The battle commenced at
1 p.m. and lasted for about three hours. This was the first and last
battle that the brigade fought in the entire war.

The battle ended in our favour. Major Zahid and Major Sher-
ur-Rehman both won *Sitara-i-Jurat*—the coveted gallantry award
equivalent to the Military Cross. The enemy withdrew, leaving
behind their dead and wounded. The enemy corpses, including
that of an Indian general's son, lay in the fields as well as on the
slopes of the high embankment of the fateful road. Some of them
had been crushed under the tracks of our M-24 tanks. The enemy
avenged his defeat later by torturing Major Sher and Major Zahid
in captivity for the alleged crime of 'mutilating dead bodies'.

Kushtia did not turn out to be as safe as Brigadier Manzoor
thought. The enemy artillery and air force, in turn, pounded his

defences and he was in no position to reply. Like an anvil, he helplessly received the strokes of the hammer. It did not take him
more than a day to realize that Kushtia was not a place to be defended. But where could he go? The Hardinge Bridge was nearby.
It could take him across the Ganges to the relatively peaceful area
of 16 Division. Perhaps there he could add to that divisions'
strength.

Brigadier Manzoor's brigade left Kushtia on the night of 10/11
December. Most of the brigade vehicles, equipment and personnel,
safely crossed to 16 Division area on 11 December. But on the
morning of 12 December, the Indian Air Force, which had so far
spared the bridge, perhaps with the intention of capturing it intact,
delivered a direct hit on one of the spans of the 1,795-metre bridge.
Now, crossing of the river would be a problem.

To make things worse, the patriotic sections of the Kushtia population abandoned their homes to follow the withdrawal of the Pakistan troops. They feared a dreadful end at the hands of the Mukti
Bahini. They preferred to share the fate of the Pakistan troops.
These men, women and children, many of whom carried their
prized possessions with them, added to the ordeal of Major Ra-
thore (Engineers) who had to ferry them across. He owed as much
obligation to them as to the brigade troops. He therefore worked
round the clock to transport them to safety. He vividly remembers
an old lady, clutching her life's savings under her left arm, trying to
climb into the ferry with her right hand. She was helped by a Pakistani soldier. She was soon on the other side of the river. That
marked the end of 57 Brigade as far as 9 Division was concerned.

Our 9 Division had thus been ripped apart: 107 Brigade was
chased to Khulna while 57 Brigade was pushed across the Ganges.
All that General Ansari was left with was a weak force consisting
of elements of 38 Frontier Force and 50 Punjab. They were first
deployed near Magura, then on the eastern bank of the Madhumati
river. The enemy did not follow. He first wanted to eliminate all
possibilities of a threat from the flanks. Two days after our 57 Brigade had crossed the Ganges, the Indian troops attacked our defences at Madhumati. Our troops stood their ground. Keeping
them busy frontally, the enemy looked for suitable crossing points.
At night, the Mukti Bahini guided him to appropriate crossing
points about seven kilometres upstream where the Indians flung a
suspension bridge across the obstacle and attacked our troops from

the flank. The battered 38 Frontier Force and the raw 50 Punjab felt shaky. On 15 December, they were withdrawn from Madhumati and redeployed west of Faridpur, the new seat of General Ansari's headquarters. They were yet to meet the enemy on 16 December when 'ceasefire' orders reached them from Dacca.

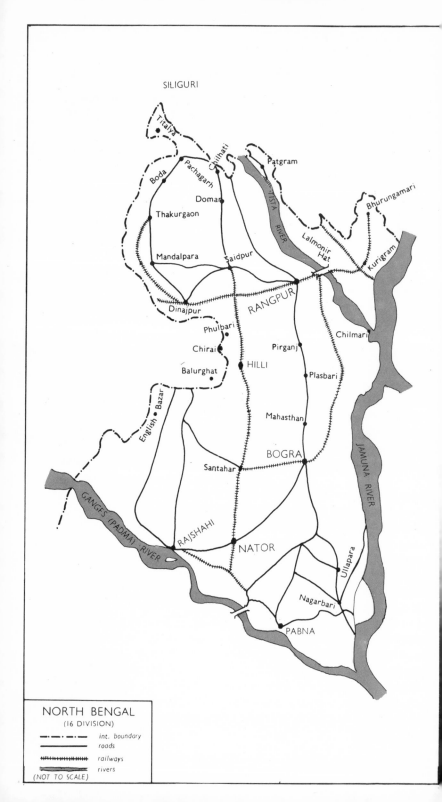

SILIGURI

Titalya

Chilhati

Patgram

TISTA RIVER

Boda

Pachagarh

Domar

Bhurungamari

Thakurgaon

Lalmonir Hat

Kurigram

Mandalpara

Saidpur

RANGPUR

Dinajpur

Phulbari

Chilmari

Chirai

Pirganj

HILLI

Balurghat

Plasbari

JAMUNA RIVER

Mahasthan

English Bazar

BOGRA

Santahar

GANGES (PADMA) RIVER

RAJSHAHI

NATOR

Ullapara

Nagarbari

PABNA

NORTH BENGAL
(16 DIVISION)

— · — · —   int. boundary
————   roads
+++++++   railways
▬▬▬▬   rivers

(NOT TO SCALE)

18

COLLAPSE IN THE NORTH
(16 DIVISION)

The vulnerable expanse of North Bengal was assigned to a broad and brave general. General Nazar Hussain Shah had been there since April when 16 Division arrived from West Pakistan to quell the rebellion. Chasing the rebels and fighting the insurgents, he came to know every inch of his area before the war.

North Bengal, with the Padma to the south and the Jamuna to the east, was the largest area that a division could be called upon to defend. It covered the northern half of the western border and the western half of the northern border. The terrain was generally dry—drier than the rest of the province. That is why the solitary tank regiment, 29 Cavalry, was stationed in this area. The only notable water obstacle was the Tista river, which ran from north-west to south-east cutting the Patgram, Bhurungamari, Kurigram and Lalmonir Hat areas into a separate sub-zone. The rail and road communications ran in a north-south direction: the railway closer to the border and the road almost in the middle. Since it was not possible to run a through train from south to north, all the divisional supplies were sent on the 103-kilometre Bogra–Rangpur road, about forty kilometres from the border.

What could be the enemy objective in this sector? Would he rush, like a torrent, from the Siliguri gap down to Bogra, sweeping aside all obstructions on the way? Or would he make a thrust to cut the Hilli–Chilmari axis? In either case, he would 'liberate a sizeable chunk of territory to establish Bangla Desh.' The division had, therefore, deployed its resources accordingly. It placed 4 Frontier Force, one of its crack battalions, at Hilli, as a part of 205 Brigade (Tajammul) which had its headquarters at Bogra. The northern approaches were entrusted to 23 Brigade (Ansari) with headquarters at Rangpur. The third brigade (34 Brigade) under Brigadier Naeem was kept at Nator while the *ad hoc* brigade, created in late September, was stationed at Rajshahi in the south to prevent any riverine operations through the Padma.

Tanks, the rare commodity with 29 Cavalry, were distributed to all three brigades. 23 Brigade deployed its share of one squadron on the Boda–Thakurgaon axis while 205 Brigade kept them in the Naogaon area with 13 Frontier Force for offensive tasks in the neighbouring Balurghat area. 34 Brigade stationed one squadron of its share near Hardinge Bridge. This squadron, which was also General Staff Reserve of Eastern Command, was to be used only with Eastern Command's permission. These were the same tanks which had been loaned to Brigadier Manzoor (57 Brigade) for a battle near Kushtia. The fourth squadron of the regiment was further split into 'troops' and distributed to other formations.

The M-24 tanks boasted a great past of World War II vintage. It was claimed that they had fought in the Korean War (1951). The gun grooves were generally worn out, resulting in shortfalls in their range. They could hardly engage a target beyond 1,000 metres. Against them, India had some very modern tanks. Her Russian acquisitions in the 'T' series (T-55, T-56) were far more versatile than any other tanks available to India or Pakistan. The Indian indigenous tanks (Vijayanta) supplemented the fire power of these imported machines. It was obviously a battle between un-equals.

Before we enter the war proper in this sector, let us briefly survey the situation as it was on 3 December. India had been paying a lot of attention to Hilli since September 1971. She had deployed 20 Division there with its full complement of armour and artillery. Shelling and mortaring had been a daily affair for several weeks, with occasional attempts to grab territory as well. But the gallant Frontier Force not only withstood all the pressure during the period but also beat back several enemy attempts to cross the railway line, which served as a no man's land between the opposing forces.

India's pressure had increased considerably since 21 November when she started a 'war of salients'. Her 7 Guards attacked Hilli and the neighbouring posts of Qasim, Babur, Navapara and Aptor. The enemy troops, supported by tanks and artillery, managed to overrun Qasim post, about 2 kilometres north of the main Hilli defences. Our platoon there suffered ten killed and twelve wounded, including the young commanding officer. From there, the enemy tried to attack Babur post on the east of the railway line, but suffered heavily in the process. Only one of their three tanks managed to climb over to the east of the railway embankment. It, too, was engaged and disabled by our recoilless rifle. The enemy tried to tow away this obvious evidence of aggression but only suffered more losses in the process. The damaged tank stayed there for several days. It was this evidence of Indian aggression that we wanted to show to foreign correspondents on 27 November when they met General Niazi over a plate of chicken *tikkas.*

The enemy maintained his pressure on Babur post, but could not capture it. Soon Frontier Force realized that the platoon at the post would not be able to withstand the pressure any longer. So it was withdrawn. The enemy later occupied it without facing any opposition. This gave him a stable foothold on the east of the railway line.

We also further strengthened our defences. A troop of tanks was borrowed from the Corps Reserve (Hardinge Bridge) and deployed at Dangapara, headquarters of 'D' company of 4 Frontier Force. A platoon of Reconnaisance and Support battalion (34 Punjab), with its recoilless rifles, was positioned a little to the north. The 4 Frontier Force platoon withdrawn from Babur post was reorganized and re-deployed closer to other troops. We felt strong enough to launch a counter-attack on Babur post but the enemy had, meanwhile, occupied it in strength and we failed to eject him. As an alternative, we deployed three companies to contain the enemy. While our two companies formed a cordon to the south and east of Babur post, Major Akram with his 'C' company chose to stay west of the railway embankment. Major Akram's position was not only a sharp irritant in the enemy flank but it also obstructed his movement along the embankment. They tried several times to overrun 'C' company positions but without success. This was the situation on 3 December.

Meanwhile on the northern border, the principal worry for the enemy there was the twenty-five-kilometre-wide Siliguri gap (only seventy kilometres from China's south-eastern border), providing the only link between the West Bengal/Bihar and Assam/Tripura areas. Nearly one third of Indian military command, which lay in the east, had to be supplied through this gap. So, they not only protected this vulnerable line of communication from any possible attack but also enlarged the gap to fifty-five kilometres by occupying our Titalya bulge and the adjoining areas. They also pushed back our defences on the Pachagarh–Thakurgaon axis, on the night of 28/29 November. In the next two days, they overran Boda and

came to the northern outskirts of Thakurgaon. This was as far as
they got by 3 December.

Before the war, they also overran parts of the Patgram and
Bhurungamari bulges to secure their line of communication running
north of the bulges. In fact, their gains in these bulges were so
substantial that we feared that they might resume, through Bhurungamari, the Bihar–Assam Railway which had lain in disuse since
the creation of Pakistan. We denied them this railway by restricting
their gains in the bulges but they managed, by 1 December, to push
us down to Kurigram and Lalmonir Hat, two important towns
and railway stations in the area. Lalmonir Hat also had an airstrip
for light aircraft. The Razakars and E.P.C.A.F., scattered in Chilmari and the neighbouring areas, were withdrawn to Kurigram on
3 December.

When all-out war broke out, Kurigram and Lalmonir Hat received uninhibited pounding from the I.A.F. The two towns had,
on several previous occasions, experienced periodic visits by Indian
jets, but these had never before poured out their wrath as they did
on 4 December. The G.O.C., therefore, ordered our troops at
Kurigram and Lalmonir Hat to cross over to the home side of the
Tista river and blow up the bridge. The withdrawal commenced
on the night of 4/5 December and continued into the following day.

The patriotic sections of the population also left their homes to
accompany the withdrawing troops. They swarmed on to the
train which carried our men to Rangpur. The major in charge of
this last train run by Pakistan in the area retained an unforgettable
impression of this journey. His account of the journey was, roughly,
as follows: 'The train was full of civilians, most of whom were
sobbing and screaming. The troops guarded them by sitting at the
windows, the barrels of their guns protruding outside. The last
compartment, which consisted of only a flat platform, was used as
a mortar position by putting piles of sand bags on the sides. We
fired a few mortar shells as well as light machine-gun bursts to
scare away the rebels who fired on the train. When we stopped to
pick up stranded Razakars or civilians, we attracted machine-gun
as well as mortar fire. When we were about to cross the Tista
Bridge, we saw a band of Razakars at some distance. We stopped
and invited them to board the train. But they did not budge. As
we crossed homeward and blew up the bridge, they jubilantly
threw up their arms in the air and shouted "Joi Bangla". They

were Mukti Bahini, who had infiltrated the Razakar ranks and passed valuable information to the enemy.'

All our troops were back in Rangpur on the night of 5/6 December. Our detachments on the Domar axis had fallen back to Saidpur the same night. A day earlier, Thakurgaon had fallen and our garrison there had taken up an alternative position at Mandalpara, north of Dinajpur. The new defence line, on 6 December, ran along the Mandalpara–Saidpur axis. Immediately behind these defences lay the Dinajpur–Rangpur line. 23 Brigade may take legitimate pride in defending this line until the end of the war, but one wonders whether the enemy would have really bothered to follow the longest route from north to south, when he had the option to find a shortcut from the western border.

The Indians found that shortcut by effecting a breach near Chirai, eleven kilometres north of Hilli, on 4 December after overrunning our platoon position. Chirai was originally held by a company of troops but after the Qasim post incident in late November, the position had been thinned to make up a deficiency elsewhere. No threat was anticipated from the area as it was full of *bheels* (marshy lakes) and *nullahs* (ravines) and seemed most unlikely for any tank manoeuvre. Moreover, there was no principal route which the enemy could develop into an approach for attack. Yet, this 'most unlikely route' was adopted by the enemy. Guided and helped by the Mukti Bahini, the enemy tanks and infantry column managed to overrun our Chirai post and started moving towards the east.

When the message was passed to the superior headquarters, the angry staff officer told the platoon commander, 'Don't imagine things. How can tanks come when there are so many *bheels*, marshes and mines there? You must have seen buffaloes.' The young captain replied, 'You may be right, Sir. But I swear the buffaloes have 100mm guns fitted on them and they are picking off our bunkers one by one.'

Although the enemy had pierced our defences at Chirai, he could not move in strength towards the Rangpur–Bogra road until he had neutralized Major Akram's company on his southern flank. Two enemy columns, therefore, rolled from north and south to attack Major Akram's position. But Major Akram beat back assaults from both sides and held out for two days. It was now 6 December. The enemy was obviously in a hurry to brush aside this dogged obstacle. Though full pressure was put on Major

Akram, he held out for a further forty-eight hours, till 8 December. 'C' company had already, by now, proved its mettle against over- whelming odds. Major Akram moved from one trench to the next to cheer on his boys who were already in high spirits. During one of these moves, a tank shell hit and killed him on the spot. That was a serious blow to his valiant soldiers. The enemy again attacked from the north as well as the south, inflicting heavy casualties. Only forty members of 'C' Company survived and they withdrew to join the rest of the battalion. Major Akram (Shaheed) was posthumously given *Nishan-i-Haider*, Pakistan's highest gallantry award.

While the main enemy thrust was directed against Major Akram's defences, a light column of armour and infantry had proceeded towards the east through Durgapur railway station. It hit Pirganj on the Bogra–Rangpur road on 7 December, unbeknown to the Pakistan Army.

The same afternoon, Major-General Nazar Hussain Shah was returning from Rangpur to Bogra by road. He was accompanied by Brigadier Tajammul and a few staff officers. As the road curved near Pirganj, they came under enemy fire. Abandoning their ve- hicles, they quickly disappeared into a grove of trees. The G.O.C. later triumphantly told me that he had seen 'enemy tanks as close as 500 metres on my right.' He and his party were helped by a God- fearing Bengali who guided them to a safe path which took them towards Rangpur.

Major-General Nazar's jeep had a two-star plate. On its reverse were three stars so that the same plate could be used for General Niazi's visits. When the plate was removed by an Indian soldier and taken to his officer, they were elated to have ambushed a three- star general—General Niazi himself. Little did they know that since the outbreak of war he had not ventured out of Dacca.

I was in the operations room of General Niazi's headquarters when, on the night of 7/8 December, news of the Pirganj incident reached Dacca. Till then, the G.O.C. was missing, presumed cap- tured. Immediately, Major-General Jamshed, Director General E.P.C.A.F. and G.O.C., 39 *ad hoc* Division, was sent by helicopter to take over General Nazar's duties. He returned after about two hours, tired and browned off. His helicopter had failed to locate the divisional headquarters at night. Luckily, General Nazar had meanwhile found his way there.

Headquarters 16 Division, though at the risk of its G.O.C., had discovered the enemy presence on its main line of communication. This could well mean a split in the division—and a division split is a division destroyed. The G.O.C therefore ordered that Task Force 'A' and Task Force 'B' be organized immediately and sent from north and south to crush the enemy at Pirganj. Brigadier Naeem who had been stuck in Rangpur since the outbreak of war was to command the northern task force, while Brigadier Tajammul was to lead the columns from the south. Nearly forty-eight hours passed, but the 'blades of the scissors' failed to click. The enemy utilized the period to build up his strength to a brigade and a regiment of tanks.

When Brigadier Tajammul reached his headquarters at Bogra after the 7 December incident, he reproved Lieutenant-Colonel Sultan, commanding officer of 32 Baluch, for neglecting the divisional line of communication. The colonel, a dutiful officer, took it so seriously that he set out immediately with his battalion to wipe out the enemy. He intended to dismount his troops from the trucks a little short of the enemy and launch the attack at night. Little did he know that the enemy had, in the meantime, extended his reach further south to Plasbari and increased his strength. Working on the basis of previous information, Lieutenant-Colonel Sultan literally bumped into the enemy defences. The advance company was mown down and Lieutenant-Colonel Sultan himself was killed. 32 Baluch, mauled and shaken, fell back. Brigadier Tajammul sent reinforcements consisting of 8 Baluch, a company of 32 Punjab and a few field guns to check the southward flow of the enemy.

The enemy presence on the Pirganj-Plasbari section of the Bogra–Rangpur road had an unsettling effect on the border defences of 205 Brigade (Brigadier Tajammul). The extended fingers in the north-west and north-east were folded back to form a fist at Bogra. In the same process, 4 Frontier Force had been withdrawn from the Hilli defences. The small posts at Fulcharighat, Bonapara and Gobindganj in the east were also evacuated.

Now the 16 Division had been decisively divided. Its 23 Brigade was cut off on the Rangpur–Dinajpur axis while 205 Brigade was pressed close to Bogra. All hopes of a link-up between these two brigades had been shattered. Each brigade now had to fight for its own life.

Since the enemy's main interest lay in capturing Bogra, a communication centre, the main pressure had to be borne by Brigadier Tajammul's brigade. He tried to delay the enemy at Mahasthan, fourteen kilometres north of Bogra. The Indians, guided by the Mukti Bahini, took a long detour to avoid our defences astride the main road, and hit the battalion headquarters in the rear. They also rounded up men and vehicles in the rear echelon and started attacking our defences from the south. Our troops, facing north, could not turn back as they were also frontally engaged.

Major Sajid, company commander of 32 Punjab, was on the eastern side of the main road. He was captured by the enemy advancing from the south, while his men continued fighting the enemy from the north. Havildar Hukamdad of Sajid's company had successfully foiled three enemy attempts to link up from the north and south. Each enemy wave was repulsed leaving one or two dead in front of Hukamdad's trench. The Indian major ordered Major Sajid, his captive, to 'stop this fanatic fellow or we will assault his position.' As Sajid showed reluctance, an Indian detachment charged on Hukamdad's position. Alone in his trench, he sprayed bullets right into the charging troops. He killed three of them. The others ducked down and crawled back.

This further infuriated the Indian major who, with a revolver at Sajid's chest, ordered him to stop 'that fanatic fellow'. Sajid obeyed. He shouted to Hukamdad, 'Stop it Hukamdad, stop it!' He replied, 'Sa'ab! You seem to have exhausted your ammunition but I still have two magazines with me. Don't worry, I have enough.'[1] The Indians finally had to kill him in his trench at heavy cost.

We left our Mahasthan defences on 12 December and came to the outer perimeter of the Bogra fortress. 205 Brigade was now deployed all round the town. The enemy aircraft and artillery alternately pounded the area. Besides the bombs, rockets and shells, the debris of brick houses splintered about with lethal effect. The casualties were collected and huddled in a nearby building. On the night of 13/14 December, Lieutenant-Colonel Sarfraz, the new commanding officer of 4 Frontier Force slipped on the verandah of a pukka building. He switched on his torch and found fresh blood streaming from a doorstep. Opening the door, he discovered a bundle of wounded soldiers suffering their agony in the dark.

[1] This was said in an expressive Punjabi dialect; 'Saab, apna amnition mukai baittey oh, per maray kal do magazin hain. Meri fikar nah karo.'

The divisional headquarters had already shifted to Nator, further to the south-west. Bogra was left to Brigadier Tajammul's care and he continued to resist the enemy attempts to close in for three days and three nights. On the morning of 16 December the enemy, on the threshold of Bogra, announced that General Niazi had agreed to surrender. He invited our troops to lay down their arms and save their lives. Surprisingly, some of them started walking to the enemy post under a white flag. When Brigadier Tajammul learnt about this, he cursed these black sheep and expressed his resolve to fight on. A little later, he received his orders from the divisional headquarters: 'Cease fire'. Leaving his troops where they were, he moved out of Bogra. He was hardly out of the city when he was caught and manhandled by the Mukti Bahini. He returned to his command, with a fractured arm, to share Indian hospitality as a prisoner of war.

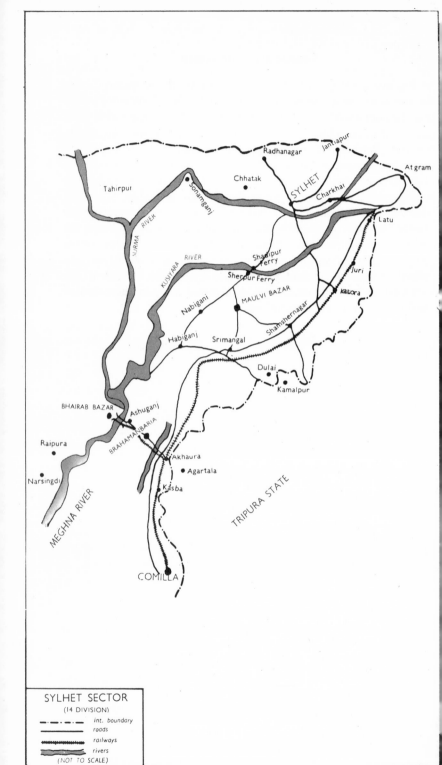

SYLHET SECTOR
(14 DIVISION)

- — · — int. boundary
- ———— roads
- ×××× railways
- ▬▬▬ rivers

(NOT TO SCALE)

19

BREAKDOWN
(14 Division)

The eastern border was like a saddle. The humps at the ends—Sylhet in the north and the Chittagong Hill Tracts in the south—were not very sensitive areas from an operational point of view. The loss of either, or both, would not have threatened Dacca. Eastern Command was, therefore, mainly concerned with the defence of the depression in the centre. It had accordingly placed a brigade each at Feni, Comilla and Brahmanbaria to protect three possible approaches which the enemy could develop into axes for an attack on Dacca. The rest of the border was left to relatively weak formations.

14 Division was responsible for the northern half of this border. Its area extended from Saldanadi, north of Comilla, to Sylhet District. It had three brigades whose total strength hardly measured up to one Indian brigade. Its strongest brigade (27) consisted of two and a half infantry battalions while the other two (202 and 313) had one and two regular infantry battalions respectively.

27 Brigade under Brigadier Saadullah was deployed on the Akhaura–Brahmanbaria–Bhairab Bazar axis while 202 *ad hoc* Brigade, under Brigadier Salimullah, was positioned in Sylhet. Brigadier Iftikhar Rana, commander of 313 Brigade, had his headquarters at Maulvi Bazar between Akhaura and Sylhet. He could put his weight in the south or in the north to influence the battle in our favour. Or, as General Niazi later told me, he could be launched against India's Tripura State with Agartala as his immediate objective.

Behind the 14 Division's border defences flowed the mighty Meghna river which provided a natural protection to Dacca. The enemy had first to neutralize the human resistance offered by 14 Division, particularly its 27 Brigade, and then negotiate a great water obstacle before he could reach the threshold of Dacca. His most likely approach was the Akhaura–Bhairab Bazar axis on which lay the tactical headquarters of Major-General Abdul Majid Qazi,

G.O.C., as well as 27 Brigade. Both General Qazi and Brigadier Saadullah were known for their courage, drive and dedication. The latter had to defend a forty-eight kilometre front from Saldanadi (north of Comilla) to Itakhola (south of Maulvi Bazar). He deployed 12 Frontier Force at Akhaura with 33 Baluch and 21 Azad Kashmir (minus) in the south and north respectively. He had also ten field guns, four tanks and a platoon from a Reconnaissance and Support battalion (48 Punjab).

The enemy had devoted a lot of attention to Akhaura and neighbouring Kasba even before the war. Both of them had long ceased to function as stations on the Chittagong-Comilla-Sylhet railway line. Since the previous October, they had hit the headlines in the national press as scenes of bloody battles. Several times they had changed hands between Pakistan and India. The railway sleepers had been removed by the occupants during their periods of control. The railway building, a brick hut, was deserted and bullet-ridden.

When India started her war of salients on 21/22 November, we anticipated a major move on this axis. Four days and five nights passed in a suspenseful lull. Finally, India showed up on 27 November when she attacked our forward positions in strength. While we concentrated on repelling this frontal attack, the Mukti Bahini, accompanied by their patrons, infiltrated from the sides and encircled our Akhaura position. We failed to relieve these besieged posts because all our efforts to link up had to be made frontally, as we were not allowed to cross the international frontier for any flanking manoeuvre.

The enemy launched a fresh attack on Akhaura on 30 November to reduce these isolated positions. One of our platoon defences eventually collapsed and the enemy, who had tested our reinforcement capabilities over the past few days, gushed forth and captured our only field gun deployed—mainly to boost the morale of our troops—behind the Akhaura defences.

As telecommunications with the forward platoons were also broken, a lieutenant was despatched to the right extension of the forward company to bring first-hand information. He found our troops retreating and the enemy column infiltrating on our right. He got the withdrawing troops to return to their trenches and reported the infiltration to battalion headquarters.

South of Akhaura was our Ganga Sagar position which had a platoon at Malik Bari and a section at Lanasar. On 1 December the enemy flushed them out with artillery and tank fire. The troops could not withstand the impact and bolted. This time, it fell to the lot of Major-General Qazi to put them back in their nests.

While the G.O.C. and the brigade commander were occupied with mending the falling defences in Akhaura and Ganga Sagar, some elements of India's 4 Guards managed to infiltrate, with the Mukti Bahini's help, to the rear of our battalion defences. Since we had no reserves to deal with such eventualities, Lieutenant-Colonel Basit of 14 Division raised a small force of batmen, military policemen and clerks. He took two of the four tanks and attacked the intruders with this 'force'. The infiltrators, who had the psychology of thieves, tried to rush back as soon as they were detected. Basit confidently gave pursuit and fired a few shots, killing some of the retreating enemy. Among those who lay dead in the field was a young observer of Indian Artillery. Among his possessions were discovered some important documents, including a 'Task Table' which showed the capture of Akhaura bridge on the Titas river (behind our defences) as the target.

When the all-out war began on 3 December the brigade commander in consultation with the G.O.C. decided to readjust his positions to receive full-fledged attacks. He decided to withdraw his troops, the following night, to the home side of the Akhaura bridge, fold back his extended arm to the south and blow up the strategic bridge.

The plan was successfully executed, except that the bridge, left intact by the hastily retreating troops, fell into enemy hands. In consequence, they crossed over the bridge on the heels of our withdrawing troops, allowing us no time to prepare and occupy our defences on the home bank of the Titas river. Brahmanbaria, 14 kilometres further west, was considered a suitable site for a prolonged defensive battle. The town had already been developed as a divisional 'strong point' with dumps of rations and ammunition for fifteen days.

We occupied our Brahmanbaria defences and waited for the enemy hammer to fall on the anvil. As before, they failed to do as we anticipated and infiltrated from the sides to threaten our rear. We also reacted as before and abandoned our position to withdraw to Ashuganj, a further 13 kilometres back, on the eastern bank of the Meghna. The withdrawal commenced on the night of 7/8

December and finished next morning. The enemy, this time, allowed us enough time to dig our new defences.

The tactical headquarters of 14 Division had, meanwhile, shifted from Brahmanbaria to Bhairab Bazar on the western bank of the Meghna. This move, which could not be kept secret, had an un-settling effect on our troops who thought that safety lay on the western, and not the eastern, bank of the Meghna. If the presence of the divisional headquarters in the forward area can be a tonic to the troops, its withdrawal can, by the same token, be demoralizing.

Brigadier Saadullah deployed his brigade at Ashuganj with a bias to the east and south—the most likely directions of enemy attack. He assigned the north-western sector to E.P.C.A.F. with a sprinkling of regular troops.

On the morning of 9 December it was learnt that the enemy was approaching Ashuganj from the north-east. The news was received with surprise: how could the enemy be in that area? Before our field guns could fire the first salvo, it transpired that the 'approach-ing enemy' was none other than our own E.P.C.A.F. personnel who, trailing their arms, were walking homeward along the river bank. They reported enemy troops and tanks in the area and did not see much point in sticking to their trenches with .303 rifles.

The E.P.C.A.F. personnel were followed by another foot column. They were believed to be friendly troops retreating from the defence perimeter. But when they approached Ashuganj, they were ident-ified as Indian troops in green uniform. They were not very far from our brigade headquarters. A handful of men was quickly collected to stop the enemy advance. Meanwhile, word was sent to pull out some regular troops from the eastern sector to deal with the new threat. Before the regular troops could arrive from the eastern sector, the *ad hoc* force had beaten back the enemy troops. The enemy hurriedly withdrew, leaving behind several dead and abandoning seven tanks in running condition. This small victory sustained the morale of our troops who had been withdrawing, step by step, since the outbreak of war.

While 27 Brigade was still in Ashuganj ready to receive the en-emy, General Qazi ordered the blowing up of the gigantic Bhairab bridge on the Meghna. His orders were immediately carried out and the iron girders splashed down into the river. The troops on the eastern bank could not help but notice this unencouraging development. What had prompted the G.O.C. to order the demolition is not known. Generally, two explanations are offered. First, it is said that the blowing up of the bridge was the only way to 'stop the troops from looking back'. They would now fight to the last on the eastern-side. Secondly, it is argued that the G.O.C. feared that the enemy column advancing from the north might capture it intact. The demolition was ordered mainly to deny this bridge to the enemy. When I asked the G.O.C. about it soon after the war, he said that he had received reports of a heliborne enemy force landing in the northern vicinity. That force, he reasoned, could have no function other than the capture of this bridge. The presence of this heliborne force, however, was not substantiated by any other source.

27 Brigade, using available rivercraft, crossed over to Bhairab Bazar on the night of 10/11 December. The new defences of the Bhairab Bazar fortress were organized the following day. The fortress had ready stocks to last for fifteen days. The brigade, benignly presided over by its G.O.C., sat there, untouched by the enemy, till the end of the war. While 27 Brigade waited 'safe in the saddle', the enemy helicopters ferried troops across the Meghna and landed them in the Raipura–Narsindgi area, about fifteen kilometres south of Bhairab Bazar. This heliborne force threatening Dacca was not disturbed by 14 Division or 27 Brigade, as it lay technically outside their jurisdiction.

That is all 14 Division was able to achieve by playing its highest trump card on the Akhaura–Bhairab Bazar axis.

Let us now turn to the other two formations of the division. 313 Brigade, immediately north of Brigadier Saadullah's position, had 30 Frontier Force and 22 Baluch deployed on border outposts from Kamalganj to Latu. Like Akhaura and Kasba in 27 Brigade area, Dulai was the trickiest border outpost in this brigade area. Held by elements of 30 Frontier Force, it had received several attacks by Indian troops and their collaborators (the Mukti Bahini) since October. In view of this, our troops were increased to a (mixed) company strength. The enemy tactics were the same as those employed elsewhere: to keep the defenders busy by frontal attacks to allow time for infiltration from the flanks. They tried this several times during the four weeks of October but without any success. On 29 October, however, they managed to isolate the Dulai post. All our efforts to reinforce or link up with the post proved abortive. Yet, it lived through the siege quite defiantly. On 31 October,

Major Javed, second-in-command of 30 Frontier Force, lost pa-tience with his helpless situation and decided to break the siege at all costs. He collected a handful of volunteers, eighteen in number, and attacked the encirclement on its southern flank. The enemy, who had waited for this opportunity, rained shells and bullets on Major Javed and his comrades. But they did not relent or return. The observer with the Indian artillery, who saw the advance of these gallant men with his naked eye, gave a fresh correction to his guns and the next salvo landed right on the determined band of men. Most of them were killed, including their leader, and the fate of the Dulai post continued to hang in the balance.

This was not the first incident in which 30 Frontier Force lost many soldiers. Up to 3 November it had suffered 160 dead inclu-ding two officers, three junior commissioned officers and 90 regular troops. The others were Razakars and E.P.C.A.F. personnel. Officially, the war had still not started in East Pakistan!

Brigadier Rana suggested to the G.O.C. and the Commander of Eastern Command that, instead of trying to link up frontally with the besieged border outpost, it would be better to cross the inter-national border and hit the enemy in the tail. He, in fact, raised a force of 22 Baluch, 30 Frontier Force and 39 Baluch (from down south) for the purpose. He also made available two field guns and four heavy mortars (from Sylhet and Comilla) to support the attack to relieve Dulai. He explained his plan, in my presence, to General Niazi during one of the latter's visits to the area in early November. Permission to cross the international border was refused. Yet Brigadier Rana was asked to use the force he had so diligently raised. The three-pronged attack went in, almost frontally, and failed. It only added to the tally of casualties attributed to the Dulai post.

The other battalion of Rana's brigade, 22 Baluch, had an equally rough time before the 'official war'. By the end of November, the enemy had nibbled away all the border curves near Latu, Kalora and Shamshernagar. On 1 December he penetrated a little deeper and established a blocking position between Shamshernagar and the border outpost. The brigade commander discovered this when he came under fire from the neighbouring Rajnagar position. Next day the enemy attacked Shamshernagar itself, making the border outposts untenable. P.A.F. help was sought and two F-86s promptly replied to the call. They flew over the home side of the border and found no enemy positions. Troops, tanks and vehicles were assembled on the eastern edge of the border but the planes could not go in to destroy them, as this would be a violation of the international frontier. They had to fly back to base without firing a single shot. That was on the eve of all-out war.

The abortive P.A.F. sortie had, at least, established that the enemy had not yet occupied Shamshernagar. So our troops were ordered to go back and reoccupy their abandoned positions. Meanwhile the isolated post east of Shamshernagar had been reduced by the enemy. Second Lieutenant Zamir is said to have stuck to his trench there till the end. He was last heard shouting to his troops, 'Look! They are turning back. You hold on to your positions. The enemy is retreating.'

It is said that the weakest links in these border outpost defences were the Razakars and E.P.C.A.F. personnel, who were the first to abandon their posts. Cowardice, they say, is contagious. The infection quickly spread to the regular troops also. Moral: Never mix paramilitary personnel with the regular troops in front line defences!

After the outbreak of war on 3 December, Brigadier Rana ordered the withdrawal of 30 Frontier Force from the border posts to Maulvi Bazar—a divisional 'strong point' and Rana's brigade headquarters. The 30 Frontier Force company, on the extreme right, was allowed to join the neighbouring 27 Brigade.

22 Baluch could not be called back as it had lost contact with the brigade headquarters. Brigadier Rana naturally worried about the troops scattered as far afield as Latu, Kamatnagar, Juri, Kalora and Mirzapur. Had the battalion been overrun? Had the troops in the border outpost been destroyed piecemeal? What could be done for the survivors, if any?

Eventually, one of the company headquarters of 22 Baluch was contacted by radio. They were asked to tell everybody to group together at convenient places to avoid total annihilation. Some of them collected at Latu and Fenchuganj, while others (about fifty stragglers) made their way to Sylhet. They walked back with their personal weapons, leaving behind their heavy equipment.

At long last, the battalion headquarters of 22 Baluch was picked up by chance on a radio receiver. It gave its new location as a tea garden, about sixteen kilometres from Kalora. The battalion was ordered to reorganize. It turned out that 22 Baluch had been splintered by a severe enemy attack which had forced the battalion headquarters to withdraw without passing the necessary orders to the companies deployed in the border outposts. In the confusion, it lost contact with the companies as well as the brigade headquarters. This happened on 6 December.

That was the day when the G.O.C. ordered 313 Brigade to link up with 27 Brigade on the Akhaura–Bhairab Bazar axis. It was essential to reinforce an axis which could affect the fate of Dacca, but Brigadier Rana expressed his inability to accomplish the task. He was asked to send down at least one battalion, but he could not. He only ordered the nearest company of 30 Frontier Force to join 27 Brigade, as I have already mentioned.

Meanwhile, the enemy had advanced on the Shamshernagar-Maulvi Bazar road. Since 22 Baluch was still dispersed, Maulvi Bazar had to be defended by 30 Frontier Force (which now had only two and a half companies) and para-military forces. The perimeter defences were organized on 5 December.

There was the small Kusiyara river between Maulvi Bazar and Sylhet. It had two ferries: Sherpur and Shadipur. The brigade headquarters with vehicles and heavy equipment moved to Shadipur ferry on the Sylhet side of the river, while 30 Frontier Force with E.P.C.A.F. and Razakars stayed in Maulvi Bazar. Enemy aircraft and artillery now launched an attack on Maulvi Bazar. They bombed, shelled and rocketed the area heavily. 30 Frontier Force took the punishment with fortitude. It stood its ground for two days and lost only five soldiers. But many others were wounded, including those who were hit by flying bricks. Finally, it was ordered on the evening of 7 December to shift to Shadipur ferry after destroying the ammunition dumps.

As 30 Frontier Force left for Shadipur ferry, brigade headquarters moved from there to Sylhet. This depleted brigade had two commanders. In addition to Brigadier Rana, Brigadier Hassan had been sent from Dacca in early December because General Niazi feared that Rana alone might not be able to withstand the pressure. He did not seem to appreciate that duplication of command is worse than a weak command.

Captain Zafar of the brigade headquarters drove ahead of his brigade commanders on 7 December. As the young officer approached Sylhet towards evening, he saw enemy helicopters landing troops on the eastern periphery of the city. He stopped, held his breath and counted ten helicopters taking off after delivering their load. Meanwhile, Brigadier Rana's jeep caught up. He was told about the helicopter landing of enemy troops. He feared that the city may have fallen to the enemy. How could they land troops without creating a safety zone there, he wondered.

Meanwhile, the enemy did not disturb 30 Frontier Force in their new defences at Shadipur ferry, as any pressure on them would have pushed the battalion towards Sylhet which would not suit the enemy, who wanted to take Sylhet while it had minimum strength to defend itself. Sylhet, with its Saluchikar airstrip and rich tea gardens, had sufficient attraction for the enemy in this sector.

As ordered by Brigadier Rana, 30 Frontier Force and the allied troops moved from Shadipur to Sylhet on the night of 8/9 December. The officer who led this column told me later that from outside 'Sylhet looked like a ghost city. It was shrouded in thick layers of darkness. The stillness was packed with awesome suspense. The only disturbance was the occasional bark of a stray dog or the periodic cracking of a rifle shot.'

But, in this 'ghost city', was Brigadier Salimullah's 202 *ad hoc* brigade. What had happened to it? 202 Brigade, with headquarters at Sylhet, had only one regular infantry battalion—31 Punjab. Its strength had been augmented by the addition of paramilitary personnel, consisting of Frontier Corps, Rangers and Razakars. The 'brigade' was also given a battery of field guns (previously belonging to 31 Field Regiment). The brigade had a long frontage in the east as well as in the north. Its area extended from Latu (the northern extremity of 313 Brigade) to Tahirpur on the northern border where Sylhet district joined Mymensingh district. Opposite Brigadier Salimullah was one Indian Mountain Division from IV Corps.

The main approaches to Sylhet were from the east and north-east. Atgram, Zakiganj and Charkhai were the successive defensive positions on the eastern approach while Jaintiapur, Hemu and Khadim Nagar lay on the north-eastern route. The other approaches to the city and cantonment were through Chhatak in the north-west and Goyain in the north, but neither was there any enemy concentration on these routes nor could they be developed into an axis for a major offensive. The brigade, therefore, gave primary attention to the Atgram side.

The entire 31 Punjab could not be deployed on the most threatened axis because the enemy, guided by the Mukti Bahini, could also follow a less sensitive route to attack Sylhet. So the battalion was split into eight groups and parcelled out to various border outposts, from Atgram in the east to Sunamganj in the west. With regular troops as the 'backbone', the positions were 'beefed up' with an assortment of paramilitary forces.

As elsewhere, the enemy had been active on this border since 15 October when 85 Indian Border Security Force, supported by a battery of field guns and a battalion (3 East Bengal) of Mukti Bahini attacked Chhatak, with the apparent aim of capturing the town and the cement factory there. The paramilitary troops guarding this path left their forward positions but held on to the town. A company of regular troops and two field guns were sent from Charkhai to stabilize the position. Later, a company of 30 Frontier Force was borrowed to counter-attack and throw back the intruders. The operation, launched on 23 October, was a success.

Our success only served to convince the enemy that he would have to commit a larger force to capture and occupy our territory. He therefore launched a brigade attack (59 Indian Brigade) on 21 November in the Atgram and Zakiganj areas. He managed to throw back our troops including regular elements of 31 Punjab. We could not dislodge the intruders, and readjusted our positions. Our new defences lay at Charkhai, thirty-two kilometres east of Sylhet. 202 Brigade received a reinforcement of two companies of 12 Azad Kashmir which arrived from West Pakistan in late November. As the new troops were unfamiliar with the local conditions they could not be given an independent assignment. They were deployed, one company each, at Charkhai and Jaintiapur.

The 'gift' of these two companies did not affect the enemy aims or tactics in the area. He continued to nibble at our territory with the help of the Mukti Bahini. By 3 December, he had sliced off the entire border length from Atgram to Tahirpur. The depth of enemy penetration varied: it was five to six kilometres at Chattak, thirteen to fifteen kilometres at Sunamganj and thirty kilometres at Zakiganj. The total area under enemy occupation in this sector measured several hundred square kilometres.

When war broke out in West Pakistan, our defences in the Sylhet area had shrunk to Charkhai in the east, Hemu in the north and Chhatak in the north-west. For the first three days of all-out war, the brigade held out on this line of defence. In fact, the enemy did not commit his forces against Sylhet until the situation on the main

Akhaura-Brahmanbaria axis had crystallized. By 7 December not only had 27 Brigade withdrawn towards the Meghna but 313 Brigade (Maulvi Bazar) had also been displaced. Now the enemy was free to decide the fate of this important border town.

Mr. Ajmal Chaudhry, a former central minister from Sylhet, came to Brigadier Salimullah's headquarters on 7 December and said that he had seen enemy helicopters landing toops in Miran Chak, about two kilometres east of the city. (After the war, he fell into the hands of the Mukti Bahini who brutally killed him.) That was about the same time as Captain Zafar of Brigadier Rana's headquarters entered Sylhet from the Shadipur ferry side. He had seven men with him.

Zafar was met by Lieutenant-Colonel Sarfraz of the local martial law headquarters who took him towards the site of the helicopter landing. They counted nine helicopters taking off after releasing their load. They looked at their watches: it was 1630 hours. They worked out the approximate enemy strength and thought that it would be impossible to dislodge two companies with seven men.

Meanwhile, Brigadier Salimullah had pulled out twenty-six men of 31 Punjab from Jaintiapur position and sent them, under Captain Basharat, to neutralize the enemy. When he approached the area, he saw a fresh wave of helicopters landing troops and guns. He thought it would be too much for his platoon to eject a 'battalion' (minus). He was content with exchanging a few shots across the *nullah*.

About the same time, nearly fifty stragglers of 22 Baluch reached Sylhet from the Latu-Kalora side. They were also sent to reinforce Basharat's force. It was, by now, 8 December. Our troops, who never made a determined attack on the heliborne force, helplessly saw the enemy extending his arm northward, apparently to cut off Charkhai from Sylhet. At the same time, two helicopters flew over the local circuit house and Kaen bridge, presumably to reconnoitre the area. Suddenly, one helicopter released a bomb which exploded in the compound of the circuit house. It injured four persons—one intelligence clerk and three policemen. As soldiers rushed out to help the wounded, the other helicopter sprayed them with bullets, inflicting further casualties.

By the evening of 8 December, two companies of 22 Baluch had also arrived in the city. In addition, there were fifty men from 30 Frontier Force and forty-five from 31 Punjab. They totalled a battalion (minus). Four field guns (two each from 31 Punjab and 22 Baluch) were made available. In the brigade headquarters sat three brigadiers—Hassan, Rana and Salimullah—to commmand one skeleton brigade.

The mixed battalion and four field guns were given to the commanding officer of 22 Baluch to neutralize the heliborne enemy force. He refused because 'exhausted troops are not in a fit state to attack. Next day (9 December), the commanding officer of 30 Frontier Force was assigned the same task but he, giving a similar reason, disowned the mission.

On 10 December, a new plan of attack was finalized. The task force consisted of two prongs—consisting of 30 Frontier Force and 31 Punjab. The former was to simulate a frontal attack while the latter was to launch a silent attack from the northern side. At the appointed hour, 30 Frontier Force 'simulating the attack' shouted, 'Charge', but the other prong failed to act.

While we considered the enemy too strong to be ejected, he wavered in his mind about the tenability of his own position. After the war, I met an Indian officer of 5 Gurkha Rifles (heliborne force) who admitted that when the first shots were fired on the night of 7/8 December, his commanding officer talked about 'withdrawing to avoid total annihilation.' But his indecision saved him. When Pakistan failed to mount any pressure, he gained confidence and stayed on.

Meanwhile, the enemy ground column advanced on the Zakiganj axis to link up with the heliborne force. The link-up was effected on 12 December—about five days after the helicopter landing which we had failed to neutralize! On December 13, we further folded our defences and sat content with parts of Sylhet town and the Saluchikar airfield under our control. The remaining areas were occupied by Indians and the Mukti Bahini. The three brigadiers, and their men, survived in Sylhet till the end of hostilities on 16 December.

20

CHANDPUR UNDER CHALLENGE
(39 *ad hoc* DIVISION)

General Headquarters passed word to Dacca, in the middle of November, that the main enemy thrust was expected from the east. General Niazi, therefore, cast a fresh look at the map and Indian troop concentrations. Aided by Major-General Mohammad Rahim Khan, Deputy Martial Law Administrator, he identified the southern flank of Comilla as the likely route of enemy penetration. Till then, the area was under 14 Division, which was stretched over too wide an area. He decided to make Rahim responsible for this 'soft belly' and gave him 53 Brigade from Dacca, and also placed 117 Brigade (Comilla) under him.

General Rahim, considered to be one of the ablest generals of the Yahya regime, left Dacca on Sunday 21 November with a handful of staff officers and an armful of operational maps, to establish his headquarters at Chandpur, east of the Meghna. With his headquarters on the main Mudarfarganj–Chandpur road, he had a brigade on either side, at Comilla and Feni. If the enemy dared come on this road, the plan went, the two brigades would clip him to death.

The border south of 39 Division area consisted of the Chittagong Hill Tracts which did not permit any large-scale military movement. Chittagong and the Chittagong Hill Tracts were placed under an independent brigade (97) commanded by Brigadier Ataullah. He had a commando battalion (2 Commando) at Kaptai, to look after the Hill Tracts, and 24 Frontier Force at Chittagong. He also had a miscellany of other troops, including two companies of 21 Azad Kashmir, E.P.C.A.F., Razakars and policemen. No serious threat was anticipated in this area except a sea landing, which was practically impossible to prevent because of the extended coastline.

The main battle was to be fought between Comilla and Belonia Bulge. The Comilla Brigade (117) under Brigadier Atif, Pakistan's famous hockey skipper, was fully prepared for it. It had developed the cantonment as a fortress and stocked it with supplies to last for one month. It had dug anti-tank ditches on its eastern flank. Its three infantry battalions—30 Punjab, 25 Frontier Force and 23 Punjab—were deployed from north of Comilla down to Chauddagram. There was one field regiment of artillery, one mortar battery and two tanks to support the divisional front.

53 Brigade, commanded by Brigadier Aslam Niazi (no relation of General Niazi) had 15 Baluch and 39 Baluch to guard Feni and Belonia Bulge. Half of this bulge had been occupied by the enemy before the war. This gave him access to the Feni–Chittagong road, the only link between the seaport and the rest of the province. The enemy could have followed this route to hit Chittagong from the north rather than taking it from the south. But General Niazi had a ready solution for this too. He created another *ad hoc* brigade headquarters (91) under Brigadier Taskeen and made him responsible for this approach. Taskeen, who had mostly E.P.C.A.F. personnel under him, received two companies and the battalion headquarters of 21 Azad Kashmir which arrived from West Pakistan in late November.

When war broke out on 3 December, its impact was first felt by 25 Frontier Force south of Comilla. Two of its companies were deployed on the border, east of the Parbatipur river, while the remaining two were at Lalmai Hills in the rear. The battalion headquarters was with the forward companies. On the night of 3/4 December, the forward companies were attacked by 61 Mountain Brigade of the Indian Army. The attack was supported by a regiment of medium guns and a squadron of tanks. The defenders tried to repel the attack with infantry weapons and knocked out three enemy tanks. But this was not sufficient to cause the enemy to slacken his pressure. The commanding officer of 25 Frontier Force asked for permission to withdraw to the home bank of the Parbatipur river but he was ordered to stand fast. While he was frontally engaged, the Indians, led by the Mukti Bahini, circumvented his position and occupied the eastern bank of the river, to his rear. The battalion soon lost contact with the brigade headquarters.

This naturally disturbed Brigadier Atif who was worried on two counts. First, what was the fate of 25 Frontier Force? Secondly, if the battalion had collapsed, what was the direction of the enemy advance? Was he heading for Chandpur or wheeling northward to envelop Comilla?

Atif sent a fighting patrol of 30 Punjab to reconnoitre. The patrol party wandered through the southern vicinity of Comilla and came back to report a total absence of enemy troops in the area. But where was 25 Frontier Force? Had it retreated south-ward? Anticipating that it had, a message was sent to 23 Punjab, in the immediate south, to get ready to receive 25 Frontier Force elements—but none reached there. The mystery was resolved by a havildar of 25 Frontier Force who reached Comilla at about 11 a.m. on 4 December. He brought the news that the commanding officer, with his two companies, had surrendered to the enemy! His report was confirmed by a proud announcement on All India Radio in the afternoon that one lieutenant-colonel with six officers and two hundred men had been taken prisoner.

This was a major setback at the very outset of the war. 23 Punjab was asked to extend its northern arm to bridge the gap left by 25 Frontier Force, but it failed to carry out the orders as it, too, was under attack from 302 Indian Brigade and a regiment of field guns. 23 Punjab, while under pressure on the night of 3/4 December, sought permission to withdraw to the home bank of the Dakatia river but was ordered to stay in its forward defences. Permission was, however, granted next morning when withdrawal was impossible! The commanding officer, Lieutenant-Colonel Ashfaq Ali Syed, decided to step back after sunset. But during the day, when his second-in-command, Major Zafar Iqbal, tried to reach him with reinforcements from Laksham, he was fired upon by the enemy who had infiltrated to the eastern side of the Dakatia river. This meant that the withdrawal route of 23 Punjab was also cut. Major Zafar reported the enemy presence to Brigadier Aslam Niazi who refused to believe the information, saying, 'You must have seen *Muktis.*'

When Lieutenant-Colonel Syed learnt of the enemy presence at his back, he felt too uneasy to wait for sunset. He packed up his battalion headquarters at 16.30 hours, left the casualties to the doctor's care, and made for Laksham through the country-side. He also passed a message to the companies to meet him at Laksham. While the companies on the flanks withdrew in time, the forward company at Chauddagram under Major Akram could not, as it was still in contact with the enemy. When this company withdrew at night, it moved in the general direction of Parbatipur, our gun position at Dakatia river, without realizing that the area was now

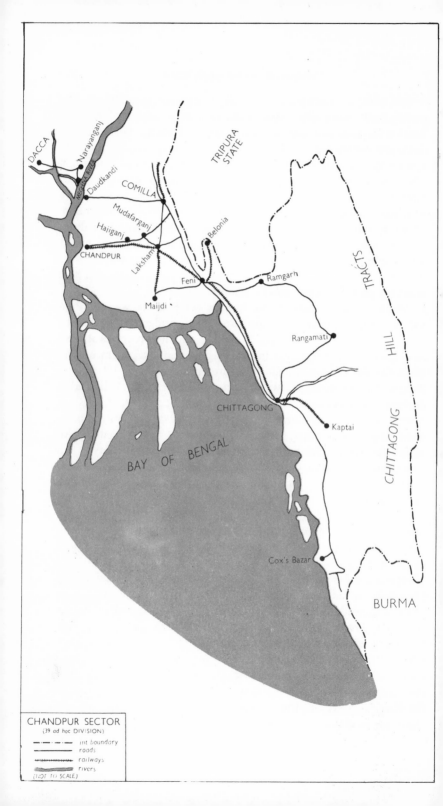

CHANDPUR SECTOR
(39 ad hoc DIVISION)

--- · --- · int boundary
——————— roads
++++++++ railways
▨▨▨▨▨ rivers
(NOT TO SCALE)

under enemy control. As a result, Major Akram ran into an enemy position and many of his men were mown down. He himself got a burst in the abdomen and lay almost dead in the fields. Next morning, when the Indians came to search their pockets, they found some sign of life in Major Akram and a few of his dedicated soldiers. They took them to their nearest dressing station. Major (now Lieutenant-Colonel) Akram still carries bitter memories and permanent scars of this withdrawal.

The surrender of 25 Frontier Force and the withdrawal of 23 Punjab created a sufficient gap for the enemy to channel a sizeable force along the Chandpur road. On the morning of 5 December Brigadier Aslam Niazi was, therefore, ordered to withdraw and assemble his brigade (15 Baluch and 39 Baluch) at Laksham, where 23 Punjab had already fallen. Laksham, about ten kilometres south of the Mudafarganj–Chandpur road, had been developed as a fortress. Lieutenant-Colonel Zaidi, commanding officer of two companies of 21 Azad Kashmir (the other two companies were in 14 Division), was also directed to join the others at Laksham. 15 Baluch, 39 Baluch and 21 Azad Kashmir did not move during the daytime on 5 December, for fear of an enemy air attack. They completed the withdrawal the following night. Instead of putting them to any immediate use, they were ordered to spend the night 'wherever they could'. They were to be briefed by Brigadier Niazi next morning. The commanding officer of 39 Baluch even rang up divisional headquarters to say that he had promptly pulled back from the Belonia side, and awaited orders! He was told that the G.O.C. would be in Laksham next morning to assign the new tasks.

Next day, 6 December, General Rahim drove out towards Laksham. A little short of Mudafarganj, his pilot jeep came under mortar and small arms fire. He cancelled the trip and returned to Chandpur, because the fire indicated that the enemy had already blocked the road. That posed a real challenge for Chandpur. Now was the time to show drive and determination. One brigade lay in Laksham, the other waited in Comilla. Above all, General Rahim with his bright professional career was in Chandpur to put his experience to practice. He could employ both the brigades to snip the enemy's tail and force the Indians to look back. But nothing of the kind happened for the next thirty-six hours. Brigadier Aslam Niazi sat in Laksham 'organizing the fortress defences' while the enemy continued his advance towards Chandpur. Comilla, with one and a half battalions, was busy with its local battle. It was not willing to abandon the security of a fortress. The Indians utilized this period of inaction to funnel more troops along the Mudafarganj–Chandpur road.

Our first column came out from Laksham on 7 December. One company of 21 Azad Kashmir and two companies each of 15 Baluch and 23 Punjab were organized into two groups, each commanded by a lieutenant-colonel. The mission given to them was to clear the enemy from Mudafarganj while the remaining troops (39 Baluch) held the fortress. The 15 Baluch column was to move direct to Mudafarganj, while 23 Punjab and 21 Azad Kashmir were to approach the target from the south-west. The first column was caught up in an exchange of fire outside Mudafarganj, while the second failed to show up because of some interference by the Mukti Bahini on the way. The 'attack' on Mudafarganj eventually failed.

Since the enemy was believed to be in strength at Mudafarganj, 15 Baluch was called back to Laksham while the other column (23 Punjab and 21 Azad Kashmir) was ordered to make for Hajiganj, further west on the Chandpur road. Lieutenant-Colonel Ashfaq Syed and Lieutenant-Colonel Zaidi, commanders of this force, decided to walk through the country-side and hit Hajiganj from the flank to avoid confrontation with the enemy on the road. They did not appreciate that the enemy, using the metalled road, would be in Hajiganj much earlier than they could hope to be.

The Hajiganj column had left Laksham on 7 December (for Mudafarganj) without carrying its essential supplies because the operation was not expected to last long. Now, it needed meals for its troops. They walked through inhospitable country-side all day and night, buying rations wherever they could and drinking water from the village ponds. They were also without cooking utensils. Cooked meals from Laksham could not be supplied as they did not follow any predetermined route and criss-crossed the fields and *nullahs*, by-passing suspected Mukti Bahini pockets.

They walked like this for thirty-six hours, shedding heavy wireless sets, surplus light machine-gun ammunition and worn out boots. Sharpened by their ordeal, their senses interpreted every trembling light in the country homes at night as enemy signals about their movement. This march turned out to be an endurance test for the hungry and fatigued troops.

Lieutenant-Colonel Ashfaq Syed and Lieutenant-Colonel Zaidi held their informal conference in the fields on 9 December and agreed to bifurcate their groups (23 Punjab under Syed and 21 Azad Kashmir under Zaidi) to reduce the chances of detection. The following day (10 December) they both surrendered to the enemy separately. This was the second major surrender in 39 Division.

Major-General Rahim realized that the enemy advancing along the Chandpur road would soon hit his headquarters. He asked for orders. When his request reached Headquarters, Eastern Command, on the night of 8 December, General Niazi was informed about the predicament of his ace general. He came out from his room wearing a dressing-gown of red printed satin. When he entered the operations room, the junior officers, including myself, were carrying on their private appreciation of the war. General Niazi went directly to the operational map depicting the latest battle situation in 39 Division area. He placed the index finger of his right hand at Chandpur and pressing it hard on the map, gave the historic decision: 'Tell Rahim to come back to Dacca. How can he stay in Chandpur with his back to the river? He has only one company to defend his headquarters.'

General Rahim, who could withdraw only by river, asked for a naval gunboat to escort his convoy. His liabilities at the divisional headquarters included two platoons of Frontier Force, one platoon of 23 Punjab, fifty-five men of a commando battalion and odd elements of ordnance, signals and supplies. Rahim raised the necessary river-craft from local resources during the day in order to be able to leave for Dacca on the night of 9 December.

The naval gunboat from Narayanganj (on the outskirts of Dacca) reached Chandpur at about midnight, but Rahim's headquarters could not leave the Chandpur jetty before 0430 hours on 10 December. An efficient river-craft would normally take four hours from Chandpur to Dacca but this unwieldy convoy was expected to cover the distance in five hours. This meant that at daybreak the convoy would only be half way to Dacca. So General Rahim, while leaving Chandpur, signalled Eastern Command to provide him with air cover during the later part of his journey. He presumably did not know that our air force had been grounded since 6 December. Alternatively he asked for another gunboat (equipped with anti-aircraft guns), but experts in Dacca ruled that two gunboats would be no more effective against an air strike than one—so why risk the second boat!

At about breakfast time—the usual visiting hour of the Indian jets—two MIG-21s attacked the convoy. The anti-aircraft guns of the solitary gunboat proved ineffective against the repeated and determined attacks of the jets. Soon, the boat was hit and its roof torn. While the others jumped out of their launches, the captain of the gunboat stuck to his vessel and skillfully manoeuvred it to the river bank. As everybody scrambled out of the boats and launches, the enemy jets continued strafing their poor victims. Four officers were killed, including Major Bilal (2 Commando Battalion) who had led the assault on Mujib's house on 25 March. Among the 'wounded' was Major-General Rahim who received bruises on the legs. He was evacuated to Dacca.

Back in Laksham, the situation had deteriorated further. Brigadier Aslam Niazi found it difficult to hold the fortress with only five companies. Moreover, what was the sense in sticking to Laksham when the enemy would soon be following Rahim to Dacca? The brigade was ordered to fall back on 9 December and join 117 Brigade at Comilla.

Laksham had 128 wounded soldiers in the Advance Dressing Station which had been established at the local civil hospital. On 8 December they had been loaded onto the train for Chandpur. As the fate of Chandpur hung in the balance, the casualties spent the dark night on the floors of third class compartments. Many of them were in a serious condition and needed immediate medical or surgical treatment. As the doctors could not attend to them all, Captain Hashmi took a kettleful of pain-relieving mixture to the train and poured an approximate measure of the liquid into the half-open mouths of the groaning soldiers. Next day, they were unloaded and brought back to the Advance Dressing Station. The question now was: could they be carried to Comilla?

53 Brigade kept the doctors and the casualties in the dark about its move. It organized the rest of its strength into two columns. The first column, mostly E.P.C.A.F., Mujahids and Razakars, left Laksham at about midnight on 10 December. Major Raishem of 23 Punjab was in charge of this mass. The second column, which left half an hour later, was commanded

by Lieutenant-Colonel Naeem. He had mainly his own troops of 39 Baluch.

Comilla was twenty-eight kilometres from Laksham and it would not normally have taken more than a few hours to cover the distance on foot. But now they had to trek three times further to avoid engagement with the Indians or Mukti Bahini on the way. Before leaving Laksham, 53 Brigade destroyed or damaged most of its heavy equipment, threw the ammunition crates into the water and burnt the ration dumps. They carried only personal weapons and pouch ammunition. Brigadier Niazi and his escort safely entered Comilla cantonment the following morning. So did Major Raishem's column. But Lieutenant-Colonel Naeem and his troops had some problems.

Lieutenant-Colonel Naeem followed an undetermined route, mostly zig-zag, to avoid the enemy. He also bypassed local *baris* (thatched huts) lest his move be detected by the Mukti Bahini. When the next night fell, he was near Janglia, about eleven kilometres south-west of Comilla. He decided to spend the night there. Next morning, when he tried to approach Comilla, he ran into an enemy position at Jaspur. This soon developed into a small battle and the exchange of fire continued intermittently until the afternoon. In the engagement, we lost some valuable lives including Major Taimur, company commander. Naeem withdrew his troops to Janglia again for the night and hoped to enter Comilla from a different direction next morning.

It was now 12 December. Naeem consulted his officers about the next move. Some of them suggested that they should make for Dacca as they had failed to enter the Comilla fortress, while others insisted that they should make another attempt to link up with 117 Brigade as ordered. So, early in the morning, they left Janglia and walked northward to reach the Comilla–Dacca road. They had hardly gone a few kilometres when the advance elements saw Indian troops between Ram Mohan and Chandina. They paused, took out their white handkerchiefs, and resumed their march towards the enemy. Shortly, the rest of the column also caught up and they all surrendered at about 10 a.m. on 12 December. This was the third major surrender in General Rahim's division.

The Comilla fortress still survived. It now had two brigadiers, two infantry battalions and two tanks. It had given up Comilla

city and confined itself to the cantonment. The city, under a
Bangla Desh flag, observed no air raid precautions. It glittered
with electric light while the cantonment was in a state of virtual
siege.

The Comilla garrison was still holding out when Dacca fell
on 16 December.

21

THE FINAL RETREAT
(36 *ad hoc* DIVISION)

Major-General Jamshed, who won the Military Cross in World War II, was known for his quiet and cool temperament. He was Director-General of East Pakistan Civil Armed Forces (E.P.C. A.F.). Since E.P.C.A.F. personnel, Rangers, Razakars and police, were placed under the operational command of General Niazi and his subordinate commanders, General Jamshed was not left with much of a force to command. He was, therefore, given another cap to wear. He was made General Officer Commanding, 36 *ad hoc* Division, which was assigned to look after Dacca and its northern areas, including the Tangail and Mymensingh districts.

The total divisional frontage of 185 kilometres extended from the eastern bank of the Jamuna (main Brahmaputra) to the western end of Sylhet district. There were only two approaches in this area, from north to south, which the enemy could exploit to descend on Dacca. They were the Haluaghat Mymensingh approach in the east and the Kamalpur Jamalpur axis in the west. The division had only two regular infantry battalions— 33 Punjab and 31 Baluch—which were grouped under 93 Brigade commanded by Brigadier Qadir, an old soldier on the verge of retirement. Brigadier Qadir deployed 33 Punjab on the eastern approach and 31 Baluch on the western. He established his own headquarters at Mymensingh.

The battalions were given the task of delaying the enemy as long as possible on the border; then, 'trading space for time', they were to fall back on the Mymensingh and Jamalpur fortresses. These two important towns, located on the home bank of *Chhota* (small) Brahmaputra, were to form the 'Line of No Penetration'.

Three memorable things happened in this sector during the war; the tenacious defence of Kamalpur border outpost, the self-defeating withdrawal of 93 Brigade and the Indian paratroop drop near Tangail, to which we will return later.

Opposite our 93 Brigade, the enemy had 101 Communication Zone, which was a misnomer. It was as good as a fighting formation commanded by a major-general. Before the war, the enemy had reinforced it with 95 Brigade. It had the usual complement of field and medium artillery, whereas we had only a battery of 120mm. mortars to cover both axes.

Of the two axes mentioned above, the main enemy thrust was expected on the Kamalpur–Jamalpur approach, which could open his way to Dacca via Tangail. The eastern approach, Haluaghat–Mymensingh, was relatively underdeveloped and was hence less likely. Kamalpur, which does not appear as more than a dot on the map, was the main stumbling block for the enemy on the western axis. He could not roll down to Bakshiganj, Sherpur and Jamalpur without first neutralizing this border outpost. He therefore paid it far more attention than it would, at first, appear to deserve.

The enemy first gingered it up on 12 June 1971, when he lobbed a few shells into it in support of insurgency operations in the border areas. He again needled it on 31 July when he sent some rebels to 'attack' it. The attack failed and the rebel force, which included defecting East Bengal Regiment/East Pakistan Rifles personnel, left behind one heavy machine-gun, twelve light machine-guns, four sten-guns, thirty rifles, one rocket launcher, and a number of corpses. This bitter experience silenced the so-called freedom fighters for over two months.

On 22 October, regular Indian troops, mixed with the Mukti Bahini, attacked the border outpost. They suffered nine casualties, including one officer, and withdrew across the border. They came again in strength on 14 November. The 13 Guards led this attack while the rebels followed it. Keeping the border outpost frontally occupied, they infiltrated to the sides and established a blocking position on the Bakshiganj–Kamalpur road. The enemy artillery intermittently shelled the area from 1200 hours to 1900 hours while the infantry staged some feint attacks. The attempt seemed to be a psychological ploy to unnerve the border outpost rather than a manly effort to assault and capture it.

We had seventy regular troops and a platoon of Razakars and Rangers at Kamalpur. They were commanded by a wiry young officer, Captain Ahsan Malik. He had three mortars of 81mm. calibre. When the border outpost was cut off, the battalion headquarters in the rear sent a link-up force under an officer. Two 120mm. mortars also struggled up from Bakshiganj, about four kilometres away, to provide supporting fire, if required. Before the mortars could be deployed or the link-up force could dismount from the vehicles, the enemy opened up from both sides of the road. Hurriedly, the troops jumped down and returned the fire but the enemy had the upper hand. Ten of our men were killed and seven wounded, including one officer. We also lost four vehicles and both the mortars. The enemy took away one of our light machine-guns. Fortune, this time, had smiled on the other side.

After this expensive link-up attempt, we had two options. Either we could have asked the Kamalpur post troops to withdraw and join the main body of men at Bakshiganj or tried to keep it supplied under all circumstances. The official policy of maintaining a 'forward posture in defence' ruled out the first alternative. The second, therefore, had to be followed.

In fact, withdrawal of the Kamalpur post would have automatically necessitated the winding up of other posts (Naqshi and Baromari) on the border. With these three posts of 31 Baluch vacated, the western flank of 33 Punjab would have been exposed. In other words, abandoning one post would have meant folding back the entire brigade defences.

After isolating Kamalpur post in mid-November, the enemy did not venture to neutralize it and it continued to survive as long as its stocks of rations and ammunition lasted. On 23 November, Captain Ahsan sent out a group of Razakars on patrol duty. It did not return to the post. Another party, of regular troops this time, was sent to search for them. It too did not come back. The message was clear. The enemy lay in strength on all sides to devour odd bands of men outside their defences. It was insane to lose a third party by repeating the experiment. The battalion headquarters was requested, by radio, to help trace the missing patrols.

The battalion headquarters sent a group of soldiers with a spare vehicle to link up with the border outpost, trace the missing men and bring back the casualties, if any. This small force was ambushed on the way. The spare vehicle for the casualties was lost, but other members of the group managed to retrace their steps to Bakshiganj. Similar efforts were made during the next three

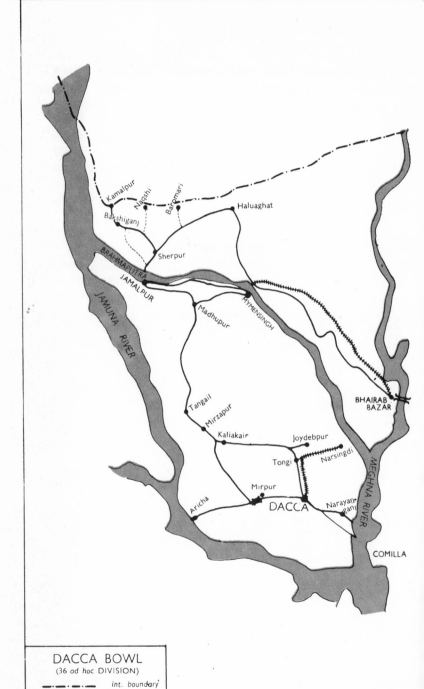

DACCA BOWL
(36 ad hoc DIVISION)

— · — · — · — int. boundary
——————— roads
+++++++++ railways
▓▓▓▓▓▓▓▓ rivers
(NOT TO SCALE)

days but with no success. Finally, Lieutenant-Colonel Sultan, commanding officer of 31 Baluch, made a determined effort on 27 November to break the encirclement of the border outpost and give it a new lease of life. He ordered three columns to advance on and astride the Bakshiganj–Kamalpur road, with the mission to converge on the border outpost. Simultaneously, small parties were sent from Kamalpur to block the possible escape routes of the intruders so that all of them could be smashed during the operation.

Meanwhile, the enemy had also reinforced the besieging troops and deployed some additional artillery in the area. An artillery observer kept a watchful eye on important approaches to the border outpost.

As soon as our three-pronged advance made some headway, the enemy observer directed a heavy rain of artillery shells on to it. Immediately, the advance column hit the ground—only to be subjected to automatic fire. The enemy Hunters, meanwhile, hovered over the border giving the impression that, if need be, the artillery fire could be supplemented with air strafing. The link-up effort eventually failed.

The following night (27/28 November), the enemy launched an attack to neutralize the isolated border outpost. The attack, which commenced in the dead of night, was spearheaded by "C" company of Indian 13 Guards. But, thanks to the concrete bunkers and the even more solid determination of the men who occupied them, the enemy was allowed to close in till he had come within the effective range of our small arms. He could not withstand the spray of bullets and withdrew. Next morning, Captain Ahsan's troops counted their night's harvest. It consisted of twenty enemy corpses, including an artillery observer. A soldier crawled up to the silenced observer and recovered the fire plan from him.

The two-week duel had brought out two important points. First, the enemy had foiled all our attempts to reinforce the border outpost. Secondly, we had foiled the enemy attempts to overrun that isolated post. Despite the trying period through which the post had passed, the troops were still in good cheer. Supplies, rather than spirits, were at the lowest ebb. The rations and ammunition, which were supposed to last till the end of November, were fast running out. Ahsan had imposed strict economy measures to conserve the valuable supplies. It was possible to live on one *chapati* less but difficult to save bullets in the face of the enemy. Some of the troops had grown so touchy that they pressed the trigger at night even if a bush rustled, a frog croaked or a jackal coughed.

The worst sufferers were the five wounded soldiers who lay in the outpost without any medical help or nourishing food. The solitary nursing assistant could merely dress and undress their wounds and minister an occasional dose of pain-killer. As to the diet, the situation was equally depressing. The doves and wild pigeons which were hunted earlier to prepare soup for the wounded, had also migrated to safer places because of the frequent exchange of fire. Yet the outpost stood, in the face of the enemy, as a symbol of unconquered defiance.

Major Ayub, a brilliant company commander, undertook a replenishment mission on 29 November. He took with him some regular soldiers and Razakars who carried crates of ammunition and bags of rations on their heads. They avoided the road and detoured through the country-side. Major Ayub reached the outpost but his followers came under enemy fire a little short of Kamalpur. They threw off their load and crawled back to Bakshiganj. Ayub's presence greatly boosted the morale of the troops, although they had only 200 rounds of light machine-gun ammunition, twelve three-inch and ten two-inch mortar shells, and 75 bullets per rifleman. Major Ayub returned to the battalion next day to give a first-hand report.

No supplies or reinforcements reached the outpost even after Ayub's return but it held out on its own till 3 December when full-scale war erupted. The escalation of hostilities seemed to have increased the fury of the enemy who now lost no time in knocking out this stumbling block. Two Allouette helicopters appeared over Kamalpur on 4 December. The exhausted faces in the trenches looked up and beamed with hopes of last minute help from Dacca. In fact, they were hostile kites weighing up their prey. On the ground, the enemy closed in from the sides to narrow the encirclement.

The same day, Major Ayub made a desperate attempt to replenish the outpost. In this heroic effort, he sacrificed his life. It was a great loss and it extinguished all hopes of help for the outpost. In the afternoon, a Bengali carrying a white flag brought a message from the Indian commander asking Captain Ahsan to surrender, to avoid unnecessary bloodshed. The messenger was despatched with a curt reply. It was sheer dogged determination that prompted this bold reply; Ahsan had nothing in store to support it with. The following night, the Kamalpur border outpost fell to the enemy.

Almost simultaneously the troops were withdrawn from the Naqshi and Baromari posts. Lieutenant-Colonel Sultan organized his new defences round Sherpur, north of the Brahmaputra. The new defence line ran through Janaigati, Kurea, Sherpur and Jagan Char. The neighbouring 33 Punjab could not remain unaffected by the withdrawal of 31 Baluch. So it too was brought back to Surcha ferry, almost in line with Sherpur, both of which had been developed as 'strong points'.

On 5 December, the left flank of Sherpur defences came under pressure. The heaviest impact was on the Jagan Char position. The officer reported from there that the positions were likely to collapse for want of ammunition. A truck quickly moved out with the necessary supplies. It had hardly reached a 'T' junction, south-west of Sherpur, when it met the retreating defenders of Jagan Char. Major Fazle Akbar, second-in-command, rushed in with reinforcements and organized new defences ahead of the 'T' junction. It was already evening by now. When it came to digging fresh trenches, the troops announced that they had no digging tools with them. On request, patriotic Bengalis came out from the neighbouring *baris* (thatched huts) with their implements and helped dig the trenches for the salvation of Pakistan.

Brigadier Qadir was not happy at the long backward leaps of 31 Baluch. He did not even approve of the Sherpur defences, so far from the borders, abandoning Bakshiganj without a fight. Now, he was displeased at the withdrawal of our troops from Jagan Char. He therefore ordered Lieutenant-Colonel Sultan to recapture the Char by attacking it from the Kurea side. But Sultan, unable to carry out this order, withdrew to Jamalpur on 6 December. It forced Brigadier Qadir to order 33 Punjab to step back to Mymensingh. As mentioned, earlier Jamalpur–Mymensingh was our last defensive line in this sector.

Enemy aircraft and artillery bombed and shelled the Jamalpur fortress on 7 December but did not cause much damage. The same day, the enemy troops reached the northern side of the river, forcing us to withdraw our forward post across the water obstacle. At about midday, the enemy commander was seen with his 'O' group (senior officers) opposite Jamalpur but he was out of range of our weapons. Later, in the same area, the commander of 101 Communication Zone stepped on a mine. He was replaced by Major-General Nagra.

For the next three days, we held Jamalpur and Mymensingh, the two strong shoulders of this defence line. The enemy could not roll south towards Dacca without neutralizing these fortresses. He would have to commit about a brigade each to invest Jamalpur and Mymensingh, which would not leave him with enough spare troops to force his way to Dacca. While these fortresses held fast Dacca was therefore thought to be safe from the north.

It was during this period that Brigadier Klere of the Indian Army sent a letter to Lieutenant-Colonel Sultan asking him to surrender. Sultan gave him a soldier's reply, enclosing a bullet in his letter. He asked him to 'give up the pen, take up the sten and fight it out'. This confident reply showed that all was well in the Jamalpur fortress. But something went wrong in Dacca which forced Major-General Jamshed to order 93 Brigade to give up the 'Line of No Penetration' and redeploy at Kaliakair on the outer perimeter of the Dacca defences. We will discuss General Jamshed's compulsions in the next chapter.

Brigadier Qadir received the withdrawal order on 10 December. He was not prepared for it. He tried to contact his G.O.C. to cancel this order but he could not. Every time he rang up Dacca, some staff officer told him, 'General Jamshed is in conference with General Niazi.' On the other hand every hour or so a phone call from Dacca checked up whether the brigade had commenced its withdrawal or not.

Brigadier Qadir passed the withdrawal orders to the battalions after last light on 10 December. They were asked to assemble at Madhupur road junction, south of Jamalpur. A company of 33 Punjab was sent in advance to establish a base there.

The Mymensingh garrison, which included a large number of E.P.C.A.F. personnel, Razakars, Rangers, West Pakistani families and patriotic Bengalis, left the fortress at 2100 hours the same night. Everybody was keen to be first out and boarded any vehicle that came along. Some civilians even stuffed the commandeered vehicles with their bedding, tin boxes, cots and goats. The Bengali drivers of private vehicles concocted various excuses to avoid transporting this load to safety—if safety there was, anywhere in East Pakistan!

33 Punjab, with hundreds of fleeing men and women, reached Madhupur junction without encountering any resistance on the way, but the story of 31 Baluch was different. When Jamalpur garrison prepared to leave, it discovered that the enemy had cut it off from all sides. Lieutenant-Colonel Sultan decided to fight his way out. He divided his command into two groups. The first group consisting of two companies was to break the encirclement, while the second was to follow with rear-guard troops, casualties and administration vehicles.

The first group, led by Lieutenant-Colonel Sultan, left Jamalpur at about 2300 hours. Soon it was entangled with the enemy. A fierce battle took place, but the losses were mostly on our side because we were caught in the open. About thirty soldiers were killed and twenty-five wounded. The enemy casualties could not be ascertained. Colonel Sultan's force disintegrated and withdrew in small parties. The second group also failed to break out of the encirclement though some did manage to trickle out through the gaps. The remainder surrendered to the enemy next day. The doctors with the sick and wounded stayed in the fortress, waiting for their captors.

So the two battalions failed to regroup at Madhupur junction as scheduled. Again, brigade headquarters could not reorganize the scattered elements into a viable force. In fact, when Brigadier Qadir and his staff did not find 31 Baluch at the appointed junction, they made their way to Tangail, leaving behind Major Sarwar's infantry company and Major E.G. Shah's mortars to receive the withdrawing troops.

Brigadier Qadir and his companions reached Tangail on the morning of 11 December.

While Brigadier Qadir and others rested in Tangail, Lieutenant-Colonel Akbar of E.P.C.A.F. continued his journey towards Dacca. He had hardly gone two or three kilometres when he saw the after-effects of a mine explosion. Lieutenant-Colonel Akbar described the sight to me later: 'A vehicle lay overturned on the edge of the road while the wounded driver pulsated on the blood-soaked dust. A little to the left was sitting twice-decorated Lieutenant-Colonel Sultan, completely shaken and dispirited. By chance, a straggler belonging to 31 Baluch passed by. Seeing his commanding officer for the first time after the Jamalpur mishap, he beamed up and gave a smart salute to Sultan who impulsively cried out,

"Where are my troops? Where is my battalion?" The straggler had no reply to offer, so he gave another smart salute and walked off. I brought Sultan back to Tangail.'

Akbar and Sultan told the brigade commander about the mine incident. It was taken as an indication that the Tangail - Dacca road was mined. In fact it was not, because many stragglers, as well as Indians, frequently used it thereafter. Brigadier Qadir debated various possibilities. Should the mines be cleared? Should he stay at Tangail?

It was now afternoon. Brigadier Qadir and a few others stood on the verandah of the white Circuit House waiting for some bright idea to come. What came instead were enemy aircraft, which started dropping men and machines in the Kalihati area, about nine kilometres north of Tangail. When they looked southward, they found more transport planes dropping their loads in the general area of the abandoned Tangail airstrip. As a piece of equipment descended beneath its parachute, an officer exclaimed, 'My God! That looks like a 3.7-inch gun!'

This development naturally irked Brigadier Qadir, who gallantly drew out his stengun and emptied one magazine in the general direction of the parachute landing. That was his way of expressing his anger. He followed it up by ordering Major Sarwar to take his company (minus) and 'neutralize the enemy. Sarwar obeyed the orders but returned within half an hour to report, 'Sir, the locals say they are Chinese.'

Although the 'news' tallied with the wishful thinking of all Pakistani soldiers, it was too good to believe. How could they land without any prior co-ordination with the Pakistani commanders? After an initial flurry of hope, Brigadier Qadir reverted to reality. He knew that Tangail had no defences. He also knew that his brigade had lost its cohesion and identity. 'Moreover, the mission given to me is to reach Kaliakair rather than organize the Tangail defences,' he said and decided to resume the withdrawal. He had a company of regular troops and Rangers, six hundred E.P.C.A.F. and police personnel and half a dozen officers. They all left Tangail for ever at about 1745 hours. The Pakistan flag on the Circuit House was left fluttering alone till it was pulled down later to make room for the Bangla Desh flag.

Meanwhile, elements of 93 Brigade, withdrawing from Madhupur towards Tangail, received small arms fire near Kalihati probably from the Indian paratroops and their local collaborators. Instead of trying to brush off this temporary resistance, our troops decided to avoid a confrontation. Some of them turned back while others decided to leave the road and walk through the country-side.

When Brigadier Qadir and his party reached the scene of the earlier mine explosion, they also heard some rifle shots and decided to leave the road and cover the one hundred and fifty kilometres to Kaliakair on foot through the fields. Since this large body of men was likely to be detected by the Mukti Bahini on the way, it was split into three groups. Brigadier Qadir kept eight officers and eighteen men with him while Lieutenant-Colonel Sultan took a few more under his wing. Those who found themselves under no one, made their way to Dacca on their own.

Brigadier Qadir and twenty-six others took three days and four nights to reach Kaliakair. Avoiding the hazards of terrain and terrorists, they walked through mud and slush, shivered at night and starved during the day. They had some money but nobody would sell them any food. Only once during this trying period did they meet a God-fearing man who allowed them to drink water from his earthen pitcher, otherwise they had to live on stolen vegetables and dirty pond water. At a crucial stage of this journey, they chewed wild leaves to draw sustenance and licked dewdrops to moisten their tongues. On the third day, when they lay exhausted in a humid jungle an officer plucked a leafy branch and, presenting it to Brigadier Qadir, said, 'Sir, chew it slowly. It kills thirst. I have tried it.'

On the morning of 14 December, they reached the Tangail road again, north of Kaliakair. During the time that they had fought against hunger and thirst and local terrorists, the enemy had occupied a major portion of the Tangail Dacca road. How far the enemy had gone on this road was not known. So Brigadier Qadir and others waited in a cluster of trees off the main road and a major went off to locate our own troops who were supposed to be in the Kaliakair area. He found none. Instead, he came across the enemy who took him prisoner and used him to track down the others. They soon came to the cluster of trees and took charge of Brigadier Qadir and his companions. That was the most prestigious bag for the enemy.

The disorganized 93 Brigade did not stop at Kaliakair. Its troops were practically leaderless and did not even know their new line of defence. They thought that safety lay in reaching Dacca at the earliest moment. Many of them arrived there on 13 and 14 December in very bad shape. I saw them arriving: they were unshaven, unwashed and even bootless. Their faces were starved, eyes sleepless and ankles swollen. They needed at least twenty-four hours to be able to participate in the defence of the provincial capital.

22

DACCA: THE LAST ACT

Mental fortifications in Dacca and physical defences on the border, seemed to hinge on each other. Fluctuations in one affected the fate of the other. If any other element had any significant influence it was the progress of war on the West Pakistan front. General Niazi, who literally flexed himself like a wrestler at the ill-founded news of our successes on the Lahore front on the second day of war, gradually lapsed into disillusionment by 7 December. At about the same time, the Indians occupied Jessore and Jhenida in 9 Division, ambushed the G.O.C. on 16 Division's main line of communication and stabbed the soft belly of 39 *ad hoc* Division between Comilla and Feni.

The same evening, General Niazi was summoned to the Governor's House to brief Dr. A.M. Malik on the war situation, because the latter was receiving contradictory reports. While General Niazi's Chief of Staff, Brigadier Baqar Siddiqi, reported gallant defence on all frontiers, panicky civil servants in the divisional and district headquarters telephoned the Governor about extensive damage to civilian life and property following army withdrawals. The Governor thought that the best way to discover the truth was to confer with General Niazi.

General Niazi's meeting with Governor Malik on the evening of 7 December was a very discomforting experience for him. Officially and publicly Niazi had maintained a posture which was not supported by the facts. Should he admit his set-backs to a civilian Governor as early as the fourth day of all-out war? Or, should he keep up a facade of defiance and fortitude? If he chose the latter course, how long would he be able to fool the Governor, the Government and the public?

Governor Malik, General Niazi and two other senior officers sat in a comfortable room at Government House. They did not talk much. Every few minutes, silence overtook the conversation. The Governor did most of the talking and that, too, in general terms.

The crux of his discourse was: things never remain the same. Good situations give way to bad situations and vice versa. Similarly, there are fluctuations in the career of a General. At one time, glory magnifies him while at another defeat demolishes his dignity. As Dr. Malik uttered the last part of his statement, the burly figure of General Niazi quaked and he broke into tears. He hid his face in his hands and started sobbing like a child. The Governor stretched out his elderly arm to General Niazi and, consoling him, said: 'I know, *General Sahib*, there are hard days in a commander's life. But don't lose heart. God is great.'

While General Niazi was sobbing, a Bengali waiter entered the room with a tray of coffee and snacks. He was immediately howled out as if he had desecrated the room. He came out and announced to his fellow Bengalis, 'The *Sahibs* are crying inside.' The remark was overheard by the West Pakistani Military Secretary to the Governor, who told the Bengalis to shut up.

That is how Governor Malik received the most truthful and convincing operational briefing on the war in East Pakistan. After the exchange of words for tears, he said to General Niazi, 'As the situation is bad, I think I should cable the President to arrange a cease-fire.' General Niazi kept quiet for a moment and then, with his head down, said weakly, 'I will obey.' The Governor sent a message to Yahya Khan accordingly. No action was, however, taken on this proposal.

General Niazi came back to his headquarters and shut himself in his room. He virtually lay in hibernation for the next three nights. During this period, I went to his room on the night of 8/9 December. Till then, I did not know about the Government House meeting. I saw him resting his head on his forearm, his face totally hidden from the entrant's view. I cannot say whether he was crying. I only remember the remark he made during the brief conversation. He said, 'Salik, thank your stars you are not a general today.' It showed his agony. I left but his words echoed in my ears the whole night and I pitied him.

Three days—7, 8 and 9 December—were very heavy for General Niazi. During this period, all the divisions lost their coherence. Many of them had been pushed even beyond the so called 'line of no penetration'. To make it worse, no gains had been made on the West Pakistan front to compensate for the losses suffered in East Pakistan. General Niazi had lost all his gaiety and had ceased to crack the jokes for which he was so famous. He saw very few people and looked agitated and withdrawn. His eyes showed visible signs of sleeplessness. The strain of responsibility obviously weighed heavy on him.

Meanwhile, All India Radio in particular and other foreign broadcasting stations in general put out exaggerated stories of our reverses. Our own Radio Pakistan tried to beat them by broadcasting equally exaggerated stories about our successes. Unfortunately the listeners, particularly Bengalis, had more faith in All India Radio and other stations than in Radio Pakistan.

During the same period, the British Broadcasting Corporation announced that General Niazi had flown to West Pakistan leaving his troops in the lurch. This directly affected his public image and he felt bitter about it. He made a surprise appearance at the Hotel Intercontinental on 10 December and said to the first man he saw in the lounge, 'Where is the BBC man? I want to tell him that, by the grace of God Almighty, I am still in East Pakistan. I never leave my troops.' After this declaration, he returned to his headquarters.

General Niazi's presence in Dacca, however, failed to reinforce the foreigners' confidence in his ability to control the situation. They were keen to jump out of the sinking ship. The United Nations arranged an airlift for them on 8 December but the runway was still cratered and the Indian Air Force attacked the airfield at least three times a day. After arranging with the Indian and Pakistani authorities, they were able to leave East Pakistan a few days later.

The feeling of uncertainty and insecurity was not confined to fleeing foreigners or beleagured civilians, it also stole into some army officers' hearts. Two of them, wearing a substantial quantity of brass on their shoulders, came to me and said, 'You have access to General Niazi. Why don't you tell him to be realistic, otherwise all of us will die a dog's death?' I parried the suggestion saying that it was too much for a press officer to influence a Corps Commander's decision on as sensitive an issue as the war. I did not speak to General Niazi.

On the night of 8/9 December, I came across Major-General Rao Farman Ali near the perimeter wall of General Niazi's tactical headquarters. I told him about the feelings of these officers. He said, 'Yes, the Governor is also concerned. But Commander, Eastern Command has some reservations. Nevertheless, we will do something about it.'

Next day, the Governor sent a signal to the President which, *inter alia*, said, 'Once again [I] urge you to consider an immediate cease-fire and political settlement.' Yahya Khan again ignored it because his man on the spot for authentic military reports was General Niazi. As long as he was confident, there was no need to seek political crutches. It was only on the morning of 9 December that Headquarters, Eastern Command for the first time admitted that the situation was 'extremely critical'. A signal to the following effect was sent:

One: regrouping readjustment is not possible due to enemy mastery of skies. population getting extremely hostile and providing all out help to enemy. no move possible during night due intensive rebel ambushes. rebels guiding enemy through gaps and to rear. airfield damaged extensively, no mission last three days and not possible in future. even extrication most difficult. Two: extensive damage to heavy weapons and equipment due enemy air action. troops fighting extremely well but stress and strain now telling hard. NOT slept for last 20 days. are under constant fire air artillery and tanks. Three: situation extremely critical. we will go on fighting and do our best. Four: request following immediate strike all enemy air bases this theatre. if possible reinforcements airborne troops for protection Dacca.

General Niazi's telegram confirmed Governor Malik's apprehensions. So President Yahya Khan took stock of the situation and delegated authority to the Provincial Governor to take the necessary steps on his behalf. The main contents of the President's telegram sent the same night to the Governor and the Commander, Eastern Command were as follows:

From President to Governor repeated to Eastern Command. Your flash message received and thoroughly understood. You have my permission to take decision on your proposals to me. I have and am continuing to take all measures internationally but in view our complete isolation from each other decision about EAST PAK-ISTAN I leave entirely to your good sense and judgement. I will approve of any decision you take and I am instructing General Niazi to accept your decision and arrange things accordingly.

This signal was followed by another signal from General

Abdul Hamid Khan, Chief of Staff, Army, to General Niazi. It repeated the main points of the President's telegram and asked General Niazi to give his frank assessment of the operational situation to the Governor to enable him to take the correct decision. Hamid also advised him to 'destroy maximum equipment so that it does not fall into enemy hands.' General Hamid's telegram, sent early on 10 December, conveyed the following message:

For Comd from COS Army. President's signal message to Governor copy to you refers. President has left the decision to the Governor in close consultation with you. as no signal can correctly convey the degree of seriousness of the situation I can only leave it to you to take the correct decision on the spot. it is however apparent that it is now only a question of time before the enemy with its great superiority in numbers and material and the active co-operation of rebels will dominate East Pakistan completely. meanwhile a lot of damage is being done to the civil population and the Army is suffering heavy casualties. you will have to assess the value of fighting on if you can. based on this you should give your frank advice to the Governor who will give his final decision as delegated to him by the President. whenever you feel it is necessary to do so you should attempt to destroy maximum military equipment so that it does not fall into enemy hands. keep me informed. Allah bless you.

Now that the decision-making authority had been delegated to Governor A.M. Malik, what steps could he take to save the situation? He had not many options open to him. If General Niazi had been able to continue fighting, there would have been no need for the above exchange of telegrams. If Niazi had lost his spirit there was little the Governor could do to bolster his falling morale. Dr. A.M. Malik, therefore, thought of obtaining a ceasefire to bring about a political settlement which would include the installation of a government run by the people's elected representatives, and withdrawal of Indian and Pakistani forces from East Pakistan. The intermediary chosen for the purpose was Mr. Paul Mark Henry, Assistant Secretary-General of the United Nations, who was then in Dacca.

Major-General Farman Ali, Adviser to the Governor, and Mr. Muzaffar Hussain, Chief Secretary, were with the Governor when the note was handed over to Mr. Henry. The President was informed accordingly, in a signal from Dr. Malik on 10 December:

For President of Pakistan. As the responsibility of taking the final and fateful decision has been given to me I am handing over the following note to Assistant Secretary-General Mr. Paul Mark Henry after your approval. Note begins: It was never the intention of the Armed Forces of Pakistan to involve themselves in all-out war on the soil of East Pakistan. However a situation arose which compelled the Armed Forces to take defensive action. The intention of the Government of Pakistan was always to decide the issues in East Pakistan by means of a political solution for which negotiations were afoot. The Armed Forces have fought heroically against heavy odds and can still continue to do so but in order to avoid further bloodshed and loss of innocent lives I am making the following proposals. As the conflict arose as a result of political causes it must end with a political solution. I therefore having been authorised by the President of Pakistan do hereby call upon the elected representatives of East Pakistan to arrange for the peaceful formation of the government in Dacca. In making this offer I feel duty bound to say the will of the people of East Pakistan would demand the immediate vacation of their land by the Indian forces as well. I therefore call upon the United Nations to arrange for a peaceful transfer of power and request. One: An immediate cease-fire. Two: Repatriation with honour of the Armed Forces of Pakistan to West Pakistan. Three: Repatriation of all West Pakistan personnel desirous of returning to West Pakistan. Four: The safety of all persons settled in East Pakistan since 1947. Five: Guarantee of no reprisals against any person in East Pakistan. In making this offer, I want to make it clear that this is a definite proposal for peaceful transfer of power. The question of surrender of Armed Forces would not be considered and does not arise and if this proposal is not accepted the Armed Forces will continue to fight to the last man. Note ends. General Niazi has been consulted and submits himself to your command.

Once the cease-fire proposal was before the United Nations, it could not be kept secret from the world. Some important foreign stations broadcast its contents. It at once weakened Pakistan's case at the United Nations where Mr. Z.A. Bhutto, Deputy Prime Minister (designate) was pleading our case to obtain a favourable decision. Consequently, a Government spokesman in

Rawalpindi denied outright the cease-fire proposal, at a press conference on 13 December. He said, 'I would like to challenge anybody to produce a document or statement in which even the idea of surrender has been suggested.'[1] Dacca was also informed that 'your proposals have gone too far' and that 'you were expected to take the decision within the framework of a united Pakistan.'

Major-General Farman Ali, generally considered to be the author of these proposals, told me later that the step aimed at nothing but obtaining a cease-fire 'to allow our commanders to reorganize their forces and regain their poise. What we meant by a government of the people's elected representatives,' he said, 'was that all those available pro-Pakistani Bengali M.N.A.s and M.P.A.s who were elected in the general elections of December 1970, or subsequent by elections, would be installed in power. If India treated it as a betrayal and resumed hostilities, we would have faced her with renewed energies.'

Irrespective of the main purport of these proposals, their rebuttal by a government spokesman in Rawalpindi froze the cease-fire issue for the time being. Perhaps, Yahya Khan wanted to allow Mr. Bhutto more time to try his diplomatic skill at the world body.

Rawalpindi invented a novel way of diverting Niazi's attention from cease-fire proposals and bolstering his morale. He was told that 'moral and material support' was being obtained from outside—specifically, that 'yellow from the north and white from the south' were going to intervene on the side of Pakistan. Dacca interpreted this as a clear indication of Chinese and American help, to neutralize Soviet support for India. This 'good news' was allowed to spread to the troops, who were under great pressure in all sectors. The leak was intended to reinforce their flagging spirits. The withdrawing 93 Brigade (under Brigadier Qadir) cherished the same illusion when it saw an Indian paratroop drop near Tangail. About the same time, I saw a batman glued to his two-band transistor radio in Tactical Headquarters in Dacca. When I passed by him, he stood up and, adjusting his crumpled beret, saluted me. 'What is the news?' I asked him casually. He replied coldly, 'There is no news about Chinese or American help.'

This Rawalpindi hoax had some temporary effect. The soldiers looked to the skies (for Chinese) and the seas (for Americans) and tried to buy time for these friends to reach them. But no one came.

[1] The *Pakistan Times*, Rawalpindi, 14 December 1971.

Headquarters, Eastern Command, impatiently rang up important sources in Rawalpindi to know the latest about the friendly intervention. Everybody said it was going to happen 'soon'. When forty-eight crucial hours had ticked by without any positive development, yet another phone call was made to Rawalpindi. G.H.Q. again said 'soon' in reply. A disgruntled staff officer overhearing the conversation said, 'Ask them how *soon* is their "soon".'

The Chinese and American diplomatic heads in Dacca were also contacted separately. They expressed their ignorance of any such move by their home governments. General Niazi himself was most reluctant to talk to General Yahya or General Hamid about this rumour. Finally, Eastern Command asked Rawalpindi, 'Tell us definitely how long have we to wait for "friends"?' 'For thirty-six hours more' was the reply. The new deadline was set for the evening of 12 December.

Meanwhile, the operational situation had deteriorated further. 57 Brigade of 9 Division had crossed over the Hardinge Bridge. 16 Division had been decisively cut in two. 14 Division had been confined to Sylhet and Bhairab Bazar. 39 *ad hoc* Divisional Headquarters had ceased to exist. The solitary brigade of 36 *ad hoc* Division disintegrated while withdrawing to Dacca. All divisional sectors were split into subsectors allowing adequate gaps for the enemy to funnel fresh troops through for the capture of Dacca.

However, viewed objectively, the enemy was still outside the 'Dacca bowl'. He had only a heliborne company in Narsingdi and a para battalion in the Tangail area. These two isolated forces could not pose a serious threat to the provincial capital, unless they were joined by ground columns from across the Meghna, Brahmaputra (Jamuna) or Ganges (Padma). India had to bring up additional troops from home territory, construct bridges on the rivers or raise a great number of river-craft to transport tanks, artillery and other heavy equipment to the Dacca side. Besides negotiating these river obstacles, she had also to neutralize some of the important fortresses which still held out. Even by a conservative estimate, it would have taken India at least one week more to mass adequate forces for a *coup de grace*.

Eastern Command lost its nerve not because it faced any heavy concentration of enemy forces round Dacca. It shivered at the realization that Dacca had no regular troops to defend this 'lynch-pin'. I witnessed Brigadier Baqar's desperate pleadings with all formations to spare a brigade, or at least a battalion, for the defence of Dacca. He asked Brigadier Atif to give up the Comilla fortress and redeploy on the eastern side of Dacca, but Atif felt it unwise to withdraw from the safe sanctuary of his carefully prepared defences. Major-General Qazi was asked to withdraw from Bhairab Bazar but he could not 'for lack of adequate riverine transport'. Major-General Nazar Hussain Shah was requested to send 57 Brigade (originally from 9 Division) but he did not. He did despatch a battalion but it failed to cross the Jamuna.

It was in this state of helplessness that Major-General Jamshed ordered 93 Brigade to pull back from the Jamalpur–Mymensingh axis and redeploy on the northern perimeter of Dacca. He avoided talking on the telephone with Brigadier Qadir lest he, too, should find some excuse to disobey the orders. Brigadier Qadir is the only commander who complied with the wishes of his superior, but his forces disintegrated on the way.

Although the situation on the ground was deteriorating fast, General Niazi, still convinced by the promises of foreign help, maintained a bold posture. He drove out of his headquarters on 11 December to visit the local combined military hospital and the anti-aircraft defences at Dacca airport. I was with him. At the hospital, he was presented half a dozen West Pakistani nurses who pleaded for protection against the 'barbaric Mukti Bahini'. He told them not to worry because big help was on the way. If the help did not come, he said, 'We ourselves would kill you before you fall into *Mukti* hands.'

From there, he drove to the airfield area and inspected a few gun positions. He gave the boys a word of cheer but said, 'Take care of the dead ground in front of your position. Keep your personal weapons ready.' As he turned back towards the cantonment, he saw a sizeable crowd of foreigners outside Dacca airport waiting for an airlift to Bangkok. He thought it a fit opportunity to 'show up' there to contradict rumours of his desertion. The journalists among the crowd bombarded him with searching questions. His answers were snappy, bitter and evasive. Some of the questions and answers ran as follows:

Q. India claims that her forces are at the doors of Dacca. How far away are they?

A. Go and find out for yourself.

Q. What are your further plans?

A. I will fight to the last man, last round.

Q. Have you sufficient force to keep the Indians away from Dacca?

A. Dacca will fall only over my dead body. They will have to drive a tank over this [indicating his chest].

The spate of questions continued unabated. Answering some, parrying others, he staged a quick retreat and whisked off to his underground headquarters.

I saw a slight change in General Niazi's mood during this hopeful spell of 10 to 13 December. He was still tense, but not completely broken. His jokes were extinct, but so were his sobs. He manfully checked his aberrations and maintained fairly good control over himself. The promise of foreign help, though empty, had had its effect.

The change in Niazi's mood had, however, no effect on the operational situation. It continued to deteriorate. By 10 December, the writing on the wall was so clear that Major-General Jamshed started exercising his duties as the defender of Dacca. General Niazi was thus relegated further to the background.

An operational map of Dacca and its outskirts was pinned on the western wall of the operations room. Jamshed held a conference there to organize a two-layer defence of Dacca. His deputy, Brigadier Bashir Ahmed, drew oval figures round Dacca to indicate new defences. The markings looked very impressive on the map. They were like curled up cobras who, it appeared, would sting the enemy to death if he dared touch them.

According to the paper arrangements, Dacca was to have outer and inner perimeters of defence. The external layer, or the covering troops, were to be in the line of Manekganj in the north-west, Kaliakair in the north, Narayanganj in the north-east, Daudkandi in the east and Munshiganj in the south-east. It was hoped that 93 Brigade (Mymensingh), 27 Brigade (Bhairab Bazar), 117 Brigade (Comilla) and 39 *ad hoc* Division (Chandpur) would fall back on Kaliakair, Narsingdi, Daudkandi and Munshiganj respectively. This hope, however, never materialized. The inner defences were to run along Mirpur Bridge, Tongi, Demra and Narayanganj. Colonel Fazle Hamid, Brigadier Qasim and Brigadier Mansoor were made responsible for these western, northern and eastern approaches to Dacca, while Brigadier Bashir was to look after the main city.

As there was no organized force in Dacca, efforts were made to collect scattered elements to fill the positions marked on the map. Another conference was held and representatives of various arms, services and paramilitary forces were asked to indicate the strength of their available troops. The total manpower representing infantry, engineers, ordnance, signals, electrical and mechanical engineers and army service corps came to about twelve companies. About 1,500 E.P.C.A.F, 1,800 policemen and 300 loyal Razakars (Al-Badr) were added to them. The grand total came to about 5,000. Surplus staff officers were pulled out from various offices to command this hotchpotch.

Most of these men had .303 rifles. To give them additional fire-power, one squadron of tanks, three mortars (3-inch), four recoilless rifles, two six-pounder guns and a few light machine-guns were collected from different sources and distributed to various axes. These 'heavy weapons' were generally deployed on the Kaliakair–Tongi axis as the Indian Para Brigade was likely to attack from this side. There was no shortage of ammunition, except for the armour and artillery.

The deployment of men and weapons may look impressive on paper but on the ground the situation was pretty bleak. The troops were demoralized, weapons antiquated, inaccurate or ineffective. The worst was that they had no will to fight. They stood in their places like dummies, ready to collapse at the slightest push.

On 13 December, a brigadier in charge of the northern sector took me towards Tongi to show his impregnable arrangements. 'Look, this cut on the metalled road is for the mines.' 'That muzzle in the dip is our gun position. Our RR's are there on this side of the Tongi–Dacca road. Tanks are further up near that cluster of trees.' Then we stepped down from the jeep to have a closer look at them. The recoilless rifles were deployed, but wrong ammunition had been issued for them. Mortars had 'bombs' but no 'sights'. One gun had been knocked out by enemy planes while the second waited for similar treatment. Only the machine-guns had both men and ammunition.

'How do you feel?' the Brigadier asked a young major near Kurmitola airfield. 'I am all right but the troops here don't feel confident enough to stop a massive Indian attack with only one mortar and two machine-guns.' 'Don't be silly. Cheer them up. Wars are never won by weapons.'

Back in Eastern Command Headquarters, Brigadier Baqar Siddiqi talked of organizing street fighting in Dacca. But somebody pointed out, 'How can you organize street fighting in a city infested with a hostile population? You will be hounded, like stray dogs, by the Indians from one side and the Mukti Bahini from the other.' The idea was dropped.

Looking at the enemy potential and our own resources, the Dacca defences were like a house of cards. So far as street fighting is concerned, it was not a part of an over-all operational strategy. It came only as a brain-wave, signifying nothing. A drowning man futilely clutching at a straw.

23

SURRENDER

Major-General Rahim, who sustained minor injuries while fleeing from Chandpur, was convalescing at General Farman's residence after initial medical treatment. He lay in a secluded part of the house. Farman was with him. It was 12 December, the nineth day of all-out war. Their minds naturally turned to the most crucial subject of the day: Is Dacca defensible? They had a frank exchange of opinion. Rahim was convinced that cease-fire alone was the answer. Farman was surprised to hear this suggestion from Rahim, who had always advocated a prolonged and decisive war against India. He said with a tinge of irony, '*Bus daney moock gaey—itni jaldi.*' (Have you lost your nerve—so soon!) Rahim insisted that it was already too late.

During the discussion, Lieutenant-General Niazi and Major-General Jamshed entered the room to see the 'wounded General'. Rahim repeated the suggestion to Niazi, who showed no reaction. Till then the expectation of foreign help had not finally been extinguished. Avoiding the subject, Farman slipped into the adjoining room.

After spending some time with Rahim, General Niazi walked into Farman's room and said, 'Then send the signal to Rawalpindi.' It appeared that he had accepted General Rahim's advice, as he had always done in peace-time. General Niazi wanted Government House to send the cease-fire proposal to the President. Farman politely said that the requisite signal should go from Headquarters, Eastern Command but General Niazi insisted, 'No, it makes little difference whether the signal goes from here or from here. I have, in fact, some important work elsewhere, you send it from here.' Before Farman could say 'no' again, Chief Secretary Muzaffar Husain entered the room and, overhearing the conversation, said to Niazi, 'You are right. The signal can be sent from here.' That resolved the conflict.

What General Farman opposed was not the cease-fire propos
itself, but the authority to sponsor it. His earlier signal on th
same subject had been rejected by Rawalpindi—once bitten, twi
shy. General Niazi disappeared to attend to his 'urgent wor
while Muzaffar Husain drafted the historic note. It was seen h
Farman and submitted to the Governor who approved the ide
and sent it to the President the same evening (12 December). Th
note urged Yahya Khan 'to do everything possible to save th
innocent lives.'

Next day the Governor and his principal *aides* waited for orde
from Rawalpindi, but the President seemed too busy to take
decision. The following day (14 December), for which a high lev
meeting was fixed, three Indian MIGs attacked Government Hou
at 11.15 a.m. and ripped the massive roof of the main hall. Th
Governor rushed to the air-raid shelter and scribbled out his resign.
tion. Almost all the inmates of this seat of power survived the rai
except for some fishes in a decorative glass case. They restless
tossed on the hot rubble and breathed their last.

The Governor, his cabinet and West Pakistani civil servan
moved, on 14 December, to the Hotel Intercontinental, which ha
been converted into a 'Neutral Zone' by the International Re
Cross. The West Pakistani V.I.P.s included the Chief Secretar
the Inspector-General of Police, the Commissioner, Dacca Di
ision, Provincial Secretaries and a few others. They 'dissociate
themselves in writing from the Government of Pakistan in order t
gain admittance to the neutral zone, because anybody belongin
to a belligerent state was not entitled to Red Cross protection.

14 December was the last day of the East Pakistan Governmen
The debris of the Government and Government House were sca
tered. The enemy had only to neutralize General Niazi and h
disorganized forces to complete the Caesarian birth of Bang
Desh. By now General Niazi, too, had lost all hope of foreign hel
He slumped back into his earlier mood of despondency and hard
came out of his fortified cabin. He rode the chariot of time witho
controlling its speed or direction.

He therefore conveyed the factual position to the President (wh
was also Commander-in-Chief) and keenly waited for instruction
In my presence he rang up General Hamid at night (13/1
December) and said, 'Sir, I have sent certain proposals to the Presi
dent. Could you kindly see that some action is taken on them soon

The President of Pakistan and Chief Martial Law Administrator ound time from his multifarious engagements and ordered the Jovernor and General Niazi on the following day 'to take all ecessary measures to stop the fighting and preserve lives.' His nclassified signal to General Niazi said:

Jovernor's flash message to me refers. You have fought a heroic attle against overwhelming odds. The nation is proud of you nd the world full of admiration. I have done all that is humanly ossible to find an acceptable solution to the problem. You have ow reached a stage where further resistance is no longer humanly ossible nor will it serve any useful purpose. It will only lead to urther loss of lives and destruction. You should now take all ecessary measures to stop the fighting and preserve the lives of rmed forces personnel, all those from West Pakistan and all loyal lements. Meanwhile I have moved U.N. to urge India to stop ostilities in East Pakistan forthwith and to guarantee the safety f armed forces and all other people who may be the likely target f miscreants.

This important telegram originated from Rawalpindi at 1330 ours on 14 December and arrived in Dacca at 1530 hours (East akistan Standard Time).

What did the Presidential telegram signify? Did it mean 'surrender orders' for General Niazi, or could he continue fighting if he so esired? I leave it to the reader to construe the above telegram or himself and draw his own conclusion.

General Niazi, the same evening, decided to initiate the necessary teps to obtain a cease-fire. As an intermediary, he first thought of oviet and Chinese diplomats but finally chose Mr. Spivack, the J.S. Consul-General in Dacca. General Niazi asked Major-General arman Ali to accompany him to Mr. Spivack because he, as Adviser to the Governor, had been dealing with foreign diplomats. When they reached Mr. Spivack's office Farman waited in the nte-room while Niazi went in. Farman could overhear General Niazi's loud unsubtle overtures to win Spivack's sympathies. When he thought that the 'friendship' had been established, he sked the American Consul to negotiate cease-fire terms with the ndians for him. Mr. Spivack, spurning all sentimentality, said in matter of fact fashion, 'I cannot negotiate a cease fire on your ehalf. I can only send a message if you like.'

General Farman was called in to draft the message to the Indian Chief of Staff (Army), General Sam Manekshaw. He dictated a full-page note calling for an immediate cease-fire, provided the following were guaranteed: the safety of Pakistan Armed Forces and of paramilitary forces; the protection of the loyal civilian population against reprisals by Mukti Bahini; and the safety and medical care of the sick and wounded.

As soon as the draft was finalized, Mr. Spivack said, 'It will be transmitted in twenty minutes.' General Niazi and Farman returned to Eastern Command leaving Captain Niazi, the aide-de-camp to wait for the reply. He sat there till 10 p.m. but nothing happened. He was asked to check later, 'before going to bed' No reply was received during the night.

In fact, Mr. Spivack did not transmit the message to General (later Field-Marshal) Manekshaw. He sent it to Washington, where the U.S. Government tried to consult Yahya Khan before taking any action. But Yahya Khan was not available. He was drowning his sorrows somewhere. I learnt later that he had lost interest in the war as early as 3 December and never came to his office. His military secretary usually carried to him a map marked with the latest war situation. He, at times, looked at it and once commented: 'What can I do for East Pakistan?'

Manekshaw replied to the note on ·15 December saying .that the cease fire would be acceptable and the safety of the personnel mentioned in the note would be guaranteed provided the Pakistan Army 'surrenders to my advancing troops'. He also gave the radio frequency on which Calcutta, the seat of Indian Eastern Command, could be contacted for co-ordination of details.

Manekshaw's message was sent to Rawalpindi. The Chief of Staff of the Pakistan Army replied by the evening of 15 December saying, *inter alia*, 'Suggest you accept the cease-fire on these terms as they meet your requirements... However, it will be a local arrangement between two commanders. If it conflicts with the solution being sought at the United Nations, it will be held null and void.'

The temporary cease-fire was agreed from 5 p.m. on 15 December till 9 a.m. the following day. It was later extended to 3 p.m., 16 December, to allow more time to finalize cease-fire arrangements. While General Hamid 'suggested' to Niazi that he accept the cease-fire terms, the latter took it as 'approval' and asked his Chief of

Staff, Brigadier Baqar, to issue the necessary orders to the formations. A full-page signal commended the 'heroic fight' by the troops and asked the local commanders to contact their Indian counterparts to arrange the cease-fire. It did not say 'surrender' except in the following sentence, 'Unfortunately, it also involves the laying down of arms.'

It was already midnight (15/16 December) when the signal was sent out. About the same time, Lieutenant-Colonel Liaquat Bokhari, Officer Commanding, 4 Aviation Squadron, was summoned for his last briefing. He was told to fly out eight West Pakistani nurses and twenty-eight families, the same night, to Akyab (Burma) across the Chittagong Hill Tracts. Lieutenant-Colonel Liaquat received the orders with his usual calm, so often seen during the war. His helicopters, throughout the twelve days of all-out war, were the only means available to Eastern Command for the transport of men, ammunition and weapons to the worst hit areas. Their odyssey of valour is so inspiring that it cannot be summed up here.

Two helicopters left in the small hours of 16 December while the third flew in broad daylight. They carried Major-General Rahim Khan and a few others, but the nurses were left behind because they 'could not be collected in time' from their hostel. All the helicopters landed safely in Burma and the passengers eventually reached Karachi.

Back in Dacca, the fateful hour drew closer. When the enemy advancing from the Tangail side came near Tongi, he was received by our tank fire. Presuming that the Tongi–Dacca road was well defended, the Indians side-stepped to a neglected route towards Manekganj from where Colonel Fazle Hamid had retreated in haste as he had from Khulna on 6 December. The absence of Fazle Hamid's troops allowed the enemy free access to Dacca city from the north-west.

Brigadier Bashir, who was responsible for the defence of the Provincial Capital (excluding the cantonment), learnt on the evening of 15 December that the Manekganj–Dacca road was totally unprotected. He spent the first half of the night in gathering scattered elements of E.P.C.A.F., about a company strength, and pushed them under Major Salamat to Mirpur bridge, just outside the city. The commando troops of the Indian Army, who were told by the Mukti Bahini that the bridge was unguarded, drove to the city in the small hours of 16 December. By then Major Salamat's boys were in position and they blindly fired towards the approaching column. They claimed to have killed a few enemy troops and captured two Indian jeeps.

Major-General Nagra of 101 Communication Zone, who was following the advance commando troops, held back on the far side of the bridge and wrote a chit for Lieutenant-General Amir Abdullah Khan Niazi. It said: 'Dear Abdullah, I am at Mirpur Bridge. Send your representative.'

Major-General Jamshed, Major-General Farman and Rear-Admiral Shariff were with General Niazi when he received the note at about 9 a.m. Farman, who still stuck to the message for 'cease-fire negotiations', said 'Is he (Nagra) the negotiating team?' General Niazi did not comment. The obvious question was whether he was to be received or resisted. He was already on the threshold of Dacca.

Major-General Farman asked General Niazi, 'Have you any reserves?' Niazi again said nothing. Rear-Admiral Shariff, translating it in Punjabi, said: '*Kuj palley hai*'? (Have you anything in the kitty?) Niazi looked to Jamshed, the defender of Dacca, who shook his head sideways to signify 'nothing'. 'If that is the case, then go and do what he (Nagra) asks,' Farman and Shariff said almost simultaneously.

General Niazi sent Major-General Jamshed to receive Nagra. He asked our troops at Mirpur Bridge to respect the cease-fire and allow Nagra a peaceful passage. The Indian General entered Dacca with a handful of soldiers and a lot of pride. That was the virtual fall of Dacca. It fell quietly like a heart patient. Neither were its limbs chopped nor its body hacked. It just ceased to exist as an independent city. Stories about the fall of Singapore, Paris or Berlin were not repeated here.

Meanwhile, Tactical Headquarters of Eastern Command was wound up. All operational maps were removed. The main headquarters were dusted to receive the Indians because, as Brigadier Baqar said, 'It is better furnished.' The adjoining officers' mess was warned in advance to prepare additional food for the 'guests'. Baqar was very good at administration.

Slightly after midday, Brigadier Baqar went to the airport to receive his Indian counterpart, Major-General Jacob. Meanwhile Niazi entertained Nagra with his jokes. I apologize for not recording them here but none of them is printable!

Major-General Jacob brought the 'surrender deed' which General Niazi and his Chief of Staff preferred to call the 'draft cease-fire agreement.'[1] Jacob handed over the papers to Baqar, who placed them before Major-General Farman. General Farman objected to the clause pertaining to the 'Joint Command of India and Bangla Desh'. Jacob said, 'But this is how it has come from Delhi.' Colonel Khera of Indian military intelligence, who was standing on the side added, 'Oh, that is an internal matter between India and Bangla Desh. You are surrendering to the Indian Army only.' The document was passed on to Niazi who glanced through it without any comment and pushed it back, across the table, to Farman. Farman said, 'It is for the Commander to accept or reject it.' Niazi said nothing. This was taken to imply his acceptance.

In the early afternoon, General Niazi drove to Dacca airport to receive Lieutenant-General Jagjit Singh Aurora, Commander of Indian Eastern Command. He arrived with his wife by helicopter. A sizeable crowd of Bengalis rushed forward to garland their 'liberator' and his wife. Niazi gave him a military salute and shook hands. It was a touching sight. The victor and the vanquished stood in full view of the Bengalis, who made no secret of their extreme sentiments of love and hatred for Aurora and Niazi respectively.

Amidst shouts and slogans, they drove to Ramna Race Course (Suhrawardy Ground) where the stage was set for the surrender ceremony. The vast ground bubbled with emotional Bengali crowds. They were all keen to witness the public humiliation of a West Pakistani General. The occasion was also to formalize the birth of Bangla Desh.

A small contingent of the Pakistan Army was arrayed to present a guard of honour to the victor while a detachment of Indian soldiers guarded the vanquished. The surrender deed was signed by Lieutenant-General Aurora and Lieutenant-General Niazi in full view of nearly one million Bengalis and scores of foreign media men. Then they both stood up. General Niazi took out his revolver and handed it over to Aurora to mark the capitulation of Dacca. With that, he handed over East Pakistan!

The Dacca garrison was allowed to retain their personal weapons for self-protection against the Mukti Bahini till Indian troops were available, in sufficient numbers, to take over control. The garrison

[1] The full text of this document is given in Appendix IV.

surrendered formally on 19 December, at 11 a.m., at the golf course in the cantonment. The troops, outside Dacca, laid down their arms between 16 and 22 December on suitable dates arranged by the local commanders.

All India Radio had started broadcasting the news of impending surrender as early as 14 December. It panicked the non-Bengali population in Dacca and elsewhere. Most of them left their homes and moved to the cantonments to share the fate of Pakistani soldiers. Thousands of them were overtaken by the Mukti Bahini and put to death. I heard hair-raising stories of these atrocities. They were enough to chill the blood and are far too numerous to be catalogued here.

The Indians had no time to protect these innocent lives. They were busy removing the plunder of their victory to India. Large convoys of trains and trucks moved military hardware, foodstuffs, industrial produce and household goods, including refrigerators, carpets and television sets. The blood of Bangla Desh was sucked so thoroughly that only a skeleton remained to greet the dawn of 'independence'. One year later, this realization dawned on the Bengalis as well.

When the Indians had transferred what they could of Bangla Desh's wealth to their own territory, they started transferring Pakistani prisoners of war to Indian P.O.W. camps. The process continued till the end of January 1972. The V.I.Ps, including Lieutenant-General Niazi, Major-General Farman, Rear-Admiral Shariff and Air Commodore Inam-ul-Haq were, however, flown to Calcutta on 20 December. 1 accompanied them.

When I left Dacca airport for the last time at 1530 hours on 20 December, how different it was from January 1970 when I had first landed there! The khaki of the Pakistani soldiers had been replaced by the green uniform of the Indian Army. The Bengalis sat still on the fence, watching the developments with bewilderment. Perhaps they were flabbergasted at a change which may well augur a new and worse era of domination. Had they merely changed yokes?

Soon after our arrival at Fort William, Calcutta, I took the opportunity of discussing the war, in retrospect, with General Niazi, before he had had the time, or the need to reconstruct his war account for the enquiry commission in Pakistan. He talked frankly and bitterly. He showed no regrets or qualms of conscience. He refused to accept responsibility for the dismemberment of Pakistan and squarely blamed General Yahya Khan for it. Here are a few extracts from our conversation: 'Did you ever tell Yahya Khan or Hamid that the resources given to you were not adequate to fulfil the allotted mission,' I asked. 'Are they civilians? Dont' they know whether three infantry divisions are enough to defend East Pakistan against internal as well as external dangers?' 'Whatever the case, your inability to defend Dacca will remain a red mark against you as a theatre commander. Even if fortress defence was the only concept feasible under the circumstances, you did not develop Dacca as a fortress. It had no troops.' 'Rawalpindi is to blame. They promised me eight infantry battalions in mid-November but sent me only five. The remaining three had yet to arrive when the West Pakistan front was opened—without any prior notice to me. I wanted to keep the remaining three battalions in Dacca.' 'But when you knew on 3 December that nothing more could come from West Pakistan, why didn't you create reserves from your own resources?' 'Because all sectors had come under pressure simultaneously. Troops everywhere were committed. Nothing could be spared.' 'With what little you had in Dacca you could have prolonged the war for a few days more,' I suggested. 'What for?' he replied. 'That would have resulted in further death and destruction. Dacca drains would have choked. Corpses would have piled up in the streets. Civic facilities would have collapsed. Plague and other diseases would have spread. Yet the end would have been the same. I will take 90,000 prisoners of war to West Pakistan rather than face 90,000 widows and half a million orphans there. The sacrifice was not worth it.' 'The end would have been the same. But the history of the Pakistan Army would have been different. It would have written an inspiring chapter in the annals of military operations.' General Niazi did not reply.

CHRONOLOGY OF EVENTS

14 August 1947
The Indian Subcontinent was partitioned. The Sovereign Dominion States of (Hindu) India and (Muslim) Pakistan came into being. Pakistan comprised two Muslim majority regions in the north-west and north-east of India. The north-eastern region comprised East Bengal while the north-western part consisted of Sind, Baluchistan, the North-West Frontier Province and part of the Punjab. Hindus who, as the majority community in undivided India, aspired to be the sole inheritors of power after the departure of the British, did not like the creation of Pakistan. A prominent Hindu leader, Gandhi, termed the partition 'a vivisection of the sacred cow'; while the Hindu Mahasabha said, 'India is one and indivisible and there will never be peace until and unless the separated areas are brought back into the Indian Union and made integrated parts thereof.'

27 October 1947
India sent troops to annex forcibly the Muslim majority State of Jammu and Kashmir. The Kashmiris, aided by Pakistani tribesmen, resisted. The Pakistan army, still in its embryonic stage joined the war in May 1948. The U.N. Security Council imposed a ceasefire on 1 January 1949, with the promise of holding a plebiscite to determine the wishes of the Kashmiris. The plebiscite was never held and the Kashmir issue has bedevilled Indo-Pakistan relations ever since. East Bengal, 1,600 kilometres away from Kashmir, was never as passionately involved in the issue as the western wing of Pakistan.

21 March 1948
Quaid-e-Azam, Mohammad Ali Jinnah, the founder of Pakistan and its first Governor-General, while on a visit to East Bengal, declared in Dacca that Urdu would be the only state language of Pakistan. The remark evoked an angry protest from the Bengali youth who took it as an affront: their language Bangla (Bengali)

was, after all, spoken by fifty-four per cent of the population of Pakistan. Sheikh Mujibur Rehman, then a university student, was among those who raised the protest slogan and was placed under detention. The Dacca University campus became the focal point for student meetings in support of the *Bangla* language.

11 September 1948

The Quaid-e-Azam died. Khwaja Nazim-ud-Din, the Bengali Chief Minister of East Bengal, succeeded him as Governor-General. Mr. Liaquat Ali Khan, a close confidant of the Quaid-e-Azam, continued as Prime Minister of the grief-stricken country.

March–April 1949

Maulana Abdul Hamid Khan Bhashani, a prominent Bengali leader, founded the Awami Muslim League at Narayanganj (Dacca). Sheikh Mujibur Rehman became one of its three Assistant General Secretaries. The party drew its strength from the Bengali enthusiasts and the disgruntled old politicians who received no share of power in the independent country. In September, another party with the same name was formed by Pir Manki Sharif in the North-West Frontier Province. In February 1950, the two Leagues were integrated. A popular Bengali leader H.S. Suhrawardy became the president of this new party, called the Pakistan Awami Muslim League.

16 October 1951

Mr. Liaquat Ali Khan was assassinated while addressing a public meeting in Rawalpindi. Khwaja Nazim-ud-Din stepped down to take his place as the Prime Minister. Mr. Ghulam Mohammad, a career government servant, intrigued successfully to occupy the vacant seat at the top.

26 January 1952

The Basic Principles Committee of the Constituent Assembly of Pakistan announced its recommendations which, *inter alia*, said that Urdu should be the only state language. It sparked off a wide wave of resentment in East Bengal.

30 January 1952

Bengalis held protest meetings in Dacca against the latest move 'to dominate the majority province of East Bengal linguistically and culturally.' The provincial chief of the Awami Muslim League, Maulana Bhashani, also addressed these meetings. It was decided to hold a general strike on 21 February, when the East Bengal Assembly was due to meet for its budget session.

21 February 1952
A general strike was observed and the procession taken out, despite the official ban imposed by Mr. Nurul Amin's administration. The students clashed with the police and three students and a number of other people were killed. *Shaheed Minars* (Memorials) were raised to commemorate their sacrifice. Later, these memorials became the rallying symbol for the Bengalis and a place of pilgrimage for provincial governors and diplomats.

17 April 1953
Governor-General Ghulam Mohammad dismissed Khwaja Nazim-ud-Din's ministry, without giving it a chance to face the national parliament. This further angered the Bengalis who regarded it a 'conspiracy against Bengalis'. Ghulam Mohammad quickly recalled Mr. Mohammad Ali Bogra, another Bengali, from his ambassadorial assignment in Washington, and installed him as Prime Minister. Mr. Bogra had no power base in East Bengal, he therefore played into the hands of his Punjabi patron, Ghulam Mohammad.

April 1953
The Awami Muslim League dropped the word 'Muslim' from its title to reflect its true secular character. The old Muslim Leaguers resigned from it and their seats were filled by moneyed Hindu politicians who later influenced its policies immensely.

September 1953
Maulvi Fazlul Haq, the 'Lion of Bengal', who had moved the Pakistan Resolution on 23 March 1940, formed his own political party in Dacca. It was called the Krishak Sramik Party (the labour peasant party). The founding and growth of the Awami League and the K.S.P. in East Bengal, on the one hand, showed the dissatisfaction with the ruling Muslim League and, on the other, reflected the emergence of secular politics in the province.

8 - 11 March 1954
Elections were held for the East Bengal Legislative Assembly—for the first time since independence. The East Bengal parties, Awami League, K.S.P. and others formed the United Front to oppose the ruling Muslim League. The first item on the twenty-one point manifesto of the Front was the recognition of Bangla as a state

language of Pakistan. Another important point was the demand
for provincial autonomy. The Muslim League won only 9 seats
in a house of 310 and Chief Minister Nurul Amin was defeated by
a student nominee of the Front.

30 March 1954
The United Front was called upon to form the government. Three
days later, the new government was sworn in, with Sheikh Mujibur
Rehman as one of the Provincial Ministers.

30 May 1954
The United Front government was dismissed by the Governor-
General because of allegedly seditious statements made by Chief
Minister Fazlul Haque, at Calcutta airport a few days earlier.
Sheikh Mujibur Rehman was also detained. Governor's Rule was
imposed in the province. The United Front distintegrated. The
Centre tried to woo the Awami League and K.S.P. separately in
pursuance of its own interests.

24 October 1954
Governor-General Ghulam Mohammad dissolved the Constituent Assembly. The new Government, without a parliament, was
formed by Mohammad Ali Bogra, with the Army Commander-
in-Chief, General Mohammad Ayub Khan, as its Defence Minister.

15 April 1955
The new eighty-member Constituent Assembly was created by
drawing members from the Provincial legislatures. The Awami
League and K.S.P. sent their nominees—a new element in the
national politics.

June 1955
Governor's Rule in East Bengal was lifted. K.S.P., which co-
operated with the Muslim League in the capital, formed the
government in Dacca. The Awami League sat in opposition.

6 August 1955
Mr. Ghulam Mohammad, an ailing intriguer finally quitted. Mr.
Iskander Mirza, a non-political crafty fellow, was sworn in
as Governor-General on 7 September. He installed Chaudhry
Mohammad Ali, a nominee of the Muslim League, as the Prime
Minister, although H.S. Suhrawardy, as the leader of the Awami
League, claimed the right to form a government. The Bengalis trea-
ted it as yet another conspiracy to deny political power to the
Bengalis.

7 September 1955
Mr. Ataur Rehman Khan of the Awami League said in the East Bengal Legislative Assembly: 'The attitude of the Muslim League coterie here was of contempt towards East Bengal, towards its culture, its language, its literature and everything concerning East Bengal. In fact, Sir, I tell you that, far from considering us an equal partner, the leaders of the Muslim League thought that we were a subject race and they belonged to the race of conquerors.'

14 October 1955
The west wing provinces of the Punjab, N.W.F.P., Baluchistan and Sind were grouped into One Unit called West Pakistan. The West Pakistan Bill had been passed, a fortnight earlier, to give a rational basis of equality between the two wings. East Bengal, the majority province, considered it a fresh move to deprive the Bengalis of their legitimate rights.

29 February 1956
The Constituent Assembly passed the country's first constitution with the relentless efforts of Chaudhry Mohammad Ali. It was enforced three weeks later (23 March). The Constitution placed the inter-wing relations on a 'principle of parity' i.e. equal representation in the Parliament. Pakistan became a Republic and the Governor-General, the President of Pakistan. Bangla was recognized as a state language, as well as Urdu.

20 August 1956
The K.S.P. Government which had, during the preceding fourteen months, survived in East Pakistan without ever facing the provincial legislature, was forced to resign. The Awami League, supported by a Hindu leader B.K. Das and his Congress Party, formed the government. Mr. Ataur Rehman became the Chief Minister.

12 September 1956
The Awami League President, Mr. H.S. Suhrawardy, formed the government at the Centre in place of Chaudhry Mohammad Ali who resigned (8 September). He was supported by the Republican Party, a new political force in the hands of President Iskander Mirza.

30 June 1957
Maulana Bhashani, the provincial chief of the Awami League, resigned as party President because of H.S. Suhrawardy's pro-West policies, including his support for the 'imperialists' on the

Suez issue, against the party manifesto.

26 July 1957

Maulana Bhashani, known for his pro-Peking feelings, formed the National Awami Party. It believed in secular politics but, unlike the Awami League, was supported by leftists.

12 October 1957

Mr. H.S. Suhrawardy was forced to resign by the withdrawal of Republican support. Mr. I.I. Chundrigar took his place but he too had to resign within two months. Mr. Feroz Khan Noon succeeded him in December.

18 June 1958

The Awami League coalition government was defeated in the East Pakistan Assembly. Mr. Ataur Rehman resigned. Two days later, K.S.P. formed the government but could hardly continue for three days. Once again, Governor's Rule was imposed.

26 August 1958

Governor's Rule was lifted and the Awami League formed the government in East Pakistan.

21 September 1958

The members of the East Pakistan Assembly, while in session fought with each other on the 'partiality' of the Speaker. Many members were seriously injured. Mr. Shahid Ali, the Deputy Speaker, was killed.

7 October 1958

With the support of General Mohammad Ayub Khan, President Iskander Mirza abrogated the Constitution, dissolved the Assembly and proclaimed Martial Law in the country. General Ayub Khan became the Chief Martial Law Administrator. This 'revolution' sealed the aspirations of the Bengalis who wanted to assert their political rights.

27 October 1958

General Ayub Khan removed President Iskander Mirza, despatched him to London and assumed all powers, taking the rank of Field Marshal. He started ruling East Pakistan with the help of hand-picked Governors. Since Bengalis had very little representation in the armed forces, they felt that they were excluded indefinitely from wielding political power. They were forced to look inwards. The repression of Martial Law nursed the feeling of provincialism.

26 October 1959
Ayub Khan introduced 'Basic Democracies', a new system of local bodies which was soon converted into an electoral college. Eighty thousand Basic Democrats were to elect the President and members of the Legislature. Bengalis and the vast majority of West Pakistanis considered it a thin political veneer to perpetuate one-man rule.

15 February 1960
Ayub Khan sought a vote of confidence from the eighty thousand Basic Democrats, 75,283 of them confirmed him in the office of the President. Two days later, Field Marshal Ayub Khan was sworn in as the first 'elected' President of Pakistan.

April 1960
Lieutenant-General Azam Khan was appointed Governor of East Pakistan. He worked hard to win the support of the Bengalis. He thereby lost the support of Ayub Khan and was made to resign.

8 June 1962
Ayub Khan gave his own Constitution to the country. Its principal features included a Presidential form of government based on the system of Basic Democracies. It retained the parity principle, with regard to the representation of the provinces in the National Assembly. The document did not enjoy popular support.

26 October 1962
Monem Khan, a Bengali, was appointed Governor of East Pakistan. He held the office till the fall of Ayub Khan in early 1969. His utmost loyalty to Ayub Khan became his greatest disqualification for the Bengalis, who hated him as an 'agent of the Punjabis'. The university graduates refused to receive their degrees from his hands.

29 May 1963
A Bengali member of the National Assembly, Mr. Mahbubul Haq, said on the floor of the House: 'East Pakistan contributed to the development of West Pakistan to the extent that, during the last fifteen years, East Pakistan has been drained out of one thousand crores of rupees of its solid assets by way of less imports and more exports. With that, Sir, West Pakistan was developed and these million acres have been created. These big people talk so loudly: "leave East Pakistan out, we can maintain ourselves..." Today is the sixteenth year we have been reduced to paupers to build West Pakistan; we are told "get out boys, we have nothing for you, we do not require you."'

2 January 1964
Presidential elections were held. Ayub Khan was opposed by Miss Fatima Jinnah, the sister of the *Quaid-e-Azam*. She was supported by all the opposition parties. Bengalis supported her whole-heartedly as they considered it an opportunity to dislodge a dictator, and open the way for the restoration of their political rights. Although Ayub Khan won the majority support of the eighty thousand Basic Democrats, he lost to Miss Jinnah in Dacca, the nerve-centre of East Pakistan politics, by 9.8 per cent of the votes.

6 September 1965
India and Pakistan went to war on the Kashmir issue once again. While it was a matter of life and death for West Pakistan, East Pakistan generally treated it as a conflict far from its threshold. Occasional visits by jets of the Indian Air Force to Dacca only heightened their sense of isolation and helplessness.

11 January 1966
Ayub Khan signed the Tashkent Declaration, which called for the withdrawal of troops by India and Pakistan. The people in West Pakistan, who believed they had won the war, treated it as a sellout. It weakened Ayub Khan's position considerably.

6 February 1966
Sheikh Mujibur Rehman announced his famous Six Points at Lahore. In essence, the Six Points advocated a political arrangement in which the Central Government was to deal with foreign affairs and defence, without powers of taxation. Mujib introduced the programme as a demand for provincial autonomy, while the people of West Pakistan considered it as a move for secession.

26 April 1967
Mr. Zulfikar Ali Bhutto resigned as Foreign Minister from Ayub Khan's Cabinet. He formed his own political party, the Pakistan People's Party, in December.

20 January 1968
The 'Agartala Conspiracy' was made public. It involved Sheikh Mujibur Rehman and twenty-two other Bengalis who allegedly wanted to separate East Pakistan and establish independent Bengal, with Indian assistance. When the trial started in July 1968, in Dacca, it evoked a totally unexpected Bengali reaction. While the prosecution wanted to dub Mujib a traitor, Bengalis made a hero out of him. The trial conferred such popularity

on Mujib that would otherwise have taken him a lifetime to acquire.

10-24 October 1968
Ayub Khan fell seriously ill. Already weakened politically by the Tashkent Declaration, his ailment also reduced him physically. The new forces of succession, both political and military, became active.

27 October 1968
The year-long celebration of the tenth anniversary of the 1958 Revolution reached its peak. The crude publicity given to the achievements of the regime, mainly in the economic field, only made the people conscious of their economic hardships. It helped awaken the dormant public resentment against Ayub who was reported to have built up a family fortune through irregular means.

7 November 1968
A student in Rawalpindi was killed by a police bullet. It gave a new fillip to the anti-Ayub demonstrations. The students found a champion of their cause in the person of Mr. Z.A. Bhutto, who led the movement to a point where Ayub was forced to resign. East Pakistanis also participated in the anti-Ayub riots as they hoped that the fall of the dictator would pave the way for their political goal.

15 February 1969
Sergant Zahoorul Haq, one of the accused in the Agartala Conspiracy Case, was shot dead while in military custody at Dacca cantonment. The Bengalis took it as a deliberate murder of their 'hero'. The anti-Ayub and anti-West Pakistan feelings shot high.

10-15 March 1969
Ayub held a Round Table Conference in Rawalpindi in an attempt to restore sanity to the street crowds by accepting the principal demands of the opposition parties. Some West Pakistani leaders insisted that Mujib should be released from jail to enable him to participate in the conference. The Agartala Conspiracy Case was withdrawn to suit this political contingency. Mujib declared before Dacca crowds, on 10 March, that parity was no longer acceptable to East Pakistan. He now wanted representation on the population (56 per cent) basis. The Round Table Conference failed.

25 March 1969
Field Marshal Ayub Khan handed over power to the Army chief,

General Yahya Khan, who imposed Martial Law in the country. The commotion in the streets subsided within twenty-four hours.

26 March 1969

The Chief Martial Law Administrator, General Yahya Khan, in his first broadcast to the nation, promised an early return to democracy and the transfer of power to the people's representatives.

28 November 1969

General Yahya Khan announced his acceptance of the one-man, one-vote principle. It was clearly designed to curry Mujib's favour, but it angered West Pakistanis who feared that it would lead to domination by the Bengalis. He also dissolved the One Unit and restored the four provinces of West Pakistan.

1 January 1970

Political activity was allowed in preparation for the first general elections, due later in the year.

THE SIX POINTS

The text of the Six Point Formula as originally published and subsequently amended in the Awami League's Manifesto.

POINT 1

Original: The Constitution should provide for a Federation of Pakistan in its true sense on the basis of the Lahore Resolution, and Parliamentary form of Government with supremacy of Legislature directly elected on the basis of universal adult franchise.

Amended: The character of the government shall be federal and parliamentary, in which the election to the federal legislature and to the legislatures of the federating units shall be direct and on the basis of universal adult franchise. The representation in the federal legislature shall be on the basis of population.

POINT 2

Original: Federal government shall deal with only two subjects, viz. Defence and Foreign Affairs, and all other residuary subjects shall vest in the federating states.

Amended: The federal government shall be responsible only for defence and foreign affairs and, subject to the conditions provided in (3) below, currency.

POINT 3

Original: 1. Two separate but freely convertible currencies for two wings may be introduced, or
2. One currency for the whole country may be maintained. In this case effective constitutional provisions are to be made to stop flight of capital from East to West Pakistan. Separate Banking Reserve is to be made and separate fiscal and monetary policy to be adopted for East Pakistan.

Amended: There shall be two separate currencies mutually or freely convertible in each wing for each region, or in the alternative a single currency, subject to the establishment of a federal reserves system in which there will be regional federal reserve banks which shall devise measures to prevent the transfer of resources and flight of capital from one region to another.

POINT 4

Original: The power of taxation and revenue collection shall vest in the federating units and that the Federal Centre will have no such power. The Federation will have a share in the state taxes for meeting their required expenditure. The Consolidated Federal Fund shall come out of a levy of certain percentage of all state taxes.

Amended: Fiscal policy shall be the responsibility of the federating units. The federal government shall be provided with requisite revenue resources for meeting the requirements of defence and foreign affairs, which revenue resources would be automatically appropriable by the federal government in the manner provided and on the basis of the ratio to be determined by the procedure laid down in the Constitution. Such constitutional provisions would ensure that the federal government's revenue requirements are met consistently with the objective of ensuring control over the fiscal policy by the governments of the federating units.

POINT 5

Original: 1. There shall be two separate accounts for foreign exchange earnings of the two wings.

2. Earnings of East Pakistan shall be under the control of East Pakistan Government and that of West Pakistan under the control of West Pakistan Government.

3. Foreign exchange requirement of the Federal Government shall be met by the two wings either equally or in a ratio to be fixed.

4. Indigenous products shall move free of duty between two wings.

5. The Constitution shall empower the unit Governments to establish trade and commercial relations with, set up trade missions in and enter into agreements with, foreign countries.

Amended: Constitutional provisions shall be made to enable separate accounts to be maintained of the foreign exchange earnings of each of the federating units, under the control of the respective governments of the federating units. The foreign exchange requirements of the federal government shall be met by the governments of the federating units on the basis of a ratio to be determined in accordance with the procedure laid down in the Constitution. The Regional Governments shall have power under the Constitution to negotiate foreign trade and aid within the framework of the foreign policy of the country, which shall be the responsibility of the federal government.

POINT 6

Original: The setting up of a militia or a paramilitary force for East Pakistan.

Amended: The governments of the federating units shall be empowered to maintain a militia or paramilitary force in order to contribute effectively towards national security.

OPERATION SEARCHLIGHT

BASIS FOR PLANNING

1. A.L. [Awami League] action and reactions to be treated as rebellion and those who support or defy M.L. [Martial Law] action be dealt with as hostile elements.

2. As A.L. has widespread support even amongst the E.P. [East Pakistani] elements in the Army the operation has to be launched with great cunningness, surprise, deception and speed combined with shock action.

BASIC REQUIREMENTS FOR SUCCESS

3. The operation to be launched all over the Province simultaneously.

4. Maximum number of political and student leaders and extremists amongst teaching staffs, cultural organisations to be arrested. In the initial phase top political leaders and top student leaders must be arrested.

5. Operation must achieve a hundred per cent success in Dacca. For that Dacca University will have to be occupied and searched.

6. Security of cantonments must be ensured. Greater and freer use of fire against those who dare attack the cantonment.

7. All means of internal and international communications to be cut off. Telephone exchanges, Radio, TV, Teleprinter services, transmitters with foreign consulates to be closed down.

8. EP tps [troops] to be neutralized by controlling and guarding kotes and ammunition by WP [West Pakistani] tps. Same for P.A.F. and E.P.R.

SURPRISE AND DECEPTION

9. *At higher plane*, it is requested that the President may consider the desirability of continuing the dialogue—even of deceiving Mujib that even though Mr. Bhutto may not agree he will make an announcement on 25 March conceding to the demands of A.L. etc.

10. *At Tactical Level*
   (a) As secrecy is of paramount importance, preliminary operations given below should be carried out by tps already located in the city:
      i. Breaking into Mujib's house and arresting all present. The house is well-guarded and well-defended.
      ii. Surrounding the important halls of the Universities — Iqbal Hall DU [Dacca University], Liaqat Hall Engineering University.
      iii. Switching off telephone exchange.
      iv. Isolating known houses where weapons etc. have been collected.
   (b) No activity by tps in the cantonment area till telephone exchange has been switched off.
   (c) Nobody should be allowed to go out of the cantonment after 2200 hrs on the night of operation.
   (d) On one excuse or the other tps in the city should be reinforced in the area of the President's House, Governor's House, MNA Hostel, Radio, TV and Telephone exchange premises.
   (e) Civilian cars may have to be used for operation against Mujib's house.

SEQUENCE OF ACTIONS

11. (a) *H Hr—0100 hrs.*
   (b) *Timings for Move Out*
      i. Commando [one Platoon] —Mujib's house—0100 hrs.
      ii. Telephone exchange switched off—2455 hrs.
      iii. Tps. earmarked for cordon University—0105 hrs.
      iv. Tps from the city to Rajarbagh Police HQ and other PS [Police station] nearby—0105 hrs.
      v. Following places surrounded—0105 hrs:
         Mrs. Anwara Begum's House, Rd No. 29 &
         House No. 148, Rd No. 29.
      vi. Curfew imposed—0110 hrs by Siren (arrange) by loudspeakers. Duration 30 hrs initially. No passes for the initial phase. Due consideration to be given only to cases of delivery and serious heart attack etc. Evac by Army on request. Also announce that there will be no newspapers brought out till further orders.

vii. Tps move out to respective sectors with specific missions—0110 hrs. (For tp alert a drill to be evolved). Halls occupied and searched.

viii. Tps move to University area—0500 hrs.

ix. Rd blocks and riverine block estb—0200 hrs.

(c) *Operations during the Day Time*

    i. House to house search of Dhanmondi suspected houses, also Hindu houses in old city (int to collect data).

    ii. All printing presses to be closed down. All cyclo-styling machines in the University, Colleges (T&T) and Physical Training Institute and Technical Institute to be confiscated.

    iii. Curfew imposed with severity.

    iv. Other leaders arrested.

12. *Allotment of Tps to Tasks* Details to be worked out by B[riga]de Com[man]d[er] (see 231–4) but the following must be done:

(a) Kotes of EP units taken over, including Sig[nal]s and other administrative units. Arms to be given only to WP personnel.

Explanation: We did not wish to embarrass the EP tps and did not want them to be used in tasks which may not be pleasant to them.

(b) Police stations to be disarmed.

(c) DG [Director General] EPR [East Pakistan Rifles] to ensure security of his kotes.

(d) All Ansar Rifles to be got hold of.

13. *Info Required*

(a) Whereabouts of the following:

i) Mujib	ix) Oli Ahad
ii) Nazarul Islam	x) Mrs Motia Chaudhry
iii) Tajuddin	xi) Barrister Maudud
iv) Osmani	xii) Faizul Haq
v) Sirajul Alam	xiii) Tofail
vi) Mannan	xiv) N.A. Siddiqi
vii) Ataur Rahman	xv) Rauf
viii) Professor Muzaffar	xvi) Makhan
	and other student leaders.

(b) Location of all police stations and of Rifles.

APPENDIX III 231

(c) Location of strong points and arsenal houses in the city.

(d) Location of tr[ainin]g camps and areas etc.

(e) Location of Cultural Centres which are being used for imparting military trg.

(f) Names of ex-service officers who are actively helping insurrectional movement.

14. *Comd and Control*—Two commands be established:

    (a) Dacca Area

        Comd—Major-General Farman

        Staff —Eastern Comd Staff/or HQ ML

        Tps   — Loc[ated] in Dacca.

    (b) The Rest of the Province

        Comd—Major-General K H Raja

        Staff —HQ 14 Div

        Tps   —Less those in Dacca.

15. *Security of the Cantonment*

    Phase I De-escalate. All arms including PAF deposited.

16. *Communication*

    (a) Security.

    (b) Layout.

ALLOTMENT OF TROOPS TO TASKS

DACCA

Command and Control: Maj.-Gen. Farman with H.Q. M.L.A. Zone B.

Troops

H.Q. 57 Brigade with troops in Dacca, i.e. 18 Punjab, 32 Punjab (C.O. to be replaced by [Lt.-Col.] Taj, GSO 1 (Int)), 22 Baluch, 13 Frontier Force, 31 Field Regt., 13 Light Ack-Ack Regt., company of 3 Commando (from Comilla).

Tasks:

1. Neutralise by disarming 2 and 10 East Bengal, H.Q. East Pakistan Rifles (2500), Reserve Police at Rajar Bagh (2000).

2. Exchange and transmitters, Radio, TV, State Bank.

3. Arrest Awami League leaders—detailed lists and addresses.

4. University Halls, Iqbal, Jagan Nath, Liaqat (Engineering University)

5. Seal off town including road, rail and river. Patrol river.

6. Protect factories at Ghazipur and Ammo Depot at Rajendrapur.

Remainder: Under Maj.-Gen. K.H. Raja and H.Q 14 Div.

JESSORE

Troops:

H.Q. 107 Brigade, 25 Baluch, 27 Baluch, Elements of 24 Field Regt., 55 Field Regt.

Tasks:

1. Disarm 1 East Bengal and Sector H.Q. East Pakistan Rifles and Reserve Police incl. Ansar weapons.
2. Secure Jessore town and arrest Awami League and student leaders.
3. Exchange and telephone communications.
4. Zone of security round cantt., Jessore town and Jessore–Khulna road, airfield.
5. Exchange at Kushtia to be made inoperative.
6. Reinforce Khulna if required.

KHULNA

Troops:

22 FF

Tasks:

1. Security in town.
2. Exchange and Radio Station.
3. Wing H.Q. East Pakistan Rifles, Reserve Companies and Reserve Police to be disarmed.
4. Arrest Awami League students and communist leaders.

RANGPUR–SAIDPUR

Troops:

H.Q. 23 Brigade, 29 Cavalry, 26 Frontier Force, 23 Field Regt.

Tasks:

1. Security of Rangpur–Saidpur.
2. Disarm 3 East Bengal at Saidpur.
3. If possible disarm Sector H.Q. and Reserve Company at Dinajpur or neutralise by dispersal Reserve Company by reinforcing border outposts.
4. Radio Station and telephone exchange at Rangpur.
5. Awami League and student leaders at Rangpur.
6. Ammo dump at Bogra.

RAJSHAHI

Troops:

25 Punjab

Tasks:

1. Despatch C.O.—Shafqat Baluch.
2. Exchange and Radio Station Rajshahi.
3. Disarm Reserve Police and Sector H.Q. East Pakistan Rifles.
4. Rajshahi University and in particular Medical College.
5. Awami League and student leaders.

COMILLA

Troops:

53 Field Regiments, $1\frac{1}{4}$ Mortar Batteries, Station troops, 3 Commando Batallion (less Company)

Tasks:

1. Disarm 4 East Bengal, Wing H.Q. East Pakistan Rifles, Reserve District Police.
2. Secure town and arrest Awami League leaders and students.
3. Exchange.

SYLHET

Troops:

31 Punjab less company

Tasks:

1. Radio Station, Exchange.
2. Koeno Bridge over Surma.
3. Airfield
4. Awami League and student leaders.
5. Disarm Section H.Q. East Pakistan Rifles and Reserve Police. Liaise with Sikandar.

CHITTAGONG

Troops:

20 Baluch, less advance party; company 31 Punjab present ex Sylhet; Iqbal Shafi to lead a mobile column from Comilla by road and reinforce S.T. 0100 hrs (H hrs) on D-Day.

Mobile Column: Brig. Iqbal Shafi with Tac H.Q. and Communications; 24 Frontier Force; Troop Heavy Mortars; Field Company Engineers; Company in advance to Feni on evening D-Day.

Tasks:

1. Disarm E.B.R.C., 8 East Bengal, Section H.Q. East Pakistan Rifles, Reserve Police.
2. Seize Central Police Armoury (Twenty thousand)
3. Radio Station and Exchange.
4. Liaise with Pakistan Navy (Commodore Mumtaz)
5. Liaise with Shaigri and Janjua (C.O. 8 East Bengal) who have been instructed to take orders from you till arrival Iqbal Shafi.
6. If Shigri and Janjua feel sure about their outfits then do not disarm. In that case merely put in a road block to town from Cantt. by placing a company in defensive position so that later E.B.R.C. and 8 East Bengal are blocked should they change their loyalties.
7. I am taking Brig. Mozamdar with me. Arrest Chaudhry (C.I. E.B.R.C.) on D-Day night.
8. Arrest of Awami League and student leaders after above accomplished.

APPENDIX IV

TEXT OF INSTRUMENT OF SURRENDER

The PAKISTAN Eastern Command agree to surrender all PAK-ISTAN Armed Forces in BANGLA DESH to Lieutenant-General JAGJIT SINGH AURORA, General Officer Commanding in Chief of the Indian and BANGLA DESH forces in the Eastern Theatre. This surrender includes all PAKISTAN land, air and naval forces as also all paramilitary forces and civil armed forces. These forces will lay down their arms and surrender at the places where they are currently located to the nearest regular troops under the command of Lieutenant-General JAGJIT SINGH AURORA.

The PAKISTAN Eastern Command shall come under the orders of Lieutenant-General JAGJIT SINGH AURORA as soon as this instrument has been signed. Disobedience of orders will be regarded as a breach of the surrender terms and will be dealt with in accordance with the accepted laws and usages of war. The decision of Lieutenant-General JAGJIT SINGH AURORA will be final, should any doubt arise as to the meaning or inter-pretation of the surrender terms.

Lieutenant-General JAGJIT SINGH AURORA gives a solemn assurance that personnel who surrender shall be treated with the dignity and respect that soldiers are entitled to in accord-ance with the provisions of the GENEVA Convention and guarantees the safety and well-being of all PAKISTAN military and paramilitary forces who surrender. Protection will be pro-vided to foreign nationals, ethnic minorities and personnel of WEST PAKISTAN origin by the forces under the command of Lieu-tenant-General JAGJIT SINGH AURORA.

JAGJIT SINGH AURORA
Lieutenant-General
General Officer Commanding in Chief
Indian and Bangla Desh Forces in
the Eastern Theatre
16 December 1971

AMIR ABDULLAH KHAN NIAZI
Lieutenant-General
Martial Law Administrater
Zone B and Commander
Eastern Command (Pakistan)
16 December 1971

INDEX

A

Adamjee Jute Mills 21
Adamjee School 76
ad hoc Brigade 126, 127, 139, 143, 149, 159, 172
ad hoc Division 126, 127
Advance Dressing Station (ADS) 178
Afra 140, 144
Afridi, Col. 144, 145
Agartala Conspiracy 2, 12, 14, 25, 222, 223
Ahsan Malik, Capt. 182, 183, 185, 186, 187
Ahsan, Vice-Admiral S.M. 16, 19, 20, 33, 34, 38, 41, 43, 45
A.I.R. (see All India Radio)
Akbar, Lt.-Col. 189
Akhaura 159, 160, 161, 163, 166, 169
Akram, Maj. (Frontier Force) 151, 153–4
Akram, Maj. (Punjab) 173, 175
A.K.R.F. (see Azad Kashmir Regular Forces)
Akyab 209
Al-Badr 105, 203
Allah-o-Akbar 133
All India Radio (A.I.R.) 95, 173, 195, 212
amnesty for defectors 91, 102, 109, 141
Amritbazar, 141
Amritsar 136
Ansar, 49
Ansari, Brig. 149
Ansari, Maj.-Gen. M.H. 82, 83, 126, 127, 140, 141, 146, 147
Aptor 150
Arbab, Brig. Jehanzeb 71, 72, 77
Army, Pakistan 64, 66, 93, 99, 102, 105, 107, 110, 213, 215; action 39, 62–3, 71–90 (also see Searchlight); action in Chittagong 79–83; action in Kushtia 83–5; action in Pabna 85–6; aviation 59, 132, 143, 209; supervision of polls 27–30; surrender 208, 213
Artillery 116, 118, 119, 120, 122, 132, 182, 185, 200, 203; field 94, 167, 170; light ack-ack 72; medium 182
Asghar, Capt. 85

Ash-Shams 105
Ashuganj 161, 162
Aslam, Maj. 86
Assam 116, 151
Ataullah, Brig. 126, 171
Ataur Rehman Khan, 218, 219, 220
Atgram 119, 167, 168
Atif, Brig. 171, 172
atrocities 51, 56, 57, 80–3, 104, 212
Aurora, Lt.-Gen. Jagjit Singh 211, 235
Awami League 1, 4, 5, 6, 13, 15, 16, 19, 28, 31, 32, 33, 34, 38, 40, 42, 45, 49, 51, 63, 64, 66, 67, 72, 73, 78, 93, 94, 109, 217, 218, 219, 220; dealings with P.P.P. 53–7; directives 56; leaders 83, 109; manifesto 225–7; proposed compromise 41; reaction to postponement of national assembly session 45–7; terrorists 51; volunteers 85, 99
Awami Muslim League 216, 217
Ayoob, Mohammad 69n
Ayub Khan, Field Marshal Mohammad 1, 221, 222, 223; Chief Martial Law Administrator 220; Defence Minister 218; hands over to Yahya 223
Ayub, Maj. 186
Ayub, Subedar 86, 87
Azad Kashmir Regular Forces (A.K.R.F.) 118, 160, 168, 171, 172, 175, 176, 177
Azam, Prof. Ghulam 15, 93
Azam Khan, Lt.-Gen. 221
Azimpura 14

B

Baba 103
Babur Post 150, 151
Badar-i-Islam 115
Baitul Mukarram 4, 108
Baluchistan 215, 219
Baluch Regiment 40, 45, 72, 73, 79, 80, 81, 82, 83, 143, 155, 165, 170, 172, 176, 181, 183, 187, 189
Balurghat 150
Banani Colony 51
Bangkok 201